Praise for *USA Today* bestselling author
Christina McDonald's "compulsively readable"
(*Publishers Weekly*) thrillers

## DO NO HARM

"Gripping and unflinching, *Do No Harm* explores the ferocity of a mother's love—and shows, in heartbreaking detail, how she'll risk everything to save her child."

—Sarah Pekkanen, *New York Times* bestselling author of
*The Wife Between Us*

"The stakes couldn't be higher in this smart, breathlessly paced, and emotional novel about love, family, and how far we'll go when our child's life hangs in the balance. Riveting, ripped from the headlines, and not to be missed."

—Lisa Unger, *New York Times* bestselling author of
*Confessions on the 7:45*

"Tense, taut, and absolutely unmissable. You'll find yourself wondering how far YOU would go to save your child's life."

—J.T. Ellison, *New York Times* bestselling author of *Lie to Me*

"McDonald takes the heart-wrenching premise that has become her trademark and ratchets it up a notch in *Do No Harm*, blurring the lines between good and evil in a doctor desperate to save her sick child. A gripping, emotional roller coaster with a sting in the tail."

—Kimberly Belle, internationally bestselling
author of *The Marriage Lie*

"Christina McDonald knows how to pack an emotional punch! *Do No Harm* is a riveting, thought-provoking novel that keeps you reading even as it breaks your heart. This might be my favorite book by McDonald yet."

—Samantha Downing, *USA Today* bestselling
author of *My Lovely Wife*

"A page-turner with a heart-wrenching moral quandary at its core. *Do No Harm* is tense, moving, and disturbingly relevant."

—Robyn Harding, internationally bestselling
author of *The Swap* and *The Party*

"Devastating, heartbreaking, and incredibly timely—this risky and brilliant examination of when the ends justify the means will captivate you from moment one. As a doctor's vow of 'do no harm' twists into 'do whatever it takes,' you'll be riveted."

—Hank Phillippi Ryan, *USA Today* bestselling
author of *The Murder List*

"With her outstanding writing, Christina McDonald tackles the moral lines crossed by a doctor desperate to save her child. A stunning gut punch of a suspense novel, *Do No Harm* expertly merges the dangers of the opioid crisis with a mother's love, leaving readers gasping for more. A breathtaking read."

—Samantha M. Bailey, #1 bestselling author of
*Woman on the Edge*

"Christina McDonald demands an answer to the ultimate question: How far would you go to save your child? One thing is for sure: your heart will be ripped out as you whip through each page to discover the answer. Highly recommend!"

—Liz Fenton and Lisa Steinke, authors of *How to Save a Life*

"Nobody writes motherhood like Christina McDonald. *Do No Harm* is a riveting thriller that braids the complexities of modern parenting with the pressures of finding a moral center in a devastating opioid crisis. Heartrending, heart-pounding, and fearless to the last word."

—Amber Cowie, author of *Loss Lake*

# BEHIND EVERY LIE

"*Behind Every Lie* is a deep, suspenseful novel packed with family secrets. Christina McDonald has a true gift for creating characters that are so well developed, it feels like you know them. An outstanding achievement!"

—Samantha Downing, #1 internationally
bestselling author of *My Lovely Wife*

"In *Behind Every Lie*, Christina McDonald brilliantly intertwines page-turning suspense with jaw-dropping family secrets. An emotionally charged domestic thriller that is sure to please!"

—Wendy Walker, internationally bestselling
author of *The Night Before*

"A clever, tense, and absorbing novel—this tale of family secrets had me racing toward the final pages."

—Emma Rous, bestselling author of *The Au Pair*

"Told in alternating narratives from Eva's traumatic life and her mother's mysterious past, the story twists and turns with one shocking revelation after another until it threatens to career out of control. But behind every lie there is always a reason, and there is a satisfying ending once everyone's hand is played out."

—*Booklist*

"McDonald starts with a bang, then builds the action steadily, a gradual unfolding of secrets and lies that will have you constantly switching alliances. Read it like I did, in one sitting and straight through to the end, because you won't want to put this one down."

—Kimberly Belle, internationally bestselling author of *Dear Wife*

"A layered, gut-wrenching domestic thriller that explores the complexities of mothers and daughters and the secrets families keep. McDonald's beautiful, emotional storytelling will leave you breathless. I don't think I exhaled until the end."

—Jennifer Hillier, award-winning author of *Jar of Hearts*

"An engrossing and utterly addictive thriller. I couldn't turn the pages fast enough!"

—Kathleen Barber, author of *Follow Me* and *Truth Be Told*

"[A] fast-paced yarn that explores the lingering effects of trauma and abuse as well as the complex bonds between mothers and daughters. Readers who enjoy character-driven thrillers will be pleased."

—*Publishers Weekly*

# THE NIGHT OLIVIA FELL

"McDonald ratchets up the suspense with every chapter, including plenty of gasp-worthy twists and turns. The suspense is supplemented by relationships of surprising depth and tenderness, providing balance and nuance. A worthy debut from an up-and-coming domestic-suspense author; readers who enjoy mother-daughter stories in the genre should line up for this one."

—*Booklist* (starred review)

ALSO BY CHRISTINA McDONALD

*Behind Every Lie*
*The Night Olivia Fell*

# DO NO HARM

## CHRISTINA McDONALD

G

GALLERY BOOKS

NEW YORK LONDON TORONTO SYDNEY NEW DELHI

# G

Gallery Books
An Imprint of Simon & Schuster, Inc.
1230 Avenue of the Americas
New York, NY 10020

First Gallery Books trade paperback edition February 2021

GALLERY BOOKS and colophon are registered trademarks of Simon & Schuster, Inc.

For information about special discounts for bulk purchases, please contact Simon & Schuster Special Sales at 1-866-506-1949 or business@simonandschuster.com.

The Simon & Schuster Speakers Bureau can bring authors to your live event. For more information or to book an event, contact the Simon & Schuster Speakers Bureau at 1-866-248-3049 or visit our website at www.simonspeakers.com.

*Interior design by Michelle Marchese*

Manufactured in the United States of America

10  9  8  7  6  5  4  3  2  1

Library of Congress Cataloging-in-Publication Data is available.

ISBN 978-1-9821-4261-2
ISBN 978-1-9821-4262-9 (ebook)

*For my brother, Daniel McDonald.*
*For beating the odds.*
*For being strong.*
*I love you.*

# DO NO HARM

# PROLOGUE

THE KNIFE BURROWED INTO my side with a moist *thwump*.

I looked down, confused. The blade was buried so deep that the hand holding it was pressed almost flat against my stomach. My pulse hammered against the steel.

And then I felt the fire. My mouth dropped open. The blood was rushing out of me too fast, I knew, soaking my shirt, turning it from white to red in seconds. It was too late. Too late to save myself.

I looked into those familiar eyes, mouthed a single word.

*You.*

The knife slid out of me, a sickening, wet sound. Blood pooled at the bottom of my throat. And then I fell, an abrupt, uninterrupted drop.

I blinked, my brain softening, dulling. Images clicked by, one by one.

Polished black shoes.

The blur of snow as it tumbled past the open door.

The two-by-fours standing against the wall.

My body felt like it was composed of nothing but air. I had failed.

# CHAPTER 1

MY BODY ACHED AND my head thudded fiercely after twelve hours of being run off my feet at the clinic. But all that disappeared as soon as I got home and heard Josh call out for me.

"Mommy, come upstairs!" he shouted.

"I'm coming!" I called. I'd never expected to work so much after I finished my residency. But here I was, bone-tired and depleted.

I shut the front door and dropped my purse onto the entry table. Upstairs, I could hear Nate whistling "Don't Worry, Be Happy" off-key and Josh giggling. The house smelled of the rich, homey scents of Nate's famous chili con carne. A ribbonlike thread of happiness wound around my heart, a gentle serenity easing over me.

Josh's room was an explosion of *Star Wars* fabrics, posters, and action figures. Nate was kneeling next to him. He was wearing the blue sweater I'd given him last Christmas, which of course made me think of this Christmas. Now that Thanksgiving was over, I needed to start shopping, decorating, planning. The only problem was finding the time.

"Hey, Emma," Nate greeted me, his blue eyes soft with love. I kissed my husband on the lips, thinking, as usual, how lucky I was. So many people call us by name, but very few make it sound special. Nate made mine feel special.

Nate tugged Josh's shirt off, revealing a handful of purple marks on his back. We both gasped.

"Joshy, what happened!" I dropped to my knees and ran a hand down my son's back.

The bruises were faint but distinct, a gruesome grayish purple. They looked like a trail of stepping-stones marching up the knobs of his spine.

"George slide-tackled me in soccer."

"Was it an accident?"

"No." Josh poked out his bottom lip. "He's a poo-poo head."

"A poo-poo head, huh?" I tried to maintain my most solemn expression. "Why'd he do that?"

"George kicked Ellie in the shin when she scored, so I told Mrs. Morrow and she took away our point. George said we would've won if I hadn't blabbed. And then he slide-tackled me!" Josh looked at Nate earnestly. "But if we won, it wouldn't be fair because we cheated. Right?"

"That's right, Joshy," Nate replied seriously. "We have to do the right thing, even if it's the hard thing."

I helped Josh pull on his pj's, then lifted him into bed. He smelled of mango-scented shampoo and fruity toothpaste. I scooched in next to him, and Nate climbed in on the other side so Josh was nestled between us.

"Pimple squish!" Josh giggled, that lovely childish giggle that made my heart melt. "I like pimple squishes. They make my heart happy."

Nate and I burst out laughing. Josh was a goofball. During last year's holiday pageant, he'd put his shoes on his hands, stretched his arms above his head, and told the audience he was upside down, just to make them laugh.

Nate drew Josh tight against him, and Josh leaned against his chest. I leaned against them both and closed my eyes with gratitude, just breathing them in.

I never thought I'd get a chance to have a normal life. Before I met Nate, I hadn't really belonged anywhere. I'd been an outsider. An orphan. Until I unexpectedly found out I was pregnant shortly after we'd started dating. But I got lucky with Nate. Marrying him, being a mom, had given me a chance to belong to a real family.

I kissed Nate's fingers where they were wrapped around Josh's shoulders. He was telling Josh a bedtime story, speaking in that soft drawl I loved, every word a lullaby.

"Once upon a time, a Native American chief and his wife had a beautiful daughter, who they were very proud of. For her thirteenth birthday, they planned a huge celebration. Swimming races and canoe races and bow-and-arrow contests. But a few days before her birthday, the girl became very sick."

"If she had Mommy, she wouldn't have been sick," Josh interrupted. "Because Mommy's the best doctor in the world."

Nate nodded, and Josh grinned at me, toothy and wide. They were always so certain I could fix anything. The truth was, I was trained to show a reassuring level of confidence, but most of the time I was as helpless as the next person. I was just better at hiding it.

Nate continued in a faux-thundery voice: "'The Great Spirit is angry with us,' the chief said. He asked his wisest men, 'What can we do to ease his anger?' One stepped forward and said, 'To stop the great sickness, one must sacrifice for all.'"

This was the point where I always jumped in. "Nate, the nice version, please."

"The chief's wife knew her daughter would die if she didn't do something. So that night she followed the trail through the forest to the Great River until she reached the highest cliff. She looked at the rocks below and said to the Great Spirit, 'Give me a sign that you'll accept me as a sacrifice.'"

Josh gazed at Nate in blue-eyed wonder, sucking loudly on his middle and pointer fingers. I should've made him stop before the habit affected his teeth but couldn't bear to take away the last traces of babyhood. At five, he was already growing up too fast.

"Just then, the moon rose over the trees, bright and yellow as a wedge of cheese. The chief's wife knew it was the sign she'd asked for, so she closed her eyes and jumped—"

"—and turned into a beautiful white bird," I interrupted.

"That's right." Nate nodded. "And her daughter was saved."

"And they all lived happily ever after." Josh yawned sleepily.

"Exactly."

Nate pulled the covers to Josh's chin, and I kissed his forehead. He felt a little warm to me. He'd been suffering on and off with a cold the last few weeks.

"Mommy, my throat hurts. Will you stay with me?"

In my peripheral vision, I caught Nate rolling his eyes. He thought I was too permissive.

"You need him as much as he needs you," Nate had said once, not exactly in a nice way.

Nate drew an *X* over his heart, then pointed at me before heading downstairs. It was our shorthand for *I love you*. I smiled.

"Course I'll stay." I lay next to Josh so we were nose-to-nose. The sight of his innocent little face on the pillow beside me cracked my heart wide open. I loved him so much.

Josh laced his fingers through mine, his tiny hands impossibly soft. "I wish we could get married when I grow up."

I smiled. Little boys loved their mamas so much. That love had changed me, made me a better person, a stronger person. "We have something even better than being married: we're mommy and son.

We share the same blood and the same DNA. That's closer than friends or even mommies and daddies. We're family forever."

He pondered that for a minute. "Would you turn into a bird for me?" he asked.

I gazed into his sapphire eyes. He was so perfect. The best thing in my life. So when I answered, I was 100 percent truthful.

"Of course," I said. "I would do anything for you."

DOWNSTAIRS, NATE was sprawled across the couch, his floppy brown hair still wet from a shower. Charlie, our elderly basset hound, wagged his tail at me from his bed next to the fireplace. I stroked his long ears, splayed like wings. Around me, the living room walls and fireplace mantel were covered with photos that narrated the family life we'd built together.

I handed Nate a bag of cookies. "I got you these on the way home."

"Snickerdoodles! My favorite." He grabbed the bag and pulled me onto his lap, kissing me hard. "Thanks, babe. Want one?"

I gave him a look. He knew I didn't allow myself sugar.

I leaned over Nate and wiped at a new stain on the arm of our dingy brown couch. "Ugh. When are we going to get rid of this thing?"

"No sense wasting money on a new one," Nate replied cheerfully.

The seams were tattered, the fabric stained, but I was wasting my breath. Nate had bought the couch before we met and was strangely attached to it. He preferred easy and comfortable over new and nice. And he was right: we couldn't afford a new one. Everything we owned was a little threadbare, a little shabby and overused.

You'd think we'd be doing well financially. Nate earned a respectable government salary as a detective, and I was a doctor. I certainly thought I'd be doing better by now. But becoming a doctor wasn't exactly cheap. Thank God we were able to rent our house from Nate's mother. We couldn't afford anything else.

Nate folded me in his arms, and I laid my head against his chest. A blanket of warmth settled over me, loosening the knots in my shoulders. We didn't have a fancy couch, but we had each other. That was what mattered.

Nate munched a snickerdoodle, his eyes on the TV, where a reporter was speaking about two Seattle policemen who'd fabricated evidence in order to win a murder conviction.

I waved at the TV. "Can you believe this?"

Nate shrugged. The washed-denim pools of his eyes were layered: sunny on the surface with dark, distant shadows underneath. "They wanted to make sure justice was served. I get it."

I was a little surprised. I'd always thought of Nate as the upholder of all that was good and right in the world. He was one of the good guys.

But I guess even good guys have their limits.

"My mom told me about Mabel." Nate's eyes swept the planes of my face.

I froze. For a moment I wanted to tell him everything. To unload about the crush of patients, the child who'd vomited on my shoes, and then Mabel's death after I'd unsuccessfully tried to manage her asthma attack with oral corticosteroids. I'd admitted her to the hospital but had received a call later from the ER. Mabel had died.

I knew Nate would be sweet and empathetic. He'd pour me a glass of wine, draw me a bath, and let me just relax. And he'd listen. But I couldn't tell him about any of it.

Sometimes the intricate and complicated nature of belonging to a family still felt unfamiliar to me. I knew I should open up. Nate was a good man, the kind of man whose heart was a home, who put his family first and gave more than he took.

Yet I couldn't get my feelings to move from my heart to my tongue.

"How'd she know?" I asked.

"Mabel went to her church. She was eighty-seven years old. There was nothing you could do."

He was saying it to make me feel better, but the words stung anyway.

*Nothing you could do.*

I turned my face into Nate's neck, letting the reassuring thump of his pulse flutter against my cheek. I didn't want him to see the tears scratching behind my eyelids, the feeling that I'd failed glowing in their sheen. I didn't cry, as a rule. I'd learned long ago that nothing good came from crying. Nothing but waves of helplessness, which I hated, and a throbbing headache, which I also hated.

Nate said I felt too much as a doctor. That I was too compassionate and needed better boundaries. But I didn't agree. My compassion for my patients was like a superpower. It made me a better doctor, a better human. Shouldn't we all care a little more?

I didn't want to talk about Mabel, so I stood, moving toward the kitchen to start the never-ending chores of a full-time working mother.

"You took Charlie for a walk, right?"

Charlie heard the word *walk* and stood, his tail wagging. Charlie had turned up on our front porch one day out of the blue. We hadn't planned to keep him. We both had demanding jobs and a small child; we didn't have time for a dog. But by the time we'd realized no one was responding to our LOST DOG posters around town, it was too late. He was family.

"Yep."

"Did you do laundry? Josh needs a clean school uniform tomorrow."

"Of course."

"Did you empty—"

"The garbage? Yep."

"Sorry. You know me."

Nate grinned, his eyes bright, his smile teasing. "You mean an overly responsible, incredibly anal control freak?"

I laughed. He was right: I got shit done. "No, a loving mother and a dependable, well-respected doctor."

I slipped a sweater on and searched for my fuzzy slippers under the table. "Have you seen my slippers?"

"I dunno. Bedroom?"

I found them in the bathroom, slipped them on, and returned to the living room. "You were wearing my slippers again, weren't you," I teased.

"I prefer your heels, dahling." Nate struck a pose, one hand behind his head, before grabbing my hand and pulling me back down onto the couch. He was looking at me that way he did, like he was hypnotized by me. He nuzzled my neck, and when his lips touched mine, shivers dusted my spine. Even now, married five years and with our son sleeping upstairs, my husband still made me feel like this. Content. Like I *belonged*. Just being with Nate lit me up from the inside.

Nate and I met when I was in my first year of residency. He'd arrested a guy who hadn't wanted to be arrested, and he'd been stabbed through the metacarpal bones of his palm for his effort.

I don't know if I believe in love at first sight, but when I saw him it was, as the Italians say, *il colpo di fulmine*. The thunderbolt. Holding his hand in mine as I stitched the gaping skin together, I felt electric.

"You're lucky you missed any major veins," I'd said.

"I'm lucky, all right."

My stomach had twisted as I met his gaze. I snipped the ends of the last stitch and wrapped his hand in gauze, declaring him fit to leave.

"Let me take you to dinner," he'd said.

He was drinking me in with his eyes, and when I spoke it was with less conviction than it should've been.

"Absolutely not." It didn't matter that my hand was still warm from his or that his gaze made my stomach feel like it had touched a live wire. "I don't date patients."

I didn't think I'd see him again, but a few weeks later I ran into him at a Christmas party my roommate had dragged me to. I'd been adrift and alone, and then there was Nate, and I chose not to be alone anymore.

Nate was different from other guys I'd dated. He cooked me dinner, showed me pictures of his family, listened when I spoke, and asked thoughtful questions. And he made me laugh. He always made me laugh. We'd moved in together after just a month, joining our lives the way soul mates and best friends do. And when I found out I was pregnant, it seemed the most natural thing in the world to say yes when he proposed.

"I have a million things to do," I murmured against Nate's mouth.

"I could arrest you, you know." Nate wiggled his eyebrows suggestively. "I have handcuffs."

I burst out laughing. "Maybe I have just a little time."

"Ooh-la-la!" Nate lifted my sweater over my head and unbuttoned my pants, rolling them down over my ankles and gazing at my body in admiration. He smiled, the left side of his mouth curving up just a little bit more than the right, and ran his fingers lightly over my bare shoulders as he bent to kiss my neck.

I kicked my pants off so I was only wearing my bra and underwear. "Now, what was that you said about handcuffs?"

# CHAPTER 2

THE FIRST OVERDOSE CALL came at 8:20 a.m., just as Detective Nate Sweeney was dropping his son off at school in Skamania, a small town pressed up against the Cascade mountain range about forty-five minutes outside of Seattle. His mind was crowded with worry as he watched Josh walk down the covered corridor toward his classroom.

He knew he hadn't been fooling Josh earlier. The cross on the eastern side of the bridge that spanned the Skamania River had been freshly painted, startling Nate more than it should've. He'd slowed the Crown Vic and stared at it, wondering who'd painted it. Robbie's mom and dad had left town years ago.

"What's wrong, Daddy?" Josh had asked from his booster seat in the back.

Loosening his grip on the steering wheel, Nate had flashed his son a grin. He was good at hiding his darker feelings. But Josh was a sensitive kid. "Nothing, buddy. You ready to fly?"

Josh nodded.

"Here we go!" Nate pulled onto the highway and hit the gas. He flashed the cruiser's lights, the car surging forward with a low growl. The engine thrummed as he accelerated to forty, then fifty, then sixty miles an hour.

Josh laughed and Nate laughed with him, twin bursts of relief and happiness expanding in his chest. Nate felt like a god when he made his son laugh. He remembered when his own father used to do this for him, the whir of the siren in his ears, the rush of adrenaline as the trees flew by.

"Faster! Faster!" Josh crowed.

But they'd reached sixty, and Nate was already easing off the gas. "We've reached the speed limit, Josh. I can't go any faster—it's against the law."

Soon Nate was pulling into the school drop-off lane. He turned to face Josh, surprised to see that he looked like he was about to cry.

"Hey, what's wrong, Josh?"

"I don't feel so good."

Josh had been complaining he wasn't feeling well a lot lately, but he didn't have a temperature. At first Nate thought his reluctance was over going back to school after the long Thanksgiving weekend. Then he remembered the bruises on Josh's back.

"Is there something going on at school you want to talk about?" he asked.

"No. I just wanna stay with you."

Nate made a mental note to talk to Josh's teacher later. "Mommy will be here to pick you up before you know it."

Nate had helped Josh put his backpack on, handing him over to the school warden who was waiting to take him to his kindergarten classroom. He watched his son drag his shoes across the pavement in the way only a five-year-old boy could. Josh was smaller than the other kids, and now, his shoulders sagging under his backpack, he seemed tinier, more vulnerable than ever.

For a moment Nate had debated going inside to talk to Josh's teacher, but he'd heard the radio crackling in the cruiser and knew he had to go. Josh peeked over his shoulder one last time, his sad eyes meeting Nate's. Nate lifted a hand good-bye.

And a second later, Josh was gone.

NATE WAS closest to the overdose, so he flipped his lights on and flew up the main street of Skamania, named after the nearby waterfall of the same name, and headed past the hospital where Emma worked. If he drove another twenty miles up he'd hit the pass, which cut the state in half, but instead he turned abruptly into the Mill Creek neighborhood at the edge of town.

The neighborhood had an air of quiet desperation about it, a mix of run-down houses with cracked windows and rusted mobile homes, the siding peeling in ugly, jagged strips. The yards were overgrown and neglected, choked with weeds, the faint scent of garbage filling the air.

Nate had been called here for domestic assaults, drug busts, and once a murder. But increasingly, the calls were about opioid overdoses. As such, the lieutenant had recently told his detectives to investigate both fatal and nonfatal overdoses in an effort to trace the drugs back to the dealers.

The overdose was a young woman of about twenty-five. She'd passed out as she was driving, the car coming to rest in the middle of the cul-de-sac, her little girl in the backseat. The paramedics were giving her naloxone when Nate arrived.

"Witness is over there," said Bill Petty, one of the paramedics. He jerked his chin toward a scrawny woman with dark, unwashed hair standing next to a squirming four-year-old.

"I live there," the witness told Nate, pointing across the street to a rusty mobile home. Her voice was scratchy, like she'd smoked too many cigarettes. "I was doin' dishes when I saw the car sorta driftin'. She was slumped over the wheel."

Nate took a few notes and thanked the woman before calling social services to get the girl. He noticed a familiar figure in the crowd gathering near the ambulance.

"Stevie McGraw," he growled under his breath. The local teenage scumbag watched the events, smoking a hand-rolled cigarette. His black hair hung in greasy sheets, gaze sharp behind horn-rimmed glasses.

By now Bill and the other paramedics had revived the mother.

"I have a headache," she mumbled, her eyes bloodshot.

"Well, of course you do," Bill replied briskly. "You weren't breathing for a while. Your brain didn't have any oxygen."

"Why don't you tell me where your dime baggie is?" Nate asked her.

Still dazed, she pointed at the glove compartment. Nate snapped on a pair of latex gloves and reached into the compartment, extracting a baggie with a couple of white pills and a lot of residual powder. He held up the pills and examined them, surprised there were any left.

"Oxy?"

She nodded.

"You could have killed your daughter."

The woman burst into tears then. Her arms, bloody from raking broken nails down them, came up to cover her face. Bill bundled her into the ambulance and closed the back door. He caught Nate's eye and shook his head. They'd known each other since elementary school, and Nate could see the stamp of exhaustion in his sunken eyes, his sloped shoulders.

"We had four overdose calls yesterday," Bill said. "This one will check herself out of the hospital as soon as she can. When will it stop?"

Nate had no answer. Most overdose patients refused further treatment. Even a brush with death was rarely a turning point for an addict.

"Get some rest tonight, Bill." He clapped his old friend on the shoulder, then waved as the ambulance whooped and headed for the hospital.

Nate sat in his cruiser and jotted a few more notes as he waited for social services to arrive.

Nate hadn't always wanted to be a cop. Just the opposite, in fact. He'd seen how hard his dad had worked for their small town, how much being a cop had taken out of him. The constant stress and resulting high blood pressure had caused the stroke that eventually cut him down in his prime. He'd worked his whole life to make Skamania a safer place. Nate couldn't appreciate that when he was young. He did now.

One night his childhood friend Robbie Sadler had gotten out of bed, written a suicide note to his parents, stolen his father's gun, walked to the bridge that spanned the Skamania River, and shot himself in the head. His body was found downstream three days later. So when Nate finished high school, he'd signed up at the police academy, determined to save lives and stop others from taking them.

From his cruiser, Nate watched Stevie through narrowed eyes. The young man exhaled, a gray cloud of smoke swirling around him as he talked to one of the neighbors. *Is it possible that Stevie dealt the oxy to that woman?* Stevie was bad news. He'd been caught hacking the school system to change his grades last year and had been picked up for dealing weed to younger kids.

Nate groaned. If he arrested Stevie, the paperwork would take him all morning. But then he remembered that white cross. Pain expanded inside him like a balloon, so tight, so intense, he wanted to slice it open to relieve the pressure.

Nate pulled out a tin of toothpicks he kept in his slacks pocket. He placed one between his pinky fingernail and the nail bed, and then slowly, excruciatingly, pushed the toothpick into the tender skin.

Searing pain burst through his fingertip, jarring and brutal. Nate gasped. He squeezed his eyes shut and let the pain remind him what he had to do.

AN HOUR LATER, Nate hurried toward the police department, a two-story brick-and-glass building in the center of town. An American flag flapped above the glass entry doors.

He'd missed roll call, but knew Lieutenant Dyson wouldn't mind. This was Skamania. There were fewer than six thousand emergency calls and criminal cases a year. It was one of the best, and worst, things about taking the detective job here after the chaos of patrolling in Seattle.

Stevie hadn't been carrying any oxycodone. But he did have an ounce of marijuana in his back pocket. Since he was under-age, Nate had booked him for possession. He'd even seized the $4.92 Stevie had in his wallet for good measure.

Nate shoved a bite of a glazed donut into his mouth as he entered the station, all he'd had time to grab for breakfast this morning.

"Don't worry, Ma," he said into his cell phone, still chewing. He nodded at Thompson, who was on duty at the front desk, and moved toward the detectives' area. He thumped Sanchez on the back and raised a hand good-bye to McManus, who was leaving. "I'll visit him later. . . . I will, promise. I gotta go. . . . Yeah. . . . Yeah. Love you too."

The police department was busy. Phones were ringing, keyboards clattering, papers shuffling. The smell of burnt coffee drifted in the air. The cubicles in the detectives' area were squished at the back of the room.

Nate crossed to his cubicle, which was decorated with the traditional swag of a detective: pictures of his family, police awards he'd won, a trophy he'd brought from Seattle. He sat down to file his report about the overdose.

"You're gonna get fat." One of the other detectives, Kia Sharpe, nodded at the donut in his hand.

Nate patted his abs and grinned, his blue eyes sparkling. "Never."

"Life is not fair," she complained.

Kia was the yin to Nate's yang: a cynical pessimist with a fractious, snappy attitude. She had bitten-down nails, shaggy hair, and a jaw so square you could park a car in it. But beneath her dark eyes and black leather jacket, she was quick-minded and wily as a snake.

Before Nate could reply, Lieutenant Sam Dyson poked his head out of his office. "Sweeney!"

Nate hustled into Dyson's office. The walls were covered with pictures: Dyson with the mayor, with his officers and detectives, riding horses with his children, holding his grandkids, a wedding photo with his wife. Medals hung on the spaces in between.

A photo on his desk showed Dyson and Nate's dad, Matt Sweeney, back when they were partners, looking young and virile, both in full uniform standing in front of their patrol car. These days Dyson looked more like a cowboy than a cop, with a gray handlebar mustache, craggy eyebrows, and a face so creased he looked like he'd slept facedown.

"Hiya, Nate. How's Emma?"

Dyson had always had a soft spot for Nate's wife, ever since she'd caught his granddaughter's diabetes and probably saved her life.

Nate smiled, thinking of Emma this morning, the way her dark hair swirled around her shoulders, her thighs peeking out from the hem of the T-shirt she'd borrowed from him. He'd never loved anyone as much as he loved Emma. And now Josh, of course. This morning he'd watched as she rinsed their son's cereal bowl in the sink and been completely hypnotized. Even doing the most mundane things, his wife was exquisite. She'd turned and caught him staring and had bent for a lingering kiss, filling him with warmth. He didn't know what he'd done to deserve a love like this, but he sure as shit was grateful.

"She's good," Nate replied.

"Good. Listen, I got a call from Seattle this morning." Dyson smoothed nicotine-stained fingers down his mustache. "One of their informants was making noises about a fentanyl deal going down out here, but he's gone quiet. They asked us to do a welfare check." Dyson tossed a file at Nate. "Name and address are there. Let me know what you find."

"No problem." Nate picked up the folder and handed Dyson the baggie of pills. "I need this filed from an overdose earlier. I'll get you the report later."

"Sure. Tell Kia to come in. I need her to give the D.A.R.E. talk at the elementary school."

Nate strode out of the office, smirking as he told Kia what Dyson had planned for her day, and headed for his cruiser. He drove past the library, the flower shop, the bank, and the hospital, turning into the Mill Creek neighborhood for the second time today.

The gloomy, tattered building before him was the worst excuse for a house he'd ever seen. Cracked windows, chipped and peeling paint, white long since dulled to gray. Overgrown bushes choked with weeds almost obscured the sagging front porch.

The wooden steps groaned under Nate's weight. He shielded

his eyes to peer through the cracked front window, but it was too dark to see inside.

Nate knocked on the door. "Hello?" he called. "Mr. Martinez?"

No answer.

Nate knocked again. "I'm Detective Sweeney from the Skamania Police Department. Can you come outside for a moment?"

Nate waited, listening. Silence. He glanced over his shoulder, feeling eyes crawling over his back. He knew he shouldn't try the handle, but he wasn't going back to Dyson with no news. He was surprised to find the door unlatched. He nudged it open with his boot, convincing himself he had probable cause to enter. Besides, his Spidey sense was going all kinds of crazy.

"Hello?" The door creaked open, an inch at a time. Nate peered inside. In front of him was a living room decorated in shades of brown and yellow. The ceiling bulged with damp, the plaster cracked down the middle.

Somebody was sitting on the couch, facing away from Nate, a TV flickering quietly in front of them.

"Mr. Martinez?"

He pushed the door open a little more. A sudden prickling oozed over his neck and back, a headlong rush of fiery adrenaline kicking inside his veins.

That's when the smell hit him.

# CHAPTER 3

TUESDAY WAS GRAY AND DAMP. By afternoon a soft fall rain had settled outside, making the clinic look tired and dirty. Sagging chairs leaned against murky beige walls. A garbage can overflowed with empty paper cups. Wet jackets were hung on the coatrack, dripping onto the grimy linoleum. Reception was a crush of damp bodies that smelled of urine and feet and unwashed hair.

Some of my patients were from the eastern side of Skamania, where the yards were cut into neat squares of green, the bushes professionally trimmed. But most were poverty-stricken, immigrants, homeless, addicts, or all of the above. They had little or no access to health insurance, suffering agonizing pain instead of seeing a doctor because they couldn't afford it. These were the people I'd gone to medical school to help.

The more cynical accused us at the clinic of having a savior complex, but I knew we were making a difference in these people's lives. We were helping.

I yawned as I walked toward the shared medical-staff office. It had been a busy day with patients, doing wellness exams, checking X-rays and lab results. And all on very little sleep. Josh had come into our bedroom too many times to count last night. When we'd first woken this morning, his fever had been too high to send him to school, so I'd called Nate's mother and she'd agreed to stay with him. Fortunately, I was good on very little sleep. It was sort of a prerequisite to being a doctor.

I dug my cell phone out of the closet where I stashed my purse. Nate had texted me an X. I smiled and shot an X back to him, loving that he thought about me during his day. I then dialed Moira before my next appointment.

"Hello, Emma." Moira's voice was brisk, the tone she always used with me. I could hear the pursed-mouth exhale of the cigarette she thought nobody knew about. I imagined her draped in her cashmere and pearls, slate-gray hair smoothed perfectly into place, a cigarette dangling out the window in secret. I gritted my teeth but kept quiet. It wasn't like we had a lot of choice of babysitters.

"Hi, Moira. How's Josh?"

"He's sleeping now. I gave him some ibuprofen."

"If he wakes up—"

"I've raised four children, and I stayed home with all of them. I know how to take care of a sick child."

I swallowed a sharp retort, resenting the insinuation that I was a lesser mother than her because I worked. I tried hard to be grateful for my mother-in-law. She was a wonderful grandma to Josh, and she and Nate were very close. I didn't understand why she didn't like me, although I suspected she was unhappy Nate and my relationship had moved so fast.

"Sure, of course. Sorry, um . . ."

Julia, a nurse practitioner I'd become friends with, tapped me on the shoulder. "Sorry!" she whispered when she saw I was on the phone. She held a cup of black coffee out to me. "Your four o'clock is in room four."

*Thank you!* I mouthed. "Sorry, Moira, I've gotta run. Tell Josh I love him."

I grabbed the coffee and swallowed a giant gulp before hurrying to the exam room. I scanned the patient's chart as I walked. She was a new patient. Fifty-four years old. Normal temperature. Slightly elevated BP. I rapped gently on the exam room door and entered.

"Mrs. Jones?"

"Yes." Alice Jones was small and frail. Her pale hair was threaded with gray and tied into a messy ponytail. Spiderweb wrinkles framed the corners of brown eyes clouded with pain. Her clothes were threadbare, a faded sweatshirt over ripped jeans, scuffed canvas tennis shoes with no socks.

Her husband, or who I assumed was her husband, sat next to her, a short, burly-chested man with shiny red cheeks, oily dark-gray hair, and a pair of round glasses on a bulbous nose.

"Her back's hurting," he said, his voice too loud in the small space. "It's been going on a long time now. It's from all that damned gardening."

I sat at my desk and turned to Alice. "I'm so sorry to hear that. I like gardening too. I have a whole freezer of vegetables I grew this summer. It's pretty tough on our back and knees, though, isn't it?"

I opened Alice's patient file on my computer and typed notes as her husband explained her symptoms.

"I need to examine you now, Alice. Can you show me where the pain is?"

Alice struggled to stand, her husband holding her elbow firmly. She bent forward at the hips and touched a hand to her lower back.

"Sometimes my legs go a little numb," she whispered.

I felt a heavy tug of pity in my stomach, the kind you'd feel for an injured bird. I examined her spine, assessed her ability to sit, stand, and walk. There was no redness or obvious swelling. The erector spinae muscles were smooth and strong, her reflexes normal. She wasn't moving with enough pain to indicate a tear in the disc or enough restriction to show sciatica. But the numbness concerned me.

Doctors are scientists who work in an uncertain world. We use statistics, odds, and probability to diagnose and treat. Good or bad, we make the best-informed decisions we can.

"I'm going to order an MRI." I typed more notes in her file.

"Can you give me something for the pain?" she asked. "I've heard OxyContin is good for back pain."

I kept my face neutral. The opioid crisis had made it difficult for doctors to know where the line was, when to prescribe pain medicine and when not to. It was a doctor's job to help people, to assuage their pain, and yet I'd watched other doctors' patients succumb to addiction. I knew about addiction firsthand, from my brother. I refused to let my patients become another statistic.

"I'll write a prescription for naproxen to help the pain." I smiled gently at Alice. "Once we get the MRI results, we'll know better how to treat it. In the meantime, ice it, and stay off your feet for the next few days, okay?"

I handed Alice a leaflet with advice on how to treat back pain, gave her arm a compassionate squeeze, and left to see my next patient.

AFTER MY last patient of the day had left, I went to find Julia. She was clearing up one of the exam rooms after seeing a patient. Tendrils of dark hair were falling out of her ponytail. Julia was conventionally pretty, with sea-glass eyes and a slight overbite that somehow made her look even more adorable. She smiled faintly, and I noticed her wrist was bandaged, her movements slow, a little delicate.

"You all right?" I nodded at her wrist.

"Oh, carpal tunnel syndrome. Lucky me." She laughed wryly. Julia was lively and cheery, a nurse practitioner who somehow did more work than all the doctors combined.

I told her about Alice Jones, and she scowled, her freckled nose crinkling. "The husband was here last week. Said he'd sprained his wrist."

"He wasn't wearing a wrist wrap."

"I think Dr. Watson saw him. She might've prescribed some OxyContin, although check his chart to be sure. Maybe he was back for more? I seem to remember he was pretty aggressive. She was glad to see the back of him, I know that."

I'd come across my fair share of angry men in the ER during my residency at Harborview in Seattle. I could still remember stitching open wounds with shaking hands, dodging drunken fists, standing near the exit to make sure I had a quick escape route.

I pulled a fresh sheet of medical exam paper over the table while Julia swiped the edges with an antibacterial wipe. We headed down the hall to the staff office. The rectangular area was bisected by a long desk with multiple charging points; on one side was a wall of cupboard space, and on the other a coffee-making station. Dr. Wallington was writing reports into a file while two of the other doctors were speaking earnestly about a patient. I pulled my coat out of the closet and turned to Julia.

"I'm glad I didn't prescribe any oxy, then."

I'd learned that what healed wasn't always in a doctor's drugs or a surgeon's blade. Sometimes it was the quieter things, like compassion, being heard and shown you mattered. I was confident I'd made the right decision with Alice. We'd wait and see what her MRI said.

"It's a tough call these days," Julia agreed. She lowered her voice and glanced around. "Speaking of oxy, watch out for Marjorie. She's on the warpath right now."

Marjorie was the medical administrator of the clinic, which was situated within the auspices of Cascade Regional Hospital. She'd worked here forever and was unnecessarily crotchety as a result. I'd only worked here for three years, after taking over for a doctor who'd decided to partially retire, so she basically scared the crap out of me.

"What's wrong now?"

"People keep leaving the medical supply room unlocked. She keeps all the samples from our pharma reps in there."

"Yikes. I'll keep an eye out."

"Hey, wanna grab a drink?" Julia slid her coat on. "It's happy hour. We can get one of those derby thingies you like."

I laughed. Sometimes I was still surprised by the collegial nature of my job. "It's a Brown Derby. Wish I could, but Josh has been sick. Rain check?"

Her reply was cut off as our receptionist, Brittany, burst through the door, her eyes almost comically wide.

"Dr. Sweeney! You need to get downstairs! Josh's been admitted to the ER!"

# CHAPTER 4

IT WAS PAST TIME to go home when Nate finally finished his report. Skamania was a small town, but it still had its share of domestic assaults, breaking and entering, and drug offenders. Murder was less common, however. The office was still buzzing with the news a day after it happened.

Two detectives were standing near Nate's cubicle gossiping like a pair of old fishwives about the murder, about the vacation to Toronto Mike Spillane was planning, about how Harry Chen had done on the sergeant's exam, and about one of the many addicts who'd been booked earlier today.

"He was so fucking on the nod it took him a full minute to realize I was shouting at him!" Chen spluttered into his coffee. "I went over and shook him to see if he had any dope. Sure 'nough . . ."

Nate usually loved the joviality of his fellow cops, but now he tried to block them out. A murder in his town. It was on. Nate had been exposed to all the terrible things people did to each other. He sure as shit wasn't letting a murderer walk the streets of his town.

He stared at a Post-it Note he'd stuck to his computer monitor. The numbers had been written on a scrap of paper that was tacked to Santiago Martinez's refrigerator. Nate had jotted them down, thinking they might be important to his investigation.

### 323 454

What were they for? Did they mean anything?

He rubbed his jaw thoughtfully, no closer to the answer. It couldn't be a phone number, which was seven digits, or a bank card's PIN, which was four. What was six digits?

If only he had some news, a break in the case, but after the last twenty-four hours processing the scene and interviewing potential witnesses, he was at a dead end. He chuckled at his own pun. Ah, good ol' detective humor.

Nate pulled a Snickers from his desk drawer and popped the top on a warm can of Coke. He'd texted Emma earlier to say he'd be home late again, but he hadn't had a chance to check if she'd replied. He reached for his phone just as Lieutenant Dyson came out of his office, forcing him to leave it in his pocket.

"You still here, kid?"

"Yup." Nate tried not to care that Dyson still thought of him as a kid. Years as a beat cop in Seattle, then promoted to detective here, and he was still just Matt Sweeney's kid. He peeled the wrapper off his Snickers and took a huge bite. "Just finishing up these reports."

"Tell me what we know." Dyson leaned against the desk next to him. He was a good lieutenant, always willing to talk out a case or jump in when needed. The way Nate's dad used to be before the stroke fifteen years ago.

Nate put his hands behind his head and leaned back in his chair. "Okay. Name was Santiago Martinez. Alias El Pulgar, the

Thumb, because years ago he got his thumb cut off. Damned if I know how that happened, but he moved oxy, cocaine, and fentanyl around Seattle, so probably one of his associates took it for him. He was running fentanyl and heroin for one of the cartels, working the supply chain from Mexico up I-5 and east to Yakima, Spokane, and beyond. He got caught selling in Seattle, did a few years in jail, and when he was released two years ago he moved out here. No sign of him dealing since then. Seattle PD are coming out tomorrow, although they haven't been super specific about what time."

"The crime guys definitely saying it was murder?" Dyson asked.

"They found a puncture at the back of his neck. Tox screen will show what killed him, but I expect it'll be an overdose of some sort of drug. And nobody injects themselves in the back of the neck."

"So somebody else did it?"

"Maybe. We found a baggie of a white substance on the floor in the laundry room. There were also digital scales, a pill press, and those little orange prescription bottles in there. A whole fucking drug factory, just without the drugs."

Dyson tapped his finger on his teeth. "Maybe the drugs were the motive for the murder."

"It's one theory so far. The back door was unlocked. Maybe someone came in, killed Santiago, grabbed the drugs, and took off."

"The guys get any useful evidence?"

"Lots of prints. We're running them now. There were a few women's things there, no clothes in the closet, but a bottle of shampoo in the bathroom, a pink toothbrush, that sort of thing."

"Girlfriend?"

Nate gulped some Coke and set the can on his desk. "Neighbors said they'd seen a woman there. We're looking for her."

Dyson rubbed his mustache, bushy eyebrows drawn tight. "What about hair and fiber analysis?"

"Working on it. No blood at the scene to analyze. Just the puncture mark in his neck. He didn't fight it."

"Maybe he knew his attacker."

"Or he was ambushed, didn't expect it. Maybe the girlfriend—"

"Excuse me." A woman's voice, shrill and nasal, cut into their conversation. "Is one of you Detective Nate Sweeney?"

Nate and Dyson whirled around. All the other cops' heads swiveled, the bustle in the place suddenly stopped. A woman and man were standing just outside the detectives' area. Cops, Nate could tell.

The woman, clad in a black pantsuit and crisp white shirt, was about Nate's age, midforties, sharp features, thin lips. Her blond hair was pulled into a tight bun, and she had the downturned mouth of an angry carp. The man was a tall, broad-chested black guy with a military-style buzz cut. The tailored navy suit he wore looked like it cost more than Nate's annual salary.

"I'm Detective Sweeney."

The woman shook first Nate's then Lieutenant Dyson's hand. "I'm Special Agent Lisa Hamilton. This is Special Agent Phil Greene. We're from the Seattle division of the Drug Enforcement Administration. You've been in contact with some of our colleagues at the Seattle PD. Sorry it took so long for us to get in touch. There were some . . . politics that needed to be sorted out."

"Why don't we talk in my office?" Dyson led the agents across the room, his lopsided swagger more pronounced than ever. Nate followed.

Dyson closed the door. Agent Hamilton sat in one of the small plastic chairs, but Agent Greene leaned against the door, his arms crossed.

"How can we help you?" Dyson asked.

Hamilton tossed a thick file on Dyson's desk. "With oxycodone use and mortality rates at an all-time high, we've been using local informants to try to find the dealers responsible. Your guy, Santiago Martinez, was one of our confidential informants. He turned state's witness a few months back to avoid jail time, and we were getting information from him until he dropped out of contact a few days ago."

Nate flipped through the file. There were police reports, news articles, a few pages detailing Santiago Martinez's past convictions. Crime scene reports, handwritten notes, printed emails. Evidence.

"A few months back he pleaded guilty in federal court to smuggling fifteen hundred grams of fentanyl and selling to an undercover agent," Hamilton continued. "He transported the fentanyl from Seattle around western Washington. After we arrested him, he agreed to help us go after a larger supplier in the chain, so we sealed the case."

Nate glanced at Dyson. "A larger supplier?"

"He told us about this gang he works with out here. Said they got themselves a bunch of fentanyl and oxy. The black-market oxy business is booming, right? And fentanyl is cheap. So this gang, they decided to take advantage and sell both. But they're smart. They've kept it small, so they've stayed off the radar. They don't get involved in land wars or killings or any of that cartel shit."

"Did he tell you who it was?" Nate asked.

"Nope. He died first," Hamilton said. Her partner leaned against the wall, hulking and silent. "We figure somebody found out he'd been talking to us."

Nate's phone buzzed against his leg, but he ignored it. He closed the folder and set it down, then leaned his butt against Dyson's desk. He studied Hamilton and Greene. They were holding something back. Their posture, as if they were waiting on a knife's edge, gave it away.

"Why me? There are four other detectives here, but you asked for me by name. What aren't you telling me?"

Hamilton crossed her arms. "Do you know much about your wife's brother?"

Nate straightened, suddenly alert. "Ben? Ben's been in and out of jail for drug dealing, petty theft, did a few years for assault. Emma hasn't heard from him in years."

She nodded. "Mr. Martinez mentioned his name a few times."

Nate gaped at her. He'd never even met Ben. From what he could tell, Emma was the smart, successful one, while Ben was the total fuckup.

"Ben Hardman might be linked to the head of this gang. Hell, he might even *be* the head, for all we know. Either way, we need to find out who's running it before more oxy and fentanyl hit the streets. We want you to be the lead detective of our local task force. You'll have additional search and seizure powers under your new federal authority, and you'll liaise with us through occasional visits and calls."

Nate gave a bewildered snort. "I can't investigate my wife's brother! That's a complete conflict of interest."

Agent Greene unfolded his arms, smoothing his fingers down a paisley-print silk tie. "We just want you to help us stop more drugs flowing into the area. Yakima's just a few hours from here, and right now it's the main drug distribution center in North America. We've got drugs being smuggled up in bodies, cars, trucks, children's toys, paintings laced with narcotics. We have to get a handle on this before more people die."

"All we need is for you to report back to us what you find when you're investigating this case," Hamilton added. "And if your wife has anything to say about where Ben is, all the better."

"You want me to use my wife to get to her brother?" Nate was incredulous.

"We don't know for sure Ben's involved," Greene said. "We're just asking you to report back to us what you find. You saw Mr. Martinez's place. This gang is cutting oxy with fentanyl. Do you have any idea how dangerous that stuff is?"

Dyson rolled his eyes, not bothering to hide his sarcasm. "I assure you, even out here in Hicksville, we know how dangerous fentanyl is."

Hamilton and Greene exchanged looks. After a minute, Agent Hamilton dropped a card on the folder and stood. "Think about it and call me in the morning. Time is of the essence here."

When they'd left, Dyson's office dipped into silence. A vent kicked on somewhere, a low gurgle and hum. Nate's gaze drifted to the picture of Dyson and Matt Sweeney just over Dyson's shoulder. If only he could talk to his dad—but the stroke had stolen speech from him too.

He took a toothpick from his pocket and rolled it between his fingers before popping it between his teeth. "What do you think?" he asked.

Dyson frowned, stroking his mustache. "I'm not saying it's strictly against policy. He's Emma's brother, not yours. But I'm not saying it's right either."

"People could die if we don't find this gang."

"Yeah."

"But investigating Ben, interviewing him, that opens us up to legal challenges down the road if he's involved."

"Yeah, it does."

"But if we don't investigate him, fentanyl could become an even bigger problem."

"Yeah."

Nate scowled at Dyson. "Are you gonna help me here or just agree with everything I say?"

Dyson sighed. "Look, Nate, you know yourself the budget

cuts we got here. The truth is, we could use a case like this to prove we deserve more funding." He hesitated. "*You* could use a case like this."

Nate drew back. "Are you saying my job's on the line?"

Dyson blinked, startled. "Course not, son! You're my best detective. I'm saying, I'm retiring next year. It's time for me to pass this job on to someone younger. I want you to apply. I'd put a word in for you, of course. More money, more regular hours with your family."

Nate's mouth fell open, a curl of pride twisting in his middle. Lieutenant? *Him?*

Dyson grabbed his cowboy hat and shoved it on his head. "You can help investigate your wife's brother, impress Chief O'Neill, and make your mark with the mayor, or you can let our community continue to be ravaged by fentanyl and oxy. I think you know the right answer."

Nate's phone buzzed against his leg again. He pulled it out as he left Dyson's office. It was a text from his mother.

**COME QUICKLY. JOSH IS IN THE ER.**

# CHAPTER 5

*JOSH'S BEEN ADMITTED TO THE ER.*

The words snapped me into action. I sprinted past my colleagues, through reception, and out of the clinic. I took the stairs two at a time, the soles of my shoes making a hollow, vibrating sound against the metal surface. An elderly woman was struggling to open the door at the bottom of the stairwell. I pushed past her and barreled through.

The emergency room was on the ground floor, at the opposite corner of the hospital from the clinic. By the time I reached the front desk, I was sweaty and out of breath.

"My son . . . Joshua Sweeney . . ." I gasped at the admitting receptionist.

"Go on in, Dr. Sweeney," she said, buzzing me through the locked doors.

I found Josh in the last exam room. One hand was grasped tightly in Moira's. Her face was wet with tears. Josh had a bloody bandage taped to his forehead, an IV attached to the back of his hand. But his eyes were open. He was okay.

Relief hit me hard. My legs went numb, made of nothing but air, and for a second I teetered there, feeling like I would collapse. "Josh!"

I tugged Josh into my arms, hot tears pressing against my eyelids.

"Mommy, I fell down the stairs," Josh said.

I looked at Moira.

"He just . . ." She started crying. Her usually sleek hair was a complete mess, her eyes rimmed with red. Her cashmere sweater was wrinkled and smeared with blood. "He fainted, right at the top of the steps. I couldn't catch him!"

Her sobs became hysterical. Mascara oozed down her cheeks, embedding into the wrinkles on her face. Her hysteria snapped me back to myself.

"It's okay." The words gusted out of me.

I touched my son's cheek and took a deep breath. Josh's head dropped against my chest, and I just held him, his hot little body pressed against mine. He stuck his middle and pointer fingers in his mouth and after a minute dozed, his breath coming in short little bursts.

The blue curtain swung back, the scraping metal rings making me jump. A doctor I didn't know entered the cramped exam room. He was young, with curly dark hair, a strong nose, and a manila folder clutched in his hand.

"Hello, Dr. Sweeney. I'm Dr. Adelman. We've put some fluids into Josh's IV to start hydrating him, but we are going to need to investigate a little more to find out exactly what's going on." He pulled over a low stool with wheels so he was next to us. "We'll take some blood, do an MRI, of course."

Josh moaned in his sleep, a small sound at the back of his throat. I tightened my hold on him, felt the heat of him seeping through my clothes and warming my skin.

"He started feeling unwell a few days ago," I said. "Sunday.

He was a little warm, but nothing to be concerned about. He had a bad cold a few weeks back, and I thought maybe he'd just gotten overtired. He, uh . . ." I closed my eyes. "His back . . ."

I gently lifted Josh's shirt, exposing the pale skin of his back for the doctor to look at. Moira gasped. The bruises marching up his spine were even darker now.

"He said he got slide-tackled at school," I whispered, horrified.

The doctor's face didn't change, but I saw the tightening around his eyes. "Let's run those tests."

WE WAITED for hours. The doctor took a few vials of blood, whisking it away to the lab for immediate analysis. Josh went in for an MRI. Another bag of fluids. More blood tests. Nate arrived at some point. My phone was still at the clinic, but Moira had called him, although only after snidely commenting that I should've thought of Nate sooner.

I ran to him and let him fold me in his arms. We sat in silence next to Josh's bed, our fingers laced tightly together. I couldn't seem to bring myself to consciously think about what those bruises might mean.

Finally a new doctor, Dr. Johnson, came in with Josh's chart. He was older, round, with fat cheeks and orange stains on his lab coat, as if he'd been wiping Cheetos dust down the front.

"Hi, Mom, Dad, why don't you come out here, and we'll have a chat. Let's let Josh keep resting."

"Go on. I'll watch him," Moira said.

Nate and I followed Dr. Johnson down the hall to a family room, our hands still laced together. It was bland, the carpets a pale brown, the walls even paler brown. Ikea couches were pressed against the wall, a wilted spider plant on a table in one corner. A clock hung over the door, ticking ominously.

A slight man with creased, weathered skin and rosy cheeks was standing next to the plant. Someone I knew from a very long time ago. I inhaled sharply. His face was etched into my memories of the worst days of my life.

"This is our oncologist, Dr. Edward Palmer." Dr. Johnson introduced us.

"Emma." Dr. Palmer nodded, not seeming at all surprised to see me. "I heard you were working here. Good to see you again, although I'm sorry, of course, for the circumstances."

It had been twenty years since I'd seen him. He was probably in his late fifties now, smaller and more stooped than I remembered. His hair was stark white, as were his eyebrows and beard. On second glance, the flushed cheeks were swollen blood vessels, the telltale sign of rosacea. But his eyes were the same warm amber, and his manner was grandfatherly.

"Nate, this is . . . Dr. Palmer." My voice was flat and wooden.

"Dr. Palmer is one of the best oncologists in the state," Dr. Johnson added. "He moved here to Cascade Regional from Harborview last summer. We're lucky to have him on the team."

Nate's gaze landed on me, heating me like an accusation. "Oncologist?"

Tendrils of panic coiled around me. Both doctors were silent for a beat.

My husband's fingers crushed the bones of my hand, and all I could do was cling to him. And then it was there, the diagnosis, coming at me slowly, and then all at once.

"The blood count came back," Dr. Palmer said gravely. "I'm afraid Josh has leukemia."

CHAPTER 6

THOSE WORDS—*JOSH HAS LEUKEMIA*—hovered in the air like wisps of smoke. Nate couldn't seem to grasp them. The diagnosis seemed as unlikely as Chewbacca walking through the doors right then.

Josh had a cold. The bruises were from being slide-tackled.

*Leukemia.*

It must be a mistake.

"Here. Sit." Dr. Palmer motioned them to a pair of cheap Ikea couches and sat across from them. Emma put one hand on Nate's knee, the warmth of her skin grounding him. He placed his arm around her shoulders, pulling her tight, as if they could ward off the doctor's words if they stayed together.

Nate studied Dr. Palmer, who reminded him of Santa Claus. In Nate's experience, most surgeons and specialists were hugely talented, with egos to match. But Palmer didn't swagger or bark orders. He smiled softly instead of grinning. He hunched his shoulders, but when he looked at Nate his eyes were calm, assured. Intelligent. The type of man you could underestimate.

Emma had gone ashen, but she didn't look surprised by the diagnosis. "How do we treat it?" she asked.

Like most habitual worriers, Emma was great in a crisis. It was one of the things that made her such an excellent doctor. But Nate knew this was simply because when the worst happened, she had sort of been expecting it all along.

"Josh needs treatment immediately." Dr. Palmer was speaking. He adjusted the silver tie at his throat, smoothed it flat against his chest. His gaze was apologetic. It made Nate anxious. "We'll do further tests and set a treatment plan."

He started talking about bone marrow and spinal fluid, but all Nate could think was that his son had *leukemia*, and didn't people die of that? How could he stop it? He felt impotent against the onslaught of medical words. It was his job to provide for his family, to keep them safe, and somehow this *thing*, this enemy, had sneaked into his son.

Nate watched Emma speaking with the other doctors. Her hair had come unclasped, glossy, dark tendrils hanging around her ears. Mascara was smudged under her eyes. And yet she still seemed so calm, asking all the right questions. She was detaching herself. But he could tell by the white of her lips, the pinch between her brows, and the hard clench of her jaw that she was terrified.

Dr. Palmer grasped Emma's shoulder, an overly familiar gesture. She leaned toward him. Just a hair, but enough that Nate noticed. This was someone so familiar that Emma could lean on him now, in the midst of their son's leukemia diagnosis. And yet she'd never mentioned his name.

Emma caught Nate's baffled expression and stiffened. She shook her head. *Not now.*

"How did I miss it?" In the harsh lights Emma's porcelain skin was so pale it almost looked translucent.

Nate thought he saw a glimmer of a tear on her cheek, a fierce sucker punch to his gut. He suddenly felt scared. Emma never cried. She was self-contained, self-reliant. He didn't know what it would mean if she fell apart.

"It's not your fault," he murmured.

"The bruises . . . I'm a doctor!"

"Em . . ." Sometimes she was her own worst enemy.

She whirled on him, her eyes blazing, raw with pain, but Dr. Palmer interjected, "Your husband's right. Those bruises could've been anything. It's easy to miss the symptoms at first. Being a doctor had nothing to do with it. You know how these things go, and that your life is about to change. With luck, we've caught it early, and can start treatment right away."

He was sharp and focused, giving them a sense of what they were dealing with and how to fight it. Nate liked that about him.

Nate cleared his throat. "Does Josh need chemo?"

Dr. Palmer looked at him, his eyes flicking up and down, as if assessing Nate's character. "First we'll need to do a bone marrow test to confirm our diagnosis."

"You don't know. . . ." Hope burst in Nate's chest.

"We *do* know that it's leukemia," Dr. Palmer said patiently. The kind but firm manner in which he said it spoke to his experience. "We found blast cells in Josh's blood. Based on the blood tests, we suspect that it's acute myeloid leukemia."

He went on to describe leukemia subtypes and consolidation therapy and bone marrow transplant, the likely outcomes and possibilities. His words knifed Nate in the lungs. His brain clouded, his eyes blurring. He nodded over and over, pretending that he understood, when he only wanted to know one thing: "What are Josh's chances of survival?"

Dr. Palmer hesitated. "We won't know for certain until we have the test results back. However, acute myeloid leukemia is very aggressive and requires quick decision-making."

Nate closed his eyes. He could hear the clock above the door ticking. It seemed to have gotten louder. How long had they been in here? How long did Josh have left?

Emma's hand snaked over to his, winding her fingers through his. Her hand was ice-cold. He squeezed it and drew an *X* on her palm with his index finger.

"There is one other treatment we could do," Dr. Johnson spoke up from where he'd been standing silently near the door.

"What is it?" Nate looked between the men. When they didn't answer he looked at Emma, but she seemed as clueless as he felt.

The *tick-tock* of the clock suddenly grew more insistent.

"Chimeric antigen receptor T-cell therapy. Or CAR T-cell therapy," Dr. Palmer finally said. "It's a type of immunotherapy that's been approved to treat children and young adults with acute lymphoblastic leukemia. Recently it has shown some impressive results treating acute myeloid leukemia."

"I've read about it," Emma said. "You withdraw T-cells from a patient, genetically modify them, and reinject them to identify and attack cancer cells."

"Yes, it's been very effective—" Dr. Palmer began.

"Then what's the holdup?" Nate asked. "When can we start this T-cell thing?"

"This type of treatment is still emerging." There was a warning note in Dr. Johnson's voice. "And most insurance companies don't cover it."

"Josh and I are both covered by the hospital plan," Emma said.

"The hospital insurance only covers about ten percent of the total cost of CAR T-cell therapy—" Dr. Palmer said gently.

"It doesn't matter," Emma said fiercely.

"—which is five hundred thousand dollars."

# CHAPTER 7

LATER THAT NIGHT, we settled Josh in a private room on the pediatric oncology floor. It was small but clean, decorated in cheerful shades of blue and orange. One wall was covered in a childish mural, leafy trees and a mountain with little rabbits hopping along the bottom. The window looked out in the direction of the waterfall.

Josh smiled shyly at Katie, the nurse who was getting him settled. She chucked him under the chin. "I'm going to call you Captain Smiley," she declared. Josh giggled.

After she left, I turned a cartoon on for Josh and sat on the couch next to Nate, leaning my head on his shoulder, while Moira settled on a chair next to us. Josh was asleep within a few minutes.

"Oh, Moira!" The door flew open and a woman with short curls dyed brownish red, sagging jowls, and a colorful patterned dress plowed across the room and pulled Moira against her massive bosom. "Thank you for texting me. We're all just so devastated!"

Moira's eyes filled with tears. "Thank you, Bertie."

Bertie handed a handkerchief to Moira, who delicately dabbed at the corners of her eyes.

"This is Bertie." Moira introduced us. "From my church."

Anger spiked through me. *How dare she.* This was personal, and we'd only just found out. It wasn't her place to be spreading it around.

"Pastor John and I are here to help." Bertie dabbed at moist eyes. "We've set up a GoFundMe account and we're organizing a bake sale this weekend to help pay for this treatment. We're all praying for little Josh."

*Thoughts and prayers*, I thought bitterly. *Like that does any good.*

"Thank you," Nate managed.

He always remembered his manners. But I couldn't bring myself to answer. I wanted to be grateful, I did. But what was selling a few cookies going to do to save Josh's life? Her thoughts and prayers weren't action. They didn't change a thing.

An awkward silence rang out in the room.

"Thank you so much for coming by, Bertie, it was really lovely of you." Moira guided the woman toward the door and almost pushed her out.

"What the fuck, Ma?" Nate snapped when she returned.

Moira flinched. She hated cursing. I gaped at Nate, surprised he'd sworn in front of her. He was a bit of a wimp when it came to his mother. In fact, I couldn't think of any time I'd heard him be so overtly critical.

I slipped my hand into his. Two against one.

"You're already telling people?" Nate scowled.

"Just church people."

"That's still people!"

Moira turned to me. "She means well," she said. "She did the same thing when Matt had his stroke. And when we moved Matt into the nursing home, she set up a schedule so someone visited most days of the week. Okay, it didn't change anything, but the support helped. I couldn't have done it without her."

I nodded, a little surprised that she was appealing to me, not Nate. When Nate and I first started dating, his whole family had welcomed me with open arms. I'd never felt more a part of a family than I had with Nate's. Except when it came to Moira. She'd been stiff and cool, strangely judgmental since the day I met her. I knew she thought I wasn't good enough for Nate.

Moira closed her eyes. When she spoke, her voice wobbled. "Emma, how hard will the treatment be on him?"

Nate's and Moira's gazes were heavy on mine. They both wanted—no, *needed*—my words to be positive ones. It was my job to reassure people, to help them understand and accept. Disappointing people hurt, but I knew it was even worse to hide the truth.

I thought about what my dad used to say: *You don't get to choose what cards you're dealt any more than you get to choose who your patients are. You just gotta make those cards work for you.*

I blew out a breath. "His best chance of survival is the CAR T-cell therapy, and the question isn't how hard it's going to be, it's how much it's going to cost." I looked at Nate. "We have to find a way to get the money for that treatment."


NATE WAS watching me with that intense, questioning look he sometimes got. He wouldn't bring it up in front of his mother, but he wanted to question me about how I knew Dr. Palmer.

Instead, I asked him to call our neighbor and see if she could let Charlie out and feed him, then brushed my lips against his and left to grab my purse and phone from the clinic.

The hospital's third floor, where the clinic was located, was quiet, the lights dimmed. The overhead fluorescents flickered briefly, a soft hum emanating from the bulbs.

I expected to use my key card, but the door to the clinic was still unlocked when I arrived. I slipped into the empty reception area and moved past battered plastic chairs, an empty water dispenser, and end tables with magazines splayed across their tops.

I hurried through the door leading to the exam rooms, but stopped abruptly when I noticed a light. Marjorie was still working in her little office at the end of the hall. I could just see her profile through the door, which was open a crack, her long graying hair hanging over her face as she stared down at a pile of folders. Her desk radio played the Eagles softly.

I didn't feel like talking to anybody, so I moved quietly across the laminate floor on my tiptoes, escaping into the medical office. I closed the door with a gentle *click* and slowly pulled open the desk drawer where I'd left my purse, careful not to let the metal drawer runners creak.

Before today, losing my parents was the single worst thing that had ever happened to me. After they died, my brother, Ben, and I went into foster care. Neither of our parents had any family who could take us, so we were left with just each other.

Foster care wasn't as bad as you'd think. Our foster parents were nice, and we were lucky we got to stay together. But they had two of their own kids, and it was clear we weren't part of their real family.

Once, shortly after my parents died, they had a birthday party for their oldest daughter, Kelly, a spoiled girl with brown eyes and bad skin. They had a cake, streamers, balloons, a unicorn piñata.

One of Kelly's uncles had them all pose for a picture. Still aching from my parents' deaths, I'd jumped into the photo, grinning like an idiot and wrapping an arm around Kelly's shoulders. My foster mother had firmly moved me out of the way.

"We'd like a picture with just our family," she said, smiling politely. *Just our family.*

That was when I realized I didn't belong. I was an outsider peering in the window.

The next few years, Ben and I coped in very different ways. Ben acted out. Sometimes he stayed out all night, sometimes for days at a time, picking up girls and drugs and bruises along the way. By the time he was seventeen, nobody tried stopping him anymore.

I coped by being careful and good and smart. I wore my responsibility like an invisibility cloak in school. But as much as I tried to be the person my parents would've been proud of, to blend in and be good and not be a bother, Ben stood out in the most horrible way possible to a good girl.

He was a bad boy.

He got kicked out of school for dealing when he was a senior and I was a sophomore. He left one day without even saying good-bye. I found out later he'd gone to juvie. He'd been making drugs in a shed in the woods by our foster family's house, and they'd turned him in.

And just like that, I was all alone. Not only had I lost my mom and dad, my brother was gone too.

I learned my lesson then. You can't take anything for granted. You can't stand by and leave things to chance. The people you love can die, and you'll be alone. You must always be alert, ready to fight.

It was almost twelve years before I felt like I belonged again. Twelve long, lonely years before I met Nate and we had Josh and became our own family.

My thumb grazed the screen on my phone, lighting up the picture on my screen saver. Josh was in my arms, looking directly at the camera, while I had my forehead pressed to his cheek.

Nate's arms were around both of us, his chin on my head. We looked happy.

I grabbed a sheet of paper from the printer and drew a line down the middle, making two columns: incoming and outgoing. I opened the banking app on my phone and scrawled our monthly salaries in the incoming column, then did a quick tally of our bills, my medical school loan payments, and my malpractice insurance in the outgoing.

I stared at the digits as fear corkscrewed through me.

I couldn't lose my son. We had to find the money.

I shoved my phone and the paper into my purse and slipped undetected down the hall. The radio was still murmuring, Marjorie singing tunelessly along.

In the hall heading toward reception, I noticed the supply closet was open a crack. I moved to shut it, remembering that Julia had said people kept forgetting to lock it. But something made me stop.

I pulled the door open and peered into the murky closet. There were drug samples arranged at the back. To my right, a stock of rubber gloves, tongue depressors, thermometer heads, bandages, antiseptic, blood pressure cuffs. And just beneath them, stacked on the shelf in neat piles, was the stock of prescription pads for all the clinic's doctors.

# CHAPTER 8

"JOSH HAS ACUTE MYELOID LEUKEMIA," Dr. Palmer told Nate and me the next day.

We were sitting in his office surrounded by gleaming rows of medical degrees, shining glass awards, and framed certificates. A handful of photos of his daughter over the years sat on the window ledge behind him.

"We've caught it early, but I won't lie, this is tough to cure. We need an aggressive treatment plan, and we need to start now. Without treatment, survival of AML is usually measured in weeks, not months. I can't promise Josh would even see the new year."

My hand flew to my mouth, and Nate gasped loudly, his face draining of color.

"We have two options," Dr. Palmer continued. "We can do a high dose of chemotherapy, followed by a targeted therapy drug and a stem cell transplant. Or we can go the CAR T-cell immunotherapy route. As I said, the hospital's insurance only covers a portion of the treatment, but it is FDA-approved so they should at least cover some of it."

"I'll call and find out more today," I told Nate.

"You might get stuck with hospital stays, blood work, extra tests," Dr. Palmer warned. "It will cost a lot, no matter which way you look at it."

"We'll do whatever it takes," I said.

Dr. Palmer steepled his hands on top of his desk, his gaze heavy on mine. "Josh is, what, just a few years younger than you were when your parents passed?"

Nate's head swiveled to face me. There had been no time last night to tell him how I knew Dr. Palmer. "Eight. He's eight years younger than I was."

"Let's be sure we're fighting to save the same person."

I swallowed hard. "Josh is all that matters. He has a chance to live if we get him the CAR T-cell therapy."

NATE CAUGHT up with me in the corridor as I strode quickly away from Dr. Palmer's office.

"You want to tell me what that was about back there?"

"What?" I didn't want to do this now.

"With Dr. Palmer. How do you know him?"

I kept walking. "It doesn't matter."

Nate grabbed my arm, forcing me to stop. "Don't do that, Em. Don't shut me out."

"What do you want me to say?"

"I want you to make me understand!"

I wished with all of my heart I could share more of myself with Nate. But the wounds from my past were too raw and deep. Talking about it, exposing them to anyone, even someone who loved me as deeply as I knew Nate did, was like rubbing them with salt. I'd taught myself long ago to lock it away, and that decision had allowed me to live.

I sighed and continued walking, slower this time. It would be easier to talk if he wasn't looking at me.

"I don't like thinking about it, let alone talking about it," I said finally.

"I want to be here for you, to support you, but I can't if you won't talk to me."

We stopped outside Josh's room. Nate brushed a finger across my cheek, his eyes creased with concern, but he didn't speak. He was doing that cop thing he did where he waited for me to fill the silence. He was much better at this game than I, and he knew it.

"My parents were picking me up from a friend's house. My dad had been drinking. He had a stressful job and he maybe didn't cope with it very well. My mom was mad at him for driving when he'd been drinking, but he wouldn't listen. When my dad got something in his head, there was no changing it. Anyway, he got a call, and Dad said we had to go get Ben. He was driving too fast on this tiny rural road. I don't remember much about the crash, to be honest. Just afterward. My mom . . ."

I gulped, hating the memory, wanting to push it away. "She died on impact. I got my dad out. . . . I had no way to get help, so I just sat there with his head on my lap. He died like that. We waited for what felt like hours, and nobody . . ." My voice trailed off and I took a shaky breath. "Dr. Palmer saw the smoke from the car. He called the police and took care of me. He saved my life."

Nate tipped my chin up so I was looking at him. His eyes were filled with such tenderness it brought tears to my eyes.

"I watched my dad die, Nate," I whispered.

"Josh is going to be okay." Nate's voice was firm. "We'll get him this treatment."

"We can't even afford to buy a new couch."

"We'll find a way."

I pulled the paper I'd tallied our bills on from my purse and thrust it at him. "How are we going to afford five hundred thousand dollars for this treatment? We barely have enough money to pay rent each month."

Most doctors didn't start earning a full-time salary until ten years after they graduated, and most primary care physicians earned barely more than what they had in medical school debt. Money had never mattered to me before. I only ever wanted my own family and to help people. But now, money was all I could think about.

Nate barely glanced at the paper.

"I'll get a loan," he said. "I have a buddy at the bank who'll help. We'll get on a payment plan with our insurance, and I'm sure my mom will help."

"She can't help! The rent we pay her covers your dad's care. Otherwise she wouldn't even be able to afford that."

"We have our pensions."

"It isn't enough!"

Nate scrubbed a hand over his jaw. "Lieutenant Dyson told me he's retiring next year. He basically said the job's mine if I can crack that murder case from a couple days ago."

I gaped at him. "You can't be serious. Josh is sick! He needs us. *Both* of us. If you take that case, we won't ever see you."

"If I get that promotion, I'll get more pay and better hours. We'll be able to pay off whatever we have to borrow."

"Sitting at a desk all day doing paperwork? Come on, Nate, you'd hate that!"

"It doesn't matter. It's not about me, it's about Josh."

Tears stung my eyes. I bit my lip, hard, the coppery taste of blood prickling in my mouth. But it was better than useless, pointless tears.

It was an impossible situation. We did need the money, but Josh needed his father too. I needed my husband.

I touched his hand. "We need money *now*, Nate. Not next year."

A flash of panic glinted in Nate's eyes. "I can do this," he insisted stubbornly. "I can provide for my family."

"Stop with the misogynistic bullshit," I snapped, losing patience. Nate was so used to being responsible for everybody, providing for his mom, his brothers and sister, the people of our community. I'd found it endearing when we first met. But he couldn't provide for Josh by getting a promotion next year. "It isn't up to just you. We're in this together."

Nate shook his head, and the air between us tightened. I stared at my husband, a dark swirl of horror winding through me. I'd always thought the best couples should complement each other, like peanut butter and jelly, cookies and milk. Nate was all sunshine and hope, while I was the realistic pragmatist. But together we made a balanced whole.

Now, though, he was engaging in blind denial when I needed certainty. I could see that Nate wasn't going to offer me that.

We'd reached an impasse.

DARK, ANGRY-LOOKING clouds were moving in from the west, pushing toward the mountains and hovering over town. I could smell the rain in the air. A gust of wind swept up a handful of leaves and slapped them against my ankles.

It was lunchtime, a crowd of doctors, anesthesiologists, and nurses gathered outside the staff entrance smoking and chatting as I hurried past. People thought that medical professionals didn't have vices. That we were these omnipotent, perfect people with Madonna-like serenity. That we didn't take antidepressants and never needed something as taboo as a line of coke to stay up studying for the board exams while moonlighting to make enough money to pay our bills at the same time. But I could say from experience, doctors were humans. We had vices like everybody else.

I pulled a crumpled pack of Marlboro Golds from the bottom of my bag and lit up as I climbed into my eleven-year-old Honda. I rolled my window down and pulled out of the parking lot, inhaling slowly. My lungs felt like they were being wrapped in a warm, downy blanket. Ash sprinkled on my open window. I flicked it away. Nate would kill me if he found out I'd been smoking.

I drove slowly down Main Street. The Christmas lights were already strung up and would be turned on tomorrow. Usually we went to the tree-lighting ceremony in town, a thermos of hot chocolate clutched in Josh's hands.

I headed out of town toward Seattle, making two calls as I drove: one to my office, leaving a message for Marjorie to call me, and the other to our insurance company, starting the claim process for Josh's CAR T-cell therapy.

Once I was far enough away from Skamania, I stopped at a cash machine and withdrew some money. I bought a couple of cheap, prepaid cell phones from Target, as well as a bag of Nate's favorite snickerdoodle cookies, and hopped back in the car. My phone chimed a text from Nate.

X

I texted an X back, then turned my phone off.

Twenty minutes later, I pulled onto a two-lane road flanked on either side by red-painted barns and overgrown fields gnarled with weeds. Douglas fir and ponderosa pines jutted angrily into the chilly blue sky.

I parked in front of a small redbrick gas station. A GENERAL STORE sign hung above the door. Below that: FISHING. BAIT. This was not your typical Exxon.

A bell jangled against the door as I went inside. The gas station was cute, with splashes of cheerful red décor and rustic cream and orange tiles. The middle of the shop was filled with neat rows of chips, cookies, and donuts. Against the back wall was a floor-to-ceiling refrigerator with sodas and beer, and one corner was taken up with a coffee station and a food-to-go refrigerator.

A man came out from a back room, wiping his hands on a cloth. He was well-built, with a few days of stubble on his jaw and blond hair scraped into a short, straggly ponytail. His faded denim shirt hung over a white T-shirt that was streaked with grease.

Nerves fizzled in my stomach like an ulcer.

"Can I help you?" he asked.

I turned to face him fully.

"Hey, Gabe."

Gabe Wilson had been my brother's best friend—and fellow dealer—in high school. Gabe was basically a walking penis. He oozed sex appeal and had a pair of dimples you just wanted to lick. All the girls fawned over him, and naturally I had a wicked crush on him. Since he was my brother's best friend, I had easy access. Plus, I had a unique talent he and Ben liked: a gift for forgery. They let me hang out with them if I'd write their absence notes for school.

Gabe and I had connected a few times while I was in medical school, and yes, by "connected," I mean had sex. But it had been years since I'd seen him. Gabe was a part of my past that I'd kept hidden from Nate.

Gabe's face went slack with surprise when he recognized me, but he smiled quickly to cover it, revealing those deep dimples I'd always loved.

"Gabriel? Is everything okay?" A very young woman appeared behind him—early twenties, long, white-blond hair, sharp cheekbones.

She had an accent. *Swedish? Norwegian?*

"Hey, babe." Gabe kissed her quickly. "Do you mind making sure pump two is working?"

She shrugged and went outside.

"What do you want?" he asked when she'd left. His voice was decidedly cooler this time.

"I need your help." I plopped my bag on the counter and pulled out a stack of prescription pads, the ones I'd stolen from the clinic last night.

Drugs had ruined my brother's life, but maybe they could save Josh's.

"I've signed a bunch of these prescriptions for OxyContin. I need your help selling them."

# CHAPTER 9

GABE REARED BACK AS if I'd reached across the counter and punched him in the teeth.

"Are you insane?" he hissed, glancing out the window. "I don't sell drugs anymore. How did you even find me?"

"Facebook."

"Well *un*find me. I got out of that game when I bought this place."

I withdrew five of the prescriptions I'd signed and thrust them at him. The signatures of my colleagues had been easy to forge. Nobody could read a doctor's signature anyway.

"Please!" I shook the prescriptions at him. "My son has leukemia. He's at Cascade Regional on an IV, for God's sake! I need the money to pay for his treatment."

Gabe looked horrified, as I knew he would. His sister had died of cancer when he was a kid, leaving parents who never really recovered from the loss. They'd eventually divorced, his dad running off and leaving Gabe with a single mother who'd been so busy trying to provide for him she'd barely been around to take care of him.

He rubbed a hand over his grizzled jaw but shook his head. "I'm really sorry to hear that. I am. But I can't help you. I have a good life now. I sold enough shit to buy this place, but now I'm out. I don't plan on getting back in."

A sluggish sort of fear wormed under my skin. I set the scripts down on the counter in front of him.

"Gabe, you have to help me."

"Why?"

"He's your son."

Gabe stared at me, his face a mask of shock that was quickly replaced by anger. "Fuck." He wrenched his ponytail out, smoothed his beach-blond hair, and retied it. "Are you sure?"

"I did a paternity test. I'll show you."

He swore again, looking irate. "When?"

"Remember right before Christmas six years ago? It was my first year of residency."

I could see him doing the math in his head. "Why didn't you tell me?"

"You were still dealing! I didn't want that for my child."

"Why didn't you . . ." He hesitated.

"What, get an abortion?"

"Well, yeah. You were all stressed out about medical school shit."

I looked away. "I didn't get to grow up with a family. Josh was my chance to have one."

"I want to meet him."

"Absolutely not. I'm married now. I'm not asking you to give financial support or do anything else. I met my husband right after that night. He thinks Josh is his, and I don't plan on telling him otherwise. I just need your help selling these prescriptions so I can save my son's life. *Our* son's life. Please."

"Em—"

"We can split the profits, fifty-fifty."

"No!"

I opened my mouth, but the bell on the door jangled. I glanced over my shoulder.

Cop.

The hairs on the back of my neck prickled, a chill racing down my spine.

The cop was massive, well over six feet, and probably almost as wide. He had a buzz cut, with dark hair curling over his bare arms and sprouting from the collar of his uniform.

In my peripheral vision, I saw Gabe quickly sweep the prescriptions to the floor behind the counter. He looked like he was going to be sick. I casually hitched my purse higher on my shoulder, letting the rest of the prescription pads drop to the bottom.

The cop's presence filled the small space. He wandered from aisle to aisle, picking up junk food as he went, a pack of Hostess cupcakes, a bag of Doritos. The refrigerator made a thwucking sound as he grabbed a Coke, then let the door slam shut. His footsteps sounded magnified in the confined space.

And then he was right behind me, his breath lifting the hair at my neck. I squeezed my hands together to hide their shaking.

"A pack of Marlboro Golds, please," I said loudly to Gabe.

Gabe stood frozen in rigid silence. There was so much in his eyes, I was terrified he would give everything away.

*Pull yourself together!* I screamed silently at him. How had he ever been calm enough to deal drugs?

I turned slowly, deliberately, and smiled at the cop while arching one eyebrow and lifting one hand. "I'm trying to quit, but I'm totally addicted," I said, opting for casual and chatty.

I knew the consequences of selling these prescriptions: each count of unlawful distribution of OxyContin by a medical professional carried a twenty-year prison sentence. One doctor in

Seattle had traded sex for prescriptions; a podiatrist had set up an entire oxy ring; a dentist had unnecessarily pulled teeth to justify prescribing opioids so he could get thousands in kickbacks. These doctors bought yachts and houses, jewelry and status and privilege.

But I wasn't in it for the money. I just wanted to save my son.

The cop grinned at me, exposing small, straight teeth and matching dimples. "I've quit, like, a hundred times. It's the job, I think. It's so stressful."

"Don't I know it!" I laughed. "I'm a doctor. I know all about stress!"

I lowered my eyelashes, all innocence, and smiled up at him, before turning back to Gabe.

"Could I get those Marlboro Golds, sir?" I asked Gabe.

Gabe finally snapped out of it, grabbing the cigarettes and setting them on the counter. "That'll be nine forty-two."

I slipped my hand into my bag and withdrew my wallet, carefully extracting a ten-dollar bill and one of my business cards with my cell phone number printed on it. I tucked the card under the bill and handed it to Gabe.

Gabe wordlessly gave me my change. I took it, waved goodbye, and left.


MY HEART was slamming in my chest as I jogged to my car. Rain had started falling in sheets. I was an idiot to think Gabe would help me, even more of an idiot to bring all those signed prescriptions inside. Now he had them. What kind of an amateur did that? I'd shown all my cards.

I'd broken two of my dad's most important rules. *Keep your hand close to your chest.*

*And never get caught drawing dead.*

"Always make sure you have a plan B, Emma," he used to say. "Because once you get caught drawing dead, you're done. It won't matter what cards you draw, you'll have zero chance of winning."

And then a horrible thought occurred to me: What if Gabe had video surveillance? Of course he did. The real question was: What would he do with it?

I drove as quickly as I dared back to Skamania, my windshield wipers swiping pathetically at the rain. I was going to have to set up an OxyContin drug ring on my own. But how, without losing my job, my family, my freedom?

I pulled up in front of my house, in the middle of quintessential suburbia. Tidy, well-maintained homes with white picket fences and jewel-green lawns were separated by neat shrubs and towering apple trees, all arranged over a gently sloping hillside with views of the Cascade foothills.

When I opened the door, Charlie went crazy, barking and baying with excitement. He pushed his nose against my knees, and I dropped to the floor, wrapping my arms around him for a doggy cuddle. He snuffled happily against my neck.

Once he'd calmed down, I went upstairs for a quick shower, then made myself a sandwich. Charlie's nails clicked against the hardwood as he followed me around, tail wagging happily. After I'd finished eating, I clipped his leash to his collar.

"Come on, Charlie."

We walked through the neighborhood at a fast pace toward the woods, where I wouldn't be bothered by people I didn't want to speak to. The rain had stopped, a chill mist replacing it. My breath coated the air in white and my fingertips quickly cooled as I stumbled, weak and numb, through the underbrush. The wind beat heavily against the naked trees.

Suddenly my skin prickled, the hairs on the back of my neck rising. A twig snapped nearby, and I jumped. I peered into the murk. The dreary mist glazed the ground, obscuring my ankles in a ghostly swirl. My teeth began to chatter. I came to a complete stop and turned around in a circle. A shadow danced nearby, but it was nothing; the movement of the wind twisting through the trees.

My imagination was going wild, my heart slamming erratically in my chest. I mentally shook myself. No one was there. I had to get control of myself. Nobody but Gabe knew what I'd been thinking.

I hurried Charlie back the way we came, icy-cold fingernails raking the back of my neck as I ran.

As I approached my house, my neighbor Jennifer was just getting into her car. Jennifer was a pert blond with twin girls just two years older than Josh. She ran a dog grooming shop in town.

She waved and crossed the grass that separated our houses, meeting me at the front door. She wrapped her arms around me, smelling of lavender and the faint musky scent of dogs. I stood stiff as a board in her soft arms. If I fell apart now, I might never be able to put myself back together.

"I'm so sorry, Emma. I heard about Josh."

"Wow, that was fast." I barely even tried to hide my irritation.

"Well, you know Brad's sister-in-law works in the ER. She told Brad and he told me."

"Ahh."

"So how are you guys doing? Do you need anything?" Jennifer asked, her brown eyes pools of liquid sympathy.

I looked down at Charlie. "Actually, yes. Would you be able to pop in and check on Charlie? Just for the next few days."

"Absolutely!"

I rummaged in my purse for the spare key and handed it to her. "He has the dog door out back, so he'll just need a few walks and some food. I'll leave it out on the counter."

"Of course. Anything to help."

I moved toward the house, hoping to get away as fast as possible. "Thanks, Jennifer. See you later."

BACK AT the hospital, I headed first to the clinic, planning to talk to Marjorie about reducing my hours while Josh was in treatment. But as I got out of the elevator and strode down the hallway, I noticed a cluster of people crowded around the clinic's entrance.

I pushed past them and entered the reception area. Marjorie, Brittany, and a handful of doctors and nurses who were working today were gathered in a little cluster near reception.

"What's going on?" I asked Marjorie.

Marjorie jumped. "Emma! I didn't see you there." Her eyes were red, like she had been crying. "It's just terrible. I found the supply closet open this morning. Someone had left it unlocked, and when I went in I noticed that almost all the Oxy samples were gone. I told Lawrence, up in administration, and he called the police. They found—"

Just then two burly police officers came out of an exam room, their mouths pressed into grim lines. Between them, her arms handcuffed behind her, was Julia.

The fluorescent lights cast stark shadows across her face, her eyes like dark bruises. She was looking right at us but not really seeing us. Her brown hair had come out of its ponytail, clinging to her neck in damp patches. She moved stiffly between the officers, as if she were a remote-controlled dummy and someone else had taken over.

A shocked silence settled over the room. Marjorie's hand flew to her mouth, her chubby throat bobbing up and down.

She lowered her voice and leaned toward me. "The police found OxyContin samples in her purse. Looks like she's been stealing them!"

"No!" My skin went cold and clammy.

Julia's head swung toward me. Her face was ashen, her eyes damp and shiny. She strained, trying to pull away from the officers, but they held her tight.

"Emma, I didn't do this!" she shouted, breaking out of her reverie. "Come on! Tell them!"

*Julia* . . . My mouth formed her name, but no sound came. My vocal cords were paralyzed with shock.

I could feel the weight of the prescription pads in my purse, the bulk of them pressing against my side. Guilt oozed, black and sticky, through my core. But nobody had noticed they were gone. The Oxy samples were so much more obvious.

I clamped my mouth shut. I needed to appear calm and unfazed, just the right amount of upset and shocked.

And then, a second later, Julia was gone.

# CHAPTER 10

NATE FLICKED ON THE television in Josh's hospital room. His mom had run downstairs to grab them something to eat, and Josh was sucking his middle finger and pointer finger, sleepily staring into space.

Nate was still trying to process the fact that Emma had never told him she'd watched her father die. He shouldn't be that surprised, he told himself. Emma could be intensely withdrawn, closemouthed about her past.

When they first started dating, she'd told him that her parents had died in a car accident when she was thirteen, but she'd never elaborated. He'd only found out the details when he'd looked up the accident report form. Her father had been drunk, double the legal limit. When a deer leaped across the dark road, he'd lost control of the car and it had flipped over an embankment.

Nate saw Emma going to the clinic every morning, working to help people, and he knew: every patient she saved mattered because she hadn't been able to save her parents.

Sometimes he watched her, folding Josh's pajamas or matching socks or scraping eggs off the pan after breakfast, ribbons of dark hair swaying down her back, her eyes focused and intense until they looked up and caught his. And the way they'd soften, just melt at the sight of him . . . he just felt awed by her. He'd pull her into his arms, running his hands over her body and pressing his lips to hers, and feel completely fulfilled. Emma meant everything to him, and he knew she felt the same.

Still, who kept the fact that her father had died in her arms from her husband? Nate knew he kept some secrets, but he also knew he couldn't have kept something like that from Emma.

And what did it say about her that she could?

Nate tapped the remote control, finally finding something Josh might like.

"*Star Wars* is on, buddy," he said.

Josh loved *Star Wars*—the robots, the aliens, the themes of good versus bad. But now he didn't seem interested. He was a million miles away.

"Josh? Want to watch *Star Wars*?" Nate repeated.

"I don't know, Daddy." He sighed. "I'm a pool of sadness right now."

He pulled Josh in for a hug. "I know. But you know what? The evil stuff in your blood is like the Empire. We just have to go to battle with it, and we're gonna win because we're the good guys."

"Do the good guys always win?" Josh asked.

Nate caressed the little tin of toothpicks in his pocket as Luke Skywalker's lightsaber flashed on the screen. "Always. Remember? Obi-Wan Kenobi and Yoda defeat the Empire, and Luke helps Anakin become good again."

"Is that why you're a detective? You wanted to be one of the good guys?"

"Well, yeah. But I also wanted to help people. I think a good detective can change someone's life for the better. There are some things worth fighting for, like you're gonna fight the Empire."

"I'm glad you're a good guy, Daddy."

Nate kissed the top of Josh's head. "Me too, Josh." Josh's bottom lip was wobbling. "Hey, what's wrong?"

Josh burst into tears. "I don't want to die!"

"Oh, Josh." Nate wrapped his arms around him, pulling him closer.

Emma came in just at that moment. She dropped a backpack on the floor and rushed to Josh. There wasn't room for the three of them in the narrow hospital bed, so Nate stood, allowing her to scoop Josh into her arms.

"I don't want to be in mud! I won't be able to breathe!" Josh's voice inched up an octave.

Nate looked at Emma, hollow-eyed with helplessness.

"Shhh." Emma spoke to Josh in low, soothing tones while all Nate could do was stand next to them feeling cold and alone, afraid he'd messed up somehow, said the wrong thing.

Emma clutched Josh to her, her strong, jutting chin clenched. "You're not going to die. I'm not going to let anything happen to you. Do you hear me? I am *not* going to let you die."

Eventually Josh's sobs subsided and he fell asleep. Nate watched his wife stroking Josh's hair, the movement strangely hypnotizing. He thought suddenly of one of their first dates. He'd dated a lot by the time he met Emma. It was easy for him to meet women. He was handsome and charming, confident, with an easy smile. Girls loved that shit. But there was always something missing.

Until Emma.

He'd spent hours cooking that day, trying to impress her. But as soon as she arrived, her hospital pager had gone off, notifying her that a patient had died. She'd been a resident at the time and off duty. But she'd grabbed her coat and slid her shoes back on.

"I have to go to the hospital," she'd said. "Her daughter has nobody to grieve with."

The humanity in those words, how much Emma cared, took Nate by surprise.

"I'll go with you," he said.

He'd stayed late into the night, watching this woman he'd just met as she comforted a stranger. He'd fallen in love with her then.

"I can't watch someone I love die again," she whispered to him now, her voice wobbly.

"Dr. Palmer, he seems like he knows his stuff," Nate said, trying to stay upbeat. "We have to trust that, right?"

Emma plopped down next to him on the couch, dropping her head onto his chest. Nate wrapped his arms around her.

"Why haven't you ever mentioned him?" he asked. "Dr. Palmer, I mean. He saved your life, and you've never said a word about him."

Emma blew out a long breath. "I asked him to stay away from me."

Nate was stunned. "Why?"

"I didn't want to remember. Dr. Palmer felt bad for me, so he visited all the time. At first in the hospital, then at the foster house where I was staying. I started playing basketball for a while, just to keep busy, and he'd show up at my games. My foster parents encouraged him, but every time he showed up it just reminded me of that night. If I could go back and change what happened, I would. But I can't. I couldn't. And it was too hard to move on with him around."

Nate tried to imagine how it would feel to be thirteen and lose your parents, to have your father die in your arms. He tightened his hold around Emma as the sound of her phone buzzing came from her purse. She bent to retrieve it, barely glancing at the screen before dropping it like she'd been scalded.

"Everything okay?" he asked.

"Yes. It's the hospital."

"But we're here."

"I mean, the clinic. It's probably just Marjorie returning my call."

Nate squinted at his wife. He got the distinct feeling that Emma wasn't telling the truth. It was nothing specific, but there was something cagey about the way she shifted her gaze that gave Nate the telltale tingle he got when someone was lying to him. Yet her face was as inscrutable as ever.

It was just the pressure they were under, he told himself. Emma wouldn't lie to him.

She pressed her cheek against his chest. "You know, I totally understand that the accident was no one's fault," she said after a minute. "Life's too messy to attribute blame so neatly. You can't blame a deer for jumping in front of a car. You can't blame a kid for not knowing how to save someone's life. There was no culpability, just fragments to pick up."

She lifted her chin and met his gaze, her eyes clear as a summer sky. "But this . . . I can't bear the thought of Josh dying because I didn't do enough to save him."

NATE WALKED outside the hospital for the first time in twenty-four hours. Autumn was sullenly sliding into winter, the bare branches cackling in the biting wind. The clouds were bloated with rain, the air smelling faintly of woodsmoke.

He climbed into his car, pointing it in the direction of home while putting the phone on hands-free and listening to a voice message. It was from his old high school buddy Jonathan Kellington, a manager at one of the banks in town.

*"Hey, Nate. Your loan application came back today and I'm, well, I'm really sorry, man, but it's been declined. Without any collateral and no disposable income, it's pretty unlikely a bank will lend*

*you that type of money.*" There was the sound of Jonathan clearing his throat. *"Again, I'm really sorry. I hope Josh is doing all right. Give me a call if you want to grab a beer or anything."*

Nate threw his phone down, his chest feeling like it had gone supernova. The phone clattered against the passenger's side floorboard.

A bubble of self-loathing expanded in his chest. What kind of man was he? He couldn't provide for his family. And now his son was sick and he couldn't do shit to save him.

Nate gripped the steering wheel and turned onto Main Street. When he reached the bridge where Robbie had died, he pulled to the side of the road and stared at the cross, remembering Robbie's last words to him.

*You're gonna be sorry, man.*

Nate had been pissed at Robbie for turning him and a bunch of the guys in for cheating on a math test. Nate would probably have detention for the rest of his senior year. That was some thanks after he'd done his best to keep the popular kids off Robbie's back the last few years. Sometime around ninth grade, Robbie had put on weight, and with his bad skin and stutter, some of Nate's jock friends had been merciless. Then he'd added fuel to the fire by tattling.

Nate was walking to his locker when he saw Robbie surrounded by a group of jocks. Robbie had called out to him, but Nate looked away, pretending he didn't see when one of the guys shoved Robbie to the floor. They could kick the shit out of Robbie, Nate had decided. He deserved it.

And they had.

Nate felt a sense of desperation descending on him, an urgent need to *do* something. He slid a toothpick from the tin in his pocket. He pressed it into the bed of his thumbnail, letting the pain wash over him.

He hated himself for doing this, the weakness, the self-loathing and embarrassment that flooded him afterward, like a teenager caught masturbating. He wished he could stop, but some horrible compulsion told him he deserved to suffer. He hadn't helped Robbie. He couldn't help Josh.

*Drip, drip, drip.* The sound of his blood hitting the seat snapped him back to the present.

Nate clenched his fist, trying to contain the bleeding. He snapped the bloody toothpick in half and tossed it in a used Starbucks cup, swiping a crumpled napkin at the drops of blood. He picked up the phone he'd thrown on the floor. His thumb was throbbing, blood pooling around the cuticle. He pulled a card out of his wallet and dialed the number. After a minute, Agent Lisa Hamilton answered.

"I'm in," he said. "Meet me at the station."

AN HOUR later Nate was sitting across from Lieutenant Dyson. He'd stopped and bought a box of six raspberry-filled donuts and was rapidly eating his way through the whole thing.

Dyson was watching him, a worried look on his face. "You sure you want this case, Nate? You got a lot going on right now. We'd all understand if you need to take a step back."

"Please," Nate said simply. He didn't want to beg, but the money he'd get from a promotion was the only way he'd be able to pay for his son's treatment. It was the only thing he could do to provide for his boy. "I need this."

Dyson studied his face. Finally he nodded. "All right. I'll give you until the end of the year, and we'll see where you're at. And I'm gonna assign Kia as your partner."

Nate opened his mouth to protest. The end of the year was barely a month away. Dyson held up a hand. "We'll see what headway you can make while also dealing with Josh's illness. I was serious when I said I want you applying for this job. But your son is sick, and that isn't something to be discounted. We can't let it affect this case. Kia can help. Besides, you know we can't have any question of bias being raised. *If* the case necessitates any direct contact with Ben, it should come from her."

Nate knew he was right. So he nodded, and Dyson called Kia into the office. She entered, shuffling her feet awkwardly and rubbing nail-bitten fingers over her square jaw.

"I'm sorry about Josh," she told Nate, looking at her feet. "We all are. We've taken a collection and donated to that GoFundMe account."

"What GoFundMe account?"

"You know, the one Pastor John and his wife, Bertie, started?"

Nate vaguely remembered Bertie saying something about a GoFundMe account, but he was genuinely surprised and humbled at the goodness of the people in this community. "That's really good of you guys. Emma and I—we appreciate it."

Agents Lisa Hamilton and Phil Greene arrived a few minutes later, carrying steaming coffees and a box of Krispy Kreme donuts that they set in the middle of Dyson's desk. Nate accepted the coffee gratefully and dumped sugar into it. He stood to allow Agent Hamilton and Kia to take the only chairs available, while he and Greene leaned against the wall.

Hamilton slid a silver-and-blue DEA badge across the desk to Nate, the metal gleaming in the light. "Keep that with you," she said. "You'll need it in addition to your detective's shield when on task force duties."

Nate fingered the badge, a strange feeling settling over him. Pride. And also guilt. Like he didn't deserve it or something, which was dumb. He'd worked hard for this.

"We're really happy you decided to join us. And we get Detective Sharpe too, it seems." Hamilton handed Kia a badge. "Let's get started. We've had a few developments."

She moved her coffee out of the way and slid a photo across the table. "The substance in the baggie found at Mr. Martinez's house tested as oxy and fentanyl powder. We found fingerprints from a woman named Violeta Williams."

"Santiago Martinez's girlfriend?" Nate asked.

"Unknown, but that is the current assumption."

A very young woman stared back at him from the picture. Long, dark hair and glittering, angry eyes; a colorful tattoo of thorny red roses climbed her right arm, disappeared under her sleeve, then reappeared at her throat.

"Violeta Williams works at a restaurant in Seattle, but she's been off the past two days. We know she was at the house with Santiago Martinez at some point. What we don't know is if she's the one who killed him."

Agent Greene spoke up. "According to footage from the restaurant's security cameras, she was last seen leaving with a man. Want to wager a guess who it was?"

Nate took a giant bite of his donut, raspberry jam oozing into his mouth. He licked his fingers. "I'm not a betting man, but I'd put money on Ben Hardman."

Greene grinned, his teeth very white against his dark skin. He fingered his Burberry tie. "Maybe you should become a betting man, then."

# CHAPTER 11

"MOMMY, CAN I GET a lightsaber?" Josh asked.

He was lying on a hospital bed attached to about a million lines snaking out of his body into a special machine that was extracting his T-cells. He seemed more curious than upset about the needle in his arm.

"Don't you already have one?" I asked.

"Yeah, but I want one with lights and stuff so I can do battle with the Empire."

I smiled. Josh had started calling the leukemia *the Empire.* "Sure, we'll get you a lightsaber."

Josh turned to the lab tech. "You're really going to turn my blood cells into mini *Millennium Falcons*?"

"That's right." The lab tech smiled. He was clean-shaven with thick, black glasses and a rash of red zits sprouting up his chin, but I could've kissed him for how well he was handling Josh. "We'll take your blood to our lab and then we'll separate the white blood cells. That's called leukapheresis. Don't worry if you can't say it; it's pretty tricky. I just call it Luke-Skywalker-esis. Once we do that, we freeze Luke-Skywalker-esis and send him off to our mother ship, where we train him to fight the Empire in your blood. That way, when we inject the reprogrammed T-cells—the mini *Millennium Falcons*—back into your body, they're all trained up."

"Cool!" Josh exclaimed.

I laughed, feeling the first sense that maybe everything would be okay. AML was a terrible disease, but CAR T-cell therapy had a high success rate. Maybe he'd be all right. I just had to make sure we could pay for it.

My phone buzzed again, but I continued ignoring it. Gabe had already texted twice, saying he needed to speak to me, but I hadn't been able to leave Josh's side.

The lab technician finally withdrew the needle from Josh's arm, capped the little tubes, and put them in a white lab envelope.

"Okay, that's all for us here. We'll see you both in about three weeks with some fighters ready to put in your blood." He gave a funny little salute and then left the room.

Back upstairs in his hospital room, I fluffed Josh's pillows, pulled the blankets over his thin little body, and flicked the TV on for him.

Because my job was more flexible than Nate's, we'd agreed that I would take the week off while he continued working as normal until we could establish some sort of rotation. Dr. Palmer had promised to let Josh go home if he was still doing well by Friday. We just had to return in two weeks to start lymphodepleting chemo. The chemo would prepare Josh's body for the reprogrammed CAR T-cells. But until then it was R & R for Josh.

Moira swept into the hospital room. She'd promised to come every day after visiting Matt in the nursing home, and here she was, bearing gifts.

"How's my little Jedi!" she sang. "I've brought you all your favorite toys. I don't know how you've managed with just TV to keep you entertained." She gave me a meaningful look, then dumped out the objects in the canvas bag she'd been carrying: Josh's favorite *Star Wars* blanket, a teddy bear the size of my upper body, a box of Lego.

"Grandma!" Josh immediately launched into an update on the *Millennium Falcon*s the doctors were preparing to put into his blood. As he was talking, my phone beeped. I glanced at the text.

> I'm here. I know someone who can help. Meet me in hospital café. G

I looked up as a shadow darkened the doorway.
*Gabe.*

He was wearing a baseball hat, his eyes obscured by the shadow the bill cast. He'd shaved, but his sharply angled jaw and full lips were instantly recognizable.

I froze, terrified Gabe would come in and introduce himself to Josh. Maybe it had been stupid telling him Josh was his son. Even stupider telling him the hospital Josh was getting treated in. But I hadn't expected him to come here, to find us.

His gaze landed for a long moment on Josh. I waited, breathless, but a second later Gabe disappeared, the doorway again empty.

I was debating what to do when my cell phone rang. I answered, my voice shaky.

"Hello, Mrs. Sweeney, this is Nicole from Avail Insurance calling about your claim for Joshua Sweeney's CAR T-cell therapy."

"Hi. Yes." I motioned to Moira that I would be right back and stepped into the hall outside Josh's room.

"I'm really sorry, but unfortunately your insurance plan doesn't provide coverage for CAR T-cell therapy."

I almost dropped the phone. I'd assumed they would cover at least *some* of it.

"What?"

"The insurance plan you're on doesn't provide coverage for CAR T-cell therapy," she repeated.

"But the therapy is FDA-approved." I parroted Dr. Palmer's words, my throat so dry I could barely speak.

"Yes," she agreed. "But CAR T-cell therapy is still so new it's being reviewed on a case-by-case basis. This is very typical when new therapies are first approved."

"What *is* covered then?"

"As I said, we're looking at policy coverage on a case-by-case basis. I've spoken to Josh's referring doctor and the administration office at Cascade Regional Hospital, and we have a policy of care we can offer for your case."

My heart leaped with hope, but it was short-lived.

"Naturally, you'll still need to pay your deductible and all co-pays, but we can cover physical removal of the white blood cells and reinjecting the cells. We won't, however, be able to cover reprogramming the cells, as those are sent to a specialist lab. The lab will bill your hospital once they've received the white blood cells, and you'll need to pay Cascade Regional directly before the cells can be reinjected into your son."

The breath left my body in one giant gasp.

A month. I only had one month.

I pressed a shaking hand to my mouth. "How much will I need to pay?"

"Ninety-eight thousand and four dollars."

I SANK onto the toilet seat in the accessible bathroom, sweat beading on my forehead. I'd grabbed my purse and the canvas bag Moira had brought Josh's toys in and escaped the hospital room, promising to bring Moira a blueberry muffin when I returned.

I yanked a handful of prescription pads from my purse. For the next few minutes I signed prescriptions from my colleagues for OxyContin as if my life depended on it. I thought about signing a few from me, but decided it was too risky.

Water leaked in a steady drip from the tap, merging with the sound of my heart throbbing in my ears. I transferred the signed prescriptions to the canvas bag, flushed the toilet, washed my hands, and went downstairs to the café, my mind made up.

Gabe was nowhere to be found, and for a second I panicked, thinking he'd changed his mind. But then I saw him outside talking on his phone. Gabe waved and made a drinking motion with one hand, asking for a coffee.

The café was busy. Most doctors went to the staff cafeteria upstairs for lunch, but the coffee was better down here. I got in the back of the line.

"Hello, Emma." Someone tapped me on the shoulder. I whirled to see Cass Robbins standing in line behind me. Cass had huge, soft brown eyes that were serene and thoughtful, matching a calm demeanor that was much admired in the ER, where she worked as a doctor. She smiled, revealing teeth that were an orchestra of chaos, her front teeth too large, her canines twisted and sticking out at odd angles.

"Oh, hi, Cass." I risked a quick glance out the window for Gabe; he was still on the phone.

"How are you? How's Josh?" Cass peered at me, her brow furrowed. Word spread fast in a small town.

"He's okay right now, thanks. How are you?"

Cass sighed. "I need more coffee. The amount of ODs coming in lately, I just can't keep up. We had two resuscitations this morning, a mother and father. Their four-year-old called nine-one-one when she couldn't wake them."

"Oh my God. Did they survive?"

She shook her head. "Poor little girl's going to grow up completely traumatized."

I opened my mouth to answer but was saved by the cashier calling me up. I ordered a blueberry muffin for Moira, a double-shot Americano for myself, and a mocha for Gabe, which I remembered was his drink of choice.

"You must really need the caffeine!" Cass chuckled, an eyebrow arched.

"Ha." I forced out a breezy laugh, busying myself with stuffing my receipt into my purse. "I'm meeting a . . . friend."

She glanced over my shoulder and grinned. "Oh my God! Your friend is hot. Maybe introduce me later."

I turned to see Gabe watching me from the other side of the glass. My stomach twisted.

The barista plopped our drinks on the counter. Cass grabbed hers and waved good-bye. I picked up the coffees and blueberry muffin and found a mostly-clean table tucked in a corner at the back. A minute later, Gabe slumped into the chair opposite me.

He took a long slug of coffee and made a face.

"Why are you here?" I hissed.

"You wanted my help, right?"

"Yes, but this is where I work!"

"I wanted to see him."

"I told you, you can't meet him. My husband doesn't know about us. He's a good man. He doesn't deserve to find out like that."

The thought of it, Gabe telling Nate he was Josh's father, triggered a sickening, clammy feeling deep inside me.

"Why didn't you tell me?"

I lifted one shoulder. "I guess I just wanted Josh to have a family. And I knew he wouldn't get that from you."

Gabe looked pained by my words. After a minute, he nodded. "I won't tell your husband. Promise. I just want to meet Josh."

"No." I shook my head. "Gabe, I—"

Gabe stood, somehow managing to both lift his chin and glare down his nose at me at the same time. God, he looked like a thumb when he did that. A very hairy thumb.

"Look, sweetheart, you want my help, I want to meet Josh. Arrange it, or I'm out."

I gritted my teeth. "Fine."

Gabe sat back down, looking smug. He reached across the table and grabbed the half-eaten ham-and-cheese croissant sitting next to me. He took a massive bite, cheese oozing out the bottom and dribbling down his chin as he chewed. I watched him impassively.

"Have you heard from Ben?" I asked.

"No. You?"

"No."

Gabe finished the croissant. He grabbed a crumpled napkin from the table and wiped the grease from his mouth.

"She wants to meet you," he finally said.

"Who?"

"The person who can help you." He thunked a small black backpack onto the table. "Here's the money for the scripts you left at the gas station. Cash. There's five K in there. She'll give you two thousand dollars per prescription, so she still owes you another five K."

I did the math quickly in my head. From what I'd read, oxy's street value was around $45 per pill. There were 120 pills in a bottle, so one prescription could bring in over $5,000. Why was she only offering me $2,000? I would have to sign 50 prescriptions to get enough money to pay the $98,000 for Josh's reprogrammed cells to be injected. Even with prescription pads for six different doctors, it was far more than I'd wanted to sell.

It was too risky.

"She also has a business proposition for you," Gabe said.

"I'm listening." I leaned back and studied him.

Gabe shrugged. "Fuck if I know. Like I said, I'm out. I just know her through a friend. She said she'll meet you tonight. Midnight. At the old Skamania Mill. And she'll give you the other five K then."

"The abandoned warehouse over by the waterfall?" I exclaimed, incredulous. "You must be joking. I'm not meeting a drug dealer I don't know at some deserted old warehouse. I know how that movie ends!"

Gabe rolled his eyes. "She isn't a drug dealer. Not like you're thinking. She isn't part of some cartel or gang. She has a job, a kid. She's smart. She just deals a little to make a bit of extra money. Like I did. Like you're doing."

I tried not to let my disdain show, but Gabe saw it. "You can look down your nose all you want, but you're just the same as us now."

I wanted to scream.

But she still had the rest of my money. "Fine, I'll meet her. But you have to come too. And then I'll organize a time when you can meet Josh. Lunch or something."

Gabe shrugged. "Sure."

I pushed one of the cheap cell phones I'd bought across the table to Gabe. "I have one just like it. I've put my number on this one and downloaded WhatsApp. Only contact me using that."

He seemed exasperated by my caution.

"I have a lot to lose here, Gabe. I'm trusting you. *Josh* is trusting you. We can't have anybody find out."

"Whatever you want, sweetheart." He slipped the phone into his jeans pocket.

"And don't call me sweetheart."

I grabbed the black backpack and the canvas bag and stood, coming around to Gabe's side of the table. I leaned close to whisper in his ear, "By the way, that ham-and-cheese croissant was here when I sat down."

I straightened, pleased at the look of horror that crossed his face.

"See you tonight," I called over my shoulder as I strode briskly away.

## CHAPTER 12

"YOU SHOULD GO HOME. Get some rest," I told Nate that night. "Charlie needs to be fed and let out."

He'd come straight from work to the hospital, not even bothering to go home and shower. He had a distracted, faraway look in his eye.

I felt a twinge of resentment pull in my chest. He wanted this promotion to help Josh, but if Josh died, the promotion would mean nothing. He was working for something in a future that might not even matter. Knowing his mind was on unraveling the tangle of a stranger's death rather than fighting for our son's life made me furious.

"I thought you said Jennifer was going to do it?"

"We still need to make sure he's okay."

Nate hesitated. "I don't know. . . ."

He looked tired, physically and mentally, dark circles under his eyes, his skin gray. He wasn't sleeping well either. But still, he looked at me and smiled, drawing me close, and as he did I softened, melting against him.

"It's fine. Honestly." I stood on tiptoe and kissed his lips, not wanting him to feel guilty for leaving.

I remembered one evening when we'd only been dating a couple weeks, it began to snow. We still lived in Seattle then, and snow was unusual enough that we decided to go for a walk. The snow fell softly, clumping into our eyelashes and melting on our lips. I'd stopped walking, drinking in the sight of this man I already loved more than I'd ever thought possible.

*I'm so lucky to have you*, I'd thought, and then I said it out loud, just so he knew.

He had gently brushed a flake from my cheek and bent to kiss me tenderly. At that moment, I felt such a deep sense of belonging. He reached for my hand and pulled me against him.

"Come here, *mo chuisle*."

"What does that mean?" I asked.

"It's Irish for *my heartbeat* or *my heart*. My dad used to say it to my mom."

"That's so sweet . . ." I struggled to think of a cute reply, then flashed back to my high school French. ". . . *mon homme*," I blurted.

We both burst out laughing. "Sorry," I said between gasps of laughter. "I'm crap at being a girlfriend. This is all just so new to me!"

"Then why don't you be my wife instead?"

For a moment, I couldn't speak. School and then the hospital were the only constants I'd had until I met Nate, kindhearted, loyal, cheerful Nate. His optimism and his love for his family were infectious, and I ached to be a part of it. He would love me, protect me. We'd get married, have a family, grow old together. I'd never felt that way before, and it was magic.

"Yes," I breathed.

I'd found out a week later I was pregnant, and when I read the

DNA results I knew exactly what I needed to do. The instant I told him, Nate proposed a second time. My face was covered in snot and tears, my heart aching, but somehow that second time was even more romantic than the first.

We were married just a couple months later.

Nate was a good man. But all his good qualities meant I couldn't tell him what I was doing now. He wouldn't understand, and he certainly wouldn't agree.

I wrapped my arms around Nate's waist, feeling the warmth of his body against mine. He dropped his chin onto my head and exhaled heavily.

"You're exhausted," I said. "Just go home and get some sleep. I'm fine sleeping on the couch here. And anyway, you have to work tomorrow."

"All right," he finally agreed. His breath was warm against my hair. "I'll be here tomorrow morning, okay?"

"Sure. Love you."

Nate kissed me good-bye and stumbled out of the room, bleary-eyed and exhausted.

Josh was sleeping soundly, the room a peaceful oasis for the next hour before I had to leave to meet Gabe and his drug-dealer friend. I checked Facebook on my phone, saw what a few college friends were up to, caught up on the news.

A doctor in Spokane had been charged with more than eight hundred counts of illegally selling opioids; a police officer in Oregon had stoned a squirrel and killed it; a murder-suicide in Tacoma. I tapped on local news, my eye snagging on a story about a drug dealer called Santiago Martinez who'd been murdered over in Mill Creek.

This, I realized, was the case Nate was working on. The case that was taking him away from us but could get him promoted to lieutenant.

The story outlined a man with a history of drug abuse and dealing, who'd left Seattle for a fresh start and gotten caught up in a turf war that had left him dead.

Nate was quoted in the article: *"I would like to appeal to anyone who was in the area at the time of the incident to come forward, if they haven't already done so. We can assure the public that the Skamania community is very safe. We're doing all that we can to establish the full circumstances of this case."*

After a while reading the news, my eyes started to droop, exhaustion smearing the room around me.

*Glass shattering.*

*My mother's scream.*

*Daddy sobbing, "Don't leave me!"*

I jolted awake, my body covered in a cold, sticky sweat. A shadow hovered over me. I gasped and lurched upright.

"Mommy?" Josh's voice. I put a hand out to touch him, felt his skin, warm under mine.

"Josh?"

"Were you having a bad dream?"

I pulled him against me, still panting. "I guess I was."

"What was it about?"

It was a memory more than a nightmare. Only somehow the images had shifted, revealing things that hadn't happened. Instead of being inside the car, I'd dreamed I was on the road watching as it careened toward me. I screamed as the car abruptly jerked to the right, hurtled through the air, and flipped onto its side. And then the dream had started over again.

Over and over I'd watched, unable to do anything to stop the accident. Unable to do anything to save them.

"I can't remember," I lied.

"I had a bad dream too." He snuggled into me, his body warm, smelling just faintly of yeast.

"What happened?"

"I builded a sand castle and then I went inside, and a big giant came and he stepped on it and everybody in the sand castle died."

My breath caught in my throat. I pulled him tight against my chest. "I'm so sorry. That sounds like it was really scary."

We lay in silence for a long time before I remembered I had somewhere to be. My eyes flew to the clock. It was almost midnight.

"Time to get back in bed," I whispered. I tucked Josh into the narrow hospital bed and kissed his forehead where a creamy slice of moonlight fell across his face. "Love you, sweetie."

He yawned and rolled onto his side. "Love you too, Mommy."

I lay on the couch, my eyes wide, staring at the ceiling. A hospital room was never dark—not totally. And it was rarely quiet. The machines in the room hissed and spluttered; doctors and nurses hurried past; lights flooded the room; there was the scrape of curtains being pulled back against metal rods and the sound of bells and beeping from different rooms. I couldn't have gone back to sleep if I'd wanted to.

Eventually Josh's breath deepened, the telltale click at the back of his throat indicating he was asleep.

I pulled on my fleece-lined ankle boots and slipped into my wool coat. Then I tucked the canvas bag with the prescriptions into my purse and crossed my fingers, hoping Josh wouldn't wake up in the next hour or so.

Outside, the night was crisp, a cool breeze cutting sharply through my coat, biting at my cheeks and fingertips. I pulled my knitted hat down and drove carefully through town. The last thing I needed was one of Nate's colleagues pulling me over right now. Fortunately, the streets were empty at this time of night, not a soul in sight.

At the edge of town, I crossed the bridge and turned down-river in the direction of the old Skamania Mill. I drove for miles, the dark road potted with holes and cracks that jarred my teeth and set me on edge.

Eventually I pulled up next to a beat-up old Ford parked in front of a chain-link fence. There was only one car. There should be two. I debated waiting around, but I was already late. I grabbed the flashlight from the glove compartment and tucked my purse over one shoulder, heart thundering in my ears. I wiped sweaty palms on my jeans.

When I got out, I instantly heard the distant rumble of the falls. A wind-driven mist rose beyond the warehouse, fingers curling over the evergreen trees, sliding over the river, and tangling at the bottom of the mill.

I slid through a gap in the chain-link fence and crossed a long-deserted parking lot. A few years back, the building had been rezoned for commercial redevelopment, but city officials had found that the steel trusses atop the walls were damaged, forcing the company to shelve the project. The building had sat abandoned ever since.

I swept the beam of my flashlight over the ground as I walked. Dead leaves and crackling branches whispered in the wind. Weeds pushed up through huge cracks in the cement. My boots crunched over fragments of glass. My neck prickled.

The warehouse itself was two stories tall, the ancient wood rotting from the constant humidity. A crumbling brick smoke-stack jutted into the sky at the far end of the building, the outline a moody and sinister shadow against the sky. The gaping holes of broken windows were like screaming black mouths.

I approached the front door, careful to avoid splintered wood pierced with rusty nails. It was locked, a bicycle padlock coiled around the handle. I moved around the side of the building, pushing past a cluster of overgrown bushes. A spiderweb clawed at my face, and I felt the tiny feet of a spider tapping on my cheek. I stifled a scream and swiped at it. It fell to the ground, illuminated in the yellow glow of my flashlight. It tried to scuttle away but I squished it with my boot, my pulse throbbing in my ears.

I stood for a moment, rigid as the stark winter trees surrounding me. Every one of my senses was screaming at me to get the hell out of here. But I was here for Josh. Nothing could get in the way of that.

I elbowed my way through the rest of the brush and moved to the rear of the building, where there was a little clearing, muddy grass rolling down to the rushing river, the waterfall churning beyond.

The back door was propped open with a large rock. Inside, the skeletons of rusted factory equipment were pushed against corrugated walls. Decaying steel beams stretched high overhead. Water dripped rhythmically down the walls. The air was thick with damp, the pungent smell of mold on rotting wood.

A lantern sat on a table under the stairs, casting a warm, buttery glow onto the floor. It took me a minute to make out Gabe sitting at a table tucked neatly beneath the stairs. He was with a woman. Her head was bent over the table; she was snorting a line of something. Cocaine? She sniffed and threw her head back, pinching her nose.

"Gabe," I whispered.

"Emma!" Gabe hurried to me, as the woman tucked a small baggie back into a briefcase on the table. "You're late." He motioned for me to sit in one of the dilapidated chairs and turned to the other woman. "See, I told you she'd be here."

"Sorry, Josh woke up." My voice sounded breathless from the nerves writhing in my stomach.

The woman was nothing like what I'd expected. She was very

young, for starters, and small, the size of a teenager, although I'd peg her as in her early twenties. She had a petite, heart-shaped face and long, dark hair that was held back with a crimson silk scarf. She wore skinny jeans with Ugg boots and a frilled white shirt under a leather jacket.

Her eyes were huge, the pupils so dilated she looked like a cartoon character. But when she smiled, her teeth were straight and white, her hand warm and soft when she shook mine.

"This is Emma," Gabe introduced me.

"Hey, Emma. Sorry you had to come out here in the middle of the night," she said. Her voice was very high, like a child's. In the creamy glow of the lantern light, I could just make out a rose tattoo creeping out from the collar at her throat. "I'm Violeta."

## CHAPTER 13

VIOLETA OPENED THE BLACK BRIEFCASE. She pulled out two stacks of cash and thunked them on the table.

"That's the rest of your money."

I stared at it, unsure if I should count it. Would she be offended?

She swiped at her nose and sniffed. "Count it. I don't care."

"No, it's okay. I trust Gabe." I dropped the money into my purse.

Violeta arched one perfectly plucked eyebrow. "Great. Now let's talk about my business proposition."

She sniffed again. It was really starting to annoy me. "Would you like a tissue?" I asked.

For some reason this made her giggle, the sound high-pitched, like a chipmunk.

"You're funny! I like you!" she said.

She swiped at her nose again, her eyes glittering. She pulled a baggie of pills out of the briefcase and dumped a few into her palm, then handed them to Gabe. He grinned and dry-swallowed two, shoving the rest in his pocket. She offered the baggie to me.

"No thanks."

"I don't do this all the time, just so you know. But it's mom's night out tonight. You understand, yeah? Sometimes I just need to, like, chill."

"You have children?" Christ, how old was she?

"Just one."

She sealed the baggie and put it back inside the briefcase. From where I was sitting, I could see that inside were stacks of cash and baggies with pills and powders. She grabbed another baggie of white powder and tapped the cocaine into a little pile on the table. But instead of snorting it, she lit a cigarette. The end glowed red in the dim light. She leaned back in her chair, the wood creaking, and inhaled deeply. Smoke hissed out between her lips.

"How rude of me." She held the pack out to me. "Would you like one?"

Again, I shook my head. She looked too young to be smoking. A little piece of me wanted to tell her to go home to her parents.

She flicked ash onto the floor. "So. Emma. Your son has leukemia."

I glared at Gabe, and Violeta giggled. "Don't worry so much! Geez, Gabe said you were uptight, but I had no idea! Your secret's safe with me. In fact, I'll tell you one of my own. My son has diabetes. That's why I do this."

"I'm sorry to hear that. Type one?"

"Yes. Did you know that the cost of insulin has gone up over *a thousand percent*?" She scowled. "I guess you do know that, since you're a doctor."

"Tell her about the plan, Vi," Gabe said. He'd pushed his chair back, and his long legs were now extended and crossed at the ankles, his hands behind his neck.

"I thought you said you weren't involved, Gabe?" I said.

"He's not," Violeta snapped. "Gabe made it clear he's only doing this to help his son."

She inhaled sharply on her cigarette, then stubbed it out on the table, ash scattering into the wood grain. She brushed it away with the side of her hand.

"So. It's simple, really. You write the scripts. I got some girls. My guy drives the girls around the state to a bunch of pharmacies. The girls fill their scripts. Once we have the pills, we deliver them to people who need them."

She tapped another cigarette from the pack and lit it, grinning. "We're the Amazon of the drug world."

"How do the girls fill the prescriptions?" I asked. "They need ID. Aren't they afraid of being caught?"

"We change them, make it so they're different each time. They all have fake IDs. Don't worry, they're very good fake IDs. And they have no idea who's involved. They only know the guy who drives them, so it would never come back to you."

"Then why do they do it?"

Violeta giggled, smoke billowing between her teeth. "Duh! They need the money!"

The plan was brilliant in its simplicity. And as long as they didn't sell too many, it was unlikely they'd be caught. I knew from being married to a detective that the cops only had the resources to investigate the big cases, cartels, gangs. And unlike heroin or fentanyl, oxy was readily available through legal means.

A few extra pills in an already crowded market would go unseen.

"When are you sending them out next?"

"Next Thursday. My guy will pick them up at Costco over by Twin Lakes. Gabe will bring your money to you. You'll get two thousand dollars per prescription."

"I want three thousand."

Violeta's cigarette froze on its way to her mouth. When she looked at me her eyes were flat and black, and suddenly she didn't seem like such a child. "I don't think you're in a position to negotiate, Emma," she said, her voice soft and menacing.

A lurch of fear darted through me, but I clenched my jaw and held my position. "Three. I'm risking a lot here."

"Sometimes you have to take big risks to get big rewards."

"Three."

Violeta blew a smoke ring into the damp air. "Two and a half."

I looked at Gabe. He shrugged and grinned. His eyes were glazed, the oxy kicking in. I would need to sell forty prescriptions in the next few weeks if I made $2,500 each. It was a risk, but I'd have enough to pay the hospital to get Josh's reprogrammed cells injected. A few more sales after that, and I could pay off the hospital bills. Then I was out, and I'd never have to see Gabe or this horrible girl-woman again.

"Okay," I agreed. "I'm in. But I have one more question."

"Yes?"

"Who is *we*?"

"What do you mean?"

"You said 'we.' Once *we* have the pills, *we* deliver them to people. If I'm going to get involved, I want to know who I'm working with."

Violeta took one last drag, then flicked the cigarette onto the floor. The light around us dimmed as the lantern flickered. "That's need-to-know information, and right now, you don't need to know."

We stared at each other, eyes locked.

"Fine." I lifted a shoulder and extracted a handful of signed prescriptions from the canvas bag. "There are a dozen here, from six different doctors. There's more once this batch is sold."

She giggled again, back to being a child, which I now saw was all an act. She rifled through them. "Genius. Using other doctors' prescription pads. Ha! I love that."

She tucked the prescriptions into the briefcase and snapped it shut, twisting the metal numbers on the combination lock and setting it on the floor. Then she turned her attention to the little pile of cocaine on the table.

"You sure you don't want any?" She waved at the white powder.

"Uh, no thanks. I never did like it."

She scraped at the pile with her pinkie nail, frowning. "Do you have something I can use?"

I dug around in my purse but couldn't find anything.

"Here." Gabe handed her a white card.

"I'm going to head off." I stood and backed away from them. The lantern flickered, casting shadows at my feet. "It was nice meeting you, Violeta. Gabe, I'll talk to you soon."

"Byeee!" Violeta called. She didn't look up, just continued cutting the powder into two thick lines with the card Gabe had given her.

Outside, I flicked the flashlight on. The light cut through the mist rolling off the falls. I jogged silently through the underbrush, the darkness like a fist in my back, propelling me forward. It wasn't until I reached my car that I realized I was shaking. But I wasn't shaking from adrenaline or fear.

I was shaking from relief.

The bag in my hand was full of cash and I had a plan in place to get the money I needed for Josh. If this worked, he could get the treatment he needed.

My hand was on the car door's handle when a shout cut through the air.

*"Emma!"*

Ice flooded my veins. It had come from the warehouse. I sprinted back the way I'd come, branches slapping my face. About halfway there, I crashed into Gabe.

"Emma!" He grabbed me by the shoulders, eyes wide with panic. "It's Vi. Come on!"

Inside the warehouse, Violeta was sprawled on the floor near the table. She was seizing, her body thudding hard against the wooden floor. Her eyes were open, the pupils dilated. Her face was a stark blue-gray, clashing horribly with the scarf in her hair.

"What's wrong with her?" Gabe screeched.

I scanned the area. The powder. I picked up the baggie.

"Gabe, what's this?" My voice was icy, steady.

"Cocaine, I think. It's what she likes."

I dropped to my knees and put my fingers to Violeta's neck. Her pulse was thready. "Check what that is!"

Violeta had gone still, the violent thudding replaced by a horrific gurgling coming from her chest. One eye was half-open. Her lips had turned blue.

Gabe tried to open the briefcase, but it was locked. He punched it over and over while I wiped foam from Violeta's mouth with my coat sleeve and began CPR.

"The baggie," I hissed. "There's something written on it."

I thrust down on Violeta's chest with the heels of my hands. The pressure forced more foamy blood to seep from the corners of her mouth. But no breaths came. After a minute, her ribs cracked and gave way under my palms.

Gabe picked up the baggie from the ground and held it up to the lantern. "Oh fuck. Oh fuck, no, no, no!" he shouted. "It has an *F* on it. *F*. Fuck. Fuck."

"Gabe, listen to me, you need to calm down. Tell me what *F* stands for."

He met my gaze, his eyes stunned. "Fentanyl. I think it stands for fentanyl."

I checked Violeta's pulse. Nothing. I kept a dose of naloxone in the first aid kit in my car, but it wouldn't be enough to combat something as strong as fentanyl.

I began another round of CPR.

By the time I stopped, my knees and my shoulders ached, and my fingers trembled. I checked again for a pulse, used my phone's flashlight to peer into her eyes. These actions calmed me, separated me from what was actually happening.

After a moment, I sat back on my heels.

I'd seen bodies before. Pronounced death. Been to the morgue. Made life-or-death decisions more times than I could count. I had watched many people die. I didn't get squeamish or overwhelmed the way some people did. I'd learned long ago to put distance between myself and the horrible things I'd seen.

But now I was entirely complicit. I needed to call an ambulance, but I also knew there was no hope for Violeta.

I looked at Gabe.

"She's dead."

*Oh my God.* Gabe's mouth moved, but no words came out.

I stared at Violeta's body, feeling numb, like I'd stepped outside of myself. Bloody foam gleamed at the corners of her mouth. The scarf in her hair looked like a slash of blood.

I closed my eyes. This couldn't be happening. Gabe was crying, a quiet keening that seemed to be absorbed by the walls of the old warehouse.

I started to dial 911—but then I thought of everything that had been discussed tonight. The drugs. The prescriptions. The plan. The money.

If we called the cops . . .

I froze.

The cops. Nate. How would I explain why I was here with a drug dealer? Scripts written on my colleagues' prescription pads were in Violeta's briefcase next to a stack of cash and drugs. There was no way he could—or would—smooth this over for me. I'd lose my license. I'd go to jail. Then what would happen to Josh?

I wasn't going to let my son die.

"Gabe, listen to me." My voice was sharp with urgency. "We have to get rid of her body."

# CHAPTER 14

WE STOPPED WHEN WE reached a small clearing in the woods and put down the body—that's what I was now calling it, *the body*, because I couldn't possibly call her Violeta anymore—and stood in the swirling mist. The air smelled earthy, like damp soil and leaves and rotting wood. I shook the blood back into my numb fingers. My arms and legs were shaking with exertion. I swiped my hair off my face. It was soaked with sweat.

A full moon peeked out from black-velvet clouds, casting shadows over the muddy path. It was gnarled with roots and mostly covered with brush and decaying leaves. The skeletons of trees jabbed into the charcoal sky.

"We have to stop," Gabe gasped. His hair was coming out of its ponytail, plastering itself to his forehead in damp, sweaty tendrils. He was still high, his eyes glassy, his stare dull.

I glanced around. He was right. The path disappeared in front of us, trees twisting together and forming an impenetrable barrier. I edged toward the sound of rushing water, carefully pushing through the brush until I reached a small ledge that hovered about five feet above the river.

"We can do it here," I called to Gabe.

We'd carried the body as far upstream as we could, to allow it to get swept up in the current and carried over the waterfall. The last thing we needed was for it to get caught in the brambles near the warehouse and lead the cops directly there.

We maneuvered the body to the ledge and peered over. I had gone to a weird place inside myself. I'd always been good at compartmentalizing. I could create separate planets in which I dealt with life. Planet work. Planet mom. Planet wife. I'd learned how to do it the night my father died. He was in so much pain before he died, and I was so helpless, completely powerless against fate.

Now, as a doctor, I'd guess his spinal cord had been torn and he'd suffered massive trauma to his internal organs. I'd always been terrified I made it worse when I dragged him from the car. He died slowly, painfully, and all I could do was sit and watch as the flames from the car slowly extinguished into the blackness of night. That was the first time I really learned how to partition my life into neat little boxes. Before, and after.

The day of Mom and Dad's funeral, I did the same thing. Ben and I were staying at a temporary foster home then. I woke early, and my whole body hurt, like ached with grief. I hadn't just lost my parents; I'd lost my home and my bedroom and all my familiar things. And then when I sat down to pee I noticed my underwear was damp with blood, and I realized I'd lost my childhood, too.

I became a woman that day. Physically and mentally.

Later I would take this night out and examine it and hate myself for all the things I should've or shouldn't have done. But for now I couldn't afford to feel anything. There was too much at stake.

"On three," I said. I didn't even recognize my voice anymore.

We started to swing the body. Tendrils of dark hair wrapped around my wrist.

"Wait, wait!" I cried. "Did you put the fentanyl in her pocket?"

"Yes!" Gabe snapped. "I already told you."

I hesitated again. A flickering ray of moonlight beamed down between racing clouds, brilliant and white as bone.

"Okay." I took a deep breath. "On three."

I stepped out of the moonlight and into the shadows, this time releasing the body.

We didn't let go at the same time, though, so the body bounced against the ledge with a horrific *thunk*, spinning in the air then crashing into the river with a splash. Gabe bent over at the waist and retched, watery bile spewing onto the damp leaves. I watched as the body sank and then bobbed up again, then was swept downstream in the current. The black water moved fast, completely nonchalant.

After a moment, Gabe stood. He wiped his mouth on his coat sleeve.

"Did it go over the falls?" I asked, peering over the ledge. "I can't see. Did it go over?"

"I don't—I don't know! It's too dark."

"It needs to go over!" I'd started to shake, my voice turning shrill.

"Emma." Gabe put a hand on my arm. In a complete role reversal, he was suddenly calming me. "I'm sure it did. Look." He pointed at the swirling water. "The current's pretty fast."

I nodded, my teeth chattering. The mist mingled with the sweat on our skin. I stared in the direction of the waterfall, hearing the power and brilliance of its roar. It was both beautiful and brutal.

When I was a kid, my family used to come hiking up here. The river sent a massive volume of water coursing over a cluster of large boulders and hurtling down three hundred feet in two tiers. Water skipped over the first tier—a broad, fan-shaped fall—to a gently domed ledge, then plunged a further two hundred feet into a narrow amphitheater gorge.

We stood, watching the water, until a severe black cloud obscured the moon, releasing a fine rain that eventually drenched my hair. Water dripped down my cheeks like tears.

"Come on, let's go," Gabe said.

Back inside the warehouse, it was cold and damp. Gabe relit the lantern, and we sat on opposite sides of the table, shivering, shocked. I closed my eyes, running images of Josh on the screen of my inner eyelids. I was doing this for him. I had to keep that in mind.

I tried to think of all the evidence we would need to hide, to think like Nate.

"Where's her car?" My eyes popped open. "There was only one car outside. Is it yours or hers?"

"It's mine. We left hers at the Target on the other side of town. She didn't know how to get here."

I breathed a sigh of relief.

In the stark shadows cast by the lantern, Gabe's eyes were hard to read. Could I count on him to stay silent? And what if he didn't? What would I do then?

I straightened. "Okay. You remember the plan?"

He lifted the backpack of cash I'd given him. "I'll set up a bank account, deposit this five K, and transfer it into the GoFundMe account for Josh."

I needed the cash to pay for Josh's treatment, but I figured it was smarter to have smaller payments, so I'd decided to split the money between the GoFundMe account and a checking account I planned to open.

"Right. I'll take the briefcase and try to open it." I thumped it with my foot. "There's cash in there we can split. And I have to get those prescriptions I wrote. I can't have anybody find them."

The other worry was how I was going to make money now. Without Violeta, I had no one to sell the prescriptions to.

I squeezed Gabe's hand. "We're in this together now, okay?"

Gabe snatched his hand away from mine, stricken. "It's not like I have a choice, do I?"

"No. That's true. Neither of us has a choice now."

"She has a kid, you know."

I rubbed my temples, which were thudding. "Shit. Okay. Does she have any relatives? We can call anonymously—"

"Her kid is with Ben. *Your brother*, Ben. Do you have any idea what he's going to do when he finds out? Oh shit . . ." Gabe thrust his hands into his hair, pulling the ponytail holder out and bending over the table, his sweaty blond hair falling in front of his face as he breathed rapidly.

I gaped at him. "Are you kidding? Why didn't you tell me?"

Gabe laughed, but not a *ha-ha* laugh; no, a mean laugh, his dimples creasing around a twisted mouth, somehow looking ominous and cruel. "Ben didn't want you to know he was involved. He doesn't want to see you, sweetheart."

That stung. I'd spent most of my life chasing my brother's shadow, just wanting his love, to belong in his life, but he'd always turned away from me. "Why not?"

He stood and started pacing, his boots echoing on the aging wooden floors. "I don't know. You know he's never been the easiest to be around."

"Why did you go to Ben? Of all the people in the world!"

"He was the only one I knew to ask about selling drugs. I *told* you. I've been out of that game for years! He said Vi could help."

"You should've told me!"

Gabe slapped both hands on the table and leaned over, glaring at me. "At which point *exactly* was I supposed to stop everything and tell you that the woman you wanted to sell drugs with was your brother's girlfriend!"

"At any point!" I snapped. "Maybe when she OD'd or when we were dragging her body up to the water or—"

"I guess maybe I wasn't thinking clearly, okay?"

I opened my mouth, then snapped it shut. This wasn't getting us anywhere. I took a deep breath.

"I thought Ben was in jail."

"He was. He owed some money to this gang he'd been dealing for. He got caught and went to jail. When he got out last year, he moved out this way. He met Violeta and they started up this thing buying prescriptions and taking the girls around to get them filled."

"Who do they sell the pills to? Who distributes them?"

"I don't know! Ben's my friend, but he's into some shady shit and I didn't want anything to do with it. I only got in touch with him about all this because of Josh."

"Let's stick to the plan," I said. "Deposit the money and pay it into that GoFundMe account. Is it Ben who drives the girls around to fill the prescriptions?"

Gabe sighed. "Yes."

"Meet him at the Crescent Lake Costco on Thursday and give him these." I handed him a stack of prescriptions I'd signed. "I'll meet you there."

"And what do I say to Ben when he calls me asking where Violeta is?"

"Say you dropped her off at her car, and that was the last time you saw her. Don't say any more than that. The less we say right now, the better. We'll try to partner with Ben instead of Violeta. And don't worry. Whatever we make, I'll split with you."

"I don't want it. I already told you, I'm not doing it for the money."

I gathered my purse and the canvas bag with the prescription pads and stood. Gabe stopped me, his hand like a shackle around my wrist.

"Just be careful you don't get addicted."

I snatched my hand away. "I've never done drugs in my life! That was you and Ben, remember?"

Gabe shook his head. "There's more than one thing to be addicted to. If you don't get addicted to the drugs, you get addicted to the money. And trust me, some things there's no coming back from."

# CHAPTER 15

NATE WAS DREAMING ABOUT Robbie Sadler when the ringing of his phone woke him. Robbie was glaring at Nate, his face red with fury.

*You're gonna be sorry, man.*

Nate fumbled for the phone on his bedside table, just as it stopped ringing. He scrubbed a hand down his face and thought about ignoring it. This was the first night his whole family had been under one roof in a week. Emma and Josh were both asleep in the bed next to him; Charlie sprawled on his back, paws in the air, at their feet.

Nate looked longingly at his sleeping wife and son. He wished he could just lie back and wrap them in his arms and stay that way for the next few hours.

And then he thought of the four days of chemo Josh needed before getting the CAR T-cell infusion. And the hospital bills already piling up. And what it would cost to save Josh's life. It was like a goddamn elephant was sitting on his chest.

He felt like he was already failing his son.

Providing for Josh meant getting that promotion, and that

meant solving this case. The only way to do that was to answer the damn phone.

Nate gently pressed his lips to Emma's forehead.

*I'll get this promotion*, he told her silently.

He grabbed the phone just as it started ringing again.

"You're gonna want to get to the morgue," Kia said when he answered. "We found Violeta Williams."

NATE RUSHED to get ready, shoveling down a bowl of Rice Krispies and slugging a cup of instant coffee. He grabbed a banana from the fridge to eat in the car and noticed Emma had written *I'm bananas for you* in black ink across the peel. He smiled. It was something she'd done when they first moved in together, and a tradition they both did occasionally.

He pulled the regular coffee from the refrigerator and scooped a spoonful into the automatic coffeemaker, setting the timer so it would be ready when Emma got up. As he moved to put the coffee back in the fridge, his hip knocked Emma's purse off the kitchen island, spilling the contents across the floor.

He cursed and gathered up her phone, her wallet, a piece of gum, a few scraps of paper, shoving it all back in her purse. He caught sight of one of the receipts in his hand: for an Americano, a mocha, and a blueberry muffin at the hospital's café.

At first he was confused. Emma didn't allow herself sugar. He scanned the date. Last week, the day Josh had gotten his blood drawn for the first phase of treatment.

Who had Emma been having coffee with while their son was in the hospital?

A terrible thought entered Nate's mind, dread leaching through his core.

Was Emma cheating on him?

He immediately dismissed it. She could've met one of her colleagues for coffee. It was her workplace, after all. Or maybe she'd had coffee with his mother. He dismissed that thought too. He couldn't imagine Emma and his mom sitting down for coffee together.

He shoved the receipt back in Emma's purse and hurried to his car, but he couldn't get it out of his head. He remembered how he'd felt like she was lying to him when her phone rang the other day. And now this receipt.

But their son was sick. They were struggling to figure out a plan for how they would pay for his treatments. Of course she was bound to act a little bizarre. They were under unimaginable stress right now.

Emma wasn't the type to cheat. He knew her. He *knew* her. Didn't he?

NATE WALKED through the front door of the hospital, smiling warmly at the woman on reception. He recognized her from high school but couldn't remember her name. She fluttered her fingertips at him.

Nate took the elevator downstairs to the morgue. He hated the morgue. The antiseptic smell never quite covered the stench of death. The harsh lights and gleaming metal surfaces couldn't distract from the blue-tinged bodies.

Here, death was on display.

In Nate's job, he'd seen a lot of death, but he focused more on the good he did—solving the case and sending the bad guy to jail—and less on the horrors of death itself. Honestly, he didn't know how Emma did it, working with sick people every day, people who could die at any moment.

He turned into the clinical, white-tiled basement room that served as the morgue.

"Excuse me." A man wheeling a body bag down the hall nudged past him.

Nate apologized and stepped aside. He pulled up the collar of his jacket. The air was frigid down here, although it couldn't hide the sting of formaldehyde. The smell reminded him of Robbie's funeral. It had been open casket, Robbie lying in repose at the front of the church. His eyes were closed, but Nate could still see the tiny black stitches holding them that way.

Nate had wanted to turn and run and keep running. He didn't want to face Robbie's parents, whom he'd known forever, or his brother, Tommy, who'd come back from college for the funeral. He was sure they'd see the shame on his face.

*You're a bad person.*

*You're cowardly. Weak.*

*Nobody can trust you.*

Nate's self-hatred expanded in his chest. It would serve him right if Emma cheated on him. He didn't deserve her.

He watched the retreating body bag and reached in his pocket for his tin of toothpicks. Guilt, he knew, was a slippery slope. He was an honorable, law-abiding detective now, working to keep his community safe, to build a good world for his son, for his family. But he couldn't help it: he shoved the sharp tip of the toothpick under his thumbnail, grunting as pain hit him.

"Detective Sweeney?"

Nate whirled around, dropping the toothpick into his pocket.

The forensic pathologist, Dr. Kathi Morris, reached a hand out to shake his. She was a small, mousy woman, quiet, more like a librarian than a pathologist, and known for her respectful manner and detailed approach.

"Oh dear! You're bleeding!" She pointed at blood that had smeared onto her knuckles.

"I'm so sorry!" he said, horrified.

"No worries. Here." She withdrew a large black leather bag from under a cabinet, rummaged around in it, and pulled out a Band-Aid. She smiled. "You're in luck, I just stocked up."

"Thank you." Nate pressed the Band-Aid to his throbbing thumb, his cheeks flushed.

He followed Dr. Morris down a long corridor to the autopsy suite at the end. The room was large, holding three metal gurneys, each with a deep sink at the top and an organ bucket lined with a red biohazard bag at the bottom. Kia was already waiting beside one gurney.

"This is Violeta Williams. Fingerprints matched those in the system." Dr. Morris flashed Kia and Nate a bright smile, but her eyes remained flat and dark. Another faker, like himself, Nate decided.

Violeta Williams's body was swollen and blue, her face frozen in a bloated grimace, her skin loose and wrinkled. One eyelid had been torn off, exposing a bulging eyeball with a milky brown iris staring accusingly at the ceiling.

"Can you tell time of death?" Kia asked.

Dr. Morris carefully brushed a strand of dark hair off Violeta Williams's forehead and straightened the white sheet draped over her chest. The action was so intensely compassionate and humane that Nate almost wanted to look away. "Hard to know for certain, as her body's been submerged. But based on the temperature of the water and skin condition, I'd estimate anywhere from six to eight days. She had markedly heavy lung weight and frothy fluid in the lungs."

"She drowned?" Nate asked.

Dr. Morris held up a finger. "Not exactly, no. She also had cerebral edema, fluid in the brain, and bladder distension. I've collected blood and urine specimens and I'm sending them out for toxicology testing. I need to corroborate with clinical evidence, but based on my findings, and the fact that I'm seeing this more frequently lately, I'd wager an educated guess on a drug overdose, *before* she went in the water."

Nate's mind flashed to Santiago Martinez's neck. "Were there puncture marks anywhere on her body?"

"Unfortunately, the skin's been compromised from being submerged for so long. It's impossible to say."

Nate looked at Kia. "We have two people, possibly linked, possibly both drug dealers, who've died in the last couple of weeks from overdoses. Santiago Martinez's wasn't an accident. What are the chances this one wasn't either?"

Kia raised a dark eyebrow. "You think someone's killing off drug dealers?"

"Possibly."

Kia pointed to the bruising along Violeta Williams's face. "Was she beaten?"

"No, that occurred after death," Dr. Morris said.

"Her body must've been carried over the waterfall," Kia said to Nate. "If there's a crime scene, it's up there."

"There's miles of river where she could've gone in. Or she could've been dumped."

Kia's phone buzzed, and she moved away to answer it.

"Any personal belongings?" Nate asked Dr. Morris.

She handed him a large plastic bag from under the gurney and turned away to jot some notes on a form. Nate rifled through a set of keys, a waterlogged wallet with a few credit cards, an empty baggie, what looked like a business card. He turned it over. The ink had been washed away from being in the water, but he could see the indentations of where the logo had been embossed.

It looked like a set of wings with a circle of some sort in the middle. He knew that logo.

"Where'd you get this?" he asked Dr. Morris.

She looked up. "In the back pocket of her jeans."

Kia spoke from behind him. "That was Dyson."

Nate sealed the plastic bag and handed it back to Dr. Morris.

"Santiago Martinez's girlfriend just showed up at the station."

NATE CHARGED out of the side entrance of the hospital too fast, knocking abruptly into Dr. Palmer, who was rolling a coin of some sort slowly and methodically over his knuckles. The coin dropped to the ground, and Dr. Palmer picked it up, slipping it into his pocket. He smiled a greeting, looking crisp and capable in a navy suit, the pink-and-white-striped shirt matching his rosy cheeks.

"Sorry about that!" Nate said.

"No problem. Actually, I'm glad to see you. I wanted to check how Emma's coping. Her son being so sick, after what she went through . . ." His voice trailed off.

"It's nice of you to think of her. She seems . . . determined, actually." Nate smiled. Emma's strength and courage were among the things he loved most about her. "She's a fighter. That's where Josh gets it from. We're both optimistic."

"Good. You should be. This treatment has a tremendous success rate. I'm glad you went for it in the end. I know it's expensive, but I think Josh will come out the other side a healthy, happy boy. My success rate with it in Seattle is why Cascade Regional brought me here. You won't regret it."

Nate was surprised by the flash of arrogance. He hadn't pegged Dr. Palmer for that type at all.

"Thank you for everything you're doing for Josh."

"I took an oath to help the injured and heal the sick. I'm only too glad to be of service."

Nate leaned against the side of the hospital. "So, you found Emma the night her parents died?"

Dr. Palmer nodded. "Yes. But I'm sure she already told you all about that."

"Not the details," Nate admitted. "Emma bottles things up a lot."

Dr. Palmer lifted his bushy white eyebrows and made a sound at the back of his throat like he agreed with him.

"I read the accident report. You found Emma at three a.m. How long was she alone with her father's body before you arrived?"

Dr. Palmer scratched his head. "It's been a long time. I'm not sure I remember what the autopsy said, but when I arrived he was cold. A few hours, I'd say."

"Poor Emma," Nate murmured. "Well, I need to get to the station."

"Certainly. Let me know if there's anything I can do for Josh."

Nate turned to leave, then stopped and turned back. "Why were you driving around at three in the morning?"

Dr. Palmer looked embarrassed. "My wife and I were going through a messy divorce and custody battle at the time. I suffered horrible insomnia, so a lot of nights I'd drive around aimlessly. It was good I did that night." He smiled, not the expression of a doctor maintaining a professional distance, but a warm, grand-fatherly smile. "Perhaps more doctors should wander the streets at night."

Nate laughed and shook his head. "Maybe leave wandering the streets at night to the police. That's what we're there for."

Dr. Palmer chuckled and clapped Nate on the shoulder. "You're a good man, Detective Sweeney."

Nate thanked him and said good-bye. In his car, he dialed Emma's number to see how Josh was doing. The line rang out, kicking to voice mail. He hung up and called the house phone, but no joy, so he tried Emma's cell again.

She finally answered, sounding out of breath.

"You all right?" he asked.

"I'm putting laundry away. I had to run for my phone," she replied tetchily. Laundry was her least favorite chore.

He asked her how Josh was, and she asked what he wanted for dinner.

"I'm really sorry, babe. I doubt I'll be able to get home for dinner tonight."

"What? Why not!"

"I have a million things to do and they all have to be done today."

He was surprised at how defensive he sounded. He'd never needed to explain his work to Emma before.

She released an irritated huff. "How late will you be? Josh will want to see you before he goes to bed."

Guilt stabbed at him, forcing him to mentally rearrange his day.

"I'll try to get off at five. I just have to make one stop by your clinic to grab the surveillance footage after work. I'll come home after that."

"I didn't know you were on that case," she said, surprised. "Is there video footage of Julia, then?"

"Well, presumably. The clinic only just installed video surveillance equipment, so I hope it's all working right."

There was a beat of silence.

"And Marjorie will just give it to you?"

"It's on her computer. I just need a copy."

"Can't you have Kia take over?" Emma asked.

"Afraid not. It would be a conflict of interest. Kia and Julia are dating, so the lieutenant asked me to do it."

"What? Julia never said she was dating Kia!"

Nate turned the Crown Vic into the police department's parking lot. "I've gotta go."

Emma sighed. "Can you just get the video tomorrow and come home after work? It would be nice to have dinner as a family for once. You've been working so much lately."

Nate hesitated. Emma had never been one of those wives who moaned about her husband's awkward hours. She never complained or asked him to put things off. It just wasn't in her nature to whine. But she was exhausted and worried and terrified about Josh's diagnosis. He was too.

"Yeah, sure. I'll come straight home after work."

"Thanks. I love you."

"Love you too."

Nate got out of the car at the police station, a toothpick clenched between his teeth. Kia was already there, sitting on the bench in front, fiddling with her phone. A gust of wind ruffled her shaggy hair, and she dashed a hand through it as she jumped to her feet.

"Lieutenant Dyson said she just appeared at the station earlier," Kia said.

"Any idea why she didn't report him missing?"

"No. Let's go find out."

The police interrogation room was small and industrial, with a long white table and three chairs. Mariana Ramirez sat across the desk from Nate and Kia. She was Hispanic, tiny, with long, jet-black hair, an overbite, and tired eyes. Her fingers nervously twisted a chain of pink rosary beads at her throat.

Kia informed her in Spanish that they would be recording, and Nate pressed Record.

"Santiago, he didn't show at my house on Monday." Her accent was thick, but her English good. "He always comes on Monday. Always, to see our son."

Nate glanced at the notes he had in his hand. "Miss Ramirez. Mariana. Why didn't you report him as a missing person?"

Mariana's eyes filled with tears. She pulled a tissue from her jeans pocket and dabbed at her eyes. "I was, *cómo se dice, enojado?*"

"Angry?" Kia provided.

"*Sí.* Yes. I was angry. I went to my mother's on Tuesday with my son. She is very sick, and I was angry at Santiago, so I didn't call."

Mariana bent over the table, the tissue pressed to her eyes. For a moment, the only sound in the room was her crying.

"Why were you angry?" Nate asked gently.

"We argued about money. I asked him for more—for our son. He needs shoes, but Santiago says he doesn't have it right now."

Kia touched her arm and murmured to her in Spanish. Nate had never been good at Spanish in school. He jotted a note to follow up with Mariana Ramirez's mother and check her alibi.

"Mariana, your boyfriend had highly illegal substances at his house," Nate said after a minute. "Do you know where he got these? Or what he planned to do with them?"

Mariana sniffed. "Santiago doesn't want to sell these things anymore. He . . . shouted on the phone a few days ago. Maybe Friday."

"Do you know who he was talking to?"

Mariana shook her head. "He didn't say names. But when the phone rang, I picked it up, and the phone said *Ben*."

# CHAPTER 16

USING JOSH TO MANIPULATE Nate was low; I knew that. I'd completely forgotten that the hospital had installed cameras in the clinic a few weeks back. I couldn't have Nate see that video. He'd wonder why I'd lied and said I'd gone upstairs to Oncology, why I'd gone into the clinic's supply closet instead. And what if, one day, investigators found out prescriptions had been stolen from my clinic? He'd easily put two and two together.

I was catastrophizing, I knew, but I couldn't risk it. I had to stop him from seeing that video.

A flash of something, the glare of light, brought my attention to the bedroom window. I spread the blinds and peered outside. There was a black truck parked across the street from my house. It was the kind drug dealers and men worried about the size of their penis drove: shiny paint, chrome wheels, double cab.

Tentacles of fear climbed up my neck. Charlie whined and nosed his palm against my knee, sensing my anxiety.

The unmatched sock in my hand tumbled to the floor. I turned and raced downstairs, Charlie lumbering behind me. I pulled the front door open, but whoever was in the driver's seat had seen me.

The truck's engine roared to life, and the squeal of tires hit my ears. I watched it disappear around the corner, my breath tight.

I shut the door and locked the dead bolt. I peered out the peephole, staring at the empty space where the truck had been, hugging myself.

Charlie whined again.

"Who was that, Charlie?" I whispered. I stroked his ears, trying to ease some of his agitation. And mine.

My heart was thudding almost painfully. The blood had drained to my feet, turning them into boulders. I slid down the door until I was sitting on the floor. Charlie clambered onto my lap. Despite his age, he still acted like a puppy sometimes, his tail flapping, tongue lolling with excitement that he had my attention.

"What am I going to do?" I murmured.

Charlie tilted his head. His forehead skin folded into a bevy of wrinkles as he gave me that wise look basset hounds seemed to have.

Stars prickled in front of my eyes. I felt like I'd been dropped down a rabbit hole with the wolf sitting right outside.

And the wolf was my husband.

I finally forced myself to stand and returned upstairs to my bedroom. I grabbed my purse from the dresser and unzipped the side compartment, pulling out my burner phone.

"Mommy!" Josh called from the living room. He was watching *Star Wars* for the nine hundredth time. The distinctive zipping sound of lightsabers set my teeth on edge.

"Just a minute, Joshy!" I called, dialing a familiar number.

Gabe answered on the first ring.

"Emma." He sounded pissed. "You have to stop calling me. My girlfriend's getting seriously weirded out."

"I need your help."

I picked up a sock and found the matching one as I told him about the video surveillance footage of the clinic. Marjorie's desk computer was chock-full of random yellow sticky notes with various passwords and reminders jotted down. The video surveillance was new, and I was guessing—hoping—she still had the log-in details written on one of those Post-it Notes.

"I need to get into her office, log in, and delete the surveillance files."

"Listen, sweetheart, this isn't my problem," Gabe drawled. "I can't get into her office for you."

I ignored him. "She always works late. I need you to break into her car. Just create a distraction so she leaves the clinic, and I'll sneak in when she's gone."

"Have you lost your mind? No way! I'm not going to jail for you. There'll be surveillance video in the parking lot too."

"Only in the southwest corner—the rest of that system broke last year. Park down the street, not in the hospital lot, and walk up."

"No!"

I lowered my voice. "You know if I get caught, we're both going down. They'll find out about the prescription pads and that will lead them to Violeta. It won't take them long before they connect me to you."

Gabe growled, a frustrated hum in his throat. He knew I was right. No matter how much he hated me, we were tied together.

"Fine."

"Meet me outside the café at six."

I hung up and went to check on the briefcase I'd hidden at the back of the closet—I didn't want it to look too hidden because it might seem suspicious. The briefcase had two locks, one on the left, one on the right. Both required a combination of numbers, neither of which I knew.

I dropped to the floor next to the briefcase and wrapped my arms around Charlie, hugging him as a growing sense of dread filled me.


"MOMMY?" JOSH came into the bedroom, his *Star Wars* blanket trailing behind him, his pointer and middle fingers in his mouth. "What are you doing?" he asked around his fingers. "Is that a suitcase? Where are we going?"

I stood and tucked the briefcase back in the closet under my clothes.

"It's just a briefcase for work. There are patient files in there, so you can't touch it." I stroked Josh's cheek, which was pale, but cool to the touch. The extra fluids from the IV had helped in the short term. Now we just had to wait until chemo started next week. "How you feeling, sweetie? Are you okay?"

He lifted his narrow shoulders. "Yeah. I'm bored. There's a bird on the fence outside. One time at school I was with Jilly Murphy and I had jam on my finger and I touched a bird's back."

I led Josh downstairs, glanced at the bird he was talking about—a giant crow that had pooped on my car—and started pulling toys out of the toy box to distract him.

By 5:45 p.m., Nate still wasn't home, and I was a bundle of nerves. The house looked like a bomb had hit it, picture books and toys scattered across the floor, interspersed with crayons and bits of colored paper. Josh had turned whiny and clingy, not wanting me to leave the room. He was sick, but bored: the worst combination for a child.

I glanced at the clock again and finally called Moira. I told her I'd left my purse at the hospital and needed to run over really quick. She came over immediately. That was the thing about Moira: no matter her problem with me, she adored Josh.

The first time we met was at a barbecue at her house a few months after I'd moved in with Nate. I'd adored Nate's family the instant I met them, and thought they liked me too. I loved the easy banter, the camaraderie, the love. I felt happy and accepted, a baby in my belly and Nate's arm around my shoulders.

A little while later I escaped to the bathroom. I was just coming out when I heard Moira and Nate's sister, Aimee, coming down the hall.

"Don't you think her maternity dress is a little . . . I don't know, *rrrarrrr*?" Moira made a sexy roar sound at the back of her throat.

I looked at my dress, which I'd scoured secondhand stores for. It was a navy body-con dress that stretched over my baby bump.

"Yeah, she's trying a little too hard," Aimee agreed.

I'd quietly shut the bathroom door, cheeks burning. Belonging to their family had been a mirage. A nice, pretty façade. I felt again like that little girl watching Kelly get her picture taken with her family: an outsider looking in.

I'd used the baby as an excuse for the first time that day, saying I wasn't feeling well and needed to go home and lie down. It was awkward with Moira after that. But then I realized that the family we were creating—Nate, our baby, and me—was all I needed. It was everything I'd dreamed of. I couldn't risk losing it.

I was in control of my family.

I sent a quick text to Nate telling him I was going to get my purse, and headed to the hospital. I was driving too fast, burning through a yellow light and not stopping at a pedestrian crossing, but I didn't care. I had to get there and back as quickly as possible.

At the hospital, I did a loop around the parking lot, but saw no sign of Nate's Crown Vic. I was safe.

For now.

A light rain had started up, coating my hair and my jacket as soon as I stepped out of the car into the night. My feet splashed in black puddles as I hurried across the pavement. The familiar sound of sirens made me stop abruptly, heart hammering. But they weren't for me; an ambulance's lights flashed as it whooped into the emergency bay.

Cass was coming out the revolving doors as I entered. She lifted her coffee cup in a wave, her crooked teeth gleaming. I smiled but kept walking, not wanting to give the impression that I could linger to talk.

I found Gabe in the café eating a bowl of teriyaki.

"What the hell are you doing?" I hissed.

He shrugged and spoke with his mouth full. "What? I haven't had dinner."

I watched as he chewed, the food sliding slowly down his throat, and had the sudden urge to shove him off his chair. Anger and fear and adrenaline coiled in my veins.

"We don't have time for this!"

"Sure we do. Sit down." He shoved a chair out with his foot. After a moment, I dropped into it. "Are you sure you want to do this?" He looked closely at me.

"We don't really have a choice."

"We could just find someone to hack into the system."

"There isn't time."

Had he always been this spineless? Back in high school, he'd been a bad boy with an attitude. If he saw a boundary, he'd cross it; a rule, he'd break it. I'd followed happily along, like a cow, stupid and naïve, desperate to be included.

He lifted both hands. "It's your funeral, sweetheart."

"Here's what we'll do. I'll go upstairs and find out if anybody's in the office. Once I know, I'll text you. You have the phone I gave you?"

"Yeah."

"Break into her car, and then come back and sit in the café. That's all you have to do."

I slid a piece of paper toward him with her license plate number, which I'd grabbed on my way in from the parking lot, written on it.

"There's a black-and-white bumper sticker on the back," I told him. "*Grateful not Hateful.*"

"What are you going to do?" he asked.

"I'll tell the security guard I saw someone breaking into her car. He'll call to let her know, and when she leaves the clinic, I'll go back in. I just need you to tell me when she heads back upstairs."

He shoveled the last of the rice into his mouth and stood. "Let's do this."

# CHAPTER 17

I OPENED THE DOOR to the clinic loudly, clearing my throat as I entered. "Marjorie?"

Marjorie came into the reception area, looking surprised.

"Dr. Sweeney! Hello, dear. Are you okay? How is sweet little Josh?"

"Oh." I gave her a faint smile. "He's the same. He's home now while we wait for the T-cells to be reprogrammed. He's scheduled for a week of chemo starting next week."

"Bless him. I donated to that GoFundMe account. I know this can't be easy for you, but we're all behind you guys."

"Thanks, Marjorie," I replied, genuinely touched. "Listen, I know we talked about reducing my work hours, but I wanted to talk a bit more about my schedule."

"Certainly. Why don't you come into my office?"

I followed her through the clinic. She shut the door and shoved aside a tower of files stacked precariously on one chair. The rest of the office was a crush of paperwork, photos, empty coffee cups, and loose papers. Her desk monitor was covered with Post-its. I hoped one of them had the log-in details I needed.

"Excuse the mess." Marjorie laughed, deep and throaty; a smoker's laugh. "I never seem to have the time to clean up."

She sat behind her desk and waved for me to sit across from her.

"My mother-in-law has agreed to watch Josh in the mornings so I can work. Would that be okay for the next few weeks?"

"Sure, of course. We'll spread your patients around to the other doctors for now. You do understand we'll need to change your contracted hours?"

Rage swelled in me. The only thing I'd ever wanted to be was a doctor. As a child, watching my dad heal people had seemed a little like watching God. I'd put myself in debt up to my eyeballs to become a doctor. There'd been no money from my parents' estate; my dad had lost it all to gambling. Even their life insurance didn't cover much after settling taxes and loans and bills and funeral costs.

And now that I needed money to save my son's life, they didn't want to pay me.

Marjorie patted my knee, her leathery face softening. "I'm so sorry."

I shook my head. "It isn't your fault."

*It's this system*, I thought. *Our medical system. It's failing all of us.*

"And, uh . . ." Marjorie cleared her throat. "You might want to remember, you'll need to maintain twenty-five hours in a week to keep your health insurance."

I nodded.

"Okay. I'll update your paperwork with human resources."

We agreed I'd come back to work on Wednesday, and I gathered my purse, scanning the Post-it Notes while trying not to be obvious.

"May I ask, what'll happen to Julia?" I asked.

Marjorie shifted her butt, the chair creaking loudly. "Well, I suppose she'll spend a little time in jail, lose her medical license."

"So you're pressing charges?"

"I'm afraid it's up to the hospital. She's committed a crime, so, yes, I believe they'll press charges. It's such a shame. Her whole career gone down the toilet, just for a few silly pills."

She tutted, throwing her gray ponytail over one shoulder. I wanted to punch her in the face. I'd never punched anyone before, but the urge was so strong it actually made my knuckles itch.

She tilted her head at me, lips parting. She wanted me to agree with her. I blinked at her slowly, then turned and left.

Addiction wasn't silly. Marjorie didn't have any clue how an addict's brain structure changed over time, how serotonin levels became warped and the brain rewired to say it needed more. All these people—medical administrators, government officials, politicians, people who didn't have a clue—discussed addiction and prescription fraud and setting up task forces to stop drugs, but what we really needed was a way for our many addicts to get treatment. They needed help, not criticism and ridicule.

Out in the hall, I checked my phone. Gabe had texted.

It's done.

I exited the back of the hospital near the ER and headed for the front.

"Sir! Sir!" I rushed up to a security guard lounging behind his desk. "Someone's breaking into my boss's car! Can you call her? Her extension is four-four-two-two."

The security guard leaped up. He called Marjorie, then took his baton out and headed outside. I flattened myself into a quiet nook behind the stairs and watched. Within a few minutes, Marjorie emerged from the elevator. Once she was outside, I rode the elevator upstairs and hurried toward the clinic. I had my keys ready, but in her haste she hadn't even bothered to lock the door.

The clinic was small, with two doors: one that patients entered and one they exited. Behind the reception desk was the medical records room, and through that was Marjorie's office, which was connected to the exam rooms by a hallway. I moved quickly toward Marjorie's office. I scanned the Post-its on her desk, little beads of sweat popping up on my forehead and above my lip, sliding into my mouth and tasting of fear. There was nothing useful, no log-in code or password.

My stomach plunged.

I ran my hand along the underside of the desk, my trembling fingertips snagging on a loose nail. Nothing. I flipped through the colossal stacks of paper and folders. My heart was booming, almost deafening in my ears.

"Shit, shit, shit," I muttered.

I rifled through her desk drawers. Phone charger, paper clips, pens, pencils, loose paper, more sticky notes, but not the one I needed. I checked the filing cabinet, looking for a video surveillance company. If only I knew the company's name.

I glanced at the clock. Seven minutes had passed. How much time was left?

I swiped my sweat-slicked palms on my jeans as I stood in the middle of the office. "Think, Emma, think."

My gaze landed on Marjorie's computer. The screen saver was on, one of those migraine-looking designs flashing in strange geometric patterns. Her log-in and password for the computer were written on a sticky note.

I sat in her chair and logged in. The screen saver disappeared, revealing a background picture of Marjorie with her husband and their two grown children, smiling in front of a Christmas tree.

As messy as her office was, Marjorie's home screen was organized with military precision. I scanned the screen, but there were no folders with passwords or what looked like a surveillance company file. I did a search for all the words I could think of on her hard drive: *password, log-in, video.*

Nothing.

Finally, in desperation, I clicked into her recent downloads. There! She'd downloaded the software for Sunshine Surveillance two weeks ago. And in the application folder she'd saved a Notes file with her log-in name and password.

"Bingo," I whispered.

My phone vibrated. "She's on her way up," Gabe whispered.

"Shit." Scalding jolts of adrenaline zipped through me. "How long?"

"She's in reception at the elevator. Maybe a minute or two."

I hung up. A bead of sweat rolled down the slope of my nose. I shook it away.

"Come on, come on." I clicked through the folders until I found Recording Log. Each recording was categorized in a dated folder beginning last week. Looking at the date the application had been installed, I could tell they'd begun recording two weeks ago, but it looked like after a week the recordings started over-writing themselves.

I clicked Disable so no more recording would be done.

*Control A to highlight all. Right-click. Delete. Accept.*

I right-clicked on the Recycling Bin and emptied it.

My phone vibrated again. Gabe.

I lunged out of the office, just as I heard the horrible metallic slide of a door opening.

Marjorie had returned.

# CHAPTER 18

I PERFORMED A DESPERATE gymnast's leap down the hall into one of the exam rooms and threw myself behind the door.

I didn't have time to close it, so I just huddled in the narrow crack between the door and the wall. My chest heaved as I tried desperately to catch my breath. My back was soaked with sweat. I couldn't remember if I'd closed the recycling bin on Marjorie's computer. What if she saw what I'd done? What if her screen saver hadn't turned back on?

Marjorie was moving around the reception area. I froze, straining to hear. But I couldn't tell what she was doing, the sounds muffled by the door. I rested my head against the wall, trying to think through my options.

I could text Gabe and ask him to come up. Maybe he could distract Marjorie. Or I could try to slip out when she was back in her office. I'd done it before, although that time she'd had music on.

My phone buzzed again. I pulled it out, my screen lighting up the small exam room. Afraid Marjorie might see the light bleeding out of the office, I curved my palm over the top.

Gabe: You out?

I replied with numb, clumsy fingers: Trapped in clinic.

Gabe: There's a bunch of cops out front!

The cops had probably come when Gabe broke into Marjorie's car.

I closed my eyes. I was on my own.

Leather creaked as Marjorie sat down. She was back in her office.

I stood silent and still for what felt like forever. Rain fell in sheets on the other side of the window, a curtain separating me from the outside world. Sepia shades of yellow cast long rectangular shapes on the tiled floor.

My eyes adjusted to the darkness. Across the room I could make out the hulking shape of the exam table, the computer on its small desk just beyond. I glanced at the tools in the room, trying to figure out what I could use now. Stethoscope. Scales. Paper towels. Gauze. Reflex hammer.

If worse came to worst, I could just knock her out. There was always gauze to bandage her afterward. I almost laughed at the absurd thoughts whirling through my brain like demented birds.

The clinic was set up like a square, reception in front, exam rooms along the corridor at the back. Marjorie's office was at the end of the hall, facing the exam rooms. Directly across from me was the hallway that led past the medical supply room and out into reception. Marjorie's office door was open, so sneaking across wasn't an option unless she was distracted.

I had to distract her.

I grabbed the reflex hammer and eased around the open door, tossing it across the corridor toward the medical supply closet. It made a solid *thunk*, and Marjorie instantly got out of her chair. I peeked through the crack by the door's hinges. Marjorie's back was to me as she bent to pick up the little hammer.

She then opened the supply closet, momentarily obstructing her view of me.

This was it.

I slipped out, scuttling to the left, then cutting right down the hallway toward reception.

I crouched behind the desk while I waited for her to return to her office, but instead she walked toward reception. I could hear her breathing, the shuffle of her shoes against tiles. My heart banged against my rib cage, my whole body flooded with adrenaline. It felt like my blood was made of fire.

I waited, sweat dripping down my nose, splashing into my mouth. Finally she turned and shuffled back to her office. I counted to ten before creeping to the front door. My palm was sweaty when I grasped the doorknob. I stepped into the hallway, shut the door with a soft click, and sprinted down the white maze of halls.

My heart slammed in my chest, *bang, bang, bang*, trying to get out. I flung myself into the stairwell—no time for the elevator—and raced down, two at a time. At the bottom, I paused in the stairway, trying to get hold of myself. I sent a text to Gabe.

I'm out.

I took a few deep, steadying breaths and smoothed my hair, wiping sweaty strands that clung to my forehead. When I pushed through the stairwell door into the bright light and moist warmth of the hospital's entry, I was still sucking in deep breaths. A few people wandered around near the front reception desk, looking lost and confused.

I hurried straight for the revolving doors in the entrance, not looking where I was going.

And ran smack into Nate.

"Nate! Oh my God!" I gasped. I rubbed my forehead where I'd thwacked into his shoulder. "What are you doing here?"

"I was just . . ." He cleared his throat and swallowed, his Adam's apple bobbing. "There was a break-in in the parking lot."

I studied Nate. He was sweating. I mean, I was sweating too, but I'd been running. He wouldn't usually be called to deal with something like a car break-in. That was a cop's job, not a detective's. And why would he start a new case right as he was on his way home? Nate was lying; I was sure of it.

And suddenly I knew he'd been about to go get the video surveillance footage from Marjorie. Behind my back. It was lucky I'd been here to catch him.

I let a smile slide into place and linked my arm through his, moving us toward the revolving doors. But Nate didn't budge.

"What are you doing here?" he asked.

"Didn't you get my text? I forgot my purse." I laughed. "It was in the bathroom all the way up on the oncology floor. Your mom's with Josh."

Nate laughed too, and nodded at my sweaty head. "And did you run all the way up and back down?"

I swiped at a loose tendril of hair glued to my forehead. "Yeah. I haven't been getting a lot of exercise lately so I thought I'd run up the stairs."

"Did you see anybody suspicious wandering around the parking lot?"

I frowned and pretended to think about it. "The parking lot?"

"Yeah. Dark clothes, beanie. Likely male."

I caught a glimpse of Gabe walking casually past the entrance. He was wearing jeans and a blue blazer, carrying a pink balloon that said IT'S A GIRL. One of the cops smiled at him and said congratulations. Gabe nodded and returned the smile, continuing past the door. Our eyes met, fleetingly. As he moved away, I caught sight of a beanie sticking out of his blazer pocket. I would've laughed if it wasn't all so completely terrifying.

"Emma? Emma! I'm talking to you."

We stepped outside, the brisk wind buffeting us as we crossed the parking lot. "Sorry. No, I went upstairs, got my purse, and then I had to go to the bathroom, so I stopped there. And then I came back downstairs."

"Did you see anyone matching that description come inside?"

"I don't think so. Maybe they came in the back way?"

"Who were you with? Did they see anything?"

"I wasn't with anybody."

Nate studied me, his eyes narrowing. Cop's eyes. Dead eyes. The ones that showed he had something cold at his core. He could turn it off and on when he wanted to, when he was on the scent of a case. But this was the first time he'd ever looked at me like that.

Nate was cheerful, but he was also a detective, I reminded myself. He was susceptible to suspicion and skepticism. I just had to convince him not to be suspicious of me.

"While it's always fun being interrogated by my husband, I'd really like to go home now," I said, letting sarcasm drape my words.

Nate smiled then, an unexpected smile, his good-cop smile. "Just try to remember."

A crackle of frustration zipped through me, but my phone chimed the arrival of a text before I could reply. It was from my colleague Julia.

I need your help.

I stopped walking so abruptly that Nate's arm jerked my shoulder socket.

"What is it?" he asked.

I showed him the text. "I think I'll swing by Julia's on the way home."

He shook his head. "Julia's in a lot of deep shit. You should stay away for now."

"She's my friend. I need to go."

"Why? Once we have that surveillance video, the courts are going to throw the book at her. If you get pulled into a drug case, it won't look good for you. And it won't look good for me if my wife is involved in even a hint of a drug case while I'm trying to get a promotion. I don't want you getting involved."

I stepped away from him. "Are you telling me I'm not allowed to go to my friend's house?" I asked, my voice icy.

"Of course not! I'm just saying, think of your career. Think of *mine*. And if you won't think of anything else, think of Josh!"

Anger kicked inside me, bitter and raw as an oozing wound.

"I can't believe you're implying I don't think of Josh. He is *all* I think of!"

Nate shoved a hand through his hair. There were mud-colored circles under his eyes. He'd been working late every night, up early every morning. Trying to spend time with Josh when he could. The exhaustion and strain were starting to show.

"He's all I think of too!" he said wearily. "That's why I'm trying to solve this case. We need this promotion, Emma."

Nate was only a few feet from me, but the distance might as well have been a mile. The space between us prickled, charged with the energy of our anger, suspicions, and fear. I stared at my husband, wanting to reach out and touch him, to pull him closer to me, but I couldn't. Instead I took another step away from him.

We were not in this together.

Bitterness stung deep in my belly.

"I can't just abandon her," I said.

I turned and got in my car. I adjusted the rearview mirror and watched as Nate stared at me helplessly, then got in his police cruiser. He started the engine and drove away, the distance growing until he turned and I could no longer see him.

# CHAPTER 19

I DROVE TOWARD JULIA'S, guilt filling my chest with an ache so fierce it threatened to crush the air from my lungs. What I was doing was very dangerous. I was risking everything. Nate's love and devotion. My son's respect. My career. My freedom.

Everything felt unstable and scary when Nate and I argued. But selling prescriptions was the only tool I had to get money to pay for Josh's treatment. I didn't know what else to do. I'd already called asking for an increase to my credit limit on both my credit cards, but neither had been enough.

I pulled into the long driveway that led to Julia's house, a small blue Craftsman with white-painted shutters, wood-scalloped rafter tails, and a cute wraparound porch.

My phone buzzed as I parked, and when I looked at the text, I saw it was from Nate. I'm sorry for being a shithead. I love you. Of course you should see Julia. P.S. Happy first kiss anniversary.

Relief gushed, warm and sweet, into my chest. I replied: I'm sorry too. I think we're both just stressed. I love you back. X

Nate always remembered. Every year. Even amid Josh's sickness and our squabbles, he had remembered.

After I'd stitched up Nate's hand at Harborview, I hadn't expected to ever see him again. But then he was there at a Christmas party my roommate made me go to. I'd invited Gabe to the party that morning as he was dashing out of my apartment. But about an hour after arriving I knew he wasn't coming. My high heels were pinching my feet, and I was feeling rejected and alone and, by that time, a little tipsy.

I'd run into Nate—literally—as I headed outside. He was looking down at his phone and we collided, red liquid from his cup spilling down the front of my dress.

"Oh, shit!" he'd exclaimed, eyes wide with horror. "I'm so sorry! I didn't mean to—I wasn't watching—I mean, I was texting my mom."

I arched an eyebrow.

"Or something less dorky." He smiled, the left corner of his mouth pulling up in a way that was completely disarming. "It's you."

And there it was. *Il colpo di fulmine.* The thunderbolt hit me. Again.

I couldn't take my eyes off him. I remember the physical sensation of relief I'd felt seeing him again. His touch felt like oxygen.

Nate held his hand up to show me his scar, a neat seam. "You'd barely know it was there. Thank you."

I flushed. "It was nothing."

"Hey, do you want me to take you home to get changed?"

"Excuse me?"

Nate laughed at my expression. "I mean, your dress. It's covered in cranberry juice."

"Oh!" I brushed at the damp patches. "I don't know."

"Don't you trust me?" He smiled.

The funny thing was, I *did* trust him. Without even knowing him, I felt a closeness that I'd never felt before.

We went back to my apartment and stayed up talking all night. We never returned to the party. And when Gabe finally called a few weeks later, I didn't answer the phone. I never looked back.

Nate had told me his dad had suffered a stroke a few years back. He told me about his high school sweetheart who'd abruptly dumped him the day before he left for the police academy. He told me about his friend Robbie, who'd killed himself right before graduation, and the guilt he carried because he'd allowed Robbie to be bullied.

I'd realized then that there was so much more to Nate than met the eye. He seemed so happy-go-lucky, sweet, with a little bit of swagger. But there was something a little broken, hidden like a bruise before it purpled the skin. I could see it in his eyes. It drew me to him as much as our initial chemistry had.

Maybe I wanted to fix him a little bit.

I walked up the gravel path almost hidden by dripping leaves and evergreen bushes to Julia's front door. As I lifted my hand to knock, it opened, and Kia Sharpe nearly walked straight into me.

I was surprised to see her—Nate had said Julia and Kia were dating, but she was a detective and Julia had been arrested. Wasn't there some sort of conflict of interest there? And why would someone as sweet and fuzzy as Julia date a prickly bitch like Kia?

Kia trained her dark eyes on me. "What are you doing here?" she asked, her usual charming self.

It was no secret that we didn't like each other. Nate had once suggested that I was jealous, but it wasn't that. Kia was just hard to get along with. She was tiny, with something sharp and complicated coiled beneath the surface that somehow inflated her size.

"Julia texted me. I thought I'd stop by and see how she's doing."

Kia stepped outside, pulling the door shut but not latching it. She rubbed a hand over her square jaw and lowered her voice.

"Julia's been released on bail. She isn't in a good place right now. Maybe come back another time?"

I let my gaze sweep Kia's face. "I think we're good enough friends that we can see each other at our worst," I said sweetly.

I moved around her, rapping my knuckles on the door.

Julia didn't answer, but Kia was watching me, her lips curled in distaste, her dark gaze making my skin itch with resentment. It was the same way Nate had looked at me earlier: suspicious. I turned away and pushed the door open.

"Julia?" I called.

The entry was dark, but the kitchen light was on at the end of the hallway. I shut the door and moved toward it. The thick oatmeal-colored carpet in the hallway cushioned my steps. To my right, a stairway led into darkness.

In the kitchen, Julia was bent over the island, a pile of pills and a crumbly line of powder in front of her.

"Julia!" I gasped. "What the hell are you doing?"

Julia jumped, a little gasp of surprise bursting from her mouth. She scooped up the pills and pushed them into her pocket. She looked exhausted and stressed, wearing a tattered old T-shirt and lumpy gray sweatpants. I felt overdressed in my cashmere turtleneck, tall brown boots, and infinity scarf.

"It's not what you think," she rushed to say.

"Really? Because I'm thinking you're crushing up pills and snorting them. Does Kia know about this?"

"God, no!" Julia glanced over my shoulder, eyes wide. "She's gone, right?"

"I think so." I studied the white powder. "Let me guess. Oxy? So you *were* stealing the samples!"

"Fine, what do you want me to say? Yes, it was me. I took them." She sighed, her eyes glittering with tears. She dabbed at them with a tissue. "But I'm not a junkie, I swear. I just take what I need to manage my condition."

"What condition?" I couldn't remember Julia being sick once in the time I'd known her.

"I have lupus."

I was stunned. Like other autoimmune diseases, lupus caused the body's immune system to attack its own tissue and organs. It caused excruciating joint pain, stiffness, and swelling. Julia was energetic, bubbly. I'd never have guessed at her pain. Maybe doctors thought we knew what people were going through, that we could read the signs and symptoms, but maybe in the end we were just guessing.

"Your wrist." My eyes flew to Julia's bandaged wrist, remembering how she'd blamed the pain and stiffness on carpal tunnel syndrome.

"Yes. It's advanced to lupus arthritis." She smiled sluggishly. "Here, let's sit."

Julia walked unsteadily toward the living room, tipping abruptly to the right and almost falling. The immediate high evident in her speech and movement came from crushing and snorting the pills instead of swallowing them. It rendered the extended-release mechanism obsolete.

"Come on." I curled my hand around her elbow and helped her to the living room. We sat on an overstuffed couch offset by blue-and-white-striped cushions. The living room was a small but neat space with rich wood panels, antique furnishings, oatmeal-colored area rugs, and a box-beam ceiling. The tiled fireplace opposite was covered in candles of every size and shape.

Julia leaned her head back and closed her eyes. She sighed as the drug wound through her system, her whole body limp as an old washcloth. When she spoke, her voice was soft and dreamy.

"I was diagnosed with lupus when I was sixteen. My older sister had it too. We both lived with chronic pain our whole lives. Stephanie, my sister, she lost her hair, her body broke out in rashes. The pain was constant. She killed herself two years ago. She couldn't cope anymore."

"I'm so sorry," I murmured. "Is that why you moved here?"

I'd only lived in Skamania for a year when Julia arrived; being the new person in a small town was one of the things that had bonded us.

She nodded. "Yes. I wanted to start over. And I was doing really well. I'd been put on a low dose of OxyContin to help the pain, and it made my life manageable. Under normal circumstances I couldn't work at the clinic, I couldn't see patients or go grocery shopping, or even get out of bed some days. I wouldn't be able to work. I would lose my home. But the oxy allowed me to reclaim my life."

She adjusted her position on the couch, her eyes bright, the pupils constricted. She used both hands to lift one leg over the other knee, wincing as she did. "But six months ago, my doctor told me he had to lower my dosage. He said the amount I was taking would put up a red flag on my chart and that would alert the DEA. You know yourself all the laws that are changing around oxy, how prohibitive they are. They're kicking people off their pain management plans so abruptly it's leaving them with no option but to head to the streets. People are killing themselves because they can't live with their pain. That's what my sister did."

Julia shook her head slowly. "I know it was wrong to take the OxyContin. I know I shouldn't have done it, and now I'm going to lose my license. I might even go to jail. But the dose I get now is too low. I have a standing order with this dealer. She's not exactly legal, but she delivers a few extra oxy to me every month.

It's been over a week since she left any, though. So I took a few extra from the medical supply closet, just to tide me over."

"You get them delivered? Where?"

"The birdhouse on my front porch." She chuckled. "Sophisticated, right?"

"No, I meant, where—who—do you get them from?"

She shrugged and looked away, not answering.

My mind was churning, too fast to keep up with. Was it Violeta? Had she delivered drugs to people like Julia? But now that Violeta was dead, there was a gap in the supply chain.

"Why didn't you tell anyone you were suffering so much?" I asked.

She snorted. "I was afraid! Pain management is such a taboo subject, you know? I was scared people would think I was a bad person for needing it."

"You're not a bad person, Julia."

"I need your help." She clutched my hand. Hers was icy-cold, the skin stretched tight over bony knuckles. "Can you prescribe me some pills? Just a few to get me through until I can get more?"

I coughed to cover my surprise. "Julia . . ."

Julia laughed, a hard, dry sound, like straw scraping against asphalt. "No, sorry. I shouldn't have asked."

She dropped her face into her hands. It took me a minute to realize she was crying. I put a hesitant hand on her shoulder.

"When did the war on drugs become a war on the disabled?" she asked bitterly.

The opioid epidemic was a complex one, not nearly as black-and-white as politicians tried to make it seem. Almost lost in the national controversy surrounding the epidemic was the reality that some people genuinely needed opioids. Badly. And these people were being forgotten, betrayed by a system desperate to look like it was righting a past wrong.

For so long, doctors had been told that morphine was evil, addictive. Then the drug industry shifted its marketing, telling the medical community that freedom from pain was a fundamental human right. And we'd lapped it up. Until people started dying and we had to cut our patients off.

All this time, I'd thought I was wrong to forge those prescriptions, to illegally sell oxy. I knew I was doing it for the right reason, but I still thought my choice was immoral.

Now I wasn't quite so sure.

My job as a mother was to keep my son alive. And my job as a doctor was to help people, not watch them suffer.

"I used to believe in justice," I told her. "I thought life was fair, that karma existed and everything would eventually roll around to equity. I don't believe that anymore. Bad people stay healthy, good people become addicted, loved ones get sick and die. Some people suffer blow after blow, while others drift along easily. The world is unfair and unjust and just really damn cruel. I wish I could help you, Julia."

"You *can*. I'm not an addict. Maybe I'm addicted, but I'm not an addict. I just need pain relief. Please. Without it, I don't know if I can go on living."

# CHAPTER 20

NATE TOSSED HIS KEYS and wallet on the console table at home, his mind still on Emma's strange behavior at the hospital. Nate questioned suspects every day, and they all displayed the same signs when lying: too many details, slowed-down movements, helpfully offering other explanations.

Her statement about not seeing anybody at the hospital included all of those hallmarks. But she'd left before he'd had a chance to confront her.

The house smelled of the rich, tantalizing scent of beef stew and freshly baked bread. Charlie loped over to him, pressing his nose into Nate's leg and licking his palm. Nate scratched him behind the ears.

The living room was a complete mess. Toys formed an obstacle course across the carpet. Picture books were scattered everywhere. Dirty plates and cups were stacked on every available surface. Nate was surprised. Emma usually ran the house, and their lives, with such military precision.

Despite the clutter, the fireplace was on, the flame flickering in the grate, making a cheerful crackling noise. If only they'd had the time to put up the Christmas lights, to hang the stockings and decorate a tree. Still, the room was cozy and warm. Like a home. A family home.

Josh was bent over the coffee table coloring while Pokémon fought an epic battle on the TV in the background. The knobs of his shoulders and arms and knees were sharp and severe, his skin a sickly shade of pasty white.

Nate's heart squeezed with a sudden fear. What if Josh died and it was all because he couldn't pay for the treatment? It would be his fault.

"Daddy!" Josh lifted his arms and waited for Nate to scoop him up. Nate gently pulled his son into his arms. Josh's body was small and vulnerable, lighter than ever. Like he was already disappearing.

"Hey, buddy." Nate's heart crunched fiercely. Josh still smelled the same, like mango shampoo and day-old socks. His giggle was the same when Nate's breath tickled his neck. "What are you drawing?"

Josh showed Nate a swirl of dark colors, thick strokes over twists of thinner ones, shades of blue and red. "Do you like it?"

"Of course I do!"

"That's you and that's Mommy. And this"—Josh pointed to a particularly dark swirl—"is the Empire. And that's all of us and we're fighting the Empire."

"Wow! It's amazing!"

"Grandma said I might be an artist when I growed up, and I said if I'm a famous artist I'd have very much money and I'd buy all the kids with cancer their medicine so they'd live."

Nate pressed his lips to the top of Josh's head, unable to reply.

"Here." Josh handed it to Nate. "It's for you."

"Thanks, buddy. I'll put it on the fridge, 'kay? Is Grandma cooking?"

"Yup."

Nate went into the kitchen, Josh and Charlie trailing behind.

Moira was bustling about, filling bowls with a bubbling stew and slathering chunks of steaming white bread with slabs of butter. The kitchen was warm, steam rising from a colander sitting in the farmhouse sink. The cabinets, breakfast bar, and dining table were rich with woodwork, giving the area a homey, rustic vibe. Moira had music playing on her phone, an old Stevie Nicks song.

Nate remembered that when his parents had bought the house, it was a complete dive. His dad had spent weekends remodeling it. He'd begged Nate to help him tear out moldy carpeting and rotten wood, paint the new woodwork, and install toilets, but Nate had refused. He was a teenager and wanted to hang out with his friends. He regretted that now. Regretted that he hadn't spent time with his dad before he'd been incapacitated by the stroke.

His parents had used the house as a rental until Nate and Emma moved back to Skamania. Now their rent helped pay for Matt's care.

"Hey, Ma." Nate kissed his mother on the cheek. "It smells amazing."

"Well, maybe you'd get a home-cooked meal more if I got to see you more," she replied tartly, but she smiled and patted his cheek to soften the words.

"Can I help with anything?"

"Nope, it's almost ready."

Josh moved past Moira. "Alexa, make a fart sound."

Alexa complied with a fart sound. "That was a long and windy one," she said.

Josh giggled, and Nate rolled his eyes, unable to hide his smile. Emma had taught that trick to him the other day, and Josh had been asking Alexa about farts ever since.

"Josh, Grandma's listening to music."

"No, no, it's fine." Moira turned the music off.

"Is Siri Alexa's best friend?" Josh asked.

Moira chuckled and kissed Josh's cheek. "You remind me so much of your father when he was your age!"

"I look like Mommy, though."

Josh looked at Nate, who shrugged. It was true, Josh was all Emma, from his dark hair to his sharp jaw. His eyes were blue, but not Nate's dark blue, Emma's lighter sapphire blue. He was strong-willed and determined, in a way Nate loved.

"But you have your daddy's smile." Moira turned to Nate. "Where's, uh . . ." Her eyes flickered behind Nate.

Nate's gut clenched with a familiar disappointment. "Emma will be here in just a few minutes."

Moira nodded and resumed serving up stew—but not before Nate noticed the scowl on her face. She'd never explained exactly why she didn't like Emma. He'd asked her once, the day Emma and he had gotten married. He'd arrived at the courthouse, and Moira had been waiting on the steps outside. She'd pulled him aside and whispered urgently in his ear.

"It isn't too late. There's no shame in canceling this."

"Mom, we're having a baby!"

"Well . . . accidents happen."

"Mom!" He'd pulled away, stunned. "What's your problem with Emma?"

"Nothing. She's lovely."

"Then you need to accept she's going to be my wife."

He'd brushed past his mother without another word.

Sometimes he felt stuck between them. As if he had to choose sides. He felt guilty, like he was doing something wrong, when all he wanted was to take care of his mother because she was all alone. He wanted to take care of Emma too, but she was fiercely independent and so strong. She didn't need him the way his mom did. And maybe he liked that a little. It was nice to feel like for once he didn't have to carry the burden all by himself. That he had a partner.

"I'm going to go wash up," he told Josh and his mom now.

Upstairs, he headed for his office, first grabbing a sheet of tracing paper from Josh's room. He pulled the business card he'd taken from the morgue out of his pocket and laid it flat on the surface of the desk.

He'd nearly shit himself when he bumped into Emma at the hospital. He'd only decided to stop by the morgue to get the business card from the evidence bag at the last minute after promising Emma he'd come home.

Maybe, he realized, he'd felt like Emma was lying because *he* had been lying.

He felt like a complete dickhead. On the spur of the moment, he opened Google and searched for the item he'd been thinking about for Emma for Christmas. He smiled as he ordered it and left a message for the seller. It wasn't much, but they didn't have a lot to spend this year. And he knew Emma would appreciate the thought more than anything.

Once he was done, he picked up the water-damaged card and turned it over in his hands.

He knew he shouldn't have just taken it. He should've checked it out in the evidence log, but the evidence bag had still been lying there under the gurney and nobody had been around, so he'd taken it. And he needed a lead. Anything that would get him closer to solving this case.

Was it the right thing to do? Nate had no idea. What was right and what was wrong was becoming increasingly blurred to him. His frustration curdled into a sharp anger. He hated himself for feeling useless and ineffective, hated that this promotion felt miles away and that he needed it so desperately.

Nate laid the sheet of tracing paper over the business card and rifled through the desk drawer. When he found a pencil he scratched it over the tracing paper, the shape of the business card, slowly revealing the embossed logo on the front.

A thick cross was surrounded by a circle, a set of wings to the left and right of the circle. Beneath that, the bold capital letters AL  GIA CE.

Nate opened Google again and found the website he was looking for. He compared the tracing paper to the website. The logo was the same.

### ALLEGIANCE HEALTH CLINIC

It was Emma's clinic.

LATER THAT NIGHT, Nate was lounging on the couch. Emma's feet were on his lap, Josh curled like a bean on hers. He was too big to sleep on her anymore, but he didn't like to be left alone, and Emma seemed to need him close. Charlie was on the floor making funny little sucking sounds in his sleep.

The TV murmured in the background, the fireplace crackling and casting a sepia glow across the screen. All of Emma's usual rules—strict 7:30 p.m. bedtime for Josh, flossing and brushing teeth, laundry on a Monday night—had gone out the window. Even her glass of wine was propped on the coffee table without a coaster, unheard of for Emma.

Emma was looking down at Josh's sleeping form, gently stroking his cheek, her eyes so full of love it made Nate's heart ache.

She looked tired. Exhausted, really. Her hair was tied into a tangled ponytail, limp tendrils hanging around her face, not a speck of makeup on. But when she looked at him and smiled, it made everything in him go warm with happiness. There was no woman in the world more beautiful than his wife.

Watching Emma watching their son filled him with a powerful sort of love and fear. He loved them both so much and was terrified he wasn't protecting them the way a husband and father should.

"We should put up the Christmas decorations," Nate said.

Emma didn't answer, just kept stroking Josh's cheek.

"Em?"

"Hmm?"

"Did you hear me?"

"Sorry, no."

"I said we should put up the Christmas decorations."

She groaned and let her head fall back against the couch. "I know. I'm just so tired."

She stared at the ceiling, not speaking, for a long time. It was hard to read her face. Nate couldn't help feeling like she wasn't really here with him. Her body was, but her mind was somewhere else.

He wondered if he was being paranoid or if it was just the stress of having a sick child. The cop in him said there was no evidence that Emma was cheating. But the husband in him wasn't convinced.

Now was his chance. He should ask her what was going on. But he couldn't seem to get the words out. Maybe a part of him didn't want to know. His son might die; he couldn't lose his wife too.

Bigger than that, though, Nate knew that if Emma was having an affair, he wouldn't be able to stay. And Josh needed both of his parents right now. Nate wouldn't jeopardize his son's health for his own paranoia and pride.

The space between him and Emma felt immense and insurmountable. He wondered what the hell was going on in her head. Sometimes he wondered if she ever thought about what was going on in his.

"Did you see the GoFundMe page?" he asked with a cheerfulness he didn't feel.

Emma shook her head.

"Someone donated five thousand dollars. It'll pay down some of the treatment costs."

Emma's eyes widened. "Seriously?"

She fumbled on the side table for her phone and checked the website for Josh's GoFundMe page. "Oh, thank God." She clenched the phone to her chest and closed her eyes, looking more relieved than surprised.

"The community's really pulling for us."

Emma glanced at him. Her face betrayed no emotion. She'd retreated behind a mask.

"Yes," she said slowly. "Maybe Moira's church?"

Nate frowned. "The donation was anonymous. I'm not sure why they'd do it anonymously."

"Honestly, I don't care who did it, I'm just glad Josh can get his treatment."

"I wish we could at least thank them," Nate said.

"Yes—oh God!" Emma shut her eyes. "But this will only help with one bill! What about the next one, and the one after that, and all our deductibles and—"

"Hey." Nate squeezed her leg. "It's going to be okay."

She clamped her lips together. "Of course. You're right."

Nate changed the subject. "Hey, um, have you seen your brother lately?"

She looked at him, confused. "Ben? No. Why?"

"Well, you know, in case Josh needs a bone marrow transplant or a kidney or something."

"That isn't how this treatment works. They take Josh's own blood cells and reprogram them."

"I know, I was just thinking for the future. . . ."

Emma shifted in her seat. "I haven't seen Ben in years. Since, God, I guess it was when I first started medical school."

Nate shrugged and looked down. He tugged Emma's socks off and started rubbing her feet.

Emma made a little sound of pleasure at the back of her throat. "That feels nice."

Nate winced as pain shot through his fingertips. He adjusted his hands and instead rolled his knuckles over the arches of Emma's feet.

Emma noticed the wince and scooped his hand into hers. "Oh my God! Are you all right?" She examined the dried crusts of blood along the cuticles, the bruises that had appeared under the nails.

Nate flushed and forced a wry laugh. "Kia slammed my fingers in the car door today. Hurt like hell."

How many times had he made excuses for his bloody nails? Emma pressed her lips to his fingers, but he gently eased them away. He had the sense that she could see right through him, but when he looked up she was already distant and distracted.

The silence stretched for a long minute.

"Do you have a patient named Violeta Williams?" he asked.

Emma frowned. "The name sounds familiar, I think. Why?"

"We found a body today. Violeta Williams. She had a business card from your clinic in her back pocket."

"That's horrible! What happened to her?"

"We're still investigating."

"Care to elaborate?" she asked.

Nate's hands stilled on her feet. "I think she may have been murdered."

Emma sucked in a breath. "You think a business card will help you find out what happened to her?"

"Maybe. I'll call the clinic and find out if she was a patient. There might be a connection."

Emma gently shifted Josh off her lap and stood, reaching her hands to the ceiling as she stretched. "Well, I wouldn't hold your breath," she said. "All the doctors' business cards are out at reception. Anybody could grab any of them."

# CHAPTER 21

I DROVE INTO THE parking lot of the Crescent Lake Costco, my whole body tense. My eyes swept the lot as I looked for the best place to park. I was a little early. Gabe had said to be here at one p.m., but I didn't see any sign of him or Ben yet. I pulled into an empty space located on a slight incline at the side of the lot. It offered the best view of the parking lot.

A pale, watery sun hovered apathetically in the sky, barely managing to warm the day. This morning the ground had been glazed in silver frost. We could see snow any day now. I could feel winter descending, its talons reaching out from the jagged mountains in the distance, sinking into the ground around me. Snow had already fallen on the highest peaks, looking like cream-dipped cones jutting into the cold, turquoise sky.

I sipped my Starbucks coffee and unwrapped the ham sandwich I'd bought to go with it. Yesterday had been my first day working mornings at the clinic. The hours away from Josh were interminable, my mind constantly drifting away from my patients to how he was feeling, if he was okay. For the first time ever, I wished I didn't have to go to work. But we needed the money, the health insurance.

I'd told Moira this morning that I would be a little late coming home because I'd be filling out paperwork for human resources. A dangerous lie: if anybody checked, they'd know I wasn't at the hospital right now. But it was a risk I had to take.

I checked the canvas bag with the prescription pads. Everything was there, ready. This had to work. Now that Violeta was gone, Ben needed a partner for his oxy ring, and I could be that partner.

We just had to make sure Ben never found out what we'd done to Violeta.

I stared at the ham sandwich in my hand. The pink meat glistened in the thin sunlight. I pressed a fist to my mouth, fighting a wave of nausea. The sound of Violeta's body hitting the river crashed through my memory. I set the sandwich on the passenger's seat, unable to eat any more.

*Get ahold of yourself, Emma.*

I flashed back to Nate telling me he'd found a business card from the clinic on Violeta's body, and the fear swelled again. Gabe must've handed her my card when Violeta was snorting what she thought was cocaine. For a moment, I wanted to kill him. Now Nate would get a warrant to find out if Violeta Williams was a patient at my clinic.

At ten past, Gabe pulled into the parking lot on a motorcycle. He'd arranged to meet Ben here, telling him he'd give him the prescriptions I'd signed. But Ben didn't know I would be here too.

Gabe parked in the middle of the lot, where he would blend into the midday Costco shoppers the most. A few minutes later a boxy white van with deeply tinted windows pulled up next to him.

Gabe got off his motorcycle and approached the driver's side window. He leaned against the van, chatting casually before handing Ben a stack of papers—the prescriptions?

Over the course of the next few minutes, six different women walked to the van one at a time, slid the back passenger door

open, and got in. Throughout it all, Gabe leaned against the driver's door, still talking to Ben.

The problem was, Ben didn't get out.

I sat in my car, uncertain what to do. The back of my shirt
was damp against my skin. I wrapped my arms tightly around
my chest, shivering with nerves.

What were they waiting for?

I couldn't stand it anymore. I texted Gabe.

**Is Ben in the van?**

I watched as Gabe pulled his phone out of his back pocket
and read my message. He said a few words to Ben before moving
away from the truck and texting me back.

**Yes. Waiting for one more girl.**

I pushed my car door open, but just as I stepped out, a shiny
black truck with chrome wheels skidded to a stop next to them. I
gasped. It was the same truck that had been parked outside my
house on Monday.

I slid back into my car and hunched behind the steering
wheel, heart thudding. Two men got out of the truck and approached Gabe where he was now standing next to his motorcycle flicking through his phone.

Both were meaty-looking, with angry eyes and swarthy skin
covered in tattoos. One had oily black hair tied into a ponytail. The
other was mostly bald, with a thin mustache and a tattoo of something on one side of his face. A dragon? A lizard? It was hard to tell.

Ponytail said something to Gabe, who replied angrily and
moved a step closer, but Ponytail unzipped his coat and flipped it
open, revealing something strapped to his waist.

My heart stopped. Gun.

He had a gun.

I fumbled for my phone, about to call the police. A sharp rap on my window made me jump.

I peered out the window, sweat pooling at the base of my spine. It took me a second to recognize the woman grinning at me. Jessica something-or-other, one of the moms from Josh's school. She blinked gold-flecked brown eyes at me. When she motioned for me to roll down my window, her glossy hair, streaked with honey highlights, swung around her shoulders.

God, I *really* hated living in a small town.

"Hi, Emma, how are you?" she exclaimed, her voice loud and high-pitched. Jessica was the president of the PTA, with the overly enthusiastic, imperious attitude to match, always pretending to be so busy, so important. "Do you want to do our shopping together?"

"Uhh . . ." I peered past her at Gabe. The guy with the gun was now laughing, although Gabe looked pissed off. "I'm actually getting caught up on a bit of work on my lunch break."

Just over her shoulder, I saw Ben get out of the truck.

Prison had clearly agreed with him. On first glance, he was no longer pale and gaunt, with hollow cheeks and glassy eyes. He'd filled out, the sharp angles of his face and body softer. He had a cigarette clenched between his lips, thin tendrils of smoke curling above his head.

He was sober.

Relief punched me in the solar plexus, but then he turned and I saw him full-on. His coffee-colored hair was unkempt, his jaw unshaven, clothes disheveled. His eyes were bloodshot and ringed with dark, as if he hadn't slept in a few nights. Guilt surged in me, and I had the absurd urge to throw myself out of the car and confess everything.

I closed my eyes, trying to ground myself by thinking about Josh this morning. He'd run into our room before the sun rose and thrown himself into bed between Nate and me, his breath coming fast. He'd dreamed he was being chased down a tunnel and just as he was about to reach the light at the other side, the tunnel had caved in, crushing him.

Nate and I had held him, and after a few minutes he'd said, "If I die, will God let me see myself when I growed up?"

He was only five. He shouldn't be thinking about death.

The memory steadied me now as I watched my brother. His pale eyes darted, here, there, everywhere, like a twitchy mouse. His fingertips constantly moved, drumming a beat against each other.

"Emma? Emma!" Jessica's shrill voice dragged me back to the present. "I said, you're a doctor, right?"

"Yes, I am," I replied, trying not to sound impatient. Why wouldn't she just leave?

Her brow smoothed in sudden understanding. "Oh, you must be calling a patient. I *love* it when my doctor calls me. It's so personal, you know? Not all doctors go the extra mile like that. . . ."

I murmured an agreement, still watching Ben. He said something to the guys that made them take a step back. They knew him, or respected him at any rate. Ponytail turned and spoke to Gabe, a sheepish look on his face. *We were just messing.*

Gabe wiped his hands down his pants, looking seriously rattled. Costco shoppers bustled by, barely paying any attention to what was going on right in front of them. It was amazing the things that could happen in broad daylight.

Jessica was still prattling on about doctors and how she'd just gone to see hers about a urinary tract infection, and did I know the difference between a urinary tract infection and a bladder infection?

I gaped at her. Did she think I wasn't a real doctor or something?

"Well, I'd best get back to work. I need to call my patient now." I waved my phone in the air, hoping she'd take the hint. But of course she didn't. She just kept right on talking, so I slowly, ever so slowly, reached for the button to roll up my window, and pushed it.

The window rolled up, cutting off Jessica's words. She looked surprised, but I smiled and pressed my phone to my ear, speaking into it as if I were really on the phone to someone.

After a moment, she walked away.

Meanwhile, Ben was plucking at his eyebrows as he listened to Ponytail speak. After a minute, he threw down his cigarette and crushed it with his boot. He turned, rapped on the van door. It opened and one of the girls got out. She was small, dark-haired, with pocked skin and terrified eyes. She was shivering, her threadbare jacket too thin in the cold morning air.

Tattoo Face grabbed her wrist and yanked her toward the truck, shoved her inside. He looked at Gabe and Ben, and there was something in his gaze. It was too watchful, his eyes too black. Tattoo Face and Ponytail climbed in the truck and drove away.

Ben moved toward the van. I didn't hesitate this time.

I threw myself out of my car and jogged in his direction.

# CHAPTER 22

"BEN!"

The icicle air stabbed at my skin. A sharp wind whipped my hair into a frenzy around my face, stinging as it lashed my eyes. I wanted to throw myself into my brother's arms, to have him scoop me up and twirl me around the way he used to when we were kids. But his hands stayed motionless at his sides, the only sign he recognized me the twitchy blink of his eyes.

Up close, I could see that his eyebrows were thin and uneven. His nose was crooked, likely broken a time or two. A jagged scar cut down his right temple.

What had happened to him in the years since I'd last seen him?

The last time I'd seen my brother, he'd been disheveled and unshaven in an alley near Pioneer Square. He'd just shot up. His eyes were glassy, his stare dull. It was impossible to tell if he even recognized me. I took him to the nearest rehab center and checked him in, maxed out my credit card to pay for treatment.

Everybody blamed Ben's addiction on our parents' deaths, but it started before that. He fell into drugs the way a lot of people do:

he experimented with his friends in high school. The more he did, the more he wanted to do.

He was always a little wild—breaking into abandoned buildings, joyrides in stolen cars, sneaking out in the middle of the night to drink with friends down at the beach. He was pretty feral for someone who lived in such a loving home. I never could tell why he was so angry. What makes people go to war with themselves? Is it self-loathing? Resentment? I still haven't found the answer.

Once he came home in the middle of the night high and giggling. He begged me not to tell, and I was so desperate for his love and approval that I didn't. I wished now that I had. Maybe he wouldn't have become an addict.

Maybe I wouldn't have lost him.

Once Ben had sobered up that time in Seattle, he immediately checked himself out of rehab. He sent me a furious text telling me to stay out of his life. I hadn't heard from him since.

"What are you doing here, Emma?" Blink. Blink. Twitch. Blink.

As if we didn't share DNA. Hadn't lost the same parents. Hadn't suffered the same pain.

I don't know what I expected Ben to say. I knew he wouldn't feel like this was some reunion, but the child who used to creep into her big brother's room when she woke shivering from a nightmare still felt her heart break in two.

I searched his face, my ready smile sliding away.

"Violeta told me to meet her here," I said.

Ben tilted his head, a flash of emotion crossing his face. "When did you see her?"

"Last Thursday. I thought you knew . . . ? She said she was going to tell you about our deal."

Ben pulled a packet of cigarettes out of his back pocket and tapped one out. He folded it between clenched lips and lit it with a silver lighter.

"You made a deal with Violeta?"

A young mother marched up to us then, her baby slung over one hip. She was blond and precisely made-up, her overly processed hair teased into a carefully messy ponytail. She was dressed entirely in brand-name gym clothes, despite the chill in the air.

"Excuse me," she called, her voice high-pitched, nasally. "Are you using that cart?"

Ben gave her such a fierce glare she immediately backtracked and turned away from us.

"Rude," I heard her mutter as she walked away.

"Yes, we made a deal. I gave her a bunch of signed prescriptions. She's supposed to meet me here with the money."

Ben plucked at his eyebrows, smoke curling up from the cigarette between his fingers, twisting like a snake in the icy air.

Finally he spoke. "Violeta's dead."

I gasped, my gaze darting to Gabe. He looked stunned too.

"What happened?"

"The police came to our place last night." Ben rubbed a hand over his face, looking tired and haggard. "I was out, but Vi's mother was there, babysitting our son."

"You have a son?" I exclaimed.

Violeta had told me she had a son, but in the chaos after she'd died, I'd failed to connect the dots to Ben.

I had a nephew.

Ben blinked at me, tugging on his eyebrows, but didn't reply.

I broke eye contact and looked down, righteous anger flaring in me. He'd raised a child in a drug ring, with a mother who was clearly a psychopath. And he hadn't even bothered to tell me, his own sister, about him.

"What'd the cops say?" Gabe asked.

"Her body was found downriver from Skamania Falls," Ben said. "They think she went over the waterfall."

Gabe and I both murmured condolences.

"How did she end up in the falls?" I asked.

"Autopsy said she overdosed. They think she shot up and then fell in the water." Ben inhaled another mouthful of smoke, letting it seep deep into his lungs as his eyes darted around. "I told them Violeta doesn't do drugs. Not drugs that take needles, anyway."

His gaze landed on Gabe, hazy and dull. "Where did you last see her?" he asked.

"I told you, man—I dropped her off back at her car in the Target parking lot after we met Emma at the mill," Gabe replied.

Ben smoked some more while plucking at his eyebrows. My skin prickled with sweat, the lie vibrating in the air. Could he see it written like ink across our faces?

Ben blinked hard. "That isn't anywhere near the river."

Fear crouched on my chest, like a pillow over my mouth and nose. Gabe's eyes flicked to mine, waiting for me to answer. When I stayed silent, he spoke up.

"She'd, uh, done a few lines of coke. She said it was 'mom's night out' so she was celebrating."

"That's true," I pitched in, finally finding my voice. "Her eyes were dilated. She had a nosebleed."

"Violeta was scared of water. She almost drowned when she was a kid. She wouldn't have gone in voluntarily." Ben shook his head. "I think something happened to her."

"Maybe those guys in the truck that was here?" I suggested. "They looked dangerous. Who were they?"

Ben shook his head. "Nah. That was just the boyfriend of one of my girls."

I started, horrified. "But, Ben, he looked like he was going to beat her!"

Ben shrugged and flicked a long strand of ash onto the ground. "Bad people get away with doing bad things all the time. It's not my problem. Or yours." He glanced at his watch. "I gotta go. Thanks for dropping that stuff off." He clapped Gabe on the back and turned to get in the van. "See ya round, Em."

"Wait." I held out a hand. "I want in. Violeta said we had a deal."

Ben side-eyed me.

"No."

He climbed in the van and slammed the door. A second later the engine roared to life.

# CHAPTER 23

THE FEELING OF REJECTION was instant and intense, an immense wave pummeling between my shoulder blades, grinding me into the pavement.

I turned to Gabe. "Stop him," I hissed, "or I'll tell him where the drugs that got him sent to prison came from."

Gabe's mouth fell open. "Wha—? But . . .you . . ."

He still hadn't moved, and Ben's van was rolling forward. I shoved Gabe out of the way and slammed my palm against Ben's window. The van stopped abruptly, and Ben rolled his window down, his eyebrows folded angrily.

"What the hell, Emma?"

"Violeta said we had a deal," I said, my tone cold.

"Go home, Emma. You don't want to be a part of this."

I stared at my brother. It hadn't always been like this between us. I missed the brother who used to carry Band-Aids in his pocket because I was always scraping my knees. The brother who'd taught me how to ride a bike, to swear, to stick up for myself when boys in my class tried to flip my dress up. Where had that brother gone?

"I have more prescriptions," I said. "Stacks more."

Ben plucked at his eyebrows. It was a nervous habit from when our father would rage at him on the nights he came home drunk.

Once I'd told Ben how much like Dad he was. He shoved me off my bed. I hit my cheekbone on the windowsill and the skin had split open, like a ripe melon. I still have a little crescent-shaped scar on my cheek from it.

I guess some people don't like to hear the truth.

"It's for my son," I said softly. "Your *nephew*."

Ben's eyes flickered. A beat of silence expanded between us.

"Violeta said you guys would help." My heart raced, the lie tingling like mouthwash on my tongue.

Ben considered this. "Fine. Give me two more prescriptions. We'll start with that."

"Five," I said. "And I can sign more. We can scale up."

"Are you insane? I'm not scaling up anything!"

That was surprising. Ben had always been an enterprising sort.

"I'm not going back to prison," he replied, seeing my look. His eyes darted. Left, right, left, right. He coughed and blinked hard. "I have a kid now. I have to stay off the cops' radar."

"What's my nephew's name?"

Pain flared in Ben's eyes, and he looked down. "Lucas."

"Lucas," I repeated. My family. I wanted to meet him, but now wasn't the time to ask. "I bet you'd do anything for him."

"Isn't your husband a cop? I'm not risking it."

"Don't you see, Ben?" I smiled, but there was no warmth in it. "It's exactly *because* my husband's a cop that we're safe. I can read his reports, check his notes, lead him away from us. Besides, no one would ever expect a doctor to be involved in an opioid prescription ring, let alone a cop's wife."

"What about the PDMP?"

The Prescription Drug Monitoring Program tracked controlled-substance prescriptions to make sure patients weren't getting numerous scripts from different doctors. But a lot of practices hadn't started using it yet, mostly because it was cumbersome and nobody had been trained to use it.

"It's informational, not regulatory," I said. "Besides, the prescriptions I'm giving you are from other doctors. Nobody will trace any of this back to us. If anybody gets in trouble, it'll be them."

Ben looked at Gabe. He smiled slowly, looking like a fox that had caught a hen. My brother was a lot of things, but he wasn't stupid. He knew when opportunity was knocking.

"Fine. Let's meet at that old warehouse next Tuesday night. Midnight. You in, Gabe?"

Gabe flashed his dimples and shrugged, looking for all the world like we were talking about what flavor of syrup to have on our pancakes. "Sure. Why not?" he drawled.

I handed Ben a stack of signed prescriptions, but he would only take a dozen. I pulled a scrap of paper from my back pocket and gave him that too.

"What's this?"

"A friend of mine. She needs oxy. I need you to deliver it."

Ben's lips curled. "I'm not your fucking delivery boy."

I leaned in closer.

"No, you're a distributor," I hissed. "So distribute. Besides, I bet you already have her details in that notebook there." I nodded at a red notebook I'd spotted in the console.

Ben scowled, and I knew I'd guessed correctly.

"Leave them in the birdhouse on the front porch," I told him. "She said she had a weekly supply being left there, but none turned up this week."

Ben snatched the scrap of paper from me. "I can't do it this week."

"Then give me some. I'll take them to her."

Ben turned and murmured something to somebody in the back. A few moments later, he handed me a small baggie of white pills.

A car pulled into the parking stall in front of us. A man and woman got out with a little girl. The man said something that made the woman laugh as she lifted the little girl onto her hip. They looked like a billboard for the traditional, perfect family. Happy. Normal.

But I knew how easy it was to hide the darker side of yourself from others, even those you loved. To hide fear and sadness, anger and hostility. The mask was easy. It was honesty, openness, and trust that were truly difficult to manage.

I turned my body to hide palming the baggie of pills. "Thanks for these."

A little thrill moved through me as I looked at them. These tiny discs of white represented hope for Julia, and for me. I smiled.

Ben watched me. "Let me tell you something, Emma. Dealing isn't a game. Nobody wins. It's just survival. Do you understand that?"

"I think I understand that better than anybody right about now."

Ben shook his head and shoved his door open, forcing me to step back. "I don't think you do. You want to be included? Part of the plan? Then you need to know what's really going on."

He yanked the back door open. Five pairs of eyes blinked at the sudden light.

The girls were all young, in their late teens or early twenties, with hunched backs and terrified eyes that suggested they were used to hiding. The girl nearest the door was the youngest, maybe seventeen or eighteen. She had vitiligo, a condition in which the melanin in skin cells stops working, leaving the patient with patches of lighter skin. These stood out most prominently on her face and hands.

I wondered how they'd gotten here, to this van, in a Costco parking lot. What sort of pain and trauma had they faced?

A woman holding a baby looked up at me, the only one to hold my gaze. Her eyes glittered, chin jutting defiantly, like she was challenging me to ask why she was there. But I didn't need to. I knew the lengths to which a mother would go.

"These girls are undocumented," Ben said. "They have a fake ID to see the doctor. We give them fifty dollars for the prescription once it's filled. They can't complain because they know we can turn them in to ICE anytime. We exploit them and send them on their way. You okay with that?"

I thought about Josh sick at home. I thought about Julia writhing in pain as she waited for relief the medical system had denied her, and this woman in front of me just trying to earn enough money to provide for her baby.

My dad had once told me that the most dramatic moment of a game of Texas Hold'em is when the player pushes all their chips to the center of the table. That's when they go all in, when they realize there's no going back. That's when they commit to either raking in the pot or losing everything.

"More harm is done by a timid doctor than a bold one," he used to say. "Inaction is what kills people. Be bold and decisive, and never quit as long as you have a chip and a chair."

I was all in. Josh's life was worth just as much as each of theirs, every girl in that van and every person in this parking lot.

I had two weeks. Two weeks to get the money that would pay for Josh's lifesaving treatment.

I'd lost enough in my life. I couldn't lose my son too.

I swallowed hard, dousing emotion with cold, hard practicality. I grasped the sliding door handle and slammed it shut, closing the girls inside. I faced my brother, jaw set.

"The end justifies the means."

# CHAPTER 24

THE ALARM CLOCK BLARED into the dark bedroom, waking Nate abruptly. He rolled over to Emma, who was just stirring.

Nate propped himself on his elbow and brushed a tendril of dark hair from his wife's forehead. The strands were silk in his hands. He dropped a kiss onto each of her eyelids. Her body was lush and he yearned for her in a way they hadn't had time for lately.

"Morning, you," he said, his voice husky.

Emma opened her eyes, blinking sleepily. "Josh didn't come in last night?"

"Guess not."

Emma stretched and yawned. "I hope he's okay. I should check." She threw the covers back. "Brrr! It's cold!"

She slid a thick wool cardigan on, her dark hair tumbling over her shoulders, a glossy sheet stark against her pale skin.

Nate tugged her back down, pressed his mouth to hers. "It's cold. Josh is still asleep. What do you say?"

Emma wiggled away. "Babe, seriously. I need to check on Josh. He's been so sick . . . and we both need to get ready for work."

He watched her walk away, feeling like he was drowning in the ocean expanding between them. Nate wanted to shout at her, *Stop shutting me out!* But Emma was doing that thing she did, turning inward.

It was normal for couples to grow apart when dealing with a child's cancer diagnosis. He and Emma were both riddled with anxiety, guilt, and fear over Josh's illness. But he worried there was something else going on.

Or someone.

"Sure," he called after her, trying to save a shred of his dignity. "I have that meeting with Chief O'Neill and Mayor Walker this morning anyway."

He didn't relish the idea of standing up in front of the chief or the mayor and admitting he didn't have a solid lead in one of the town's biggest cases in years, a case that was directly linked to the flow of oxy to his community. He could feel his hopes of a promotion to lieutenant slipping away, and with them any chance of providing for Josh.

Black thoughts whirled through his head like crows: horror stories of medical bills making people go bankrupt; Josh dying because he couldn't get the right help; Emma leaving him for another man, a better man.

*I can handle this,* he told himself. *That's what cops do, we fix things. I will fix this.*

Nate peered out the slatted blinds. The sun was just rising across the valley, mist glittering in strips in the distance. The rooftops of the surrounding houses were sheeted in white. Frost coated the patchwork lawns and shrubs, turning the tree-lined street an ethereal silver hue. It looked cold out.

Nate went to the tiny walk-in closet and rummaged around for the box of winter things Emma kept there. When he didn't find it, he shuffled through Emma's hanging shirts and dresses.

"Hey, Em, where's the box of winter stuff?" he called.

He pushed aside a cluster of hangers. Underneath, perched in the corner, was a black briefcase he'd never seen before.

Emma came in then, catching him kneeling in front of the briefcase. "What are you doing?" she snapped, looking annoyed.

"What's this?" Nate lifted the briefcase, turning it over in his hands. It looked expensive. Soft Italian leather. Gold metal feet on the base. Twin combination locks.

"I borrowed it from the clinic to carry patient files. That's why it has the locks. Josh was trying to play with it the other day so I stuck it in here."

"Ahh." Nate set the briefcase back under the clothes. "Where are the winter clothes?"

"I'll get them." Emma disappeared, then returned a moment later with a large box.

Nate rummaged through and found his favorite fleece-lined hat, scarf, and gloves, a gift from Emma for his birthday last year. The doorbell rang and he heard Charlie bark, then his mom's voice as Emma let her in.

Nate finished tying his tie and rushed downstairs, despair and desperation making him hurry out the door, the draw of the toothpicks in his pocket a call he couldn't refuse.


NATE HUNG up after updating Agent Hamilton on what he knew about the case so far, which was damn near nothing. Hamilton and Greene weren't happy, Chief O'Neill and Dyson weren't happy, and Mayor Walker sure as hell wasn't going to be happy when she heard that he had basically zilch on this case.

He leaned back in his chair and stared at the computer on his desk. The clock said 8:45 a.m. Fifteen minutes until his meeting with the mayor. Dread lodged firmly in his throat.

Muriel Walker was a former district attorney who'd won that office on the strength of a campaign to reduce homelessness back in 2012. She'd ridden the success of that campaign up the chain to become mayor last year, promising to fix the oxycodone problem in the region.

Now that there'd been four more oxy overdoses in the last two days, it had become a priority to find out why there'd been such an increase on the streets, who was distributing it, and how fentanyl had gotten introduced into the mix. Nate had to deliver an update on Santiago Martinez's murder and how it fit into the wider drug distribution in the area. If only he had something new to tell her.

Nate unwrapped his eighth Bit-O-Honey. He savored the honey-flavored taffy, enjoying the tug and pull on his teeth. He let it dissolve in his mouth before slugging it down with a mouthful of lukewarm coffee. Ahhh, sugar and coffee. The breakfast of champions.

When Nate was a kid, his dad used to keep a bag of Bit-O-Honey in his police car, sneaking them to Nate whenever he'd come on a ride-along. He felt horrible that he hadn't kept his recent promise to his mom to visit. He didn't want to tell her how difficult he found it.

His dad had been a good man, a larger-than-life father and husband, an honorable and noble cop. Once Nate remembered seeing Matt coming out of a motel parking lot in Seattle. Matt had told him he was checking on a woman and a little girl after a domestic. Nate had felt proud that his dad went the extra mile for victims. That he cared.

Seeing him the way he was now, a shriveled ghost of his former self, sickened Nate. Self-loathing howled inside his head.

*You're a bad person.*
*You're cowardly. Weak.*
*Nobody can trust you.*

Nate looked at his bloodied fingernails and longed for the familiar sharp thorn of the toothpick. The phone on his desk rang.

"Detective Sweeney, this is Dr. Kathi Morris at Cascade Regional."

The pathologist. "Yes, hi, Dr. Morris."

"I received the tox screen back from Violeta Williams. I've emailed you the results, but thought I'd give you a call as well. The cause of death was ruled combined toxic effects of fentanyl and cocaine. The chemical structure of this particular type of fentanyl is quite unique, however. The precursor chemical is something called NPP, N-phenethyl-4-piperidinone, but there's also a small amount of MDMA mixed in."

Nate flipped through the files on his desk and pulled out the autopsy report he'd received on Santiago Martinez a few days back. He shuffled to the tox screen page, and there it was.

Martinez's cause of death: toxic effects of fentanyl. The chemical structure included N-phenethyl-4-piperidinone and MDMA.

Santiago Martinez and Violeta Williams had been killed by the same chemical structure.


THE CRAMPED meeting room on the top floor of the police station was freezing, the air-conditioning turned up to max even though it was December. Nate, Lieutenant Dyson, Chief O'Neill, and a handful of cops and detectives sat around a table listening as Mayor Walker spoke in tight, clipped tones. The mayor was a petite, wiry black woman with a Colgate smile, a cropped salt-and-pepper Afro, and eyes of steel. She seemed enraged rather than appeased by the news that Santiago Martinez and Violeta Williams had been killed with the same drug.

"Let me get this clear." Her icy gaze swept the room. She smoothed her severe navy suit. "We have an unknown quantity

of pills and fentanyl missing, likely somewhere in our community, plus a soaring opioid death rate that could be linked to
these dealers. We have a known drug dealer turned informant
who was murdered a week and a half ago; and now this Violeta
Williams died from the same fentanyl approximately one week
ago. How do we not have a firmer hold on this case?"

Nate cleared his throat. "We're trying to find out where the fentanyl is coming from and how it's being dispersed into the community. When I spoke to the pathologist, she said that overdose deaths
from opioids are at an all-time high, and more frequently they're
laced with fentanyl. We found oxy laced with fentanyl at Mr. Martinez's house, so we're working on the theory this is all connected."

"Any hard evidence?"

Nate's gaze flickered to the chief, who was scowling, then to
Lieutenant Dyson, who looked too hopeful for Nate's liking.
"Nothing yet, ma'am."

Mayor Walker gave him her most withering glare and stood
abruptly. "Find out where the drugs came from. And do it fast. The
media are having a field day with this. Voters are getting angry."

Walker was up for reelection next year. A worsening opioid
epidemic would cripple her campaign.

"And organize a press conference. People need to be reassured." Her piercing gaze landed on Nate. "I don't think I need
to explain what it would mean for future funding if we can't stop
the drugs flowing into our town."

Her meaning was crystal clear: *Solve this murder and stop the
flow of drugs into my town or that promotion you want is just a pipe
dream, bud.*

NATE HELD the door for Kia as they headed down the stairs to
their desks. They were quiet, the sound of their footsteps echoing

in the stairwell. Nate was already logistically trying to organize the press conference Muriel Walker had foisted on him.

The press conference and the added pressure from the mayor meant more time away from Josh while he was sick, less time helping Emma. But the only other option was to recuse himself. He couldn't do that.

At the bottom of the stairs, Nate stopped at a vending machine next to the front desk. He nodded at the duty officer and fed some change into the machine, waiting for it to thrust out his Snickers bar.

"Hey, did you check the video surveillance at the hospital clinic?" Kia asked.

Nate unwrapped the Snickers and took a bite, speaking around a mouthful of nougat and chocolate. "I tried. I checked the computer it should've been stored on, but there was nothing there. Looks like they never even started recording."

Without it, building a case against Julia would be hard. Even though the pills had been found in her purse, a clever lawyer could claim a pharmaceutical rep had given them to her or that someone else had put them in her bag. But he couldn't tell Kia that without compromising his case.

"You know, Julia was at home that night. I checked her home video surveillance log. She entered the house at six thirty and was there all night. There's no way she could've taken those pills the night in question."

Nate grunted, still chewing.

"Maybe someone put those pills in her purse," Kia suggested.

"She'll have to prove it."

He knew he sounded flippant and rude but couldn't help himself. He was too on edge lately, stressed and testy, a far cry from his usual sunny self.

"You okay, Nate?" Kia asked.

"Never better." He finished his Snickers and moved toward the roll-call room, where the staff were given their orders every morning. The daily board, hanging crookedly on the far side of the room, summarized the criminal activity and arrests for the past seventy-two hours.

Kia sighed, knowing not to push him, and hurried to catch up. "I went out to Violeta's yesterday. Did you know she and Ben have a son?"

"Really?"

"Yeah. Cute little guy, Lucas. Violeta's mom was with him. She wouldn't let me in. Actually, she wouldn't even open the door for me—kept it on the chain. I thought it was weird, so I ran her in the system. She's a model citizen. Not even a driving ticket on her record. Her husband, though, now deceased, was killed by police in a drug bust when Violeta was a kid. I don't see her talking to us anytime soon. If we want any more information about Ben, we'll have to find him ourselves."

"Do you think Ben lives there?"

"Maybe. Only way to find out for sure is to get someone sitting outside the house, though. And we don't have resources for that."

"Do we have anything else matching Ben to either Martinez or Williams?"

"Not from the scene," Kia said. "Hair and fiber analysis at Martinez's came back with Williams's hair. Her fingerprints were there too, so she was definitely there. But so far nothing matching Ben. I'm not sure he was ever in that house."

He thought about the numbers he'd seen on Martinez's refrigerator. "I found a piece of paper on his refrigerator with some numbers on it. Two sets of three digits. Can't figure out what they could go to. The crime guys didn't find anything that needed a combination, so I'm not sure what they're for, or if they're important at all. Let me know if you can think of anything."

On the far side of the roll-call room they exited a door into the detectives' area. Someone had halfheartedly decorated the cubicles for Christmas: a few strings of red and silver tinsel, an artificial tree with a handful of gold baubles. In Nate's cubicle was a large box, sealed in yellow tape.

"What's that?" Kia asked.

Nate peered at the label. "It's the files on Ben I requested from Seattle." He slit the box open and began unpacking folder after folder.

"Holy shit." Kia gaped at the files. She lifted one file and flicked through it. "Battery. Dealing. Possession. Dealing. Don't people ever learn?"

"There are the baddies and the goodies in the world. I think Ben's made too many bad choices to ever really change." He handed her half the stack of folders. "Here, you start on those."

Kia separated the files into neat piles on her desk, her movements quick, determined. Nate pulled a flip chart over and together they built a timeline for Ben. Once they'd finished, Nate read it out loud.

"So Ben first got busted for doing drugs when he was fourteen. Looks like his father hired a fancy lawyer and got the conviction dropped."

Kia snorted. "Helps having a big-shot doctor for a dad."

"He got caught joyriding, stealing, was arrested and released for fighting at school. Then his parents were killed in a car accident. Shortly after that, he got caught selling homemade MDMA to an undercover. Turned out he was using basic lab equipment and old chemistry manuals to make drugs in the woods behind his foster parents' house. MDMA. Heroin. He got sent straight to juvie."

"Christ. He was a teenage Walter White," Kia said.

"Yeah, but when he got out he started doing drugs as well as selling them. He was in and out of jail, using and dealing. He ended up owing money to one of the Mexican gangs. He started selling oxy for them to pay off his debts but got caught with enough in his possession to be booked as dealing after someone tipped off the Seattle PD."

Nate flipped through a few more pages. His mouth dropped open with a little pop.

Kia tilted her head at him. "What?"

Nate was too stunned to answer. She grabbed the top sheet from the file and read the name of the source who'd turned Ben in to the Seattle PD.

"Holy shitballs!" Kia's eyes gleamed. "Emma turned him in? Her own brother!"

Nate read the rest of the file in his hand. Ben had been caught and sent to prison six years ago, shortly after Nate met Emma. And she'd never said a word. In fact, she'd told him just a few days ago that she hadn't seen Ben since she was in medical school.

Emma had lied to him.

If Ben knew that Emma was the one who'd tipped off the Seattle PD, she could be in real danger.

Kia turned over the paper she held and shook it at Nate. "Ben Hardman and Santiago Martinez were bunkmates at the Washington State Penitentiary."

A slow smile spread across his face. This was the link he'd been looking for.

"Gotcha, Ben."

CHAPTER 25

"DON'T WORRY. JOSH IS FINE," Moira said. The sound of smoke hissing between her teeth came down the phone line. "He's sleeping and that's the best thing for him right now."

I pressed my cell phone tight against my ear as one of the doctors pushed past me into the shared staff office.

"Okay, thanks, Moira. I'll see you this afternoon."

Josh had been sick since starting his lymphodepleting chemotherapy yesterday. He'd spent most of last night vomiting, but instead of being with him right now, I was here at the clinic, taking care of other sick people I didn't really care about.

I hung up and slid my phone into my pocket, returning to the desk space where I was jotting notes from my morning patients.

The brightly lit office bustled with activity, doctors moving in and out, writing notes, opening cupboards, grabbing quick cups of coffee. It wasn't the most peaceful environment to work in, but I liked the sense of belonging I felt around my colleagues.

I looked at the patient file I had open on the desk. Alice Jones, who'd arrived nearly two weeks ago with the bad back, hadn't shown up for her follow-up appointment yet. I rifled through the notes from the specialist. She hadn't gone for the MRI I'd ordered either. But that made perfect sense if she and her husband had been trying to get oxy from me.

"Would you like a cup of coffee?" I looked up to see Dr. Calvin Harper smiling down at me.

"That would be great, thank you." I put my pen down and stretched. Nate and I had taken turns with Josh all night, and I was exhausted.

The morning had been crazy. Back-to-back immunizations, flu shots, another case of the strep throat that was going around, a few routine diabetes checks, a little girl with a suspected broken bone in her heel whom I'd sent over to the emergency room. Primary care physicians were the gatekeepers of the medical world. We regulated access to specialists and collaborated with various organizations to act comprehensively for the good of our patients.

"No problem, darlin'," Dr. Harper said.

I knew I shouldn't take offense. He called everybody "darlin'." It was one of the phrases he'd brought with him from the South when he'd moved here last year. But I didn't feel like being patronized.

He poured coffee into two mugs and set one in front of me.

"Thanks, schmoopy." I smiled and lifted the cup in a mock cheers. Fair's fair.

He seemed surprised but chuckled, no offense taken.

I sipped the coffee, making a face. It was disgusting, thick as tar and burned. But there was no time to run down to the café.

"Can you believe it about Julia?" Dr. Harper shook his white head. Julia called him Colonel Sanders behind his back, and I had to agree. "How silly! I thought the girl had more sense than to go stealing drugs from her office. I reckon her career is over now."

"Lots of people have done terrible things for good reasons," I argued. "Look at Edward Jenner. He invented the smallpox vaccine and saved millions of lives, but he performed medical experiments on children and babies. Or Jonas Salk. Same thing. He developed a cure for polio and saved millions of children from death and disfigurement, but he performed medical experiments on his own kids."

"Now, hold your horses there." Dr. Harper looked surprised by my argument. "Jenner's experiments worked. So did Salk's. They were for the greater good."

"Sure, but they still tried untested theories on babies and children. The experiments worked, so we think of them as medical heroes. If they hadn't worked, Jenner would be an evil villain who gave a bunch of random kids smallpox, and Salk would have paralyzed or killed his entire family."

Dr. Harper stroked a hand down his white beard. "That sort of mind-set has been the impetus behind many a cruel medical and social experiment. It could easily result in deliberate deafness to suffering."

I opened my mouth to argue, but Brittany peeked her frizzy head through the office door and asked if I would see one of Dr. Wallington's patients.

"It's an emergency walk-in, and Dr. Wallington isn't back from his honeymoon yet."

I glanced at my watch. Josh had his second dose of lympho-depleting chemo in just a little bit, and I couldn't be late.

I felt the tension grow in my temples and massaged them with my fingers. It was my duty as a doctor to help if a patient was in need. I could still make it to Josh's chemo appointment before the drip went in.

"Sure, put them in exam room four." I slugged back the last of my coffee and dragged myself to my feet.

Dr. Harper put a hand on my arm. "Forgive me for saying, darlin', but I think it should be noted what a commendable job you're doing. As a doctor and as a mother. I know your boy is sick. It can't be easy."

"No, it isn't," I agreed. "He started chemo yesterday."

"Ahh." Dr. Harper bobbed his head in understanding. "And you wish you could be with him."

"Of course. I feel completely helpless."

"You are incredibly strong."

"Any parent could do what I'm doing. When your kid's sick, you go to the appointments, get them treatment, do whatever you can to pay for it. This is just normal parenting to the one millionth degree."

He patted a gentle hand on my arm. "That attitude is exactly what makes you an excellent mother."

Up at reception, I grabbed the patient's file from Brittany.

"Thanks for doing this, Dr. Sweeney," she trilled in her too-high voice. "The patient is in room four."

As I started to open the file, I felt someone's eyes on me. I lifted my head slowly, skin prickling with alarm. My mouth went instantly dry, my heart suddenly hammering against my ribs, as my eyes met a pair of familiar ones.

It was one of the girls from Ben's van. The teenager with the patches of lighter skin on her face and hands.

I watched as the puzzle pieces slotted into place right there on her face.

She recognized me.

*SHIT. SHIT. SHIT.*

I rushed down the hall, my heart pounding so hard it felt like it would burst through my ribs at any moment. I staggered into the staff bathroom and locked the door, a cruel, angry fist squeezing my chest.

I greedily gasped for oxygen, breath hissing in and out too fast. I turned the tap on and splashed at my face. Panic ramped up my breathing, the room revolving around me.

Sweat prickled over my skin. I peeled my lab coat off and tossed it to the floor, slumping onto the toilet and dropping my head between my legs. Stars danced across my vision. She knew who I was. Would she turn me in?

A tap came at the door.

"Dr. Sweeney? Are you okay?" It was Brittany.

I inhaled, trying to catch my breath. My whole body was trembling.

Brittany knocked again.

"Be right there!" I squeezed out.

*Focus,* I told myself. *Breathe.*

My cheeks were flushed when I looked in the mirror, strands of dark hair escaping my ponytail.

I smoothed my hair back and washed my hands, letting the cold water slide over the insides of my wrists as I took long, slow breaths. Finally I collected my lab coat off the floor and pulled it back on, taking a deep breath.

*I can help you. I belong here. I will save you. I don't sell drugs illegally.*

Brittany was waiting when I opened the door, her overplucked eyebrows arched high in concern. "Are you okay, Dr. Sweeney? You looked like you were going to be sick."

"Oh." I pressed a hand to my cheek and forced a smile. "I'm a little overtired, I think. Sorry."

"That's okay. You have a lot going on. Here." She handed me the file I'd dropped in my hurry. "It's for your next patient."

"Thank you."

I took the file and watched her disappear down the hall. After a minute I followed, peering cautiously around the corner at the waiting room. A tacky plastic Christmas wreath hung on the door. A small, limp tree with too many baubles stood next to the magazine table. A handful of kids on iPads. Frazzled moms soothing fussy babies.

But the girl was no longer sitting where I'd seen her.

I scanned the room again. There she was—in the corner next to the door, whispering frantically to a dark-haired, acne-ridden teenage boy. The patches of lighter skin around her eyes and mouth were stark against her shiny black hair. Her hands were blotchy with pigment, her fingers long, her nails ragged, as she gestured toward the reception desk.

I saw her mouth moving: *That's her!*

She saw me then. Her almond-shaped eyes—an unusual shade of amber—widened when they collided with mine.

The air shimmered between us, an electric tingle that vibrated with unspoken words. My stomach hollowed. Horror and fear caught in my throat, made my legs wobbly as my heart thundered in my chest.

We moved at the same time: I strode toward her while she grabbed the boy's arm and tugged him out the door. I crossed the reception area, careful not to appear too urgent, and threw the door open.

But they were already disappearing into the stairwell.

Gone.

# CHAPTER 26

I SAW MY LAST patient and murmured an excuse to Brittany before leaving in a rush. In my car, I took out my burner phone and texted Gabe:

> One of the girls from Ben's van came into my clinic.
> Think she recognized me.

Gabe replied almost immediately.

> Shit. Tell Ben. He can talk to her.

But what if he didn't get to her in time? No, I couldn't just sit around waiting for my world to crash around me.

I had a half hour before Josh's chemo appointment, so I drove to Julia's house. I parked on the street and sent a quick text to Nate reminding him about Josh's appointment. He wasn't the type to forget something so huge, but he'd been so busy with his case, acting like a promotion would change everything, that I thought I'd remind him.

I'll be there, he texted back.

And then a second later: X

I smiled and tucked my phone in my bag.

Julia answered the door looking fresh and chipper in khakis and an oversize dove-gray turtleneck, a stark contrast to the last time I'd seen her. Now that I knew, I could tell she'd taken painkillers. But even as a doctor it was difficult to spot the signs.

"It's good to see you. Would you like anything to drink? Tea? Coffee?"

I hung my purse and coat on the coat hook by the door, my fingers brushing against something hanging from one of the hooks as I did.

"Sure. Coffee, thanks." I followed her into the kitchen. "I just thought I'd stop by and see how you're doing?"

Julia lowered her gaze, shamefaced, and turned to fill the kettle. "I'm so sorry for asking you to prescribe me oxy. I really shouldn't have tried to drag you into this. I was just desperate."

"It's fine," I assured her. "Seriously. I just hope you understand why I had to say no. Are you . . . feeling better now?"

She put the kettle on the stove and pulled two mugs from the cupboard. "Yes. I'm all . . . sorted out now." I noticed the slight hesitation. She'd received the pills I'd put in her birdhouse last night, then.

"Good. Someone must be looking out for you." I figured slipping the oxy I'd gotten from Ben into Julia's birdhouse was the least I could do for her. She could lose her job, her license, her ability to pay for pain medication, all because I hadn't locked the medical supply room door after I'd stolen the prescription pads.

Julia side-eyed me, but I smiled innocently, confidently. Even if she suspected it was me, I'd learned my lesson at the clinic and had been on the lookout for any video surveillance cameras. I'd found one directly above the door and had made sure I was never in frame. There was no evidence I'd left the pills.

"So, what's your lawyer say about the drug charges?"

"I'm meeting with him later today. I was able to give him the alarm system footage here at home, which proves I wasn't at the clinic the night they're trying to charge me for. At the very least, it'll cast reasonable doubt."

"But you said you did take the samples."

She shrugged, her mouth pressed into a hard line. "So sue me."

I frowned. I'd never seen this side of Julia.

The kettle whistled, and Julia scooped instant coffee into the mugs, pouring water over.

"You take your coffee black, right?" she asked.

"Yes, thanks."

We took our mugs to the living room and sat on the couch, sipping our coffees as we spoke for a few minutes about Josh and chemo, Nate and his big case, the bake sale Moira's church had run last week to raise money for Josh.

I set my coffee on the table and stood. "Excuse me, I think I hear my phone ringing."

I hurried down the hallway to the front door, where I'd left my purse. Darting a quick glance over my shoulder, I rifled through Julia's coats, looking for the item I'd noticed when I arrived.

Julia's hospital electronic key card was hanging under a navy puffer coat. I was a little surprised security hadn't taken it, but maybe this was her spare. We were all given two. I plucked it from the coat hook and slipped it into my purse, feeling ashamed and horrified of the person I'd become.

Back in the living room, I sat and picked up my coffee. "So, how's Kia handling it all?"

"It's been tough on us. Our relationship is so new, and she

can't really be seen as supporting a lawbreaker. It looks really bad for her." Julia blew gently on her coffee.

"Does she know about the . . . delivery method?"

"God, no! She'd definitely turn me in!" Julia laughed, but stopped abruptly, the smile falling from her face. "You won't turn me in, though, right?"

I smiled at Julia and patted her knee. "I swear, my lips are sealed."

BACK AT the hospital, I parked and slipped Julia's key card under the spare tire in my trunk.

Guilt swirled fast and thick in my gut, turning to bile in my throat. I would never need it, I assured myself. It was just insurance, really. If things went bad and vitiligo girl turned me in, somebody had to take the fall for setting up an opioid drug ring. Julia and I looked vaguely alike, and we both worked at the clinic, but only one of us was being investigated for stealing.

Like my dad always said, never get caught drawing dead. And now I had a backup plan.

I just hoped it never came to that.

I hurried through the staff entrance and took the elevator to the pediatric oncology floor. A Winnie-the-Pooh mural greeted me, a Dr. Seuss aquarium, a wall of children's books. All around me were children in wheelchairs, some wearing oxygen tanks and others too weak to get out of their beds.

Moira, Nate, and Josh were already in the infusion center, a large room that held six reclining chairs with IV poles and bags of clear liquid hanging from them. Each chair had a television that could be pulled out of the arm, like on an airplane, equipped with headphones and a wireless video game controller. There was another boy at the far end of the room, maybe a year or two

older than Josh. He was completely bald. His mother was reading a homeopathy magazine while he played a video game.

Josh's eyes lit up when I entered and he smiled, a tiny, feeble
curl of his lips. I pulled him into my arms, my heart pinging
with those agonizing sympathy pangs mothers get when they see
their child in pain.

"Hi, sweetheart. How are you feeling?" I murmured.

He sighed faintly. He was so weak. Even before starting
chemo, the cancer had been eating him alive. I would be glad
when he got the reprogrammed T-cells injected next week.

As long as I had the money to pay for it, that is.

Josh sniffed and swiped at his nose. One of the side effects of
chemo was a mess of flu-like symptoms. Josh's eyes were red-
rimmed, his skin pale and cold, making him look even smaller
and more vulnerable than he should.

"My tummy hurt this morning, but I'm better now. Grandma
made me some soup, and it was yummy. I have these things in
my mouth that hurt, though."

He opened his mouth, and I peered in. The moist pink skin
along his gums and under his tongue was riddled with white-
edged mouth ulcers.

"Poor baby. Those look sore." I handed him a bottle of water,
feeling impotent and useless, and stroked a hand over his silky
hair only to have a tuft of it come off in my hand.

I met Nate's eyes, seeing my horror mirrored in his face. Tears
flooded my eyes. I clasped my hand over my mouth and turned
away so Josh wouldn't see my reaction. The antiseptic smell in
the room burned my throat as I stared at the hair in my palm.

This was hair I'd washed and brushed and cut since Josh was
an infant. And soon he would have none.

If only I'd noticed the bruises on Josh's small body sooner.
Would his chances be better now?

I thought suddenly of when Josh was a baby, the early stages of my pregnancy, when I'd been so terrified about that paternity test. How I'd had to go back into the hospital when I'd unexpectedly started bleeding at twenty weeks. How I'd gone into labor three weeks early, and he'd been born underweight and yellow. How he'd broken his leg jumping off the top of the slide when he was just three. But it had all been fine, everything normal and ordinary and just, magically, fine.

Until now.

I had to get that money.

I don't know why I did it—maybe even then I couldn't let go—but I shoved Josh's hair into my pocket.

Dr. Palmer came in, casting a quick glance at me. Josh grinned a greeting, and Dr. Palmer's creased face lit up. My boy. There was nobody who didn't like him.

"Hey, Captain Smiley. You're looking good!" Dr. Palmer pulled a round, wheeled stool over to Josh and gave him a fist bump.

I bit down hard on my bottom lip. "He was very sick last night."

"It might take a few days for us to find the right combination of antinausea meds. I hope it'll settle down by tomorrow."

"Dr. Palmer, did you know that snails are very old?" Josh asked.

"I didn't know that," Dr. Palmer replied seriously. "What makes them old?"

"Because they're very slow. So we hafta take care of them."

"I think that's very wise."

The nurse, Katie, came in and prepped the bag of fludarabine and cyclophosphamide—the lymphodepleting chemotherapy regimen—that would go into Josh's arm.

"Are you ready, Josh?" Dr. Palmer asked.

"Accept the challenge, I do," Josh answered in a funny Yoda impression.

Nate and Dr. Palmer laughed, but I could barely bring myself to smile. I was so tired and so sad and so, so angry that this was happening to us. Angry that I was so helpless. Angry at this thing we couldn't see eating away at Josh's insides.

Katie leaned in with the needle, and I closed my eyes, trying not to think about it sliding into the blue vein on the back of my baby's hand.

LATER THAT NIGHT, Nate and I tucked Josh into bed together. It was nice having Nate home instead of working for once. I leaned against him, feeling the warmth of his body against mine. Charlie clambered onto the bed, excited that everybody was home. Josh wrapped his arms around him, and Charlie dragged his tongue across his face.

Josh giggled and it was pure magic. Even though his face was thinner than ever, his skin sallow, dark circles ringing his eyes, the antinausea meds seemed to be working. He'd only vomited a few times since the chemo drip. Now he was sleepy and clean, and we were all together, smooshed onto his bed.

Nate and I lay on either side of Josh, with Charlie at his feet.

"Pimple squish." Josh smiled, although he lacked his usual energy. "Can I go back to school tomorrow?"

"Not tomorrow, buddy," Nate said. "Soon, I hope. You have your infusion next week, and if that goes well and you're feeling better, you can go back to school after that."

"But it's boring at home. And I miss my friends."

"We know, sweetie." I stroked a hand over his hair gently. "You know I love you so much?"

"I know, Mommy. I love you so much back. More than belly buttons."

"I love you more than noodles."

"I love you more than poop-heads." Josh was giggling now.

I burst out laughing. "Wow, that is a lot. I'm a very lucky mommy."

Nate stood, shaking his head. But he was smiling when he moved toward the door. "You little weirdos."

I got up too. "Can I have a kiss?" I held my cheek out to Josh, and he kissed it.

"You can have all the kisses," he said somberly. "Days and nights and up until I'm dead."

That word—*dead*—sent a spike of adrenaline shooting through my veins. I froze, wishing I could call Nate back to help me deal with this conversation.

I didn't want Josh accepting it, acting like it was an inevitability. He had to fight.

"That isn't going to happen for a very long time," I said.

Josh's face pinched with too much sadness for a five-year-old. "I might. We all die. George told me that his hamster died and he didn't even want him to die."

I wanted to kick that little jerk in the knees.

I sat on the edge of the bed and put my hand on Josh's chest.

"I don't care what George told you. Sometimes we can stop it. That's why I became a doctor, and sometimes I stop it. And that's what this cancer treatment is about. You're going to live a long and happy life. I promise you. Remember what Daddy told you? The good guys always win. And we're the good guys."

He smiled faintly.

"Do you believe me?"

He thought about it for a minute and then nodded.

"Good." I pulled the blankets to his chin. "It's time for you to get some sleep now."

"Will you stay with me?"

"Always."

I lay next to him, and he snuggled into me. After a moment Josh's breathing evened, the way only a child's can in sleep.

From downstairs I could hear the gentle murmur of the TV. The heating kicked on, a pleasant hum. I breathed in the scent of Josh and felt my body relax, and before I knew it, I was drifting off too.

# CHAPTER 27

GLASS SHATTERING.

*My mother's scream.*

The sound of gravel crunching, someone knocking on glass, a voice calling, *"Hello? Hello?"* A curse, like someone was in pain.

*Help*, I wanted to shout, but the word was stuck in my throat.

The scent of smoke was thick in my nose. Everything was dark.

My head felt funny. The way it did when I did a handstand in the backyard for too long. Something warm was dripping down my face.

"Emma." The sound of my name made me jump.

That was when I realized I was upside down.

I was in the car. We'd been driving home and then the brakes had screeched. A scream. Glass shattering. And then nothing.

I fumbled to release my seat belt, falling directly on my head when I did. Pain jolted through my temples and down my neck.

"Mommy?" I whimpered. I couldn't remember the last time I'd called my mom that.

"Emma." Dad's voice floated to me, riding the crest of a moan. "Help."

I tried to open my door, but it was stuck. I moved to the other side and pushed the door open. The night air was cold, bringing a sharp awareness along with the bite.

I looked at the car. It was a shattered mess, twisted metal and shards of glass everywhere. Orange flames licked out from under the hood. The smell of gas coiled with the scent of smoke.

I yanked at the driver's door, my hands shaking.

"Help . . . me . . ." Dad moaned.

I reached over him to unfasten his seat belt. I squeezed my eyes shut, trying not to look at my mother's fixed stare on the other side of the car.

Dad's body landed heavily. "I can't . . . move my legs."

The crackle of fire reached me. I tugged on my dad's arms, straining, finally getting him out and away from the car. The fire was spreading, flames leaping higher now, a roar as it engulfed the battered vehicle.

"I have to get Mom," I panted.

Dad grasped my wrist, an iron shackle. "No. Don't go. She's dead."

I snatched my wrist away, horrified at his words.

"No. I have to—"

The explosion pushed me back, a hot ball of fire punching me like a fist. Sounds dimmed, and I lay motionless on my back for a long time.

I rolled over, choking on blood that had pooled in my throat, and scooted closer to my dad. I gently moved his head so it was on my lap. His breath was coming in short, shallow bursts. Blood flecked his lips and smeared across his hair. His mouth was twisted in pain.

*Crack.*

A twig popped somewhere nearby.

"Who's there?" My voice was thin and trembly.

Nobody answered, but a shadow moved over near the bushes by the road. My heart leaped. The shadow darted into, then out of a pale slice of moonbeam.

"Help us!" I shouted, louder now. "Please!"

But the shadow had already disappeared. . . .


I JERKED AWAKE, disoriented. The nightmare clung to my throat, sticky like jelly.

My eyes flew to the clock. It was almost time to meet Ben and Gabe. Josh was sleeping soundly. Where was Nate?

I slipped downstairs to find my husband crashed out on the couch. Charlie was asleep at his feet, his ears dangling over Nate's ankles. The TV murmured quietly in the background.

Nate's head was propped on the edge of the couch, one arm thrown carelessly over his forehead, his mouth hanging open slightly. Gentle snores rumbled from deep in his chest.

I watched him, thinking of Violeta and Julia and vitiligo girl and the drugs that tied us together. I thought about the lies I'd told. Big lies and small lies. Half-truths and tiny fibs. To Nate. To his whole family. To Ben. Even to Gabe.

Especially to Gabe.

The lies were woven around me, a spider's web, swirling, tightening. I was becoming more and more entangled. I didn't know how to get out now.

Nate was a pretty heavy sleeper, but if he woke and found I was gone, he'd have questions I couldn't answer. I moved to wake him, to convince him to go upstairs to sleep, but caught sight of an envelope that had been torn open and left on the coffee table. It was addressed to me.

I snatched up the envelope, annoyed that Nate had opened something of mine. My fingers went numb as soon as I read the contents. It was the hospital bill.

I sat on the edge of the coffee table.

*Summary for patient: Joshua Sweeney.*
*Please pay amount due within 30 days of the statement date.*

Below that was an itemized list of treatments that Josh had received so far. Above that, in bolded black letters, was the amount owed.

Even after the insurance company had paid, there were still too many digits. They wobbled in front of me. The money in the GoFundMe account wouldn't cover it. And this was only the first month. It didn't even include the amount I needed to pay the hospital for Josh's infusion next week.

"It's going to be okay." Nate's voice was raspy with sleep, making me jump. Charlie lifted his head at the sound and wagged his tail. "We'll get there. This whole town is rallying to help Josh get this treatment."

I stared at him, unable to reply. He was so blind. We'd had a trickle of $5 and $10 donations, plus the $330 from Moira's church's bake sale, but that was it until the lump payment that Gabe had deposited. This town wasn't doing anything. *I* was.

Nate was only inches from me. His hair was tousled from sleep. He needed a haircut. It had grown out from his usual short cut. It made him look younger, gave him a boyish air. If I wanted to, I could reach out and touch him with my fingertips, feel the warmth of his skin on mine. And yet I couldn't. I was too separate from him, disconnected and alone, as if I were on a wooden raft floating out to sea.

"Why don't you go upstairs and get some sleep?" I said. "I'm going to read for a bit. I can't sleep."

Nate's eyes were unreadable. "Why didn't you tell me you turned your brother in to the police?"

I went very still. "How did you know about that?"

"It came up in my investigation."

"Ben came up in your murder investigation?"

He didn't reply.

"I guess I figured you didn't need to know," I said finally. "I know I shouldn't have turned him in, but I wanted to protect him. I thought jail was the safest place."

"Where'd you get all the drugs you planted on him?"

"I—I—didn't plant anything. He already had them. I just called it in." I set the hospital bill down slowly, trying not to give away my shaking hands.

Nate's mouth narrowed into a thin line. He didn't believe me.

"You can't understand!" I burst out. "You belong to a family that hasn't been broken. Watching someone you love injecting himself and destroying his life, it's not a happy place. I'd have done anything to keep him from dying."

I thought of Ben the day I'd found him passed out in the alley. A teenager had approached me—dark, oil-slicked hair, pimply skin. He told me Ben owed his brother some money. A lot of money.

"He has to pay off those debts or . . ." he'd said. Not cruelly or anything. He actually sounded apologetic, a little regretful.

"What can I do to help him?" I asked.

He'd looked down at me, sitting cross-legged next to my brother on the filthy pavement. "You can't help him. You are . . . helpless."

He left then, telling me he'd be back soon to get the money Ben owed him.

After that, I knew I couldn't just sit by and let him get killed. Not by the drugs, and not by that kid's brother.

So I'd stolen needles and tourniquets from the hospital. I'd begged Gabe to get me a bag of heroin that I could sell to help me pay my bills. I told him I couldn't make my student loan payments, that I was about to be evicted and hadn't eaten in two days. I didn't give up until he got it for me. The rest I got from a guy I'd never met before on the street. I went downtown and bought a couple of bags of heroin. It was easy to get drugs, I'd learned.

Too easy.

The opioid epidemic was, at its basest level, a case of supply and demand, and supply was never in doubt. So many others, just like Ben, had started on opioids. They'd had a bad back or had broken a leg or torn a tendon, and a doctor had prescribed OxyContin or Percodan. Then when their opioids were taken away, they turned to the streets. To heroin. To fentanyl. Sometimes to meth. It was a genie that couldn't be put back in the bottle.

Ben had been passed out in the same alley when I found him the next time. I stuffed his pockets with everything I had. Then I called the police. I watched, stony-faced, from across the street as they arrested him.

"You know Ben was released from jail two years ago, right?" Nate said. "If he contacts you, you need to let me know. We're looking for him. I can't tell you why, but you need to know he's out there. And if he knows you're the one who turned him in, you could be in danger."

A buzzing came from beside the couch. My eyes jumped to my purse. Nate looked at me, his gaze heavy and judgmental.

My phone.

One of my phones.

"Are you going to get that?" Nate's voice was laser-sharp.

"No, we're talking right now. It's probably just Julia."

He didn't reply.

I stiffened. He knew I was hiding something. The girl at the clinic. The canvas bag of prescription pads. The pills I'd left for Julia. The briefcase at the back of our closet. Ben and Gabe waiting at the warehouse.

"This is all so unfair." My voice cracked. "I've lost my whole family. My parents. My brother. And now Josh is sick. What if I lose him too? And what if we lose our insurance and . . . ?"

"I know." Nate's gaze softened and he put a hand on my knee. His eyes, when they met mine, were bloodshot. "I'm scared too. I've got this case living inside my head and only a few weeks to prove I can solve it. I feel so damn helpless."

Nate dropped his head into his hands. It took me a minute to realize he was crying. I didn't think I'd ever seen my husband cry. He was bulletproof. To see him fall apart terrified me.

I could tell he was reliving Josh's life, just like I was. The newborn who'd had his days and nights mixed up. The giggly baby who'd loved to snuggle. The inquisitive toddler who'd gotten into everything he could get his hands on. The precocious little boy with a flair for the dramatic. The sunny kid who made everyone smile.

I touched a hand to my cheek and realized I too was crying.

"Nate, it isn't all on you. Getting this promotion, becoming lieutenant, it's all great, but it isn't up to you to save Josh all by yourself."

"What do we do?" he whispered.

"We make sure we can pay for the CAR T-cell therapy."

"I'm going to solve this case," he replied fiercely. "I'll catch whoever murdered Santiago Martinez and I'll find out who's running these drugs. Once I get that promotion, we'll have the money to pay off the bills. Josh will get better," Nate said before I could speak, almost like he was trying to convince himself. "We'll be fine. We'll all be fine."

An optimistic cop. Was that an oxymoron?

I sighed and stood, stretching my arms above my head, and just left the words there. Tension fizzled between us.

"I'm going to make myself some warm milk. Maybe that'll make me sleepy. Want any?"

Nate shook his head, getting to his feet. "No thanks. I think I'll head up to bed. Wake me if you need help with Josh."

He kissed me on the lips, a soft, warm pressure. I melted, leaning forward, yearning for more of him even though I was irritated, but just as suddenly as it began, the kiss ended and Nate turned away. A moment later, he disappeared up the stairs.

# CHAPTER 28

A HEAVY SNOW WAS falling by the time I left the house, fat flakes swirling in the orange streetlights. The world I walked into now was a completely different one from the one I'd inhabited just hours before. The shrubs were white-tipped, the ghostly evergreens dancing a choreographed ballet in the rising wind. My breath misted in the numbing air, snow kissing my eyelashes. Christmas lights flickered, still lit around my neighborhood, even at this time of night.

My own house, though, was sad and dark. I hadn't yet been able to prepare for the holidays. We hadn't bought a tree, no lights were strung outside, no stockings hung above the fireplace. I hadn't gone shopping or chosen toys for Josh. How could I when he might—

The thought of losing Josh calcified inside of me, hard and razor-sharp, like I'd swallowed glass.

No. I cut the thought off.

Only yesterday Josh had asked if Santa would remember him if he was in the hospital. I couldn't let him think Santa had forgotten him. I needed to make more of an effort, to keep things as normal as possible for him right now.

I resolved to get the house decorated and buy presents to-morrow.

For Josh's sake.

The drive to the warehouse should've been a quick ten-minute journey, but the snow turned it into a white-knuckle twenty. About halfway there, I noticed a car behind me. The headlights were high, beaming directly into my rear window.

The lights followed me around the loops and bends in the road. My knuckles ached from clenching the steering wheel so tightly. I ignored the turn to the mill warehouse and headed into town, pulling into the hospital parking lot. Behind me, illuminated in the glow of the streetlights, was a big, black truck with shiny chrome rims.

The same truck from Costco.

It drove past and disappeared down the road. I sat in the parking lot, shaking despite the heat blasting from the car's vents. One of vitiligo girl's friends had left in that black truck. Vitiligo girl had recognized me yesterday. They had to be connected in some way.

After a few moments, I left the hospital and continued driving up the mountainous road. I turned right to cross the bridge and parked about a quarter of a mile away from the warehouse on the shoulder, grabbing my hat and the flashlight from the glove compartment.

My breath misted as I ducked through the gap in the chain-link fence. I stepped carefully over the white ground. Footprints had turned the snow to mush. Gabe and Ben must be inside—I guessed they were the ones who'd boarded up the windows on the bottom floor since I was last here.

When I reached the back door, Gabe and Ben were speaking in low tones. Ben pointed at a page in the red notebook from his van. Gabe leaned in to look. He had a nail gun in one hand, a stack of cardboard panels, and a few pieces of wooden two-by-fours on the floor next to him.

"I don't know, Vi usually did this part." Ben's voice floated toward me. I paused, hearing the anguish in it.

Gabe replied softly, and Ben said, "I'm sorry, I'm just tired, man. I mean, you knew her, she was fucking crazy, but she was *smart*." Pause. "I miss her. Lucas misses her. He won't stop crying. I don't know what to say. How do you have that conversation with your kid? 'Your mom's dead. I think someone murdered her.'"

Ben's voice broke a little, and Gabe looked horrified. I decided it was time to break up their little chat before he said something we both regretted.

"Hello!" I called loudly.

They both fell silent.

"Hey," Gabe said.

He looked terrible. His eyes were rimmed with black shadows, a few days of stubble on his jaw. He'd lost weight in the last few weeks. I wondered if his sleep was broken with nightmares too. If he still heard the sound of Violeta's body as it thunked against the rocks before splashing into the river.

I pointed at the two-by-fours. "You guys trying to keep it warm in here?"

"We didn't want anybody seeing in," Gabe explained. "How's Josh?"

I dusted snow from my coat. "A little better. Just two more days of chemo. Once he's feeling better, you can come meet him."

"So you had Gabe's kid, huh?" Ben raised his sparse eyebrows at me, blinking too fast. "And you let another man raise him." He whistled. "That's pretty low."

I flinched, remembering the day I'd found out I was pregnant, hurrying to order a prenatal paternity test, my surprise at the results.

"I don't think you can judge me for wanting the best for my child when you're raising yours in a drug den," I said coolly.

I stormed over to the wooden table tucked under the stairs and threw my purse and canvas bag on it.

Ben opened his mouth, but Gabe moved between us, hands up, the odd peacemaker in our twisted little trio. "It's fine. I'm sure Emma wishes some things were different. I know I do."

That wasn't true. I didn't regret a thing. I'd made the best decisions for my baby then, and now. But I tossed him a grateful smile anyway.

I needed him on my side.

I wasn't sure why it surprised me that Ben was so angry at me. Our relationship had been strained for a long time. He was jealous and resentful before our parents died, angry and hateful after. When I was a girl, he was my hero, but somewhere along the way he decided I was spoiled, a princess with daddy wrapped around her little finger.

Once, when Ben was about thirteen, Dad came home late very drunk and very angry. He'd lost a lot of money at the casino. He went to the kitchen to make himself some toast and found crumbs in the butter. Dad lost it, blaming Ben and raging about what a loser he was.

"Can't you do anything right?" he'd snarled.

Ben had just sat there plucking at his eyebrows. He didn't bother telling Dad that I'd been the last one to use the butter.

Later, I asked him why. "What would've been the point?" he'd said, stony-faced. "You can do no wrong with him. He would've turned it around to be my fault anyway."

He was probably right. Mom used to joke that I was Dad's Mini-Me. And Dad loved that I was so much like him. Even as a kid I liked to jump higher, run faster, go farther than others.

Maybe Ben got a little lost in my wake.

"I think someone was following me," I said.

Ben straightened. "Shit! Who?"

"It was a big black truck. Chrome wheels. Double cab. It looked like the one that was at Costco. You know, the one that guy who took the girl out of your van was driving? Like that."

"Why'd you come here then?"

"Relax, Ben. I'm not stupid. I went to the hospital first. Nobody followed me here. Who is it?"

Ben scowled. "His name's Carlos Martinez. I shared a cell with his brother, Santiago, in prison."

The world tilted around me. "Santiago Martinez?"

"Yeah."

Santiago Martinez was the murder investigation Nate was working on. Ben had been in prison with Santiago. That's why Nate had been asking me about my brother. He was investigating Ben for murder.

I stepped away from my brother. Fear trickled ice-cold down my spine. I didn't know this man anymore. What had I gotten myself into?

Nate's words replayed in my head.

*If he knows you're the one who turned him in, you could be in danger.*

"Are you close with Santiago?" I strained to keep my voice neutral.

"I told you, we shared a cell. After we got out, we worked together. But he and Vi never really got along. Vi was pretty suspicious of people, and Santiago was a cagey fucker."

Ben sat on the bottom step and rubbed a hand through his hair. He looked sad and drained. The loss of his girlfriend, the mother of his child, was wearing on him. He didn't look like a man capable of murder, but what did I know?

"A few weeks ago, she told me she thought he was sharing information with the feds," Ben said. "I didn't believe her. I told her there was no way he'd do that to me. She was pissed, and we had a huge fight about it. And then he turned up dead, and a few days later so did she." Ben blinked hard, that twitchy blink, and lifted his shoulders. "I think Vi killed Santiago, but who killed her?"

"Maybe Carlos?" Gabe suggested. I glanced at him leaning against the damp stairs, but his face was completely blank.

"Maybe," Ben said. "He thinks I had something to do with Santiago."

"You need to lie low," I warned. "Stay away from him for a while."

"Thanks, *Mom*. I know."

"That girl in your van with the patches of lighter skin on her face and hands," I said. "Does she work for Carlos too?"

"No. She was working for both of us. I wouldn't have allowed it if I'd known. But Bea—Beatrice Flores—she only works for me now."

"She came into my clinic this morning and recognized me. She knows I'm the doctor writing the prescriptions."

Ben plucked at his eyebrows and frowned. "You don't need to worry about her."

"If she tells anybody—"

Ben got to his feet. "I'll talk to her. She came up as a drug mule last year. Swallowed fifty balloons of coke. I'm pretty sure she doesn't want to do that again."

I let it go for now, but I didn't believe that she'd stay quiet.

Ben waved for me to follow him. "Come here. I'll show you what we're doing."

He strode quickly to the other end of the warehouse, his boots echoing loudly, and disappeared into a darkened doorway.

I peeked my head inside. The room was gloomy and dull, enclosed in crumbling brick and lit only by a lantern Ben was holding. It looked like an old boiler room. A smokestack had been bricked off years ago. A series of metal tables, rusted pipes, and broken hoses rimmed the wall, along with giant cylinders and ancient, rusting generators blackened from years of disuse and covered with dust. The thick mustiness clawed at my throat, claustrophobia folding around me like wrapping paper.

"Check this out." Ben motioned me to a metal table at the back.

Scattered across it were a handful of small baggies filled with powder, along with a number of bottles of prescription pills. I picked one up. Oxy.

"What's this?" I pointed at an odd-looking contraption.

"A pill press," Ben said.

"Why do you need that?"

"This is what Vi and I were working on. People love oxy, right? We figured, if we cut the oxy with this"—he held up one of the baggies—"it'll go further and cost less. Plus, by cutting it we vary the drug's molecular fingerprint. It'll look like there's more than one gang supplying the drugs."

"What's that powder you're cutting it with?" I asked.

"Fentanyl. It's cheap and powerful. Plus I add in a little pinch of MDMA to keep people happy."

"Have you lost your mind?" I exclaimed. I looked between Gabe and Ben. They looked pleased with themselves. I wanted to smack their stupid faces. "Do you have any idea how dangerous fentanyl is?"

Gabe looked contrite; he'd seen Violeta die, after all. But Ben just shrugged.

"Where did you get it?"

"It's all over the dark web. Easy."

"You know the DEA can track that shit, right? They can track you!"

Ben jeered at me. "They can't track me. I'm not the one who ordered it."

I glanced at Gabe, but he shook his head.

"Who did?"

"None of your damn business."

"People could die!"

"So?"

I stared at him, stunned. What had happened to my brother to make him like this?

Research has shown that opioid use literally reshapes every part of the brain, even after drugs aren't being used anymore. As addiction progresses, the structures in the brain lose the ability to communicate with one another, leading to trouble reasoning and thinking, and sometimes hijacking emotions, obliterating any sense of loyalty, morality, or duty.

But still, I was shocked by his level of apathy. My brother had truly lost the plot.

"Don't act like you have a moral high horse to sit on, *Dr. Sweeney*," Ben sneered. "You've already written all those prescriptions. We've sold the drugs. You want to save your son, right? All we're doing is making the product stretch further."

I shook my head. This was a very dangerous plan. Fentanyl was one hundred times stronger than morphine. Small doses could be fatal.

But then I remembered what Dr. Palmer had said: Josh might not live to see the new year if we didn't get him that treatment.

Ben had given me the $30,000 we'd agreed on for the first batch of prescriptions, which meant I had a grand total of $35,000 in my newly set up checking account. It wasn't enough. At this rate, I wouldn't be able to pay the remaining $63,000 to get Josh's reprogrammed CAR T-cells injected in just over a week, let alone cover the copays, the deductible, and any new hospital bills, which were quickly piling up.

This was the only way.

"If you mess up, if you get even one grain wrong—" I began.

"I won't."

"You have to swear you're clean. That you're not going to use this stuff or mess up the dosing. If you aren't clean, you won't be able to do it right."

"I've been clean since I got out of prison. I was in a drug program inside and haven't touched anything since I got out."

I studied my brother's face. "Won't this be harder? You'll be closer to it."

"Nawww, I'll be fine. Besides, this way the urge can't sneak up and surprise me. I'm staring the beast down."

"Look." Gabe tapped the red notebook in Ben's hands. "Here are some of the people Violeta was distributing to. These are people who've been cut off by their doctor. If it weren't for her, they'd have already turned to heroin. They'd probably be dead."

I reached for the notebook, but Ben snatched it away.

"Why don't you come with us on Thursday?" he said. "I'll show you the people you'll help."

That word—*help*—caught me.

"Just stop arguing, sweetheart," Gabe said, exasperated. I glared at him, wanting him to stop calling me sweetheart, but then he smiled slowly, those dimples flashing, and said, "We'll get more money faster, and then we'll be done with it. It's what you want. Right?"

I nodded, relenting. Just a few more weeks, and I'd be out of this. "Okay. You're right. But I can't lose my license. Nobody can find out about my involvement."

"Obviously," Ben said. "This way we'll need fewer pills. Just keep giving me your signed prescriptions. Gabe will take the girls out to get them filled. He'll bring the pills back to me. I'll cut them, and Gabe will deliver them to our customers."

"You have to be careful. It's a myth that you can die from touching fentanyl, but in a room this small, particles can be released into the air. You'll need a—"

Ben held up a gas mask and goggles.

"Okay, good." I turned to Gabe. "Are you all right with this? I thought you said you were out?"

Gabe shrugged. "It's for a good cause."

A gentle thrill pulsed through my core. It was stupid. Juvenile. I was a grown woman. But I liked the sense that we were bound together. Not just by our past, but by what we were doing now. Gabe and Ben and me. No matter what happened now, we couldn't unstitch the fabric of what we'd become.

"Let's do it," I said.

# CHAPTER 29

I STARED OUT THE clinic window, my gaze on the rain falling in sheets onto the parking lot below. The snow had melted, the pavement filled with shimmering puddles. Gray light, the color of old socks, slanted through leafless tree branches.

A steady stream of water was falling from an overhang somewhere above the window. A spider did a sad little back-float through a puddle on the ledge, its legs waving frantically in the air. I thought about opening the window, to set the spider free, but I didn't move. Eventually a cascade of water gushed onto the ledge, washing the spider away.

I pulled my burner phone out of my lab coat pocket and checked WhatsApp.

There was a text message from Gabe.

We need to get out of this. I think Ben's using again, and it's too dangerous. If you get caught you lose everything. If I get caught, I go straight to prison. It just isn't worth it.

My heart sank. Ben was using again?

I sipped my coffee, thinking. Gabe had never cared before when Ben was using. His cowardice was becoming a liability. Ben had given me another $30,000, bringing my total to $65,000 hidden in my secret checking account. We were so close; we couldn't stop now.

I thought for a minute before tapping out a reply.

**Come meet Josh on Wednesday before his infusion. Hospital café, 10:30 a.m.**

He didn't reply for so long that unexpected tears of fury and frustration filled my eyes. I wiped at them angrily. I needed to get it together. But sheer exhaustion made it feel like my body had become detached from my brain. Too many sleepless nights were wearing on me.

Last night I'd woken from another dream about my father. I was holding his head on my lap and he was begging me to put an end to his pain. He wept and trembled and moaned, his cries reaching a fever pitch. The sound filled my ears, making my head feel swollen, every breath a bruise. It was so loud I thought my skull would explode.

I held my hands over my ears but the sound continued, a brutal wailing that filled my chest and throbbed in every fiber of my muscles. I finally shrugged out of my coat and held the fabric over my dad's nose and mouth until it was quiet. Peacefully, finally, quiet.

I'd woken with a jerk, the tears falling sideways down my cheeks and filling up my ears. I hadn't smothered my dad, and the fact that my subconscious suggested it disturbed me. What kind of person was I?

The dream played vividly behind my eyes for hours as I tried to sort it from reality, only falling into a restless sleep shortly before the alarm went off.

I finished jotting notes in a folder and was just putting it away when the burner buzzed.

It was a message from Gabe.

**See you tomorrow.**

The sound of a commotion came from the front of the office—muted shouts, a high-pitched scream, a thud. I hurried out to reception.

A man I vaguely recognized had been tackled by security and now stood slumped between two guards. He was small but burly-chested, gray hair hanging in oily strands. His red cheeks were shiny, wet with tears.

It was Alice Jones's husband. My patient with back pain who hadn't shown up for her appointment last week.

"Mr. Jones?" I came around the side of the reception desk and approached him. The other patients in the room were staring. A palpable tension filled the air. One mother was clutching her child to her chest, her eyes filled with fear.

"Let this man go," I demanded of the security guards.

"Dr. Sweeney—" Brittany shook her head at me in warning.

I turned toward her as Mr. Jones lunged. I saw him in my peripheral vision, a dark shadow hurtling toward me. Adrenaline kicked in my veins as I turned my body sideways, expecting the impact. But the security guards caught him just in time, hauling him back and wrestling him to his knees.

"You!" His eyes glittered, and spittle flew from his mouth. "She's dead, and it's your fault!"

The blood drained from my face. "Who's dead?"

"My Alice. She was in pain, and you wouldn't help her! You wouldn't give her anything. She went to the streets to get pain relief and now she's dead!"

He tried again to lunge for me. "Let me go!"

Nausea burned in my belly, my whole body shaking.

"You're done!" he shouted as the security guards heaved him out into the hall.

Or had he said *You're dead*?

I STUMBLED on wooden legs back to the medical office.

Alice Jones was dead.

I hadn't helped her when she'd needed it, so she'd turned to illegal drugs. And where had she gotten those?

The thought was as fleeting as a hummingbird, there and then gone.

I should've prescribed her something to help the pain when I had the chance.

I had to get out of here. I grabbed my coat and purse and hurried out of the clinic, down the stairs, and outside. People rushed past, huddled under umbrellas to escape the pelting rain. The wind blew my hair, cutting straight through my wool coat to my bones. My hands and ears went raw with cold.

I was pulling an umbrella from my bag when someone tapped me on the shoulder. I let out a little shriek.

"I'm so sorry!" Dr. Palmer looked surprised.

"No, I'm sorry!" I forced a smile, letting myself slide back into my other persona: Dr. Sweeney, calm and capable. "I'm just overtired."

"It's understandable." Dr. Palmer hunched his shoulders against the cold. The small blood vessels across his nose and cheeks were starker than ever. I wanted to suggest a topical vasoconstrictor like oxymetazoline, but it seemed inappropriate.

"I'm so sorry you're going through this. It's incredibly unfair. I wish—"

I held up a hand. "You've done so much for me my whole life. And I know you've helped Ben too. I heard you helped him get a place to live after he got out of prison."

"I met him one day while visiting you. He seemed so broken up. So when he called me after he got out . . . I just wanted to help."

"We—*I*—owe you everything." I put a tentative hand on his arm. "And now I owe you an apology. I'm sorry I didn't stay in touch. I was really messed up for a long time. I'm sorry."

Dr. Palmer pulled me into a tight hug. At first I stiffened, unused to public displays of affection and a little worried that a colleague might see. But it was nice to be hugged by someone who reminded me of my father. He even smelled the same, like Old Spice and well-worn leather and just faintly of cigarettes.

We pulled apart and laughed a little awkwardly.

"I better . . ." I motioned to my car.

"Yes, off course."

I dashed across the parking lot and was just opening my car door when the sound of sudden revving jerked my attention to my right. The now-familiar black truck accelerated past me, sending rainwater arcing into the air. I jumped out of the way, avoiding most of the splash as the truck drove away.

But not before I'd seen who was driving.

Prickly adrenaline crawled along my skin.

The guy with a ponytail and a gun at Costco. Carlos Martinez. Santiago Martinez's brother.

I TEXTED Moira that I had to work late, then drove to an address out near Crescent Lake. Finding a private gun seller had been easier than I expected. A plethora of websites allowed you to purchase a gun with no questions asked. Like Craigslist for gun sales. I'd told the man on the phone I wanted a weapon for protection, as I often worked late.

The rain had stopped by the time I pulled onto the gravel road. My car bumped through water-filled potholes. The road was lined with thick brush, the wind hustling through the naked branches.

I parked next to a neat chalet-style farmhouse with a brick chimney belching smoke into the gunmetal-gray sky. A man came out and stood on the front porch. He was older with a small pot-belly, floppy white hair, and a casual but alert wide-armed stance. Even from here, I could see he was armed.

*Breathe*, I reminded myself. *Smile. Be normal.*

"You Dr. Sweeney?" he called as I got out of my car.

I nodded. I'd told him my real name because I wanted him to look me up and see that I was a reputable doctor, not some scuzzy drug dealer looking for an illegal murder weapon.

He hopped off the porch and shook my hand. "I'm Harry Donohue."

"I'm Emma."

"Nice to meet you, Emma." He pulled a small gun from his back pocket. "This here is the Glock forty-two from the listing. You know much about weapons?"

"A little."

"This girl is a hair over four inches tall and just under six inches long. It holds six rounds of three-eighty ammo and weighs less than eighteen ounces. It's perfect for deep conceal, but you gotta get yourself that conceal permit like I said on the phone."

I nodded and smiled. "My husband's a detective. He already explained it to me. I'll head over to the sheriff's office and do that next."

"You know how to shoot?"

"Yep." Nate had insisted I learn to use a gun when we first

moved in together. He'd said that because he was a cop, there would always be weapons wherever he lived, and he wouldn't feel comfortable until I learned how to handle one. He'd given me lessons at the shooting range until he'd declared me "competent."

"Good, good." A gust of wind blew hair into Harry's eyes and he pushed it back. "Now, normally I don't sell unless you already have a permit, but since your husband's a cop, I'm sure he'll make sure you get it."

I gritted my teeth at his patronizing tone.

Harry handed me the gun, an ankle holster, and a small box of ammunition. I handed him an envelope with cash, and he counted it quickly.

"Make sure you apply for that permit," he reminded me as I got in my car.

"I will," I lied.

I slammed my door and started the engine, blocking out any more conversation. I pulled away too fast, the wheels of my car spinning on the wet gravel. I tapped the brakes, slowing to a crawl as I made my way down the road.

Just before I rounded the last corner, I glanced in my rearview mirror. I swallowed hard, my lungs suddenly feeling as if a vise were squeezing them.

Harry was still standing there staring after me, as if he was memorizing my face.

Or maybe just my license plate.

# CHAPTER 30

"WELCOME TO YOUR PILLHEAD TOUR," Ben said the next day.

He turned his van onto the eastbound highway, into the rural stretches along the foothills. The old van clunked and rattled as he shifted gears. I was in the middle, Gabe in the passenger's seat.

The rugged, white-tipped Cascades soared above us. Soft streaks of sunlight slanted low across the horizon; a simmering excitement bounced between my shoulders. Oxy abuse had initially exploded in these remote communities only a few years ago. While it had spread to cities like Seattle, Tacoma, and Spokane, we didn't have to go far to see its effects.

I checked my phone, aware that coverage out here could be spotty. I'd lied to the clinic and said I was staying home with Josh, then lied to Moira and said I was going to work, and if I was honest, it worried me a little. The trouble with lies is they breed like mice. You start with one, then you suddenly have a dozen, then two dozen. You tell lies to cover those lies, and more lies to cover them. Before you know it, the infestation has taken over.

Ben turned off the highway and wound along the hidden dirt roads that traversed the terrain of cool blue lakes, rushing rivers, and gullies carved into the mountain foothills.

"A guy named Paul lives there." Ben pointed at a rusty single-wide trailer across the river. "He used to work in the tech industry. His company was about to go public when the dot-com bubble burst. He lost everything. He started working with a roofing company and fell off the third story of a building. Broke his back. He's in chronic pain but can't afford health insurance."

"That's so sad," I murmured.

One of the most important things you learn in medical school is "do no harm." But what should doctors do when our patients need something we know could potentially be harmful? It was a quandary for doctors: chronic pain versus addiction. If we prescribed the medicine that could help, our patients could become dependent. In trying to solve one problem, we simply created another.

We crossed a bridge and headed north, parallel to the river. Ben pointed at a tired-looking log cabin. "An Iraqi vet named James lives there. End-stage prostate cancer. Sometimes his insurance has problems authorizing his oxy. We help him when he needs it. Oh, and see that tent there? That's where Kelly Anne lives." He shivered as a private memory rolled over him. "She's a skank. Stay away from her, or she'll knife you in the back. We don't deliver to her anymore."

"How long have you been doing this?" I asked.

"Years. I had some suppliers a few years ago." He snorted a laugh. "Before I went to prison, I mean. You wouldn't believe, one of them was a grandma. She'd never done drugs, so she sold all her OxyContin to me, just to pay for all her other medication. But now we've got a doctor on board. And with the fentanyl, we can sell even more." He smiled faintly, looking a little haunted for a minute. "Vi always said we were a boutique pill shop on wheels."

Ben crossed a tall bridge and turned down an incline to a dirt road that held about a dozen trailers. He parked next to a neat single-wide with white and gray siding and a tiny brown porch and turned to me. "I want you to meet somebody."

"No! Ben, I'm not meeting anybody!" I hissed, startled.

"Give it up, Emma. Nobody cares who you are." He unbuckled and got out.

"Come on." Gabe nudged me and got out the other side. "It doesn't look too bad."

I craned my neck, looking around. Gabe was right: no graffiti, no snarling dogs, no broken bottles or used needles lying around.

I sat for a moment in the front of the truck. My gaze landed on the red notebook in the console. I quickly picked it up and flipped through the lined pages. There was Julia's name and address. Beneath it, a few patients from my office—patients I'd specifically not given oxy to. And a couple of dozen addresses from Snoqualmie to Cle Elum, Seattle to Whidbey Island.

I returned the notebook and shoved a baseball cap on my head. I could feel eyes on my back as I hurried after Ben and Gabe, but when I turned to look, there was no one there. The windows in the other trailers were dark.

The trailer door was opened by a dried-out wisp of a woman with sad, tired eyes, graying hair, and an angular face.

"Ah, so you're the doc." She reached a hand out to shake mine.

I shot Ben a glare, furious he'd told her I was a doctor. "Uh, hi."

"This is my sister, Emma. Emma, meet Pamela."

"Come on in, then," she said. "Meet Eugene."

She shut the door behind us and slid three locks into place.

"We have a crazy neighbor," she explained. "She'll snort or inject anything she can get her hands on. I remember her from high school. Hard to believe she was a cheerleader. You just can't look at somebody and tell, you know?"

She led us into a tiny living room, the couch almost reaching the walls on either side of the room. The air smelled clean, if a little stale. A man was sitting on the couch, a crocheted blue blanket tucked over his lap. He was probably in his early thirties with long, greasy hair and eyes sunken in the sockets. When he saw us, he struggled to stand, but Pamela pressed him down onto the couch.

"Come on, Mom," he complained.

"No need to get up for us, Eugene," Ben said. He turned to Gabe and me. "Eugene had his left hip replaced last year. The surgery left him with nerve damage. He used to live in Tacoma, but he moved out here after he lost his job. Now he has to drive once a month back out to Tacoma to get his prescription."

"Just had the dosage cut again," Eugene said. He lifted one leg with both hands, wincing.

Pamela left the room and returned a minute later with one white pill and a plastic cup of water, like what you'd give a child. She handed both to Eugene. "I've had to lock them up. And the gun."

The word hung heavy and black in the room. A flush of pity bloomed on my cheeks, but I was glad to have my gun in my ankle holster.

"Come on out here with me." Pamela moved toward the compact kitchen. "I'll get you a coffee."

The three of us followed her and accepted mugs of steaming black coffee. She slipped Ben an envelope, and he dropped a baggie of pills into her desperate hands.

I looked away, my gaze briefly catching Gabe's. He looked as gloomy as I felt. The story of prescription opioids wasn't just one of addiction and overdose, but one of people like Eugene who were becoming increasingly desperate to stay pain-free. But the moral and legal implications were huge. I knew that.

"How much is Eugene taking?" I asked Pamela.

"Two hundred and forty milligrams a day."

I tried not to look surprised, but she'd already seen my face.

"You have no right to judge, missy!" she snapped. "You don't know what he's been through."

"I'm not—" I stopped because it didn't matter. "Just get some naloxone. You can get it from any pharmacy."

Pamela glared at me. Ben grabbed my arm and tugged me toward the door, Gabe hurrying after us. "We'd better be heading off. Talk to you later, Pamela!"

I stumbled down the steps after him.

"What?" I asked. "Why was she so mad?" My voice was shrill in self-defense.

"Sometimes you're *too* helpful, Emma," Ben snapped. "It makes you seem . . . I don't know, bossy. A know-it-all."

I got in the truck. "She doesn't need to lock up the gun; he could overdose on oxy any day! Naloxone could save his life!"

"You don't think she knows that?" Ben exclaimed. "She already gets all that suspicion from other people. *Is he really in pain? Has he tried physical therapy? What about some ibuprofen? Does he ice it?* She doesn't need it from us too."

"Well, I *am* a doctor," I said.

"I know. That's why these people need you. What they don't need is your judgment."

"Why did you tell her I'm a doctor?" I angrily snapped my seat belt into place as Gabe slid in next to me.

"Don't worry. You're not the only doctor I've worked with."

My mouth dropped open, but before I could answer, something smashed against the hood.

"Hey, you!"

It was a woman. Wild red hair. Pointy chin. Face pinched and desperate. She smashed her fists against the hood again, eyes glittering.

"What the hell are you doing?" Ben shouted, rolling the window down.

"You have them!" The woman dug both hands into her hair and ripped. Hair came out of her skull, trailing from her hands like seaweed.

Ben, Gabe, and I gaped at her in disbelief.

"I guess that's the neighbor," Gabe murmured.

"I know you!" She pointed a clawed hand at Ben. "I saw you with that other guy last time. I need 'em!" She took a knife from the waistband of her pants. It was huge, gleaming with menace in the pale sun.

"Knife!" Gabe shouted, scrambling to lock his door.

"Shit!" I exclaimed. "She's coming around!" I smacked Ben on the arm. "Lock your door!"

Ben locked his door and pressed the button to roll up his window, but it was too slow. The crazy lady thrust her hand inside. I screamed as she slashed wildly back and forth, looking for meat to cleave. She shrieked as the window closed on her arm. Ben punched her hand. Once. Twice.

The knife clattered to the floor mat, and she yanked her arm out, howling in rage and pain.

Ben floored the truck in reverse down the dirt road, gravel pinging against the undercarriage. He did a quick one-eighty, and we accelerated away.

"That," Gabe said, his voice shaking, "is exactly why I got out of this business."

I was breathing heavily. A solitary drop of blood rolled down Ben's forehead to his chin.

"You're bleeding!" I exclaimed.

Ben wiped at his head. "I'm fine. The knife nicked me."

"What the hell are we doing?" Gabe moaned, bending forward. He rubbed his forehead hard with his fingertips. "We can't do this, it's too dangerous!"

"What did she mean?" I ignored him and turned to Ben. A drop of blood fell off his chin, plopping onto his T-shirt and expanding, crimson against white. "Who were you here with before?"

Ben gave me a look: *You silly little girl.*

"Don't forget why you're doing this," he finally said.

# CHAPTER 31

NATE WAITED AS KIA ordered a low-fat turkey sandwich from the deli at Safeway. No mayo. No cheese. Whole wheat. He looked at the Christmas-themed M&M's he held in one hand, the turkey, cranberry, stuffing, and bacon sandwich in the other. Grease was already leaking through the paper.

"Yes, you should eat healthier, Nate." Kia answered his unspoken question without looking up from her phone.

"How'd you know I was thinking that?"

"I know you."

Nate grinned, shifting the M&M's to glance again at his phone. Still nothing from Emma. He felt bad leaving things the way they had last night. He should've stayed downstairs and talked to her more, but he couldn't bear to have her tell him that getting a promotion wouldn't help Josh. It was the only way he knew how to help.

He'd been gone before she got up this morning, and though he'd texted an apology, she hadn't replied yet.

He moved away from the deli counter toward the flower department and dialed the clinic while standing under a giant Santa balloon.

"Hey, Brittany," he said to the receptionist. "Is Emma free? I'd like to talk to her."

There was a long pause. "Emma called in sick this morning, Detective Sweeney. She's home with Josh."

Nate stared up at the Santa balloon. Emma was not at home; he'd spoken to his mother about Josh a half hour ago. Where the fuck was his wife? And who was she with?

His phone beeped an incoming call: Lieutenant Dyson. He thanked Brittany and switched over.

"We just had a call from a pharmacist over in Lynnwood," Dyson said. "She had a prescription come in for OxyContin signed by Dr. Chad Wallington from Allegiance Health Clinic."

"Okay?"

"She said Dr. Wallington's on his honeymoon right now. His new wife is her sister, so she knows for a fact. She doesn't think he wrote that script. I already spoke to Special Agents Hamilton and Greene. They've asked you to report back what you find."

"Sure. Text me her details," Nate replied.

"Will do. Hey, Nate?"

"Yeah?"

"It's getting close to the end of the year."

Nate's throat tightened. "Yep."

"Maybe it's time to let someone else take over Mr. Martinez's case? Josh has his treatment soon. He's gonna need his dad."

"You taking my case away?" Nate asked stiffly.

Dyson sighed. "Course not. You still have till the end of the year. Just remember where your priorities should be."

Nate hung up. He knew exactly where his priorities were.

The Santa balloon bobbed above him, his cheerful grin now a judgmental smirk. Nate punched the Santa in the face.

"Wow, what's your problem with Santa?" Kia asked from behind him.

Nate whirled. "Well, he's a bit of a prick, isn't he?"

Kia eyed him. "Do you want to tell me what's really going on?"

*I think my wife's cheating on me. My son might die. I need this promotion so I have the money to get him the treatment he needs and I'm running out of time. I'm weak. A coward. A failure.*

But he couldn't say any of it out loud. He could change a flat tire, save a newborn baby, stop the bad guy from hurting the good guy, but he couldn't admit weakness in front of a colleague. If word got around, they might take his badge. His gun. And then who would he be?

He stuck a toothpick between his teeth and smiled. Everyone loved Nate for his smile, his cheerful disposition. The problem was, the feelings crammed in his chest were getting harder and harder to ignore.

"That was Dyson." He told her about the call from the pharmacist. She whistled long and low.

"Do you think someone from Allegiance Health Clinic is fraudulently signing prescriptions of oxy?" Kia asked.

"That or someone got hold of Wallington's prescription pad."

Dyson's text pinged on Nate's phone just as Nate caught sight of a familiar face barreling toward him. One he hadn't wanted to ever see again.

Robbie's mother hadn't aged well. Her eyes were as droopy as Nate's basset hound's. The lines on her face were so deep they looked like they'd been carved into her skin. The peculiar dull throb of old grief and guilt battered him.

"Nate! Nate Sweeney!"

Sweat prickled on his skin. He had to get out of there. Nate thrust his sandwich and M&M's at Kia and yanked his phone out of his pocket.

"Gotta make this call." He strode quickly outside.

The season had turned surly, the air pricked with a gray mist. The threat of more snow hung heavy in the air.

Nate hunched low in the driver's seat, his hands clutching the steering wheel. His fingernails had dried, blood caked under the nail beds. He dialed the number Dyson had texted him.

"Hello, Lynnwood Pharmacy," a cheery voice answered.

"Hello, may I speak to Maryanne Rosenstein?"

"Speaking."

"This is Detective Nate Sweeney. You called the Skamania Police Department about a prescription signed by Dr. Chad Wallington."

"Yes! Dr. Wallington's my brother-in-law. He married my sister two weeks ago, and they're on their honeymoon in Barbados. I don't think he signed this prescription."

"Can doctors postdate prescriptions?"

"Some, yes. But not usually for opiates like OxyContin, which are highly controlled and regulated. A doctor wouldn't postdate it past a week."

"Did you call Dr. Wallington?"

She hesitated. "I don't know my brother-in-law very well yet. I thought it best to call you first."

Nate assured her she'd done the right thing and then requested she email a copy of the prescription and the patient's details to him before hanging up.

"What the hell, Nate?" Kia asked as she got in the car. She tossed his sandwich and M&M's on his lap, looking annoyed as hell.

He couldn't tell her this either. Kia was dating Julia. Julia was his prime suspect. A person who'd stolen OxyContin samples was more than capable of stealing prescription pads.

"Sorry," he muttered, unwrapping his sandwich.

She opened her mouth to issue a reply, but he was saved by the ringing of his phone. It was Lisa Hamilton.

"We found Mr. Martinez's car. It's parked outside the Sonora Motel near Sea-Tac Airport. Can you meet us there in an hour?"

"We're on our way," Nate said.

NATE PULLED up behind an old Ford Thunderbird at the edge of the motel's parking lot. The lot was scuzzy and weed-choked, the motel seedy and dilapidated. The car had been sectioned off with yellow tape. Lisa Hamilton and Phil Greene stood next to it, a tow truck parked nearby.

He checked his phone again before he got out of the cruiser; still no reply from Emma.

"Figured you'd need it towed to your department to process," Hamilton said as she shook Nate's and Kia's hands. She was dressed in a severe black pantsuit, her hair slicked back into a bun, her mouth in a line.

"Keys were in the ignition." Greene tossed Nate the keys.

*Probably doesn't want to get his fancy Italian suit dirty,* Nate thought.

Nate and Kia both slipped on latex gloves, and Nate opened the driver's door. A half-drunk bottle of Coke sat on the floor of the passenger's side, a plastic Taco Bell bag in the console. A Seahawks sweatshirt in the back.

"Video recording from the gas station across the street shows the car arriving here a few hours after we think Mr. Martinez was killed," Hamilton said.

"Was Martinez driving?" Nate asked.

"Can't tell from the video. It's too far away. But the car's GPS shows that it left the house shortly before one a.m. and drove about forty-five minutes, straight here."

"The killer drove his car here," Nate said.

The four of them crowded around as Nate popped the trunk. They breathed a sigh of disappointment. It was empty.

"Wait." Greene leaned in and pried at the edge of the trunk's floor. He lifted it to expose the spare-tire well. But instead of a tire, a black briefcase rested inside.

Nate pulled the briefcase out, turning it over in his hands. Soft Italian leather, gold metal feet, twin combination locks. It looked familiar. It took Nate a moment to realize why.

It looked exactly like the one in his closet at home.

Nate felt the ground beneath his feet tilt. Emma had a briefcase matching a murdered drug dealer's. She'd borrowed it from the clinic. Someone at the clinic was signing fraudulent prescriptions for oxy.

Everything led back to the clinic.

He had to talk to Emma. Did all the doctors share that one briefcase? Who'd used it before her? Was it Julia?

He opened his mouth to tell the others, then snapped it shut. If he told them, they'd scream conflict of interest. His wife worked at that clinic. He'd be yanked off this case so fast he wouldn't even have time to get his balls out of his throat. And he could kiss that promotion good-bye.

"Anybody have any idea what the combination might be?" Hamilton asked.

"What were those numbers you found at Santiago Martinez's house?" Kia turned to Nate. "Maybe it's a combination."

Nate tried the numbers: *323 . . . 454*

Nothing happened.

"Okay, let's take it back to the station," Kia said. "Let the nerds try to crack it."

Kia's phone rang, and she stepped away to answer it.

"Anything new to report?" Hamilton asked.

"No sign of Ben yet." Nate told Hamilton and Greene about Violeta's mom refusing to allow them in. Hamilton agreed to pay for an agent to sit on the house.

"We'll get someone out there this week," Greene said.

He trained his dark, unsmiling eyes on Nate for a moment too long. Nate felt his face warming under the scrutiny. He scratched the nape of his neck, wondering if Greene could tell he was holding something back.

Kia hung up the phone, her face white.

"Excuse us, we need to go. It's an emergency," she said to Hamilton and Greene.

Kia hustled to the cruiser and Nate followed, grateful for the interruption. "What's going on?" he asked.

"That was Julia. I think she's overdosing. I've called an ambulance. She said she took birdhouse pills."

"What are birdhouse pills?"

"I don't know. But Nate, she said, 'Tell Emma.'"


*TELL EMMA.*

Julia's words echoed in Nate's mind as he unlocked the front door to his house. He was furious that a known drug addict was pulling Emma into her drama. What would it mean for Emma's career, for *his*, if he proved Julia was behind this opioid ring?

Nate set the groceries on the floor, and Charlie woofed and shuffled to him, his whole body wiggling with doggy glee. Nate patted Charlie's head and went into the living room, where Moira was watching a soap opera. The fireplace was lit, cheerful crackles filling the space. Four Christmas stockings were hung from the mantel, including one for the dog. The Christmas tree twinkled in its warm glow.

He bent and kissed his mother on the forehead.

"Josh is having a nap," Moira said, looking like she needed one too.

"Where's Emma?"

"Working late."

Nate turned away to hide his scowl.

"I got a call from your dad's nursing home today. He has pneumonia again."

Nate sat next to his mom and grasped her hand. "Oh no."

Fear ripened in his belly. Pneumonia was dangerous for stroke victims, and his dad had suffered far too many bouts lately.

"You need to go see him. I know it isn't easy, but it's time."

Nate scrubbed a hand over his jaw. It had been a few days since he'd shaved. There had been no time. He only had a few weeks to crack this case, maybe less if Kia put together the pieces and zeroed in on Emma's clinic.

"Sure, Ma. I'll go soon."

Nate moved to stand, but Moira put a firm hand on his knee. "Nate. Sit down."

Nate sat back, surprised. Moira wasn't the type to be pushy or dogmatic. She'd always given her opinions and let him choose his own course, raising him with a strong sense of justice, of right and wrong, good and bad.

Tears glittered on Moira's eyelashes. "I think it's time you knew the truth about your father."

Nate stared at his mother. "What do you mean?"

"You've built him up to be this god, and he just isn't. He was a loving father, a wonderful husband, a pillar of the community. But he did things—unforgivable things. . . ." She faltered and looked at her hands.

"What'd he do, Ma?"

When Moira lifted her eyes, Nate could see red spiderwebbed across the white. "He used his job to protect drug dealers and took kickbacks for it."

"What? No way." Nate stood abruptly. Moira stood too, facing him.

"I'm sorry, but it's true. I found a stash of money after the stroke, and I spoke to one of the dealers when he called the house."

"Jesus Christ," Nate swore, even though he knew his mother didn't like it.

"We are all capable of great and terrible things. Your dad did some terrible things, and you need to know that. You refuse to see flaws in the people you love. You need to see your dad as he really was, not as you wish he was. That way you can say good-bye properly."

Nate flashed back to seeing his father coming out of that motel parking lot. He'd been so naïve. What had Matt been doing in Seattle when his jurisdiction was Skamania? He should have known something was wrong.

He shook his head and pulled his mother into his arms, resting his chin on her head. She seemed so small lately, small and brittle.

"I'll go soon, Ma, I promise."


EMMA GOT home as Nate was starting dinner.

He'd washed the four naked game hens in cold water and lined them up on a piece of parchment paper and was roasting coriander, cumin, and fennel in a dry pan when she came in.

"Mmm, smells good," Emma said as she walked into the kitchen. "I saw your mom leaving when I pulled up."

"She had to get to the nursing home to see Dad."

Emma kissed his cheek and knelt to scratch Charlie's ears. "You're home early."

"And you're home late. Must've been a busy day at work," he said.

"Yeah. It was pretty hectic."

A sick, furious spasm twinged in his belly at her lie. He yanked the mortar and pestle down from the cupboard and dumped in the toasted herbs, bashing the pestle aggressively.

"You okay?"

He didn't answer for a minute. When he spoke, it was quietly, still not looking at his wife. "Where were you today, really?"

"I was at the—"

"Don't lie to me, Emma." He slammed the pestle down, and Emma jumped. "I called you at the clinic and they said you'd called in sick. Where have you been? Are you . . ." Bile rose in his throat. "Are you having an affair?"

Emma's mouth dropped open, but almost instantly her face hardened as she retreated behind a cold, perfect veneer. The switch was fast and unnerving.

"I can't believe you would even ask me that," she whispered, her face pale. For a second Nate actually doubted himself: the receipt that clearly showed coffee with another person, the midnight texts, the lies about being at work. "You and Josh are my world. How could you think that? Everything I've ever done has been for you!"

He tipped the crushed herbs into a bowl of Greek yogurt and spooned the marinade over the game hens.

"Then tell me where you were today."

Emma's lips folded into a thin line. He huffed angrily and began chopping crusty bread into small squares to make stuffing.

Emma sighed. "Fine, you want to know where I was?"

He faced her. "Yes!"

"I was with my brother."

"Ben?" Nate had not been expecting that.

She nodded.

"Why?"

"When you mentioned Josh needing a bone marrow transplant or a kidney, it got me thinking. What if Josh does need any of those things and we can't help him? I messaged him. We met up for lunch today."

Nate narrowed his eyes. "You went to lunch?"

"Yes."

"Where'd you go?"

Emma looked pissed, but could she blame him for asking? "McDonald's. Here. You want proof?" She grabbed her purse off the counter and rummaged in it, then pulled out a crumpled receipt and thrust it at him. The date was today's.

Nate knew he should be relieved, but instead he felt furious. She'd once again excluded him from a major part of her life, just like with her parents, just like with Dr. Palmer.

"I told you to stay away from him. And to let me know if you heard from him!"

Emma stiffened. "Maybe it hasn't occurred to you, Nate, but I don't have to do everything you tell me."

She whipped out of the kitchen, Charlie at her heels, leaving him to work in silence as anger gnawed at his belly.

The lingering scents of chopped onion and sage made him feel queasy; the heat rising from the oven suffocated him. He shoved the stuffing into the birds, sparking a sudden memory of coming home after baseball practice one day and finding his dad in the office stuffing a load of cash into an envelope.

"I'm saving up to buy your mom something special for her birthday." He'd winked at Nate and shoved the envelope into the back of the filing cabinet. "It'll be our little secret, right, son?"

Nate stared at the birds. His brain felt like someone had taken it and shaken it up, a snow globe full of garbage.

Stuffing an envelope. A filing cabinet. The briefcase.

The thought came so unexpectedly, he almost dropped the

knife. He took the stairs to his bedroom two at a time. He found Emma's briefcase nestled under her clothes and lifted it onto the bed, his mind flashing to the numbers on the scrap of paper at Martinez's house.

*323 454*

Downstairs, he could hear Emma calling for him.

"Nate? Where are you?"

And then the sound of her feet on the stairs.

Nate turned the numbers on both combinations. The briefcase clicked open, the sound loud and metallic.

A sense of unrest churned in his stomach. Nate lifted the lid as Emma entered the bedroom.

Baggies of white powder. Cash. An old cell phone. And pills.

Lots and lots of pills.

# CHAPTER 32

"WHAT THE HELL IS THIS!" Nate's voice cracked with shock.

Violeta's briefcase was open on our bed in front of him, an old Nokia cell phone in his hand. I felt the blood drain from my face. A wash of cold swept over me, like I'd stepped into a shadow.

He dropped the cell phone and picked up a baggie filled with white powder.

"Don't touch it!" I lunged across the room and grabbed the baggie out of his hand.

Nate looked at me like I'd lost my mind. I pressed a shaky hand to the bed and dropped the baggie back into the briefcase. How had Nate found out the combination?

"We don't know what that is." I tried to explain my panic. "It could be anthrax, for all we know!"

"What the hell is going on, Emma?"

I squeezed my eyes shut. I'd known all along there would be a time when I'd have to lie directly to Nate. Now that time had come.

I'd been very careful to let Ben do the bulk of the work, in order to keep my hands clean. And if he ever tried to point at me, well, his history with drugs was incriminating. Nate already knew I'd turned Ben in for drugs before. It would look an awful lot like revenge if Ben tried to blame me without any proof.

"It's Ben's."

Nate stared at me, speechless.

"I told you I met up with him today, but it wasn't the first time. A few weeks ago, he asked me to hold this."

"Just out of the blue?"

"Yes. I mean, with Ben it's always out of the blue. He pops in and out of my life. I'm just happy he isn't dead somewhere."

"You didn't think to ask what was in it?"

"Of course I did! He said it was paperwork to get custody of his son. That he and his girlfriend were splitting up. He didn't want her to find out." I swallowed hard and glanced at the briefcase. Baggies filled with white powder. Stacks of cash. At least a dozen prescription bottles filled with pills. The cell phone. And there, peeking up from under the baggies of powder, were the prescriptions I'd signed.

"How'd you open it?" I had to keep Nate's attention on me. "Ben didn't give me the combination."

"The combination was on the refrigerator of the murder victim I'm investigating."

"Santiago Martinez?"

He nodded.

My brain spun slowly over this information. Nate's murder victim was linked to Violeta; Violeta was linked to Ben. "You think Ben was involved?"

He opened his mouth to answer, but snapped it shut.

"That's impossible," I said. "Ben's been in rehab."

"Did he say that?"

"Yes."

"We'll check if that's true. We'll dust for fingerprints as well." Nate rubbed an angry hand through his hair. "Shit, Emma. Do you have any idea how bad this looks? My wife was covering for her brother who has a briefcase of drugs and may be connected to a murder investigation. I could get taken off this case, and then what happens to paying for Josh's treatments? Have you thought about that?"

"I didn't know there were drugs in there," I snapped. "I wanted to help my brother! You don't understand what it's like, Nate. Your family's normal. You've never lost anybody!"

He gave me a withering look. I shook my head, trying not to look at the prescriptions. How the hell was I going to get those before Nate saw them?

"I know your dad had a stroke, but it's not the same."

"This isn't a pissing contest, Emma," he growled. "Who's suffered the most, who's lost the most."

"No, because I would win!" Tears—angry, grief-stricken tears—pricked my eyes. I blinked furiously, determined not to cry. Tears didn't help. They didn't change a damn thing. "I've lost *everything. Everybody!* I've had to get my own brother thrown in jail just to keep him alive. Do you know how hard that's been? I betrayed him."

"I know you just want to help him. You're a good person, Emma. A good mother. A good doctor. But you aren't responsible for your brother. He is a parasite. A fucking drain on society. He's using you. You can't save him. Only he can save himself."

"Mommy? Daddy?" Josh's voice came from our bedroom doorway, Charlie trailing behind, like a sentinel guarding something precious.

Josh was clutching a teddy bear in one arm and dragging his red-and-white *Star Wars* blanket behind him, his middle and pointer fingers in his mouth. His bald head shone in the overhead light. He looked fragile and vulnerable, like an overgrown baby. My heart squeezed with pity.

Nate pushed past me to kneel next to Josh. "Hey, buddy. How you feeling?"

Josh rubbed his eyes. "Okay. I dreamed that we found a black dog and we keeped him so Charlie had a friend."

"Kept," I automatically corrected him.

Nate's phone rang, and he stood. "I've gotta get this." He angled his body slightly away as he answered. I took the opportunity to take a tiny step closer to the briefcase.

"We got the budget? . . . Good. Get a man over to Williams's house tonight. If he shows up . . . Yeah . . . Yeah. Okay, bye." Nate hung up and turned to me. "I have to take this briefcase in to the station to document the evidence. I'll tell Lieutenant Dyson you were holding it for Ben and you didn't know what was in it. You're going to have to come in for questioning, though. Do you know where Ben is now? We'll need to question him too."

I snorted. "Haven't you been listening to me? Of course I don't know where he is! Ben *never* tells me where he is."

Nate snapped the briefcase shut. "I've gotta go."

"Where are you going, Daddy?" Josh asked.

"I just have to go back to work for a little bit, but I'll be home soon, okay?"

"'S okay. You gotta catch the bad guys."

He thought his dad being a cop was cool, like *Zootopia* or something: *catch the bad guys, keep us safe.* But who was the bad guy now? Who was really keeping who safe?

Nate squeezed his shoulder. "That's right."

He moved to kiss me, but I sidestepped him, dropping to my knees and pulling Josh in for a hug. I saw hurt spark in Nate's blue eyes, and guilt rushed in. Guilt and a little bit of anger. Anger that he could ever think I was having an affair, and anger that I couldn't tell him the truth: that we were on very different teams right now.

And anyway, I couldn't risk Nate feeling the gun strapped to my ankle, or the two phones in my pocket, or the prescriptions I'd swiped from the briefcase when his back was turned. I just wished that the physical distance didn't instantly result in an emotional one.

I suddenly remembered our first date, how he'd come with me to the hospital when one of my patients had died.

"I'm here for you," he'd said, squeezing my hand as we strode through the revolving doors together. And I knew right then what a good man he was. Deep and loyal and true.

At the time, I was working up to a hundred hours a week, my head throbbing, my eyes gritty. I downed energy drinks and drank coffee like it was water. I'd get to my car and fall asleep before I could even drive home and crawl in bed. I'd hesitated to go on our first date because of that, but those words—*I'm here for you*—were a grand gesture more romantic than any of the meals he could've made. I knew in that moment he was the one for me.

I wanted to reach out and touch him now. To let him fold me in his arms and tell me everything would be okay. I'd spent so much of my life feeling lonely, wanting to belong. Finally I had it, and I was pushing Nate away. He didn't deserve this.

"You know, we missed date night," he said sadly.

I floundered for a reply. Once a month, Moira babysat so we could go be husband and wife, not just mom and dad. He was right, we'd missed it this month. Worse, it hadn't even occurred to me.

"I'm sorry," I finally said.

He stared at me. "Yeah, that makes two of us."

My eyes burned, but I held his gaze. After a second, Nate took a step back. He drew an *X* over his heart and pointed at me. *I love you.* Then he turned and left the room.

A few seconds later, I heard the front door slam shut.

Nate was gone.

# CHAPTER 33

AS SOON AS NATE LEFT, I texted Ben.

> Nate's getting someone to sit on Violeta's house. I think
> they're waiting for you. Stay away.

He didn't reply, but I could see he'd read my message. After
I'd finished preparing the dinner Nate had started, I thought
about Gabe's earlier text.

> Ben's using again.

Okay, so I'd thrown Ben under the bus a little, but only out of
necessity. It wasn't like I wanted Ben to go to prison again, but
maybe he needed to go.

Like last time.

I texted Ben again. **Maybe you should stay at the warehouse.**

He didn't reply, and this time he didn't read the message. I found
myself increasingly agitated as the evening wore on, even as I sat
down with Josh while he watched *How the Grinch Stole Christmas*.

My phone rang. It was Cass Robbins.

"Hey, I'm not sure if you've heard, but Julia's in the ER right now," she said. "She was brought in a few hours ago."

"Oh my God!" Wanting to tune out the lyrics of "You're a Mean One, Mr. Grinch," I stood and moved into the kitchen. "What happened?"

"It looks like she overdosed on some oxy. One of the paramedics who brought her in said she was ranting about birdhouse pills."

"Birdhouse pills?" I echoed weakly.

*You're a monster, Mr. Grinch. Your heart's an empty hole.*

"Yeah. It doesn't make any sense. Maybe that was the logo on the pill. Do you think drug dealers have started naming oxy pills like they did ecstasy?"

I shook my head even though Cass couldn't see me.

*Your heart is full of unwashed socks, your soul is full of gunk, Mr. Grinch.*

"How's she doing?" I asked faintly.

"The paramedics gave her naloxone, but there's a lot of swelling in her brain. We've put her in a medically induced coma to give the swelling a chance to reduce. Check in tomorrow, and we'll see how she's doing. I'm sure she'll want to see a friendly face when she wakes up."

*If she wakes up.*

We both heard the words, even though neither of us said them out loud.

"Look, I've gotta get back to my shift," Cass said. "I just thought you'd want to know."

I thanked her and hung up, returning to the living room to sit next to Josh. Charlie jumped up onto the couch and curled into my side. I stroked one hand down his silky ears. After the movie had finished, I took Josh upstairs and tucked him into bed.

When I came downstairs, I checked my phone again, but there was still no response to my texts. I started on the dishes, thinking about Josh's CAR T-cell infusion tomorrow. I had the money in my secret checking account, ready to make the final payment tomorrow.

The tension that had kept me going for the last few weeks eased a little at the thought.

Soon this would all be over.

But I couldn't get something Gabe had said to me out of my head. When we'd stopped at McDonald's during the pillhead tour, Ben had gone to the bathroom, leaving Gabe and me on our own.

"What will you do after this?" I'd asked him. I waved a fry in the air so he knew "this" meant selling drugs, not just lunch.

He'd shrugged, chewing a massive bite of burger. "I'd like to get to know Josh. See what he's like."

"Gabe." I shook my head. "You know I can't allow that."

He didn't answer, just kept chewing.

"What about your girlfriend? Maybe you should settle down, get married, have kids. You'd be a great dad."

"Maybe." He seemed to think about it.

I stared at a grease-drenched fry, my stomach turning. "Will you and Ben keep going? Will you keep selling?"

He took another giant bite, shrugging. "Maybe. I don't know. Never hurts to have a little extra cash. I kinda have the perfect way to wash the money."

I snorted. "Cute. Illegally earning money to support an honest living."

He stared at me, still chewing. "What about you? Say Josh lives, you get everything paid off, what'll you do?"

"I'll go back to the way it was: working at the clinic, helping people, being a loving wife, dependable mom, and respected doctor."

Maybe my dreams were humbler, but at least they were honest, born from love, not greed.

It was his turn to snort. "You organized an opioid drug ring. People will be addicted because of you. They may die. You're not innocent here. . . ."

The sound of Josh crying wrenched me from my thoughts. I raced upstairs, Charlie at my heels, heart thudding with fear as I burst into Josh's bedroom. The room reeked of urine. Josh was sitting in bed, sobbing pitiful, jagged sobs that reached into my chest and wrenched at my heart.

"I'm sorry, Mommy!" he wept. "I peed myself!"

"Oh, my love." Tears scorched my throat. I knelt and drew him into my arms. "You don't have to be sorry. It's okay. It's not your fault. It's the chemo."

I held him as he cried, trying to reassure him, but he was mortified and inconsolable that he'd wet himself. It was a long time before he stopped crying, but once he'd calmed down I filled the bath with warm water and carefully lifted his fragile body in.

"My legs hurt so bad," he sniffed.

"I know, baby. I'm so sorry."

"And my fingers. Look." Josh lifted his fingers. Water slid off the wrinkled skin. My throat constricted.

His fingernails were peeling off the nail beds.

"Oh, Joshy. Let me get you the ice." I ran downstairs and filled a Tupperware bowl with ice and water. We'd been told to keep his hands and feet in ice baths to reduce the chances of him losing the nails, but it didn't look like it was working.

I put the bowl of ice water on my lap and he dipped his fingers in.

"Does it hurt?" I asked.

"A little."

I kissed Josh's bald head. "Not much longer. The Luke-Skywalker-esis is all trained up and you'll get your infusion tomorrow. Dr. Palmer will send those mini *Millennium Falcon*s into your blood and they'll start fighting the Empire, okay?"

Josh nodded.

"Are you worried?" I asked.

He shrugged

"You know, it's okay to feel lots of things at the same time, Joshy. You can feel scared and worried and excited. That's all okay. Those feelings are how you prepare for new challenges."

He looked at me from lashless eyes and asked: "Am I going to be sick?"

I hesitated, not wanting to lie, but desperate to reassure him. Nate and I had been warned that neurotoxicity and cytokine release syndrome, a form of systemic inflammatory response, were the most common side effects from CAR T-cell therapy. CRS could range from mild to severe, and was sometimes even fatal. But not every kid got it. We'd agreed that the short-term pain was worth the long-term gain.

"I'm not sure," I said, as honestly as I dared. "You might feel like you have the flu and you might throw up some."

My dad used to say, sometimes you're dealt a losing hand, and that really sucks. But if you always fold, you'll have a pretty tough time in life. Keep playing, keep fighting, and sometimes you can make that losing hand a winning one.

"Sweetheart, I am so, so sorry this is happening." My vision blurred with tears. "I would do anything to fix it for you."

"It's okay, Mommy. You didn't make me sick. It isn't your fault. And I'm really strong. I can keep fighting."

I choked out a little laugh. My sweet boy. He got it.

"You're doing so well, Joshy." I brushed my thumb across his cheek, tenderness throbbing in my belly. "You're so strong and you're going to fly through this. And Mommy and Daddy will be right here with you. Okay?"

Josh nodded and closed his eyes again. "Okay. Can I go back to bed now?"

"Of course."

I carefully lifted Josh out of the bath, wiping a fluffy towel over ribs that poked out like a skeleton's. I gently applied moisturizer to his skin, which was dry and flaking, and changed him into his too-baggy *Star Wars* pajamas.

I couldn't believe we'd only found out about Josh's illness less than a month ago. This horrible waiting felt like our new normal.

*Tomorrow,* I told myself. *Tomorrow he'll start getting better.*

Charlie flopped in a corner of the room as I put fresh sheets on Josh's bed. I lay next to him as he drifted off to sleep, letting myself remember when I was pregnant with Josh, his body floating inside mine, the tiny pings of his feet as they brushed against the skin that separated us. How strange it was that there was never a time in your life you could be so close to someone, but still so very, very far away. He was inside me but I couldn't hold him, couldn't touch him.

I'd watched him roll under my hands and ached for him to arrive. I wanted a family so much. I *deserved* a family.

After Josh was born, the doctor had lifted him onto my chest. I'd felt completely and hopelessly lost. He was so tiny; he'd arrived too early and his skin was a disturbing yellow. The nurses swept him away to get the care he needed. But even once he was better and we went home, I felt strangely disconnected.

As the days and nights wore on, I went through all the motions. I slept next to Josh, Nate almost relegated to a helper as I held our son, swaddled him, fed him, changed him. I wanted my mother. I wanted my father. I felt alone and adrift.

It wasn't until a few nights after we came home that the strange distance eased. Josh started crying and I stumbled to him, exhausted and delirious. But as soon as I picked him up he quieted, nuzzling into my chest, his tiny fingers gripping mine. I sat in the rocking chair, his little body pressed against mine, chest rising and falling, his soft newborn smell twining around me.

He'd looked up at me with that somber, wise expression infants have. And right there, in the stillness of night, I'd realized *this* was my family. Right here, in my arms.

I finally belonged.

Now Josh's breath came in wheezy little pants, his eyes pinched shut, as if even in his sleep he was warding off waves of pain. I felt so helpless. All I could do was hold him and tell myself that this treatment would fix him.

I was no longer a weak, helpless girl. I'd worked hard to shed her like a snake sheds its skin.

I would save him.

# CHAPTER 34

AFTER JOSH HAD FALLEN back asleep, I went downstairs, my mind returning to Gabe's text: Ben's using again.

I tried calling Ben, but he still wasn't answering. I was terri-fied he'd overdosed and was lying on the cold warehouse floor, his heartbeat slowing, his breath crushed in his lungs.

I called Gabe, but there was no answer from him either. Breaking my own rule, I tried his personal phone. He didn't an-swer, and when I tried calling again he'd turned his phone off.

I paced the living room, Charlie watching with large, inquisi-tive eyes from the couch. Finally, desperate and plagued by a fear of something I couldn't quite name, I went upstairs, wrapped a sleeping Josh in a big blanket, then bundled him into the car. I'd have to find Ben myself.

Josh woke as I pulled up next to the chain-link fence by the warehouse. "Where are we, Mommy?"

"I just need to check the tire. Stay here, okay? Don't get out or let anybody in no matter what, you hear me?"

Josh nodded and snuggled down under the blanket, seeming to go back to sleep. I hovered between my instinct to not leave my child in a dark car in the middle of the night and my fear that something horrible had happened to my brother.

I locked the car doors, slipped through the fence, and jogged quickly over the cracked cement. The moon cast silver streaks across the ground, lighting my way. Frost shimmered on the trees, the chill of darkness and a freezing wind pressing a heavy bleakness on me. My hands were stiff with cold. In the distance, the sound of the waterfall was a menacing roar, plumes of mist coating the air.

I passed a battered old motorcycle pushed into a large bush at the side of the warehouse. Ben's?

"Ben?" I stepped inside, instantly hit by the smell of damp.

The building was warmer than the last time I'd been here, but I shivered anyway. Water dripped insistently from the ceiling, a mournful, haunting sound that gave me the creeps.

"Ben?"

No reply.

I swept my flashlight over the cavernous space. The light cut through the murky darkness, revealing an open door next to the one leading to the room where Ben had been making the pills.

I crept toward it. "Ben?" I hissed.

I peered inside. A lantern flickered warily from the floor. The room was small, maybe an old storage closet, and stank of sweat and dirty clothes. I saw a backpack and a pair of old tennis shoes sitting atop a camper bed. I felt a wash of relief—Ben had gotten my warning text in time; he'd obviously packed up his stuff and come here.

Then I saw a figure on the floor.

"Ben!"

I rushed to him, dropping to my knees. I tugged on his shoulder and rolled him onto his back. His arm flopped limply against his chest. Something fluttered out of his hand onto the floor. A slash of crimson, like blood.

Damp, covered in mud, it was still unmistakably the silk scarf that Violeta had been wearing the night she died.

My stomach plunged. It must've come off when Gabe and I dragged her to the water. And Ben had found it.

I shoved the scarf into my back pocket. My brother's face was tinted a horrible bluish gray, and when I shined my flashlight in his eyes, his pupils were tiny, like flecks of pepper.

"Oh, no, no, no!"

I shoved my fingers against his carotid artery, checking for a pulse. He was alive. Barely, but his heart was still beating. The bigger problem right now was how shallow his breathing was. Respiratory depression.

I thought of the naloxone in my car. If Ben was overdosing from oxy, it would work. But I didn't have a high enough dose to treat fentanyl. Still, it was worth a try.

I raced back the way I'd come, shoving past the overgrown bushes at the side of the warehouse and staggering to my car. I threw open the trunk and fumbled with the zip of my first aid kit. I grabbed the naloxone and the needle, slammed the trunk closed. In the backseat, I saw Josh jump and twist to look at me with wide, frightened eyes. I put a finger up, motioning that I'd be right back.

In the warehouse, I knelt next to Ben.

"Come on. Come on."

I ripped the orange top off the vial and jabbed the needle into the top, carefully drawing the naloxone into the syringe.

My heart was thumping, but my hands were steady, the way I'd been trained. I yanked the collar of Ben's sweater down and plunged the needle into his shoulder.

Nothing happened.

"Ben, wake up!" I slapped him hard across the face. Still nothing.

I started on rescue breaths. I was on my third breath when

Ben twitched. His eyelids fluttered open. I sat back on my heels, tears blurring my vision.

"You're okay," I whispered, pulling his head onto my lap. My tears splashed onto his face. "Don't do that again! You're okay! Don't do that again!" I said over and over.

Ben blinked at me, dazed, then rolled onto his stomach and retched, dopesick and trembling.

"We have to get you to a hospital," I told him.

If there were enough opioids in his system, he could overdose again as soon as the naloxone wore off. The problem was, the hospital would report him to the police. He might go to jail. And what then? Would he talk?

No, of course not. Besides, I had Violeta's scarf now. And information that would keep him quiet.

"Come on." I grabbed Ben's coat and yanked it on him, then put an arm under his armpits and helped him to his feet.

He staggered next to me, disoriented and weak, teeth chattering, as I guided him to the car. "V . . . V . . ."

"Shhh." I heaved him into the front seat. "Everything's gonna be okay."

"Why . . . do you always . . . try to save me?" he slurred.

I reached across to buckle him in, but didn't answer. The truth was, I couldn't give up on him. Family was family. As long as there was breath in his lungs, I wouldn't give up hope that he could be saved.

*But you can't save someone who doesn't want to be saved,* an insidious voice whispered.

Suddenly headlights flashed and tires crunched as a car pulled up next to mine.

"You all right there?" a woman's voice called.

I straightened too fast, bashing my head against the roof. I rubbed my throbbing skull and squinted. The driver was an older woman, with sad, droopy eyes, snow-white hair. A stranger.

"We're fine," I called out.

"You sure?" She pushed her door open and started to get out.

"We're fine," I snapped, sounding harsher than I'd intended. "I'm a doctor. I've got it."

The woman hesitated, then climbed back in her car. "All right, if you're sure. Bye then."

I shut Ben's door and hurried around to the driver's side.

Josh was staring at me with wide eyes.

"Josh, this is your uncle Ben."

NATE AMBLED into the emergency room, throwing waves and grins like candy from a parade float. Kia followed like a dark shadow in his wake, looking like she'd eaten a sour grape.

I watched my husband and rubbed my forehead. How did he do it? He never appeared to hurry, to worry. Only I could see the strain in his eyes, the pinch at the corners of his mouth. The toll his latest case and Josh's illness were taking.

"Hey, babe. Thanks for calling me." He kissed my cheek with his eyes open. He knelt and stroked a hand over Josh's head, which was on my lap as he dozed.

I couldn't have Nate finding out Ben was here from someone else, so I'd called him as soon as the doctors had admitted Ben, telling him my brother had called me from Target. I'd been waiting here since Cass had wheeled him into the emergency room. Before she'd come to get him, Ben had stared at me with wide, questioning eyes from where he was lying on a gurney.

"V . . . V . . ." He could barely wrap his tongue around his words, the sound pouring slow as wet asphalt from his mouth.

"Everything's going to be okay," I'd reassured him.

"Vvvv . . . !" He was getting agitated.

I pressed him down onto the gurney. "Shhh!" I hissed. I bent lower and whispered to him: "That scarf you have, was it Violeta's?"

He nodded.

"I saw it in Gabe's back pocket. He had it when he met me at the hospital."

Ben's eyes widened. My gaze darted to Cass, who was approaching.

"Listen to me carefully," I whispered. "Nate thinks you killed Santiago. He's going to question you, maybe arrest you. Don't say a word. He doesn't have any evidence, just theories. I'll fix this for us, but you just have to stay quiet."

Ben had slumped back onto the gurney, eyes closed, as Cass arrived. He nodded, and I knew I'd bought myself a little time.

"What's going to happen to Ben?" I asked Nate now.

He sat next to me. "Ben's a person of interest in our case. Kia will question him and find out if he has any information once he's stable. When he's released, we'll likely bring him in for more formal questioning."

"You mean you'll arrest him."

"Only if he refuses to be questioned."

"He didn't kill that guy, Nate. He's been in rehab."

"I already told you, Em." Nate's shoulders tensed. "I'll check. Just let me finish my investigation."

Fury and helplessness overwhelmed me. My husband's unimpeachable sense of right and wrong was something I'd loved when we first met. But now it felt like a trap. *Good*, I'd learned, meant different things to different people. I wanted to lie on the ground and scream and rail against the unfairness of it all.

I was a fool. I'd thought Ben could stay clean. I should've known addiction was indiscriminate and eternal. It invaded the homes of rich and poor, black and white, young and old. Its effects were far-reaching, its causes deep. And it never, never went fully away.

As a family, we'd never told people about Ben's problem or talked about it with friends. It was a secret. Our family's nasty little secret. The night my parents were killed, they'd been picking me up from a friend's house when Dad's cell phone rang. It was one of Ben's friends calling to say they couldn't wake Ben up.

As with so many other things, Ben was to blame for our parents' deaths.

I shouldn't have trusted him, and now people were dying. How high had he been when he'd been mixing the fentanyl with oxy? Too high to use the right measurements, that was for sure. Julia had overdosed today. Alice Jones had died. Had they both taken the pills he'd mixed? How many others were at risk?

I looked at Josh asleep on my lap. A rush of tenderness filled me as I watched his eyelids flutter in sleep. He was the biggest love of my life. Being his mother was what gave me meaning, what made everything in this whole crazy world make sense.

I traced the shape of his face: his small, pert nose; his sharp chin, so much like mine. But the rounded hillocks of his cheekbones, his generous mouth and wide smile, the glint he got sometimes in his eyes, those were his father's.

I thought of the paternity test I had in a sealed envelope at the bottom of my jewelry box.

I should throw it away. Gabe had become a liability, and it wasn't like I needed him anymore. I'd been lucky so far; Gabe was sexy but not particularly bright. He'd never even asked where I'd gotten his DNA for a comparison match. I'd only offered to show him the paternity test because it didn't show a name. It just said *Probability of Paternity* and *Alleged Father*. I'd only kept it at the time because I was worried Nate would ask for proof that Josh was his baby. He knew I'd dated someone before we got together.

But he'd never asked.

For a cop, Nate could be very blind. Sometimes he only saw what he wanted to see.

I gathered Josh in my arms and stood, giving Nate a cool good-bye. "I'll see you at home."

And I turned and walked away.

# CHAPTER 35

NATE OPENED THE BOX that had arrived on his desk at the station this morning and looked at his Christmas present for Emma. Even though it had been tense between them lately, his wife was still the dream of his heart. Things would get better, he had to believe. As soon as Josh got this treatment and he cracked this case, they would go back to the way they had been.

He smiled as he pulled a sheet of wrapping paper he'd bought out of his desk and wrapped the gift. She was going to love it.

He signed the tag and tucked the present in a drawer, then hurried outside. There was one more thing he had to do today.

Nate squinted against the early-morning sun as he parked at the Northwestern Nursing Home. With its gleaming red brick and fluted white pillars wrapped in twinkling lights, it looked more like his college fraternity house at Christmas than his dad's nursing home.

He signed in and followed the hallway to the back. He could hear carolers singing "Jingle Bells" in the common room. The smell of pumpkin pie and evergreen trees hung in the air, Christmas lights flashing cheerfully in the hallway. Nate caught sight of his own pale, drawn face as he passed the silver ornaments on the Christmas tree.

Christmas was only three days away. He had just over a week until Lieutenant Dyson took the case from him.

Matt was sitting in a wheelchair next to his bedroom window, staring glassy-eyed outside. The left side of his face drooped, a line of drool dripping down his chin. He looked tiny and frail, but at least he was up and out of bed. It was a damn sight better than what Nate had expected, seeing as he'd had pneumonia last week.

"Hey, Dad."

Nate kissed the top of his head and used a tissue to wipe the drool away. Matt didn't look at him. Sometimes Nate wondered if his dad even knew he was there. But his mom was right: it was time he stopped hiding from what his father had become and accepted him for who he was now.

He tucked a faded blue blanket over Matt's lap and wheeled him to a corner table in the nursing home's indoor garden.

He sat down, moving the old Nokia he'd found in the briefcase from his trouser pocket to his coat, a reminder to stop by Best Buy and grab a charger for it.

After a minute he started talking. He told Matt how Josh was, how Moira was coping, and how proud he was of Emma's work.

"Mom told me about the dealers. The money," he said. "I can't figure out if I should be grateful to you or . . ." *Hate you*, he finished silently. He stared at his hands, not sure where to go from there.

"Unhh." The unexpected sound startled Nate. Matt was trying to move, trying to roll his neck.

"Are you okay, Dad?" Nate knelt in front of his father, and for just a second, a fleeting, beautiful second, Matt met his gaze.

"Unhh." A solitary tear dripped from the corner of Matt's eye. Nate watched it slide down the roughened, wrinkled skin and plop onto the blanket on his lap. "Unhh."

Nate grasped his father's bony hand. "I know, Dad." He pressed his forehead to his father's, swallowing back tears. "I know. You did your best to take care of us. I get it."

Matt's eyes fluttered shut, as if he didn't have the strength to keep them open any longer. They'd lapsed into silence when a woman approached.

"Nate? Remember me?"

It was Robbie's mom, Marsha Sadler.

"Mrs. Sadler. Yes, of course I remember. Here, sit here." Nate pulled over another chair.

She sat next to him. "I wasn't sure you did; you ran out of the grocery store so fast when I saw you the other day!"

"Sorry, I had a call. Work." He gestured to his suit and tie. "I'm a detective."

"Yes, I heard. Wade told me you're a fine detective. You're married to that doctor now."

"Wade?" Nate barely remembered Robbie's dad.

"My ex now. We divorced. After Robbie . . . there wasn't much to save, you know? But we stayed friends. He had a stroke a few months back. That's why I'm here." She looked at her hands. "We're both proud of you. All the good you've done."

Nate flushed. *Good.* A word he'd spent his life failing to live up to.

He rolled a toothpick between his fingers. "Mrs. Sadler, I've wanted to tell you something for a long time." Nate took a deep breath. "Robbie was being bullied at school. The day he . . . I was angry because he'd ratted me out about a test me and some of the other guys had cheated on. They beat him up, and I didn't stop them. I'm so sorry."

"Oh, honey, Robbie told me what happened. But you didn't do anything."

"That's exactly it. I knew what they were going to do and I didn't do *anything*."

Mrs. Sadler nodded slowly. "And now you regret that?"

"I was a coward." Shame burned in Nate's stomach.

"The way I figure it, being able to feel regret is the strongest sign of a good person. People who regret nothing are either saints or stupid. Those people do destructive things without insight. And they cause irreparable damage to their families and friends."

Mrs. Sadler reached for his free hand, cradled it in hers. Her fingers were bony and cold, the nails long, painted a garish pink. She stared at the dried crusts of blood and purple bruises on his fingernails. Nate pulled his hand away, suddenly embarrassed by the way he eased his pain.

"Sometimes we make decisions that might not be the smartest ones, but they teach us who we are and who we want to be. But don't use regret as a stick to beat yourself. Use it as a tool for doing better." She met his gaze. "No one action defines us—it's the journey that determines if we're a good person or not."

Nate saw nothing but compassion in her eyes. Forgiveness. Something cracked inside him then. Maybe he'd just needed to hear it out loud, to feel Robbie's mother's grace, before he could forgive himself.

"Thanks, Mrs. Sadler."

"Of course." She clapped her hands on her knees and stood to go. "Hey, how's your wife? I saw her last night near the old Ska-mania Mill."

"You saw Emma?" Nate tried to hide his surprise.

"Yeah. I recognized her from a picture Wade showed me. She was helping a guy who looked a little worse for wear. Were they all right?"

"Yes," Nate said slowly.

Emma must've found Ben at the old mill warehouse. So why had she told Nate she found him in the Target parking lot?

He thought of the icy glare Emma had given him when he'd admitted he was probably going to arrest Ben. He knew his wife, and something was up.

Something to do with Ben.

He was terrified to find out what it was.

THE ELEVATOR doors dumped Nate into the hospital's main entrance. He'd stopped by the clinic upstairs and spoken to Marjorie. Turned out the patient who'd filled the suspicious prescription for OxyContin signed by Dr. Wallington wasn't registered there. And when Nate had done a quick online search with the state's Department of Licensing, he'd learned that person had died in a car accident four years before.

Somebody was signing prescriptions and using fake IDs to fill them for dead people.

It had to be Julia. She had access and she'd been caught stealing oxy. Plus she was clearly using her own product.

But Julia was in a coma. He couldn't talk to her. Nate growled in frustration.

What he really wanted to know was how many other doctors' prescription pads she'd stolen.

Nate suddenly had a horrible sinking feeling. What if Julia had stolen Emma's pads too? Would the scandal, the investigation that would likely come, damage her career?

Nate glanced at his watch. He needed to call Agent Hamilton and update her. She would probably have to kick this upstairs in the DEA, and if Emma became a focus of the investigation, there was no hope he'd be allowed to stay on the case. But first, Josh was getting his reprogrammed cells injected today, and Nate had to be there for his son.

He rounded the corner and spotted Josh and Emma in front of the hospital café. Emma was talking to a tall, broad-chested man with streaky, beach-blond hair tied into a stubby ponytail. His jaw prickled with a few days' stubble, and he had those deep dimples women always found so attractive.

Emma caught sight of Nate. It was only brief, the widening of her eyes, but he saw it.

Guilt.

A rush of hot jealousy bloomed bitter and thick in his throat. Emma had been lying to him, Nate was sure of it. She was having an affair after all.

"Nate, hi," she said.

Nate ignored her and picked Josh up, hoping to cover the storm of emotions filling him. "Hey, buddy! You ready for your infusion?"

Josh nodded listlessly, his fingers in his mouth.

"Nate, this is Gabe Wilson," Emma said. "We went to high school together. He's visiting family here."

Nate put on his most charming smile. "Nice to meet you, man." He turned to Emma, already blocking Gabe out. "Ready to go?"

He clasped Josh to him like a shield and turned and walked toward the elevators, giving her no choice but to jog after him.

Moira was already waiting for them upstairs in Pediatric Oncology.

"Thanks for coming, Ma." Nate kissed her cheek.

"You know I wouldn't miss this!" She hugged Josh gently. He giggled and Emma watched him, smiling.

At the sound of Josh's giggle, the band that had been cinching tighter and tighter around Nate's chest this last month eased just a little. As long as Josh was okay, that was all that mattered.

They followed Katie to their private room. Dr. Palmer came in as she was giving Josh a dose of Tylenol and Benadryl. "It'll reduce his chances of having an allergic reaction to the preservative the T-cells have been frozen in," Katie explained.

"You ready to go to battle, Captain Smiley?" Dr. Palmer fist-bumped Josh.

"Let's do this!" Josh made lightsaber noises, slashing his pretend weapon through the air.

Katie fixed a line into the catheter connected to Josh's port. It was attached to a huge machine, where the T-cells had been warmed and readied for injection.

"Is that it?" Josh asked, eyes wide.

Katie laughed. "That's it."

"Now what do we do?"

"This will only take about two minutes, but you'll have to stay here for a few hours so we can make sure you're all good, okay?"

"I s'pose so." Josh rested his head back in the chair, his eyes drooping.

"You feeling a little sleepy?" Katie asked.

Josh nodded.

"That's perfectly normal. It's the Benadryl. Go ahead and get some rest." She turned to Nate, Emma, and Moira. "I'll check on him every half hour, but ring the bell if you need me. If everything goes well, we'll let him go home in three hours. Hopefully the new T-cells will start killing the cancer cells within a week."

After she and the doctor had gone, Moira stood and announced she was going to grab a coffee from the family room, leaving Emma and Nate in a thick silence punctuated only by Josh's gentle snores.

Katie bustled back in with an envelope. "Jill up at the front desk asked me to give you your receipt." She handed the envelope to Emma and left.

Nate looked at Emma. "Receipt for what?"

Emma's face had drained of all color. She swallowed hard, her eyes darting around, like she was looking for somewhere to run. She was trying to come up with a lie.

Before she could react, he swiped the envelope out of her hands.

"Nate!" she protested, grabbing at it, but he'd already slit the envelope open and was holding the receipt in his hand.

He couldn't seem to make sense of it, though.

Emma had paid Cascade Regional Hospital $98,004.

Nate's fingers went numb. The receipt fluttered to the floor as he tried to comprehend what he was seeing. Where the fuck had Emma gotten $98,004?

"Emma," he whispered. "What have you done?"

Emma's face had gone stony, her jaw set. "I think it's best if you don't know."

# CHAPTER 36

NATE STRODE QUICKLY ACROSS the hospital parking lot away from his wife. The sky was the color of a bruise, wet leaves slapping against his ankles. His pulse kicked hard in his veins. His stomach was tied in knots.

Kia had called to say they'd gotten Violeta's credit card statement, and he'd jumped at the chance to get away from Emma. She was still refusing to tell him where she'd gotten the $98,004 to pay the hospital.

He couldn't wrap his head around any of it. All Emma would say was that it had been required for Josh to get the infusion, although she'd promised to explain everything later, when they got home.

"We have to focus on Josh right now," she'd hissed. "We can't jeopardize his recovery."

So while Kia headed to the hospital to interview Ben, Nate left and drove to the gas station where Violeta had made her last purchase.

The gas station was about a half hour away, and Nate spent

the entire time trying to work out where the money could have come from. His windshield wipers shoved desperately at the rain, his aching head pounding with every swipe. He knew that Emma had received some money from her parents' life insurance. He thought it had all been used up on medical school, but maybe she'd had some left.

Or maybe it had come from Ben.

Which begged the question: Was it legal money?

Had Ben stolen it? But from whom? There had been no reports of large sums of cash being stolen in the area.

Nate's head hurt. All the jigsaw pieces he'd been putting together in his mind were shifting and reassembling in a different order, but he still couldn't see the whole picture.

Nate parked outside a small redbrick gas station. Inside the old-fashioned building were rows of snacks and a wall of soft drinks. A very young woman with white-blond hair smiled at him from behind the cash register.

"May I help, please?" She had a thick Scandinavian accent and eyes so blue it made Nate think of canoeing on Lake Chelan with his dad as a kid.

"Hello, are you the owner?"

"Oh no." She giggled, a cute, childish sound. "That would be my boyfriend. He isn't here right now."

"What's his name?"

"Gabe. Gabe Wilson. Shall I tell him you were asking for him?"

Nate felt like the girl had punched him in the throat.

Gabe Wilson.

The same man who'd been with Emma this morning.

Nate didn't know what the connection was, but it felt important. His Spidey sense was buzzing, and he knew never to ignore his Spidey sense. He put his elbows on the counter and leaned in closer, offering the girl his most charming smile.

"Well"—he read the name tag pinned to her shirt—"Kari. I'm Detective Nate Sweeney. I have a murder victim who last used her credit card here."

The smile dropped off Kari's face.

He pointed to the video camera above the counter. "How long does that record for?"

"Thirty days."

"I'm going to need to see it."

"I . . . don't know if that's allowed."

He thumped his badge on the counter. "I suppose I could always question you down at the station. You'd need to grab your ID and lock up the gas station, of course."

Kari's eyes darted sideways. "Gabe, he should be here soon—"

"This is time-sensitive, Kari. You understand."

Her shoulders dropped. "Okay, come with me."

He followed her to a back office with a desktop computer, floor-to-ceiling filing cabinets, and a printer. She clicked the mouse and pulled up the video surveillance footage. Nate gave her the date of Violeta's purchase, and she opened the file, then got up so Nate could sit and watch it.

The footage was grainy, opaque, but he could make out Violeta buying two packs of cigarettes, a pack of gum, and a handful of junk food from Gabe. There was no audio, but they spoke for a few minutes, Violeta saying something and Gabe laughing. After a moment, Gabe grabbed his coat and locked up the shop, and they left.

Nate watched in fast-forward as the night passed and moved into the next day. Gabe came in and opened the shop, Kari entered, then exited. There was nothing that stuck out. So he clicked into the day before. People came in and out, paying for gas and buying food from the grocery section.

And then he saw something that made his stomach drop. A

woman putting a sheaf of small, square papers on the counter in front of Gabe.

His wife.

NATE DROVE FAST, his lights flashing. He pulled up to Stevie McGraw's home, a rusting double-wide trailer parked on an end lot in Mill Creek. The trailer had an air of neglect about it. The tiny yard was overgrown, shingles falling from the roof, the yellow siding peeled and cracking.

*The perfect hideout for a teenage scumbag,* Nate thought unkindly.

He hammered on the door. Stevie opened it and scowled at Nate, black hair tangled in a gnarled rat's nest. He looked weird without his horn-rimmed glasses, younger somehow.

"I need your help."

"Why would I wanna help a cop?"

"Because I can make those possession charges from a few weeks ago disappear."

Stevie smiled widely. "In that case, come on in, man. *Mi casa es su casa.*"

The trailer was a mess—stacks of newspapers on the dining table, dishes in the sink, clothes strewn across the furniture. The faint smell of pot permeated everything.

Stevie crossed to a woman asleep on the couch and pulled a blanket to her chin. He caught Nate watching and shrugged, grabbing his glasses from the coffee table and shoving them on. "My mom has MS. Today's a bad day. Anyway, what do you want my help with?"

Nate tried not to look surprised. "I need some video footage enhanced. Do you know anybody who has that sort of technology?"

"Why don't you take it to your guys?"

"Come on, I'm sure you know people who have technology capability five times better than my guys'."

"Let me have a look," Stevie said.

Nate emailed Stevie the file from his phone and followed him down a narrow hallway. They passed a room with black light bleeding under the door.

Stevie shook his head. "Don't look over there."

In contrast to the rest of the house, Stevie's bedroom was surprisingly neat. Pushed against the far wall was a single bed made with military precision. A white bedside table held a couple of cute little cacti and a stack of books by French poet Charles Baudelaire. Nate squinted to read the title of the top one: *The Flowers of Evil.*

Stevie's desk took up most of the rest of the room, with two extra-large monitors, a couple of huge speakers, and a sleek Mac-Book Pro.

Yesterday Nate would've bet his annual salary that this stuff was stolen. But today? Shit, what did he know?

Next to the desk Nate spotted a couple of plastic storage containers, each meticulously labeled: EXTENSION CORDS, CABLES, PHONE CHARGERS.

Pulling the old Nokia phone from his pocket, Nate held it up and pointed at the containers. "Do you have a charger for this?"

Stevie looked at the phone. "Probably."

He popped the lid off one of the storage bins and rifled through, finally tugging out a cord that was precisely wrapped into a neat figure eight. He found an empty socket and plugged the phone in for Nate, then sat in front of his computer.

Stevie's fingers flew over the keyboard as he clicked into some fancy-looking video software. He opened the file to the time stamp Nate had given him.

"There!" Nate pointed at the screen. "Can you see what she's giving him?"

Stevie clicked the mouse. The grainy shot gradually cleared. He zoomed in and did the same again. Eventually a pixelated but clear shot emerged. The paper Emma was holding out to Gabe was a signed prescription for OxyContin from Allegiance Health Clinic.

Tightness banded around Nate's ribs as all the pieces started clicking neatly into place.

He thought about Emma meeting Gabe this morning. Her lie about picking Ben up at Target. He thought about the business card from Allegiance Health Clinic that had been found on Violeta Williams's body and how she'd died of the same drug used on Santiago Martinez. He thought about the prescriptions being signed by Dr. Wallington and Emma's reaction when he'd found the briefcase.

And then he thought of Julia.

*Birdhouse pills.*

*Tell Emma.*

Nate suddenly felt very, very naïve for thinking it was just an affair that Emma was involved in.

Someone from the clinic was fraudulently signing prescriptions for opioids.

Someone who needed money fast.

Someone connected to Ben, who was connected to Martinez, who was connected to Williams. It was all tied together. The drugs. The murders.

And he knew. Maybe on some level he'd known all along.

Emma was involved in all of it.

# CHAPTER 37

MY CELL PHONE VIBRATED.

Not my usual phone. My secret one.

Moira glanced up from her book, sending me a questioning look over Josh's sleeping form. She'd heard it.

I made a phone-call motion with my thumb and pinkie and stepped into the hall. In the accessible bathroom, I locked the door and pulled my secret phone from my back pocket, quickly returning Gabe's call.

He was speaking so fast I could barely understand what he was saying.

"Gabe, slow down!" I hissed.

"Your husband was here, at my gas station! He looked through the video surveillance recording!"

"Shit." I sat on the toilet, my legs weak.

I'd planned to tell Nate I'd paid for Josh's treatment with money I'd saved from my parents' life insurance. He would be mad, but not *you've-been-illegally-selling-oxy* mad.

But if Nate had seen the video footage of me giving Gabe the signed prescriptions, there was no way he'd believe that.

I felt the silken threads of the web I'd created tightening around me.

"That briefcase of Violeta's," I said. "He got it open."

A moan, sharp and barbed, came from Gabe. "What was inside?"

"Drugs and cash. And an old Nokia phone. What was on that phone? Did you text her on it?"

"No. But Ben did."

"What'd he say?"

"I don't know for sure, but they definitely arranged for Vi and me to meet at Target and then meet you at the warehouse." A strangled moan rose from Gabe's throat. "This is a fucking nightmare, Emma! I can't go to jail."

"Shut up, let me think," I snapped.

I closed my eyes. I didn't regret it. Not a thing. The prescriptions I'd written, the drugs I'd helped sell, every single lie I'd told—they had all made it possible to pay the $98,000 I needed for Josh's treatment today.

But now Nate knew.

And he would be coming here looking for more answers.


I WAITED outside the hospital entrance until Nate's cruiser pulled up. The sky was now a muted shade of pewter. The air was sharp with cold and frost, smelling of woodsmoke and the copper-kettle scent of impending snow.

My fingers tingled with nervous energy as Nate strode toward me. All that was left to do was tell him the truth. Josh was his son, and he was a good father.

Nate stopped in front of me, his eyes hard and closed off.

"It was you all along," he finally said.

I neither confirmed nor denied it. I simply turned and strode inside, tossing over my shoulder, "Let's find a private room."

I passed the towering Christmas tree in reception and headed toward the emergency room. I pushed open the door to an empty family room, the same room where Dr. Palmer had told us about Josh's diagnosis just a month ago.

I sat on the couch, but Nate remained standing.

"Tell me."

It was too late to hide anything, and to be honest I was tired of all the lies. So I told him the truth.

"I set up a drug ring selling oxycodone to make enough money to pay for Josh's immunotherapy treatment."

"Is that how you got the ninety-eight thousand?"

"Yes. When I tried to start the insurance claim for Josh's treatment, they told me they would only pay for his T-cells to be harvested, not reprogrammed. They said I had to pay the ninety-eight thousand dollars directly to the hospital for him to be able to get the infusion."

Nate blinked, his mouth pressed into a grim line. "So you stole prescription pads from your clinic and forged your colleagues' signatures."

His words struck me, staccato bursts that smacked me hard across each cheek.

"Yes. There was no other way to get that much money that fast."

"It wasn't Julia."

"Julia did steal oxy samples. She's addicted to it for her chronic pain. But, no, she didn't take the prescription pads."

"And Ben?"

"He's helping me."

A muscle in Nate's cheek flexed as he put together the pieces he knew. "At the warehouse, right? That's where you're making pills."

I hesitated.

"Someone I know saw you with Ben there. I figure that's where you're doing it. All these autopsy reports on overdoses I've seen lately, the one thing they have in common is oxy with elevated levels of fentanyl. Where'd you get the fentanyl?"

"I didn't get any fentanyl," I objected.

Nate pulled out a phone—the old Nokia from the briefcase—and read a text out: "Meet Gabe at Target in Skamania. He'll take you to warehouse to talk to Emma. I'll get fentanyl from the doc."

I frowned. Had he meant *for* the doc, not *from* the doc?

And then I remembered: Ben had said I wasn't the only medical professional he'd worked with.

"That doc isn't me," I said. "I didn't give them the fentanyl. Ben already had it. I just did the OxyContin prescriptions."

Nate's gaze was skeptical.

Despair, black and sticky, clawed at me.

"I'm telling you the truth!" I insisted. "I stole the prescription pads from the clinic. I took them to Gabe and asked for help selling the scripts because he used to deal. He put me in contact with a woman named Violeta Williams, Ben's girlfriend. But I never got any fentanyl."

"What happened to her?"

I chewed my lip, thinking about the red scarf I'd hidden under the spare tire in my car. It was nearly time to use it.

"After I left, she snorted some fentanyl thinking it was cocaine. Gabe called me in a panic saying she was overdosing. I told him to take her to the hospital. I thought that was the end of it until I saw on the news she'd been found in the river."

Nate looked horrified, his face the gray of the very ill. "How could you keep that from me? You knew I was investigating her death. Hers and Santiago Martinez's. Do you know what happened to him?"

"I swear on my life, Nate, I have no idea. I never met the guy."

Nate rubbed his hands over his face. When he dropped them and his eyes landed on mine they were dark, repulsed. He shook his head. "I thought I knew you."

I stiffened. "You *do* know me. I'm your wife, the mother of your son, and I will do *anything* to make sure he lives. Don't act like this hasn't changed everything. It has. Because of *me*, Josh will live. *Me!* I *saved* him."

"You need to stop this."

"I can't."

"Emma, people are dying!"

"Regrettable collateral damage. Ben messed up the dosage, but it won't happen again. We are helping more people than we're hurting."

"What, it's okay if a few people die, as long as you're helping some others?"

"Not just *others*, I'm helping Josh. *Our son.* He's my priority."

I moved to stand directly in front of Nate, taking his hands in mine. "If I hadn't done this, Josh would've died."

"You don't know that."

"I do. I've read the literature on children with his type of leukemia. I've read the statistics on recovery. This treatment is the only one on the market that holds any hope. He would have died, Nate."

Nate shook his hands free and stepped away from me. "You *know* this isn't right."

"It isn't *ideal*. But that doesn't mean it isn't right," I corrected him. "Sometimes we have to do the wrong thing for the right reason. Maybe it was wrong to sign those prescriptions, but Josh will live because I did. The ends justify the means. Everything I've done is for the right reason. You know that."

Nate pressed his lips tight together. "No. *How* we get to our goal is just as important as achieving it."

"Then call me as a bad person, I don't care. I don't regret anything I had to do to save Josh's life. At least I *did* something. I'm not sitting here helpless, watching him die."

Nate pinched the skin between his eyebrows.

"The overdose rate would've increased with or without me," I said. "I'm helping people who have genuine pain. Sometimes they've been cut off by doctors, or their insurance doesn't cover it, or they can't afford it. These people aren't overdosing—"

"Except the people who took the pills with too much fentanyl in them," Nate cut me off viciously.

"I'm *helping* people," I repeated.

"You're a drug dealer hiding behind a white coat."

I bristled at that. Ben was a drug dealer. Gabe was a drug dealer. I wasn't dealing anything. I was helping people, and in the process saving my son.

"Josh is all that matters."

"You think our son's life is more important than somebody else's?"

I couldn't believe he was even asking me that.

"Yes," I exclaimed. "Josh is *the* most important thing. He's why I did this. For him, for us. For my family."

Nate's hands clenched at his sides. "Saving Josh won't bring your parents back."

Silence cracked through the room, and sharp nerves needled my stomach.

"Are you done?" he asked after a minute. "Is it over?"

I didn't answer right away. "Josh could still die. We have to make sure he gets every treatment he needs."

Nate stared at me like he didn't recognize me. "So that's a no?"

"It's an 'I don't know.'"

He shook his head again. "Everyone always thinks their thing is the right thing, but we can't all be doing the right thing. That's why we have laws."

"Are you going to turn me in?"

Nate's mouth flopped open, then closed. "I . . . I don't know. I don't know what the right thing to do is here."

I crossed the room, ran the leaves of the wilted spider plant through my fingertips. When I spoke, my voice was cold and harsh. "How would turning me in be the *right* thing? My career would be over, we'd lose my health insurance, I'd go to jail. You think they'll promote you to lieutenant after finding out your wife was running an opioid drug ring? And, what, you conveniently never knew? Some detective." I snorted derisively. "We'd never be able to pay for any of Josh's treatments. He could die and it would be your fault. That wouldn't be the *right* thing!"

Nate's face had gone an even starker shade of gray. He searched my face, his eyes tortured.

"Emma. Shit!" He collapsed into the couch. "What have you gotten us into?"

Nate's phone beeped, and he glanced at it. "I don't suppose you know anything about a girl named Beatrice Flores?"

I tried to place the name.

He held his phone out to me. On the screen was a mug shot of a girl, maybe seventeen or eighteen, with dark hair and patches of lighter skin on her face and hands.

Dread bloomed black and bilious in my stomach.

Beatrice Flores. The girl with vitiligo who'd seen me at the clinic.

"Her body was found this morning in the forest over by the old mill warehouse," he said.

I could no longer get enough oxygen into my lungs. Pain circled my chest, swirling and unbearable.

I'd told Ben she'd seen me.

I slumped onto the couch next to Nate. A misty veil of tears covered my eyes, turning the fronds of the plant beside me to bony, accusatory fingers. Everything was falling apart. I was losing control of all of it.

How do you defuse a bomb of your own making?

Nate knelt in front of me. "Tell me, Em," he said urgently. "Tell me what you know. We can get through this. We can still do the right thing."

I looked into Nate's eyes and realized what he was offering me. An olive branch. A slim, tenuous branch to grasp onto. One he would use to pull me out of this.

He needed a fall guy. Someone to blame for everything. And I would give it to him.

I leaned forward, my breath hot against his cheek, and whispered one word.

"Ben."

# CHAPTER 38

NATE BACKED AWAY FROM EMMA, his fingers already on his phone.

"What are you going to do?" Emma asked. Her voice was shrill, the sharp pitch of an out-of-tune violin.

The truth was, he didn't know what he was going to do. He shook his head, twisted the doorknob, but just as he was about to leave she called him back.

"You need to trust me, Nate."

He looked at his wife, understanding that her words were a warning. Emma's face betrayed no emotion. She was cool and calm, retreating behind the cold mask he'd been seeing more and more. No softness, no vulnerability.

He wanted to trust her. He always had. He'd trusted her empathy and her compassion, her desire to help others. He'd trusted what a wonderful, devoted mother and wife she was. He just couldn't reconcile those parts of her with what she'd done.

*The ends justify the means.*

But what if they never reached the end?

Emma had done something wrong. But could he really turn her in to Hamilton and Greene when she'd done it for the right reason? Could he risk Josh getting even sicker because they couldn't pay for his treatments, watch her get arrested, ruin her career, *his* career, their marriage, their family?

He backed away from her.

"Nate?" Emma drew an *X* across her chest and pointed at him. *We're in this together*, she was saying. *Tell me you still love me.*

She needed reassurance. She needed him on her side.

Nate opened his mouth to reply, to say something, but he realized he couldn't. There were no words left to say.

NATE DROVE too fast away from the hospital, the familiar mantra ricocheting like golf balls through his head:

*You're a bad person.*

*You're cowardly. Weak.*

*Nobody can trust you.*

Maybe if he hadn't been so focused on Ben. Or Julia. Or on thinking his wife was having an affair. Maybe he would have seen it: her desperation to save Josh. Maybe he could've stopped it. But he'd missed it, and now he had no idea what to do.

No matter what, he'd lose something: his wife or his integrity.

Nate raced up the road toward the location Kia had texted him. He turned right to cross the bridge and was greeted by flashing lights as he parked next to the hiking path that led to the bottom of the waterfall.

He followed the path along a series of sharp switchbacks. The clouds were rushing like freighters through the sky. It was colder here, the air saturated with moisture from the waterfall's spray. Small pellets of freezing water dashed against his head. The light quickly turned gray as the woods closed around him.

Nate had always loved the woods. When he'd lived in Seattle, surrounded by so much pavement and tall glass buildings, he'd missed the cool, peaceful beauty of the forest, the sharp call of crickets and the gentle murmur of the leaves rustling in the wind. Now, of course, everything was dying, the plants saturated, the ground muddy. But the evergreens still kept their glossy coats, even in the deepest depths of winter, a reminder that life continued around us, even in the darkest season.

Now he could hear the distant thrum of the waterfall pounding over the rocks. He could never hear that sound without remembering Robbie's suicide, the temporary grave his body had found in the river.

Something prickled up the skin of Nate's neck and he stopped, looked around. He felt a pervading sense of menace, something dark descending. He heard voices and saw Kia standing next to a few uniforms. Dr. Kathi Morris, the pathologist, was bent over a body on the ground among the trees about fifty feet from the path.

Nate greeted them and bent to look at Beatrice Flores as he pulled a pair of latex gloves from his pocket and slipped them on. She looked younger in death than she had in her mug shot, her eyes closed as if she were sleeping. Her skin was tinted a bluish color, patches of lighter skin marbling through the dark.

"She was found by a woman walking her dog," Kia said quietly. She nodded at a pale elderly woman and a small dog being attended to by paramedics farther along the path.

"Overdose?" Nate asked.

"Most likely."

"It's a strange place for it." Nate turned to Dr. Morris. "How long has she been out here?"

"A few hours," she replied. "Rigor mortis is established around her neck and jaw but less marked elsewhere. So I'd say three to four hours. Livor mortis is on her right side, but she was found flat on her back, indicating she was dumped here."

Nate pinched the bridge of his nose. His bruised fingers throbbed.

Kia looked at him curiously. "You okay?"

Nate nodded. He had to get a grip.

"Can you check the back of her neck?" he asked Dr. Morris. "See if there's a puncture wound."

Dr. Morris wrapped an arm around Beatrice's shoulders and heaved her onto her side. The girl's long hair slid over her face. Nate knelt and scooped it off her neck, gently tucking it behind her ears.

They peered closely at the skin on her neck.

"There," Kia said. She pointed at a tiny drop of blood that had formed just above one of her vertebrae. She met Nate's eyes. "Just like Martinez."

"We'll need a tox screen," he told Dr. Morris. "See if it's the same thing that killed Mr. Martinez and Ms. Williams." He turned to Kia. "Did you question Ben this morning?"

"I couldn't; he was asleep and the doctors wouldn't let me in."

"Let's arrest him. We need his statement."

Kia frowned. "We can't do that. There hasn't been a shred of evidence linking Ben to Martinez. No DNA, hair, fingerprints, nothing. Only Martinez's girlfriend's word that she saw Ben's name on the phone. That's not concrete enough. And you know we'll never get through a grand jury with just circumstantial evidence."

Nate made a frustrated sound at the back of his throat. Emma had told him Ben was involved, but he couldn't tell Kia that without telling her everything else.

"He's gonna flee as soon as he can."

"We can't arrest him when there's no evidence he committed a crime. And you heard Dr. Morris; this girl has only been dead a few hours. Ben's been in the hospital all that time. He didn't do this."

Nate pressed his fingers into his thighs. Hard.

She was right. So why had Emma implicated Ben?

More important, why had Nate believed her?

"We still have to question him," Nate said, thinking fast. "He has a track record of making and dealing drugs. At the very least, maybe he knows who's behind all of this: the murders, the drugs, the prescription fraud. It's all tied together, I can feel it. Head back to the hospital and question him. See what he knows."

Kia studied him, her face disapproving. She knew he was hiding something. He waited for her to challenge him, to ask what was going on, but she just shook her head and slipped her plastic gloves off with a *snap*. She tucked them in the trash bag at the edge of the crime scene and disappeared up the path without another word.

The CSIs had already roped off the area, little yellow evidence flags waving in the breeze. Nate stepped carefully from one to the next, trying to piece together the scene. The person who'd dropped Beatrice's body had clearly tromped through the woods with her, rather than bringing her down the path.

Nate followed the broken branches through the woods for a good half mile. Whomever it was had been strong. Strong enough to carry a body this far through dense brush and trees. Although it didn't look like the body had been dragged. Maybe two people had been carryng it? Eventually Nate emerged from the forest onto the road. Wheel marks were traced into the gravel. Nothing that could identify the vehicle, but definitely enough to indicate a car had been parked here.

Nate turned his flashlight on and took his time sweeping the area in a neat, precise grid. He didn't stop until he reached the makeshift blanket beside the road, where all the evidence had been collected, tagged, and laid out. There, already bagged and tagged, was a black-and-white poker chip. Nate picked up the baggie, turning it over in his hand. The initials engraved on the back were *JH*.

"Shit. I think I know who this belongs to," he called to a CSI. He held up the bagged poker chip. "Mind if I take it to question the owner?"

She nodded. "Sure, let me check it out." She jotted something in the evidence log.

Nate walked quickly back through the woods to Beatrice's body. He flashed back to another body. For years he'd used regret over Robbie as a stick to beat himself with. Now here he was, standing on the edge of a forked road, choosing between right and wrong once again.

Nate blinked, seeing Josh's smiling face in his mind.

*You're a good guy, Daddy . . .*

How could he look Josh in the eye and say he was one of the good guys if he let Emma continue down this path? What she was doing was wrong, and he couldn't cover for it.

He wanted to be the man his son thought he was. More than that, he wanted to teach Josh to be good, to do better than him, to respond courageously to every challenge. Maybe it would still result in heartache and tragedy, but at least he'd be doing the right thing.

He fingered the chip in his pocket, deciding to call Lieutenant Dyson and tell him everything. But first he had one more question for Emma about the owner of this chip.

He snapped off his gloves, threw them in the trash, and slipped the evidence bag into his pocket, his knuckles brushing against the tin of toothpicks he kept there. He pulled it out and opened it, extracted a toothpick, and rolled it between his fingers. After a moment, he slipped the toothpick and the tin into the trash bag.

Nate knelt and squeezed Beatrice's hand.

"I'm sorry," he whispered. "I'm going to make this right."

Nate's phone rang, and he straightened and answered it, his shoes crunching on gravel as he moved closer to the water. The waterfall hissed in the distance.

"Nate?" Kia sounded out of breath, as if she was running. "Ben's not here."

"What? What do you mean, not there?"

"One of the doctors said he left around lunchtime. He wasn't under arrest, so they couldn't hold him. Nobody knows where he's gone!"

# CHAPTER 39

I RETURNED TO JOSH'S ROOM, rage and anxiety swirling in my belly. Everything was unraveling like a cheap sweater. How could Nate do this to me? To Josh? How could he think there was any choice at all?

Moira was sitting next to Josh reading a book, the gentle sound of his snores filling the room. Her phone was playing Christmas songs, which reminded me it was only three days away. It certainly didn't feel like Christmas.

I sat on the other side of Josh and watched him sleep. After a moment, Moira put her book down. She looked at me, then down at the floor, and took a deep breath.

"I know we haven't always seen . . . eye to eye, Emma," she said. "I just wanted to apologize if I've ever come across as, well, cold."

I didn't answer, so Moira continued. "I was on my own for a long time after Matt had the stroke. Nate helped out more than I really should've let him. Maybe I relied on him too much." She fiddled with the corner of her book, her eyes on her lap. Finally she looked up. "When your child is small, he needs all of you. Everything. But as he grows he needs you to be separate from him, otherwise he'll feel like he's taking something from you. Sometimes I worry I didn't let Nate go soon enough. I wanted him to be a son first and a husband second, and for that I'm so sorry."

She swallowed. "I want you to know I respect how hard you're fighting for Josh. He's still small and he needs someone fighting in his corner."

"Thank you, Moira. I really appreciate that."

Katie came in to check Josh's temperature then.

"It's spiking a little bit," she said, looking worried.

"Is he okay?"

"He's fine," she reassured me. "Temperatures tend to increase during the first few days after immunotherapy. But we'll keep an eye on it."

I leaned my head on the edge of Josh's bed. Moira picked up her book and continued reading. The gentle noises of the hospital washed over me: rhythmic beeps, the soft murmur of doctors talking, the swish and squeak of tennis shoes on linoleum. Before I knew it, I was asleep . . .

. . . I was running through a maze. The walls were built of iced evergreen shrubs that towered above me in a wintry forest, so high it blotted out the sky.

Snow swirled in chaotic currents; a snow globe that had been shaken. It landed on my eyelashes, freezing my tears into icy drops on my cheeks.

I ran through the maze, turning this way and that, pulse pounding as I tried to find a way out. I turned a final corner, emerging into a small, confined square. At the center of the square was a short wooden platform.

Knotted above it was a hangman's noose.

I stumbled backward and ran away, boughs ripping at my hair and clothes. I finally turned another corner, but again I was in that same square. The hangman's noose mocked me.

Again and again I ran away, but every time I emerged at the same place. And then I realized.

It was the only way out—

A sharp ringing pierced my consciousness. I jerked awake, grappling for my phone.

"Hello?"

"Where is he?" Nate shouted.

I scurried out of the room. "Who?"

"Ben! Your goddamn brother. Where is he?"

"He's in the ER."

"No, he isn't! Kia went to question him and he's gone. He walked out."

Icy needles prickled down my back and up my arms.

I leaned against the corridor wall. A clown bustled past, busily tying balloon animals. Behind him strode a cluster of doctors, deep in consultation.

"I have no—" I stopped abruptly.

The warehouse. That's where the drugs were. That's where Ben would go.

We reached the conclusion at the same time. "He went to the warehouse, didn't he?" Nate said.

Adrenaline surged through me. "No!"

But Nate had already hung up.

I hurried to the accessible bathroom and locked myself inside. I dialed Gabe on the other phone with shaking fingers.

"You need to get to the warehouse. *Now*," I hissed when he answered. "I'll meet you there."

"Already on my way. Ben called. Said to meet him there ASAP."

My mind stuttered. Ben had called him?

"Nate's on his way there right now," I said. "We need to move everything. Fast."


I STRODE down the hall to Josh's room, peeked in. Moira was still reading her book. Josh's cheeks were flushed, but he was sleeping soundly. With a last glance in the room, I went to the nurses' station.

"Can you check on Josh again?" I asked our nurse, Katie. "I need to run out to my car."

She nodded, and I hurried toward the elevator.

Outside, night was descending, and tiny flakes of snow were just beginning to fall. Cold wind buffeted my cheeks and snaked beneath my coat. I hurried across the parking lot to my car, my shoes slapping against the wet pavement.

The warm lights of the hospital quickly disappeared as I drove as fast as I dared up the mountainous road and over the bridge, turning down the road that wound along the river's edge in the direction of the warehouse.

About five miles from the mill, I saw a flash of blue lights. I braked abruptly. Police cars were blocking one side of the road. A crime scene crew was working behind yellow police tape.

I recognized Kia as I drove slowly past. Her short dark hair blew in the breeze, snow landing on her police jacket, her jaw clenched as she scowled at something on the ground.

I mentally cursed. *Why* did I have to live in such a small town?

A cop waved me around the roadblock. I kept my eyes fixed ahead, hoping Kia wouldn't recognize me. But just as I thought I was clear, she turned in the direction of my car.

In the rearview mirror, I saw her staring after me.

I drove the rest of the way to the warehouse in white-knuckled terror that Kia would follow, my fingers gripping the steering wheel so hard they ached. I finally pulled over, parking in front of the broken chain-link fence, and got out. Nate's cruiser was parked on the shoulder a little way down.

He was already here.

Gabe was waiting on the other side of the fence, stomping his feet to keep warm. There was no sign of Ben's motorcycle, although that didn't mean he wasn't here.

I grabbed my hat and flashlight and got out of the car. Gabe held open the broken chain-link fence, and I ducked to get through. I stumbled, letting my body fall against Gabe's. He lifted his arms to catch me, allowing me the second I needed to slip Violeta's scarf into the pocket of his black parka.

"Thanks," I said. "Have you seen Ben? We have to hurry."

"No, I just got here."

I put a hand on his arm. "That girl, Beatrice. She's dead. Nate told me they found her body this morning."

Gabe darted a glance up at the warehouse, looking worried.

"Do you think Ben . . ." I hesitated, leaving the sentence unfinished.

Gabe didn't answer. I tugged at the thick wool of my scarf, nerves needling the skin at my neck and chest. The cold was already biting at my fingers.

Did I really think Ben was capable of murder? Yes. But Beatrice's? It just didn't make sense. And anyway, what could I do if he had?

That familiar feeling of helplessness washed over me in short, sharp bursts.

"Gabe?"

Gabe ran his fingers between his forehead and his beanie hat.

Tufts of blond hair stuck out underneath. His beard was thicker now, his eyes sunken and dark. "Ben's a lot of things, but I don't think he's a murderer. Maybe she overdosed."

I let go of Gabe's arm, nodding. "You're right."

I flicked the flashlight on, and we crossed the parking lot, snowflakes igniting like fireflies in the beams. Our shoes crunched against the broken glass. Our feet seemed to instantly melt the snow, forming muddy little footprints.

The rumble of the falls sounded very far away now, the snow muting it, turning it to a gentle murmur. White drifted slowly from the leaden sky, covering the trees and the ground in a fine, glittering coat as we circled the building.

My phone buzzed from my pocket. I put a hand on Gabe's coat to stop him. "Hello?"

"Emma, where are you?" Moira's voice was loud, panicked. She was crying, hot, moist sounds hurtling down the phone line. "Something's wrong. Josh's temperature went up really high, and all the machines started beeping, and then he started having a seizure. The doctors rushed in and pushed me out of the room! I don't even know what's happening! Where are you?"

"Oh my God." My blood curdled, her words piercing me like a twisting dagger. "Where is he now?"

"He's still in his room." *Okay*, I thought, *not moved is a good sign*.

"What's wrong?" Gabe asked.

"Josh. He's had a seizure."

"Is he okay?"

"Who's that?" Moira asked, sounding suspicious.

"It's . . . Nate."

"Well you both need to get here right—"

Suddenly the still air of night was ripped apart by the sound of a gunshot.

Gabe's and my eyes met, and my entire body seemed to go completely numb.

"Nate!" I screamed.

I RAN like hell, scrambling over roots and pushing past the prickly bushes along the side of the building. Branches snapped and broke, slashing at my skin. Hard gasps stung my throat. The flashlight beam bounced along the ground in frenetic little jerks.

I felt like I was running in water. My limbs weren't moving fast enough. The world had slowed down.

Gabe was right behind me, his breathing heavy. We'd just hurtled around the last corner when I slipped on a patch of wet gravel. The world was suddenly upside down. And then I slammed hard into the ground, my palms scraping against it as I tried to break my fall. I rolled instinctively onto my back, the impact punching the air from my lungs.

The flashlight clattered onto the ground. Stars pierced my vision as I lay on my back, stunned. Snowflakes floated, tiny feathers dancing in the wind, as if someone had ripped open a pillow and flung the stuffing around. Dampness soaked into my jeans, muddying my coat.

A voice came to me from very far away.

*"Emma!"*

It was Moira.

Miraculously, I was still clutching the phone in my hand.

*"What was that!"*

I pressed End and scrambled to my feet, tension strung tight through my entire body. Pain flared in my knees, and when I looked down, my palms were bloody.

*Josh.*

Josh had collapsed.

But Nate was inside the warehouse, and I had no idea who had fired that shot. He could be in danger.

It was a horrible choice, one I wouldn't wish on my worst enemy. Leave my husband, who was very possibly in danger from my own brother—or turn away from my son, who definitely was in danger? But Josh was in the hospital. He had doctors and nurses and Moira to care for him. I had to go to Nate.

I shoved my phone in my pocket and pulled the Glock from my ankle holster, surprised on some weird, slightly unhinged level that it was still there. I checked the ammo clip, sliding it into place with a click.

Gabe's eyes widened when he saw the gun. He stepped away from me. "Emma, what the—?"

"Shhh," I hissed. "Get the flashlight."

Looking terrified, he complied, snatching it up.

We moved carefully across the icy ground toward the warehouse's open door.

And then the crack of another gunshot rang out.

# CHAPTER 40

"DROP IT!" NATE SHOUTED. "Drop the weapon!"

The smell of sulfur filled the warehouse. The ensuing silence echoed almost as loud as the gunshot itself.

Nate kept his gun trained on the man. The sound of Ben moaning yanked his attention across the warehouse. Ben was on his knees clutching the side of his head. Blood spurted from between his fingers.

"He fucking shot me," Ben moaned.

"I'll shoot you again if you don't tell me why you killed him!" the man—Nate had no idea who he was—shouted. He had greasy dark hair tied back in a ponytail, angry eyes, mouth twisted in a grimace. His neck was more ink than skin.

"I didn't!" Ben wailed. "I swear!"

Feeble rays of light from the lantern on the floor next to him turned his skin a sickly yellow.

"I said, drop your weapon! Now!" Nate repeated.

"No!" the man shouted. The inked veins in his neck pulsed, his eyes nearly popping out of his head. "I've finally found him; I'm not gonna stop until he tells me the truth."

"Okay." Nate recognized a man on the brink when he saw one. "Then tell me who you think he killed."

"He killed my brother."

"Your brother?"

The man turned and fully met Nate's eye. "Yeah, my brother. Santiago Martinez."

Nate's breath caught. "Ben killed him?"

"It couldn'ta been no one else! We worked together, dealing the same shit. His guys, they deal out here; my guys, we're in Seattle. Santiago told me he was working for some task force agent. They had him on a drug charge and the only way out for him was to rat his guys out. He told me so I could get out before he did it. He thought Violeta heard him on the phone with the agent, and right after that Santiago turns up dead, and then Violeta turns up dead. Ben did them both."

"I didn't do it!" Ben shouted. "I thought Violeta killed Santiago!"

"She didn't do it, *puto cabrón*! We went together to Santiago's house to get the fentanyl. She was with me when we found him!"

Nate was so stunned he almost lowered his weapon. "Then who killed Santiago?"

A sound drew his attention to the door.

*Emma? What the hell?*

And Gabe Wilson was right behind her. His wife's jeans were wet and muddy, leaves clinging to her hat and coat. She had a gun clutched in her hand.

Nate's eyes widened. What was she doing here, and where had she gotten a weapon?

Emma's arrival was the brief distraction Carlos needed. He squeezed the trigger, pointing his gun first at Nate, then at Ben.

Nate threw himself to the ground.

"Get down!" he shouted at Emma.

He dropped and rolled to hide behind a steel barrel, but popped up again almost immediately. Carlos was sprinting across the warehouse, his gaze trained on Ben. He lifted his gun, readying to shoot Ben in the head. Ben's eyes widened, then squeezed shut, as if preparing for his final moment.

"Stop!" Emma raised her gun while still on her knees.

But Nate squeezed the trigger first.

Carlos staggered backward as two bullets hit his chest.

*Thump.*

*Thump.*

He crumpled to the ground.

"Don't move!" Nate shouted at Emma and Gabe. "Stay where you are."

Nate hurried to where Carlos lay and kicked the gun out of his reach. He scooped it up and shoved it in the back of his pants for safekeeping, then checked Carlos's pulse.

Dead.

Nate's heart was pounding from adrenaline, a raw, manic throb. He inhaled in slow, measured breaths, trying to still his heart. It had been a long time since he'd discharged his weapon.

He mentally began making a list of things he needed to do: call for backup; call Special Agents Hamilton and Greene; cordon off the scene. He thought of the poker chip he'd found and how it fit into this whole messed-up puzzle: Emma, Ben, Gabe, Santiago Martinez, Violeta Williams, the drugs, the murders. And he knew. He didn't know why, but he sure as hell knew who was running this show.

"That's the man who's been following me." Emma stared at Carlos's body, her gun now hanging by her side.

"He thought Ben killed his brother." Nate pried Ben's hands away from his head to assess how bad the wound was. The bullet had ripped his ear off, leaving just a bloody stump. "He was probably trying to get to him by following you."

He glanced at Emma's gun again, recognized the shock settling across her face. "Why don't you set that gun down, Em? Kick it over to me."

Ben moaned. Nate turned to look at him. "You'll be fine. It's just a flesh wound. You're lucky the bullet only got your ear, not your damn head."

He yanked his handcuffs from his belt and cuffed Ben. The adrenaline was draining from him suddenly, leaving him furious and aware of a bone-deep chill. His fingertips were red-raw, the bitter air gnawing at his exposed skin.

Snow was falling heavier now, a barrage of white blowing in through the open door.

Emma handed the gun to Gabe and wrenched her hat off, dropping to her knees next to Ben.

"Give me your tie," she told Nate.

He ripped it off and handed it to her. She used it to tie her balled-up hat against Ben's ear. Her movements were brisk, businesslike, her face betraying no emotion. But then she glanced up at him and her face softened, a raw vulnerability there that made him ache.

Nate suddenly thought of all the things that could've happened to her, how close she'd come to being shot. He could've lost her. He wanted to reach out and touch her, to reassure himself she was still here, she was safe.

And he understood then that people weren't morally infallible. Not his wife. Not his father. Not himself. He understood why she'd done what she'd done.

*I love you*, he opened his mouth to say. *I love how much you love our family, the lengths you'll go to to protect us.*

But Ben's agonized moan interrupted.

Nate turned to him. "Were you telling the truth? You didn't kill Martinez?"

"No! Fuck, man! Could you just call an ambulance or something? I'm bleeding to death here!"

"Nate! We need to call nine-one-one!" Emma said sharply.

Gabe hovered on the periphery, looking uncertain, the gun Emma had given him now hanging limply from his fingers.

"Then who killed Santiago Martinez?" Nate looked between them. Gabe. Ben. Emma. The body of Carlos Martinez. "And where did you get the fentanyl?"

# CHAPTER 41

"WE NEED TO GET to the hospital," I told Nate. "It's Josh. Your mom called. Something's gone wrong with the treatment—he had a seizure." I looked at Ben. "And Ben needs to get to the ER. He's losing a lot of blood."

Nate pulled his phone out and started to dial.

"Stop!" Gabe shouted.

He was pointing my gun at Nate. Nate slowly raised his hands.

"Gabe, what are you doing?" I hissed. "Put the gun down."

"No!" he said. His eyes darted wildly around the warehouse. "All of this will be for nothing if we let him call the cops. Don't you see? They'll find everything we have here. We'll go to jail."

"He *is* the cops. Don't you get it? It's over for us!"

"No. I'm not getting arrested. I'll lose my gas station. Your career will be over. We won't be able to get the money for Josh."

I froze. I had to be very careful what I said right now.

"Gabe, listen to me," I said, speaking very slowly. "We have to get to the hospital. My son is very sick. Remember?"

The gun trembled in Gabe's grasp. I thought about trying to grab it from him, but he was too far away. Nate was farther behind me still, and Ben was on the floor, his hands cuffed behind his back. I took a tiny step toward Gabe, one hand held out.

"Gabe. It's Gabe, right?" Nate's voice was too strong, too loud in this empty space. I wanted to tell him to be quiet, to stop talking. His police negotiation tactics wouldn't work right now. Not with Gabe. But he kept on speaking. "You've known Ben for a long time. Look at him. He's losing a lot of blood. We need to get some help. Why don't you just put down the gun? Everything's going to be a lot worse for you if you hurt somebody."

Gabe's face hardened at the underlying threat.

"Gabe. Look at me. We need to think about Josh." I took another step toward him.

Gabe's eyes were hot on mine.

"Please."

Finally he nodded. He dropped his hand abruptly, but turned to Nate. "I'm not doing this for you," he said roughly. "I'm doing it for my son."

Nate's eyes flickered in confusion. My heart nearly stopped beating.

"No," I whispered.

Nate looked between us. "Your s—?" He took a half step back, stumbling away from me. The betrayal on his face sent ice scattering across my spine. "Josh is . . . ?"

"No!" I exclaimed. I reached for Nate's hand. It was cold, limp in mine. He stared at my fingers as if he'd never seen them before. "No! Of course not. Josh is *your* son. You *know* that!"

"What the hell?" Gabe's voice was a question. A warning. "What are you talking about? You said he was mine."

I turned to Gabe and inhaled deeply. When I'd found out I

was pregnant, my first thought was of Gabe. We'd slept together shortly before I met Nate, so I assumed it was Gabe's baby. I didn't want to deceive Nate, to move in with him, let alone marry him, if I was pregnant with another man's baby. So I'd ordered a prenatal paternity test.

But even before the results came back saying Nate was the father, I knew what I was going to do. I had no intention of letting Gabe near my baby. I chose to marry Nate because he was a good, decent man. The kind of man who would always put his family first. I loved him in a way I'd never come close to loving Gabe.

"I'm so sorry, Gabe. I lied to you. I knew you would only help me if you thought Josh was yours."

He stared at me, dumbfounded. "But the paternity test . . ."

"It matched Nate. I'm sorry." I turned to Nate. "Gabe and I were together before I met you. I did a prenatal paternity test, and it matched you. I have it at home. It's in the bottom of my jewelry box."

Gabe's mouth widened into a silent O. "You . . . *lied* . . . to me." He rubbed a hand over his face, like he was trying to wake himself from a bad dream.

"I know. I'm so sorry. I needed your help."

"All of this—everything I did was for you. For *him*. The drugs. Violeta. Beatrice."

"Beatrice?"

"She was going to the cops. We had to stop her."

"We?"

Gabe's eyes darted to Ben's. A look crossed between them, and Ben shook his head, a short, sharp jerk.

"Who?" I insisted.

I took another step closer to Gabe.

"You fucking—fucking—" He seemed lost for words, ripped apart by hurt and grief and then, when he met my eyes, by an incandescent fury that hollowed him out and then filled him up.

"This is *your* fault!" Gabe lifted the gun just as I leaped for him.

We tumbled to the ground in a heap of arms and legs. But Gabe was stronger than me. He grabbed a fistful of my hair and slammed my face into the wooden floor. Fireworks sparked behind my eyes. A dizzying pain crashed into me as the cartilage in my nose made a wet *crunch*. The taste of copper gushed into my mouth, and I went limp.

"Let her go!" Nate's voice came to me from somewhere far away. His gun was trained on Gabe.

Gabe snaked an arm around my throat and yanked me to my feet, using my body as a shield. The pressure from the crook of his arm squeezed tighter and tighter, the gun pointed at Nate. My breath was trapped in my chest, leaden and blazing. Pressure built inside me, burning, swelling in my rib cage.

I flailed weakly against him. I caught sight of the stack of wooden two-by-fours leaning against the wall. I twisted, trying to grab one, but missed. I gasped for air, clawing at Gabe's arm.

I didn't mind dying if Josh lived. If he could grow up and go to his senior prom and go to college and meet a girl, get married, have a child of his own, and know the depths a parent would go to for their child.

So I did the opposite of what every instinct screamed at me to do—I stopped fighting. My body abruptly became a deadweight in Gabe's arm. He stumbled forward, releasing the pressure on my neck ever so slightly.

I gasped, inhaling cool, soothing breaths of air. Then I dug my heels into the ground and shoved myself back, ramming into Gabe as hard as I could. We flew backward, slamming into the wall.

He grunted, the impact knocking the breath from him, and his arm relaxed. I twisted out of his grasp and lunged away from him.

Gabe raised the gun one last time. He stood straight-backed, his arm a perfect arrow. I reached for a two-by-four and turned, ready to hurl it at him, but the gun was trained on my chest. Gabe's eyes on mine were expressionless.

"Emma!" Nate jumped toward me.

Everything slowed down, with the sharp, dark quality of a nightmare, but I couldn't stop it.

The sound of the gun firing ricocheted throughout the warehouse.

The silence was suddenly, terrifyingly vast. I opened my eyes and looked down. There was no pain. No blood. Nothing.

Nothing but Nate.

The bullet had struck him when he'd leaped in front of me. Blood bloomed in a scarlet rose on his chest.

Nate sank to his knees and slumped onto his back.

"Nate!" The two-by-four in my hand clattered to the floor.

I scrambled to Nate's side and pressed my palms to his chest. My hands were instantly warmed by his blood, pulsing from the raw open wound. "No, no, no, no, no!"

Gabe dropped the gun, shocked. It fell to the cement floor with a horrible *thud*. And then he turned and ran.

Blood gurgled from Nate's mouth, spilled out of his lips and down his chin as he tried to speak.

"Baby, stay with me!" I cried.

But he was already leaving me. I could see it in his eyes, the way they were fading. I'd seen it before when my dad died, his head propped on my lap the same way Nate's was.

"No! No! Please! Nate, I love you! I love you so much."

Nate squeezed my hand, pressed something cold and smooth into it. Slowly, ever so slowly, he drew an *X* over his heart.

And then his arm went limp. His eyes rolled up to the ceiling.

I pressed shaking fingers to his throat, but the reassuring thump of my husband's pulse was no longer there.

"Come back!" I screamed. "Nate, come back to me!"

But he was gone.

# CHAPTER 42

I SAT WITH NATE's head on my lap, tears streaming down my cheeks. A horrible, surreal sense of déjà vu draped over me. Shock had left me numb but reeling, unmoored from everything.

My insides turned to liquid.

Nate was dead.

And it was my fault. If only I hadn't started selling these drugs with Gabe. If only I hadn't lied to him about Josh. If only, if only, if only, Nate would still be alive.

Grief squeezed my guts so viciously I almost threw up. I wanted to lie down in the pool of his blood, to curl myself around Nate's body and never get up.

I told myself to stop crying. Nothing good came from crying. Hadn't I learned that long ago? Only helplessness, and that didn't change a thing. But I couldn't stop. The tears kept falling, dripping onto Nate's perfect face.

I became suddenly aware of something in my left hand. It was the object Nate had pressed into my palm. It took me a few seconds to place it. When I did, a horrible tightness cinched in my stomach, looping and squeezing until I could no longer gasp a full breath.

The back of the black-and-white poker chip was engraved with my father's initials, *JH*: Dr. Joshua Hardman. We'd named Josh after him when we found out our baby was going to be a boy.

What I couldn't understand was why Nate would have this poker chip on him when he died.

I'd given it away a long time ago.

My name drifted to me from somewhere far away. Urgently. Demanding my attention.

"Emma!"

It was Ben.

I lifted my gaze. Blinked.

Ben.

I slipped the chip into my pocket and fumbled in Nate's slacks for his keys, finally finding the one I needed.

In medicine, you're faced with impossible choices every day. Where does the line lie between good and bad, benefit and harm? Radiation and chemotherapy kill healthy cells and damage a patient's body, but can also save their life. We amputate limbs to save someone's life from, say, gangrene or flesh-eating bacteria. Under narrowly defined circumstances, assisted dying gives patients a means of dying with dignity.

Saving a patient's life or, in some cases, terminating it humanely justifies the pain of chemo or the loss of a limb or handing a patient the pills that will help ease their suffering.

I guess what I'm saying is, sometimes we have to harm to heal. To get justice in an unjust world.

I unlocked the handcuffs binding Ben's wrists. My tears were already cooling on my frozen cheeks; soon they would turn to ice.

"Gabe killed Violeta," I told Ben. "I saw him do it. He gave her the wrong bag of drugs because he wanted the money in the briefcase, and then he pushed her body into the river to get rid of the evidence. I swore I wouldn't tell you because I wanted help getting the money to save Josh. I'm so sorry, Ben. I should've told you sooner."

Ben staggered to his feet, blinking hard over and over. He twisted his wrists to get the blood moving. He threw the hat and tie I'd knotted around his head to the ground. His eyes burned with a crazed light. Blood from his mangled ear streaked his jaw and neck.

I picked up the gun and held it out. "I'll take care of everything."

Ben grabbed the gun and lurched toward the door.

"Ben!" He glanced over his shoulder. "You weren't here for this. You and Carlos fought earlier. He shot you. But you weren't here for this."

Ben nodded, and a second later he disappeared into the whirling snow.

I turned to study the scene. I let my breathing slow, my mind going blank, my thoughts receding. I didn't have much time. Trace evidence would show hair, fiber, blood, fingerprints, tissue. Probably even the drugs.

Now more than ever I had to stay calm. Focused.

What I did now would determine my future. Not just mine, though. It would determine Ben's and Josh's as well.

I was at another fork in the road: Do the right thing or the necessary thing. Tell the truth or protect those who were left.

Nate was dead.

I couldn't lose anybody else.

I gathered all the little bottles of oxy, the baggies of fentanyl, the scales, Ben's backpack of clothes, his little red notebook of customers. Every scrap of evidence I could find. I wiped everything down that I had touched.

The drugs and notebook I buried a little way up the path under a gnarled root growing in an arch from the frozen ground. I used a sharp stick to score a hole under the root, and covered everything with dead leaves and twigs. The snow was falling so hard it would, I hoped, be covered by the time the crime scene techs arrived. I hefted Ben's backpack and the scales into the swirling water.

I ran back to the warehouse, using the branch of an evergreen to sweep at my footprints in the snow.

Somewhere in the distance, the faint crack of a gunshot ripped through the icy air. A stutter of silence. And then another.

My chest clenched. Ben had done it, then. That was why I'd given him the gun, wasn't it? To get rid of Gabe? I didn't feel any regret, though. No, only relief. An eye for an eye.

I hurried inside and knelt over Nate's body. I touched his cheek where the blood had cooled into little icicles

"I am so, so sorry," I whispered, closing his eyes with my fingertips. I kissed each eyelid and traced an *X* over his chest. "I won't fail you. I won't fail our son."

I didn't have to fake the tears that fell then, the horrible, awful keening that wrenched from my throat when I dialed 911.

## CHAPTER 43

I WOKE SLOWLY, emerging into consciousness like a baby deer into a clearing, timid and uneasy.

Early-morning light filtered through partially open blinds, falling in watery sepia stripes on the floor. A numbing fog curled around my head, hovering over me like a mushroom cloud. Rhythmic beeps. The quiet shushing of shoes on linoleum.

Clutched in my hand was my father's lucky poker chip.

I blinked and turned my head slowly to one side, seeing an IV stand, its thin tubing snaking under white sheets. And then I remembered.

The IV was in Josh's arm.

Nate was dead.

Gabe was dead.

Ben was missing.

My heart blistered in my chest, turning into charred black ash. I curled my knuckles to my face and wept with horror and rage and regret, burying my head in the pillow and wishing the darkness would block out the guilt.

So much guilt.

It sat like a thorn in my throat, piercing my defenses and leaving a scar that would never heal.

A gentle knock came, and Jodie Finch, my family liaison officer, entered. Jodie was a doe-eyed young woman with a sober manner and shapeless beige clothes. Her mouse-brown hair was scraped into a tight bun, her thin lips pale and bloodless.

She'd been assigned immediately after Nate was killed, and had been a shadow stuck to my side ever since. Noting my tear-stained face, she wordlessly handed me a tissue, then moved the giant Santa-dressed teddy bear—a Christmas gift from Dr. Palmer—out of the way and sat down. Josh had woken only sporadically the last week. He didn't realize Christmas had passed or that his father had died.

I wiped my tears and pulled myself to a sitting position on the couch the nurses had set up for me in Josh's room. He'd been moved out of intensive care yesterday, a week after he'd collapsed. A week since my entire world had imploded.

"How are you today?" Jodie said, her voice soft and husky. Her voice was her best quality, warm but gentle. Soothing. Maybe I didn't want her to leave. I couldn't bear the thought of being alone.

I rubbed the skin between my eyebrows. "I'm okay."

"And Josh?"

"He isn't out of the woods yet, but the doctors are optimistic." Every day Josh was getting a little bit stronger.

Last week after the immunotherapy, Josh's temperature had spiked to 107°F and he'd collapsed, having seizure after seizure. He was diagnosed with cytokine release syndrome. He'd been on oxygen therapy and antihypotensive agents for low blood pressure, but so far the doctors had been able to avoid any antibiotics, which could negate the effect of immunotherapy.

"The funeral procession starts at one p.m.," Jodie reminded me. As if I could forget.

I glanced at Josh to make sure he hadn't woken and heard her. The last thing I wanted was to harm any chance he had of recovering by telling him about Nate's death.

There would be time for that later.

"Can I get you anything?" Jodie asked gently. "A coffee? Or I can go to your house and get you something to wear."

"No, I'll do it," I said quickly. I didn't want her in my home. "I need to see my dog, anyway."

Moira had been a complete rock, checking on Charlie every day, organizing Nate's funeral, coordinating the funeral procession with the police department. By contrast, I had done nothing but sit by Josh's side the last week, silently begging him not to leave me too.

Another knock came at the door, and Kia peeked in.

"Emma? Do you have a minute?"

"I'll stay with Josh," Jodie said.

I followed Kia down the corridor. "Julia was released yesterday," she said. "She's asking for you."

"I'm so glad to hear that. I'll stop and see her when I can."

She pushed open the door to one of the hospital's family rooms and waited for me to enter. The rectangular room had soft gray carpeting and ivy-green accent walls. Four leather chairs faced inward around a small glass table.

A man and a woman, both in black suits, stood when I entered. The woman had sharp, angled features and thin lips; the man was tall, with a military-style buzz cut, his suit beautifully tailored.

"This is Special Agent Lisa Hamilton and Special Agent Phil Greene," Kia said. She smoothed a hand over her unruly dark hair. Her fingernails were bitten-down, her eyes red from too many sleepless nights. "They're with the Seattle division of the DEA."

I shook their hands, my heart doing acrobatics inside my chest.

"Here, sit." Agent Hamilton gestured at the chair across from her.

"We want to extend our deepest condolences," she began. "I assure you, we will investigate your husband's death to the full extent of the law."

"Thank you."

"I'm not sure if you were aware, but Nate was working on a case with us."

"No, I didn't know."

"Nate was looking for Ben Hardman. Your brother. We had reason to believe he was involved in an opioid drug ring, and Nate was looking into it."

I kept my face cool and expressionless, but I hadn't expected that.

"Have you heard from Ben?" she asked.

"Not since the night I brought him to the hospital when he'd overdosed."

"And you didn't see him at the warehouse before Gabriel Wilson shot your husband?"

I shook my head. "No."

Agent Hamilton looked at some notes she had on her lap. "Can you refresh my memory? Why did you go to the warehouse again?"

I sat back in my chair. The male agent had his arms crossed and was looking at me beneath half-lowered lids.

I glanced at the door. "I need to get back to my son."

"Sure. Let's make this quick then." Hamilton smiled. Her teeth were very small.

"Nate called me and said Ben had disappeared from the hospital. He thought Ben was going to the warehouse, so I headed there too."

"Did Nate say he needed you there?" she asked.

"No, but Ben's my brother. I wanted to make sure he was okay."

"And was he at the warehouse when you arrived?"

"No."

"I appreciate this is very painful, but can you tell me again what you saw when you arrived?"

Tears welled in my eyes. Kia handed me a tissue.

I took a deep breath. "I heard a gunshot when I was parking."

"One gunshot?"

"It was two. *Bam. Bam.* I ran in and found Nate standing over a body. Carlos Martinez, I learned. I thought Nate had shot him. But then I saw Gabe. He had a gun too."

"So Ben wasn't at the scene?"

"No."

"We found spots of Ben's blood on the floor."

I shrugged. "Maybe he was there at some point, but not when I was."

She glanced down at her notes, conceding the point. "You know we found Ben?"

I straightened. "Where is he?"

"He's in a rehab center over near Seattle. We questioned him yesterday. He says he left the hospital around noon that day. He went to buy pills from Carlos Martinez at the warehouse. They argued, and Carlos shot Ben."

My hand flew to my mouth. "Is he okay?"

Agent Hamilton looked at me closely. "He's fine. He's lost most of his left ear, but he's fine. According to Ben, at that point he realized he had a problem and decided to check himself into rehab."

I stared at her, wondering how much Ben had paid to get someone to change the time he was admitted to rehab.

"Were you able to ascertain why Gabriel Wilson was with Carlos Martinez?"

"From what I could gather, they were involved in an opioid

ring. Nate said they'd been arguing about one of their partners, someone called Violeta Williams. Gabe . . ." I swallowed hard. "He grabbed me and put the gun to my head. We struggled. I managed to get out of his grasp and he tried to shoot me, but Nate jumped in front of me. That's when he . . ." The tears spilled over. I sobbed into the tissue for a minute.

"I'm so sorry for your loss, Dr. Sweeney," Agent Hamilton said softly. "I'm sure we can trust you to give us a call if you think of anything else?"

"Yes. Of course."

Hamilton and Greene stood. After a brief handshake they left, leaving Kia and me alone in the family room. A long silence stretched between us.

Kia stared at me, her dark gaze malicious. "We found a scarf with Violeta Williams's DNA on it in Gabriel Wilson's jacket."

"Did he kill her?"

"That's the working theory. You're sure you didn't see your brother at the warehouse?"

"Yes." My voice tipped over into irritation before I could stop it. "Why do you keep asking me that?"

Kia's eyes narrowed. She didn't believe me, but she had no evidence to back up whatever theories she was constructing. Ben's blood and fingerprints had been found in the warehouse, but she couldn't prove when they'd gotten there. I was the only witness. A doctor. The wife of a murdered police officer. My credentials were unimpeachable.

As far as they knew, Carlos and Gabe had run the drug lab. Their fingerprints were all over too.

"After Gabriel Wilson shot Nate and ran away, you said you heard a shot?"

"Yes. He must've . . . killed himself out of guilt."

"Was it just one shot you heard?"

I hesitated, trying to remember what I'd said before. "I think so." I looked down at my hands tearing the tissue into little pieces. "It's hard to remember now."

"The thing is, Gabriel Wilson was found with two bullet wounds. Most people trying to kill themselves don't shoot twice."

She looked at me for a long time then. "The bullets that killed Gabe matched the bullet that killed Nate. The same weapon killed them both."

I didn't say anything, so she continued.

"We never found the gun used to kill Nate. Do you know where it might've gone?"

"Presumably it was with Gabe."

"Did you kill Gabriel Wilson?"

I drew back, repelled by her words. "Are you seriously asking me that?" I hissed. "How dare you. My son is gravely ill. My husband has been murdered."

"All the more motive."

"I'm not a murderer!"

She sat back in the chair. "There were partial footprints along the path near the water. Someone followed him."

I stood, furious, and walked to the door. "I'll speak to Lieutenant Dyson about this."

She stood and faced me. "Please do. In the meantime, I'll continue doing my job. And trust me"—she narrowed her eyes—"I'll find out what really happened to Nate."

She brushed past me, striding down the hall with angry, purposeful steps. But then she stopped and returned, withdrawing something from an inner pocket. It was small and square, wrapped in red and green paper. She handed the box to me.

"We found this in his desk."

I turned the box over. My name was written in Nate's familiar slanted scrawl on the gift tag attached.

"If you know anything," Kia said, her eyes hard, "anything at all, you owe it to Nate to speak up."

"I know exactly what I owe my husband, Detective Sharpe."

After she'd left, I unwrapped the box slowly, imagining Nate's face the day we were married, the way he'd watched me as I turned the corner at city hall. We hadn't had the money for a fancy wedding or honeymoon, and anyway, I was pregnant. I'd arrived after a busy shift and he'd been waiting for me, patient and handsome in his black suit and striped tie.

"*Mo chuisle,*" he'd whispered into my hair as he pulled me into his arms. His eyes were soft and warm, like moonlight on my face. "Are you ready?"

And I was.

I opened the box and pulled a delicate necklace from its nest of white silk. All the oxygen left my lungs and tears rushed to my eyes, my knees threatening to give out as I realized exactly what it was.

The pendant tying the delicate sterling silver chain together was a jagged line, up and down, up and down, mimicking the EKG wave of a heartbeat.

*Mo chuisle.*

My heartbeat.

And I knew. No matter what I had done, Nate had loved me. Eternally.

# CHAPTER 44

BACK IN JOSH'S ROOM, I asked Jodie to grab me a coffee. After she'd gone, I sat next to Josh and watched him sleep. I traced his face with my eyes. He was so thin now, I could see the sharp ridges of his cheekbones, the point of his chin. His skin was milk pale, translucent, the tiny veins stark just beneath. His eyes moved under hairless eyelids and he stirred, bringing a hand to his shoulder before relaxing into sleep again.

I pulled my father's poker chip out of my pocket and rolled it over my knuckles, the way Dr. Palmer had taught me when I was a teenager.

"Use your thumb to push the coin across the back of your finger, then raise your middle finger and push the side of the coin down so it flips onto the back of your middle finger," he'd said.

Sometimes when he visited, I couldn't understand why he bothered. I was a morose girl, lonely and insecure. And yet he continued visiting, every two weeks, like clockwork.

I'd asked him once why he kept coming. "There's a Chinese proverb that says, if you save a life, you're responsible for that life.

I found you, Emma. A piece of you is in me now. I'm responsible for you."

That's when he'd pulled the coin from his pocket and showed me how to roll it over my fingers. "I taught this to my daughter when she was about your age," he'd said.

A sharp rap came at the door, and Dr. Palmer peeked in.

*Speak of the devil*, I thought wryly, slipping the poker chip into my pocket.

"How's our boy?" he asked softly.

"You tell me."

He crossed to the monitors attached to Josh's small body and read one of the printouts.

"He's looking really good, Emma." Dr. Palmer pressed his stethoscope to Josh's chest, so smoothly that Josh didn't even wake up. "Our ultimate goal was to avoid any organ toxicity, and the systemic corticosteroid use has worked really well to do that and to reverse the symptoms of the cytokine release syndrome without compromising his immunotherapy."

He listened to Josh's chest for a minute, then spoke softly to me. "We'll continue monitoring him closely for infections and fluid imbalances, and we'll do daily echocardiograms to monitor ejection fraction and ventricular wall mobility. I don't want to promise he's out of the woods yet, but I think we can feel positive now."

Jodie entered with my coffee just then and handed me a cinnamon roll.

"Thanks." I didn't know how to tell her I didn't eat sugar, so I took the coffee and the oil-splattered bag. "I'm going to run home," I said. "I need to have a shower and get changed. Can you watch Josh? Moira should be here soon."

"Of course."

"Dr. Palmer . . ." I wanted to say more, to ask more, but I didn't have the words, and anyway, I'd learned that sometimes strategic inaction is better than action. "Thanks."

I left quickly, dropping the cinnamon roll in a trash can outside the front of the hospital.

A bitter, coppery taste filled my mouth as I thought about the poker chip in my pocket. Sorrow and also fear, because I knew this wasn't over yet.

THE HOUSE was still and quiet. Oppressively so. I'd barely been back since Nate died. Moira had been the one to come back, bring us clothes, feed Charlie.

Everything was where I'd left it: clothes still unfolded, toys scattered across the floor, a half-filled cup of coffee Nate had left on the dining room table, a pile of mail on the coffee table. Charlie came loping over to me. I bent to hug him, and he dragged a tongue across my cheek.

I shook dog food into his bowl and topped up his water as he crunched the kibble. On the dining room table I noticed an unopened bill. I slit the envelope open. It was from the hospital. My stomach clenched painfully as I read the amount due.

I moved to the laptop in the living room and opened the GoFundMe account that had been set up for Josh. Charlie flopped onto my feet.

I scrolled through the recent donations. There had been a number from the people in our community since Nate had died, but the total in the account was still too low. I scrolled back, but there were no large donations.

Gabe hadn't made a payment for at least a week before he'd died.

I felt sick.

I had no money, and no way to get access to the bank account Gabe had set up to donate from. Since the investigation was ongoing, it would be months, maybe years, before Nate's life insurance paid out.

I looked again at the total amount due printed on the bill. And that wasn't even factoring in the chemo or any of the emergency treatments Josh had needed this last week. Nor everything he would need going forward. But at least he would live. I was grateful for that.

The police had already searched Gabe's apartment and gas station, but I'd heard nothing about cash being found.

I showered quickly and dressed in navy slacks and a matching blazer, carefully applying makeup to cover eyes that were swollen from a week's worth of crying. I'd lost so much weight I looked skeletal, my cheekbones sharp, my lips tattered.

I went to the kitchen, trying to decide if I would be able to eat anything. A sound startled me, and I jumped.

"Charlie?" I moved in the direction of the sound.

The shadow of a man loomed in my living room. My scream came out mangled, dying halfway up my throat.

"Ben!" I threw a hand out to steady myself on the wall.

He was sitting in the armchair, Charlie panting happily at his feet. There was no dressing on his wounded ear; just a neat stitching job, black threads peeking out from the side of his skull.

Dangling from his hand was my gun.

Tentacles of fear clawed at me, my pulse racing. I eyed my brother warily.

"You're out of rehab?" I asked.

He raised an eyebrow. "They told you I was there?"

I nodded. "That agent. She said they questioned you. That Carlos shot you when you tried to get drugs from him."

He laughed, a paper-dry, mirthless little laugh. "Carlos was always too hotheaded. Santiago was calmer. I'll miss him. No matter what they think, I didn't kill him."

"Who did?"

Ben rubbed a hand over Charlie's long ears, not answering. "I'm heading out of town. I wanted to give you back your gun before I left."

He held it out to me. I gingerly took it, checked it was disarmed, and slid it into my purse.

I wanted to beg him to stay, to plead with him not to leave me. Family is family. Yes, our relationship was complex, but complex relationships, the ones you worked at the hardest, were sometimes the most important ones.

I didn't want to lose him.

But all I said was: "What about Lucas?"

"He's with Violeta's mom."

"Bring him here," I said. "He's my nephew. I'll keep him safe."

Ben squinted at me. "He doesn't even know you. No, he'll be happiest with his grandma." His shook his head, looking sad. "Violeta was a good mom, but me . . . I'm just a fuckup. I don't want him raised around an addict. I got enough of that from Dad."

"You think Dad was an addict?"

"You don't?"

I thought of how Dad drank, his gambling problems. How much of a workaholic he was. Substances weren't the only addiction a person could have.

"Addiction's in my blood," Ben said, "it's in my brain. Maybe I can beat it if I go away this time."

"Addiction is about escape. It's about numbing painful emotions and detaching from reality. Running away won't change—"

"Stop," he cut me off, his voice like a shard of glass. "This is my life, not yours. You don't get to tell me what will or won't work."

"I'm . . . I'm sorry, you're right." I looked down, embarrassed.

I was ashamed of what I'd done to Ben, turning him in to the police and getting him thrown in jail. I'd cut him off from friends, family, community. It was my fault he'd been isolated. My fault he'd hooked up with a lunatic like Violeta. My fault even that he'd become addicted again.

Maybe everyone, no matter how imperfect, is capable of finding their own way, given the right support. I wanted another chance to be that support.

Ben stared at the fireplace mantel, an old photo I'd framed of Mom, Dad, Ben, and me at the beach when we were young. "You know, I blamed myself for Mom and Dad dying for a long time. If I hadn't been off my face that night, maybe they wouldn't be dead."

"Dad was drinking," I reminded him. "It wasn't your fault. But if you keep using, you're going to end up dead just like them."

"I know. That's why I need to get out of here." He kicked a duffel bag I hadn't noticed on the floor toward me. "Here. That's all the money I have left. Take it, for Josh."

"Ben . . ." I searched his face.

"Take it. But promise me you won't do this shit anymore. Things will go wrong, and you'll get caught or you'll get addicted. To the money, the drugs, the power. Take this and get out while you still can."

"Thank you."

Ben moved toward the door, but hesitated. "I never told you how proud I am of you. You pulled your life together after Mom and Dad died. I love you, Emma. I always mess it up, I know, but it's not because I don't love you. I do love you."

Tears clogged my throat. "I love you too, Ben."

He turned to go, and the emptiness I felt was vast and cavernous. I knew it probably wasn't good-bye forever, but every good-bye with Ben felt like the last one we'd ever have.

Charlie tried to follow Ben, but I called him back.

"Ben!" I called out. "Who were you working with?"

He stopped abruptly. "Just leave it alone," he warned. "Trust me, some stones are better left unturned."

And then he was gone, an icy wind curling in through the open door, ruffling Charlie's fur and stirring my hair. A minute later, I heard the roar of his motorcycle as he sped away.

# CHAPTER 45

MOIRA WAS ALREADY AT the funeral home when I arrived. She was dressed tastefully in a pale-pink dress suit, her slate-gray bob immaculately styled, contrasting with the raw red of her eyes.

Two police officers with their badges covered in black tape guided us into the backseat of a black SUV. The funeral procession began, nine motorcycles flanking the car that held Nate's flag-draped casket in front of us. A line of police cars stretched behind us.

We rode through town in silence, people on the sidewalks stopping to stare as we passed. Moira reached across the back of the car and held my hand. Before all of this, we could barely stand each other. Now I had nobody else.

Patches of dirty snow clung to the edges of the roads, gathered in little piles along the shoulder. The day was cold and bleak, the kind that never seemed to warm up. More snow was forecast for later.

The procession finally turned in at the stone-and-glass community center, which was the only place with an auditorium large enough to accommodate all the mourners. The flags at the entrance had been lowered to half-staff. Rows of servicemen on either side of the road saluted Nate's casket as we drove by.

Lieutenant Dyson helped Moira and me out of the SUV. He accompanied us up the walkway, the soaring evergreens and snow-encrusted Cascade Mountains towering in the distance. His limp was more pronounced than ever, his face gray with grief. For the first time, I realized he looked like an old man. I'd heard he'd announced his impending retirement shortly after Nate was killed. I wondered who would take his place now.

At the entrance to the community center, one of the police officers took over, leading us to our seats at the front. Moira and I sat, both of us numb with shock and grief.

"Hey, stranger," I heard behind me.

I whirled around and stood. "Julia!"

She leaned her metal cane against the chair and hugged me; her body was thin and frail. Her dark hair was tied into a tight ponytail, freckles stark on her pale skin.

Julia's lashes glittered with tears. "I'm so sorry," she said.

"Thank you. How are you feeling?"

"I'm feeling . . . lucky. I must've been off my head to take so much. To be honest, I don't really remember a lot from the last few weeks. Everything's a little . . . murky."

I studied her face. She didn't seem suspicious in any way. "It's understandable."

The pastor began speaking, and Julia returned to her seat. The service sped by in a whirl of music and pallbearers and blurred tears. The mayor spoke, as did Lieutenant Dyson and a few others from the police department. Moira got up to speak, and then it was my turn.

I looked out across the sea of faces, surrounded but alone.

I fingered the heartbeat necklace Nate had bought for me, the metal cool against my sweaty fingers. Everybody was here. Nate's brothers and sister. My colleagues from the hospital and friends I'd made in the last few years. Marjorie. Julia. Kia. Dr. Palmer. Josh's nurse, Katie. I caught my breath, tears filling my eyes. I couldn't seem to stop them anymore. I wanted desperately to throw myself into the casket with Nate.

"The first time I met Nate, he'd been stabbed through the hand. I was the doctor who stitched him up. Nate said he was lucky he'd been stabbed because he got to meet me." I laughed, a weepy little gasp. "I fell in love with him because of his commitment to his family, his friends, and his job. He was a good man. An honorable man. He always said we have to do the right thing, even if it's the hard thing, and he taught our son to believe that good overcomes bad and right always overcomes wrong.

"Nate lost his life while trying to stop a man who wanted to kill me. A man who wanted to destroy everything he'd worked so hard to defend. Nate is my hero." I took a deep breath, tears now cascading down my cheeks. "But it isn't how Nate lost his life that makes him a hero. It's how he lived it. Nate was a devoted father, a loving husband, a dedicated cop, the protector of the innocent. He was a man of great love and compassion. We're all better people for having known him. I think, in the end, we're the lucky ones. . . ."

A raw sob caught in my throat and I bent over, teardrops smearing the notes on the lectern.

Moira hurried to me and helped me down the stairs. I stumbled back into my seat, sobbing, unable to catch my breath.

How would I survive without Nate?


BACK AT the hospital, Josh was awake and howling for Nate and me.

I hurried into his room to find him curled in a ball on his narrow bed, sobbing, one of the nurses trying desperately to comfort him.

"Hey, shhh . . ." I lay on the bed, pulling his thin body against mine.

"I thought you were gone," he sobbed.

"I'm right here," I soothed. "I'm not going anywhere."

His tears finally stopped, and he popped his fingers in his mouth. His eyes drooped, and I thought he would go back to sleep, but he struggled to a sitting position, wincing as the IV tugged at his hand.

"Where's Daddy?"

"Sweetie . . ."

"Where is he? I want Daddy."

I'd been waiting for this moment, planning what I would say, how I would say it. But now that it was here I couldn't speak. My throat closed around those ever-present tears.

"Josh," I began. "I have some sad news to tell you. You know that Daddy had a dangerous job. He protected all of us, but sometimes there were risks. . . ." I gulped, tears already falling. "Daddy loved you so much. . . ."

Josh's lower lip trembled.

I took a deep breath. "Josh, Daddy died. I'm so sorry, baby."

Josh's tears spilled over, tumbling down his pale cheeks in glistening streaks.

"Did he die instead of me?" He choked on the words, and I wrapped my arms around him, feeling the sharp angles of his ribs under my hands.

"No, sweetie, no. Daddy's a hero. He was the good guy and he will always be the good guy. And he would never have gone away if he had a choice. You were the most important thing in the world to him."

Josh pulled away and lay down, facing away from me. He stared at the door as he cried, fat, silent tears streaking his wan cheeks. I stroked a hand gently over his smooth skull.

"I know you're sad. I'm sad too."

He didn't reply, so I kept going. "You know in *Star Wars*, how Obi-Wan sacrificed himself so that Luke and the others could get away?"

Silence.

"Well, that's like what Daddy did. But even though he's gone, just like Obi-Wan, he's always there, living inside the people who loved him."

More silence, and then a raspy whisper. "Daddy was the good guy. Why did the bad guy win? Daddy said the good guys always win."

AFTER JOSH was asleep, I slipped outside to have a cigarette.

The temperature had dropped dramatically. Flakes of white drifted to the ground. I huddled behind a copse of evergreens next to the hospital parking lot and lit a cigarette with shaky hands.

Josh's words echoed in my head. *The good guys always win.*

*No*, I wanted to scream, *the good guy doesn't always win.* The truth hovered over me like a shadow, blocking out any light. I wasn't the good guy. I didn't deserve to be the one who lived, and as he got older, Josh would realize that. He would wish Nate had lived instead of me.

I wished it now.

I inhaled, letting the smoke warm me from the inside. It caressed my skin, curling into my hair, my eyelashes. Through the veil of the evergreen boughs, I saw a flash of movement and heard the angry lilt of voices.

I peered through the trees and recognized the crisp navy suit and bright white hair of Dr. Palmer. He was tucked behind the corner of the staff entrance. His back was to me, but when he shifted his feet I could just make out over his shoulder the person he was arguing with.

Ben.

I wanted to move closer so I could hear better, but I didn't want them to know I was here. They argued for another minute while I strained to listen. Snatches of words floated to me as snowflakes speckled my hair and melted on my hands.

". . . drugs . . . she . . . forget . . . know . . ."

Finally Ben stepped away from Dr. Palmer. His face was red, his eyebrows drawn tight with anger.

". . . what really happened that night," Ben said.

It made no sense. I was there that night; I knew exactly what had happened to Nate.

Ben stormed toward the back of the parking lot, while Dr. Palmer walked the short distance to his black Mercedes and climbed in. I tossed my cigarette to the ground, grinding it into the dirt before hurrying to my car.

I followed Dr. Palmer's Mercedes away from town. Orange streetlights shimmered in the murky air. He headed uphill, turning right and crossing the bridge.

I knew where he was going before we arrived.

The old mill warehouse looked more dilapidated than ever, the ancient rotting wood bowed and bending. The crumbling brick smokestack was barely visible in the murky light.

I left my car parked around a bend in the road and headed into the swirling snow. To my left, the winter forest stretched into the mountains; to my right, a narrow strip of brambles and evergreen trees snaked and snarled toward the river and the churning waterfall in the distance. A cruel wind bit at my face. The fall leaves, beaten by heavy rains, were now covered in snow.

I swept my flashlight over Dr. Palmer's car, catching sight of my reflection in the window. Faded black circles rimmed both my eyes, thanks to Gabe cracking the cartilage of my nose. My skin hung loose and gray on my frame, my cheekbones sharp, lips cracked and bloody.

The car was empty. Fear prickled in my mouth, bitter as a dandelion green. Where had he gone? Why was he here, and why had he been arguing with Ben?

I stepped lightly, keeping my footsteps quiet as I moved to the rear of the warehouse. I knelt, pretending to tie my shoe, and scanned the narrow snow-flecked lawn that sloped from the warehouse to the river. The dark space behind me was a fist against my back.

I slipped soundlessly inside, my senses on high alert. Water dripped rhythmically down the corrugated walls and from the steel beams, a melancholic melody that left dark puddles on the floor.

The crime scene tape had been cleared away. The only signs anybody had ever been here were the cardboard on the windows, a handful of two-by-fours leaning against the wall, and the bloodstain on the floor.

I skirted the inside perimeter of the warehouse, peering behind rusted factory equipment. But there was nobody here. Finally I dropped to my knees next to the dark stain. I pressed my fingers to it and closed my eyes for just a moment.

Nate had once told me that modern crime techs never used chalk to outline a body because it would contaminate the crime scene. Instead, they took pictures, along with measurements to fixed reference points. But I didn't need a picture. All the images from that night were burned forever into my mind.

Isn't it funny how in a crisis, your brain starts taking pictures? All those snapshots of color and light and sound and smells, ready to be held up and turned over and examined at arm's length. The iciness of the velvet night. The mist of the waterfall rising over the river. The smell of woodsmoke in the air.

My neck prickled with unease, and I stood. I peered through the murky darkness and there he was, emerging from a room at the back of the warehouse. He strode toward me quickly, his face open and friendly. He smiled. It was the smile that made me drop my hands. Relief peeled away my defenses and everything in me relaxed.

But then I saw a flash of silver. I started to turn away, but it was too late. The knife burrowed into my side with a moist *thwump*.

I looked down, confused. The blade was buried so deep that the hand holding it was pressed almost flat against my stomach. My pulse hammered against the steel.

And then I felt the fire. My mouth dropped open. The blood was rushing out of me too fast, I knew, soaking my shirt, turning it from white to red in seconds. It was too late. Too late to save myself.

I looked into those familiar eyes, mouthed a single word.

*You.*

The knife slid out of me, a sickening, wet sound. Blood pooled at the bottom of my throat. And then I fell, an abrupt, uninterrupted drop.

I blinked, my brain softening, dulling. Images clicked by, one by one.

Polished black shoes.

The blur of snow as it tumbled past the open door.

The two-by-fours standing against the wall.

My body felt like it was composed of nothing but air. I had failed.

And now Josh would be left alone.

# CHAPTER 46

DR. PALMER LOOKED DOWN at me with stoic, dispassionate eyes. He grabbed my purse and opened it, pulling out my gun and shoving it down the back of his pants, the bloody knife still clutched in one hand.

"Where are they, Emma? Where'd you hide the drugs?"

I pressed my hands to my side, trying to staunch the blood where he'd stabbed me. I kicked my feet out, trying to scramble away from him, but my back almost instantly hit the wall. I had nowhere to go.

"The fentanyl," he pressed. "Ben said he doesn't have it. You were the last person here."

I closed my eyes.

*Don't worry. You're not the only doctor I've worked with.*

Answers clicked into place.

The fentanyl. The briefcase. The confusing text on the old Nokia: *I'll get fentanyl from the doc.*

Pamela's greeting: *So you're the doc.*

Ben's cagey answers to all my questions.

Ben had been working with Dr. Palmer.

"You got the fentanyl," I whispered. "You killed Santiago. Beatrice."

"Yes, of course," he said, impatient now. "Santiago knew too much, and Beatrice was going to the police. You should thank Gabe and me for stopping her."

He knelt next to me, his face softening. "Look, it was just business. I'm not some crazy drug lord who goes out of his way to hurt people."

"Why?" I whispered.

"You can thank Ben, actually. He wanted me to sign a prescription for him. He was high, jonesing for another pill. He had some . . . delicate information on me. So I did. He kept coming back, so I suggested a partnership. I figured we might as well both make money from our mutual misfortune. He likes drugs, and I like money."

Pain rocketed throughout my body in hot, bloody waves. Darkness danced around my peripheral vision. I wanted to lie down, to melt into the cold, damp floor where Nate had died and join him. I glanced at my hands, still gripping the wound. The freezing temperature had slowed the blood flow. A warm numbness was settling over me now.

But there was Josh. Always Josh

"Ben had information on you?" I asked.

"Remember this?" He lifted his palm, exposing a long white scar slicing from pinkie to thumb.

I nodded. He'd gotten it when he'd bent to lift me up the night my parents died, accidentally pressing his hand into a piece of glass on the road.

"Ben read the accident report and knew there was no glass where I found you. You'd pulled your dad away from the car. He guessed I'd been there earlier, and he was right. I cut myself when I was trying to get you out of the car."

A memory of the accident that had killed my parents rose from a dark pocket of my mind, bobbing like a bottle adrift in the ocean.

. . . *The sound of footsteps crunching on gravel. Knocking on glass. A tug on the door handle. "Hello? Hello?" And then a growl of pain: "Ahhh! . . ."*

"You were there."

He smiled sadly and nodded, pushing a strand of hair off my forehead. I squeezed my eyes shut.

"I don't suppose it makes it any better, but it truly was an accident. I'd had far too much to drink. Like your dad, it turns out. He was going too fast to stop when I pulled out of the intersection. He overcorrected, and the car flipped off the embankment at the side of the road."

"Why didn't you get help?" A solitary tear rolled slowly down my cheek. "My dad could've lived."

"I'm a doctor. You know the power of that responsibility. I'd have lost my license, and my calling is to help people. Think about it: if I'd turned myself in that night, I wouldn't be here now to save Josh's life. The end of what I did justified the means. It was clearly for the greater good: to make sure I could serve society with the medical skills I have. It wasn't personal, I assure you."

He stood, his knees cracking. He twisted side to side, as if working out the kinks in his lower back. Then he tightened his grasp on the knife, and I realized for the first time that he was wearing latex gloves. Tears of pain and grief and fury dripped down my face.

"This is your last chance, Emma. Tell me where the drugs are."

"I don't know," I whispered. He was going to kill me no matter what.

He moved toward me, and I shrank away.

"No, wait!" I cried. "This—the poker chip!"

Dr. Palmer assessed me, curious.

"My pocket." I motioned to my pants. "Can I . . . ?"

He nodded, watching closely, his hand hovering over the gun tucked into his waistband as I slipped the chip from my pocket. Pain rocketed through my core at the movement.

"Remember . . . when I gave it to you?" My voice was thin in the icy air.

His eyes flickered as he reached for it. "I thought I lost it."

I closed my palm. "Nate had it. He knew . . . about you. They all do. You won't get away with this."

His eyes darkened, fear flickering across his face. He snatched at the chip, but I tossed it a few feet away. It landed inside the dark stain left by Nate's blood.

Dr. Palmer turned to pick it up. I reached behind me, my hand closing around the end of one of the two-by-fours. Lurching to my feet, I swung it like a baseball bat into Dr. Palmer's head.

His skull ricocheted off the wood, making a low, hollow *thud*. He crashed to the ground. The gun skittered out of his pants, across the room. I staggered to it, clutching my seeping wound with numb fingers. I expected him to come after me as I flailed for the gun with blood-soaked hands.

But he didn't move.

He was breathing, but stone-cold unconscious.

Typically someone knocked out remains unconscious for a minute or so. I didn't have much time. But I couldn't seem to make myself move.

I stared, frozen, at Dr. Palmer. Was he right? Did the good he'd done helping Josh discount his responsibility for my parents' deaths? What about all the people who were now addicted because of him? What about my father? He'd still be alive if Dr. Palmer had done the right thing. Would I trade my son for my father?

Fury opened in my veins, oozing through me, black and bilious. He was corrupt. Greedy. Arrogant.

He'd taken *everything* from me.

Maybe Nate had been right. Maybe how you got to your goal showed the sort of person you were. But I didn't care.

I knelt next to Dr. Palmer. "You're right," I whispered. Just like him when he stood there and let my father die, I had nothing to feel sorry for now. "The end does justify the means."

A rush of power, terrifying and immense, swept over me.

I wiped the gun down with my shirt and pushed it into Dr. Palmer's limp hand. I wrapped his fingers around the cold trigger. I pressed the barrel to his temple.

And I pulled the trigger.

# CHAPTER 47

I FINISHED RECORDING NOTES on my Dictaphone, tidied the blood forms, called in a handful of prescription refill requests, sent an email requesting a chest X-ray. Once I'd finished, I closed my laptop and went to the medical staff office where Julia was writing up patient notes.

After news of Dr. Palmer's involvement in the distribution of opioids got out, the Skamania Police Department had recommended the DA drop all charges against Julia in exchange for community service and time at a rehab center.

"Hey, Julia." I sat next to her, trying not to wince. The knife wound in my side had been slow to heal and sometimes still pained me. But I was alive. I had to be grateful for that. "How are you feeling today?"

She smiled. "Really good, actually. My new trial drug is really helping."

"Good, good. I'm heading off. I'll see you at Josh's birthday party tomorrow, right?"

"I wouldn't miss it!"

I wandered through the hall, shutting doors and making sure everything was in order. It was quieter than normal for a Saturday.

"Bye, Marjorie!" I called. "Want me to lock up the supply closet?"

"Goddamn it!" Her bulk shifted in the leather chair as she stood. "People still can't seem to remember." She came along the hall and reached past me to lock the door before patting my shoulder. "Thanks, Dr. Sweeney. You enjoy your weekend with your boy."

It was a balmy July day, the sun bright, the air clean and clear. Summer's breath hovered gently on the breeze. The jagged mountains and sweeps of evergreen trees stood out against the cornflower-blue skies.

I got in my car slowly, grimacing in pain. I knew I was lucky. If Dr. Palmer had stabbed me just a fraction of an inch to one side, he'd likely have pierced my bowel, which would've led to sepsis and eventual death without treatment. Instead, my quick movement meant I'd been stabbed in the side, and he'd missed all my major organs. The cold temperatures had also helped slow my blood loss.

After I'd shot Dr. Palmer, I'd staggered to the drugs I'd hidden under a tree root and filled his pockets with the baggies of fentanyl. I used his phone to send a brief suicide text to Kia Sharpe, admitting everything.

The guilt was too much for him to bear.

Thank God for hills. And gravity. And adrenaline. They'd all worked to help me roll Dr. Palmer's body down the incline between the warehouse and the river. I then hurled the gun into the rushing water. I still needed to get myself a new one.

A ruling of suicide was later confirmed by the coroner's office.

After receiving Dr. Palmer's suicide text, Kia and Lieutenant Dyson had concluded that he and Gabe had been partners in the town's prescription drug ring. They'd found fentanyl and stacks of cash hidden at Dr. Palmer's house, as well as DNA linking him to Santiago's murder. Violeta's scarf was found on Gabe's body, and after he'd been named as a suspect in the opioid ring, his girlfriend turned in a backpack of cash and drugs that he'd hidden at the gas station.

I'd stayed home for a week after Dr. Palmer stabbed me. I'd left the wound open to drain, treating it with high doses of antibiotics, cleaning, and regular irrigation. And of course, I had a large supply of oxy at my disposal to manage the pain. I'd stashed the entire supply from the warehouse, as well as the cash from Ben, in a special pouch I'd created in Nate's couch—the one he'd always insisted we couldn't get rid of. Nobody would ever think to look inside the carcass of a dingy brown couch for anything.

I pulled out of the hospital parking lot and headed for Skamania State Park at the base of the waterfall. The vibrant rhododendrons along the road were a riot of colors, the brilliant purple lilacs and yellow irises and cheery-faced dahlias bursting into bloom.

Moira raised her hand in greeting as I crossed the parking lot to where she was sitting on a picnic bench. Josh was on the playground dangling from the monkey bars.

I winced as I sat down.

"Are you okay?" Her face creased with concern.

"I'm fine." I forced a smile, absently touching the metal of the heartbeat necklace at my throat. "I think maybe I tore a muscle."

"Well, please get yourself checked out. I can't . . ." She swallowed wetly. "I can't lose you too."

Matt had passed away a few months back, and Moira was struggling under the double loss of her son and husband in just a few short months. She'd asked Josh and me to move in with her, and I was considering it. She didn't want to be alone right now. Neither did I, to be honest.

"I'm not going anywhere, I promise."

She hugged me, her fingers digging tightly into my back. I let her hold me, but didn't return the hug. I wanted to; wanted to feel something. Anything. But these days I just felt frozen. I was starting to wonder about the coldness inside me. I'd murdered a man, yet I felt nothing. My heart had hardened to stone. A new person had formed inside me, forged from the devastated rubble of this new life.

"Mommy!" Josh shouted when he spotted me. He dropped to the ground and ran to me, throwing himself into my arms. I tried not to flinch at the impact of his body against mine. The pain was my punishment and my reward.

"*Mo chuisle*," I whispered into Josh's hair.

For a minute I felt that new person inside me soften, melted by the warmth of Josh's love, the precious delight of his breath on my neck, the endless promise of his life, which I held in my arms. I closed my eyes, cherishing the feeling, enjoying the weight of his very alive body against mine.

The CAR T-cell therapy had literally worked a miracle on my boy. His hair had grown back. His long eyelashes left spidery shadows across his creamy skin, which was flushed, rosy with life. The endless loop of doctor appointments had ended, the smell of hospital was gone from his clothes. We could finally say the treatment had worked.

Josh was perfectly healthy now.

I tucked him under my arm. "You excited for your birthday tomorrow?"

It felt good to say it out loud. *Your birthday*. Josh was alive and had made it to another birthday. We'd suffered one of the greatest losses a family could suffer. The future I'd imagined with Nate was gone. But I'd promised to save Josh, and had.

My grief was a motivator of sorts. I was determined to make Nate proud, and looking at Josh now, I was sure I *had* made him proud. Our son was still here, still surviving, still going forward. That meant something. It was a gift I wouldn't waste.

Josh bobbed his head up and down, grinning. "I hope you got me a bike. Or a science set. Or a tarantula! Yeah, I want a tarantula!"

I gave an exaggerated shiver but laughed. The shiny red bike he'd been asking for since last year was sitting in Moira's garage right now.

Josh's face fell. "I want . . ." He looked at his hands, his chin quivering.

"What is it, sweetie? What do you want?"

He turned his face into my shirt, his words muffled. "I wish Daddy could come to my party."

My throat closed. Moira's white, dismayed face turned quickly away, but not before I saw the tears welling in her eyes. Grief in children, I've learned, is like a murky pond. The true depths are hidden from sight even as brief glimpses bubble to the surface.

Josh's therapist had warned me it would take a while for him to process Nate's death. But he was a survivor. Like me.

"Shall we go down to the river?" Moira suggested.

"You guys go ahead. I have a little paperwork to finish up," I replied.

"I don't wanna go without Mommy." Josh thrust his jaw out stubbornly.

"Go with Grandma," I urged him. "I'll be down in just a few minutes."

Moira took his hand, and I watched them walk away. After a moment, Josh sneaked a peek back at me. He smiled, just a small smile, the left corner of his mouth curving up just a little bit more than the right. With his floppy brown hair and bright-blue eyes and sunny smile, he suddenly looked so much like Nate it took my breath away. I missed him fiercely then, a hot ache squeezing through my middle.

Something moved in my peripheral vision, and when I turned I saw that a tiny black bird had landed on the picnic table. It stared at me, its beady eyes dark and judgmental.

I stared back, remembering the Native American story that Nate had told Josh before my world fell apart. The chief's wife had thrown herself onto the rocks, sacrificing herself for the daughter she loved in order to save her life.

I'd sacrificed everything to save Josh.

That's what a good mother does.

I pulled Ben's red notebook out of my purse. It had been six months since I'd taken it out of the little hole I'd dug under a tree root near the warehouse.

Like my dad always said, sometimes you're dealt a losing hand you might win, sometimes you're dealt a winning hand you might lose. You never win if you fold, but sometimes it's better to live to play another hand.

And my next hand was now.

The money Ben had given me had helped us get through until Nate's life insurance payment had kicked in. But now even the life insurance money was almost gone, chipped away at as more and more medical bills arrived.

Now the bills were piling up. The fear of Josh relapsing always hovered nearby. I had to stay on top of this thing. Now that Nate was gone, Josh was all I had.

There were many in the oxy supply chain to blame for addiction, from manufacturers to distributors to pharmacies to the doctors all too ready to write a script. But until someone fixed it, I could use the failings of the system to help myself and my loved ones.

Clouds were chasing the birds through the sky. A crow cawed somewhere in the distance. I swiped an OxyContin hidden in my purse and dry-swallowed it, then looked up at the indigo sky, waiting for the blessed relief from the pain Dr. Palmer had left me with.

Some criminals are born. Others are formed by circumstances.

After a few minutes, the first fuzzy tendrils of warmth from the oxy hit my blood. Before I knew it, I couldn't feel a thing.

I looked down and opened the red notebook.

# ACKNOWLEDGMENTS

My biggest thanks goes to my agent, Carly Watters, who's made so many things possible. A huge thanks also to my editor, Kate Dresser—your insight and wisdom have been invaluable. Thank you to the phenomenal team at Simon & Schuster and Gallery Books: Jen Bergstrom, Molly Gregory, Michelle Podberezniak, Anne Jaconette, Kathleen Lynch—authors write a story, but you all create a book, and I'm so grateful to have you on my team. And thank you to my TV/film agent, Addison Duffy, for being such an amazing advocate of my work.

A special and heartfelt thanks to Officer Michael Eastman of the Seattle Police Department, who patiently answered my questions about being a detective in Seattle, how task forces work, and street lingo for various drugs, and to Lisa, who facilitated those conversations. And thank you to Dr. Robin Bliss, MD, for answering my medical questions, even the weird ones like, Where is the best place to stab someone so they'll still live?

As always, my heart and soul go to my husband, Richard, who has been a constant champion, and to my boys, Adam and Aidan. Thank you for always being interested in my writing. I love you all.

Thank you so much to Kathleen Carter. Your enthusiasm and publicity magic have meant the world to me.

Authors are nothing without the other authors who've supported them. Heather Gudenkauf, Jennifer Hillier, Wendy Walker, Samantha Downing, Kimberly Belle, Kathleen Barber, Megan Collins, Emma Rous, Karen Katchur, and so many other writers who've read and supported my books, thank you from the bottom of my heart.

And most of all, thank you to you, my readers, reviewers, and book bloggers. I wouldn't be here without you, and I'm grateful to each of you who have bought a copy, shared a review, or posted a picture of my books. You are the reason I write.

# DO NO HARM

## CHRISTINA McDONALD

*This reading group guide for* Do No Harm *includes an introduction, discussion questions, and ideas for enhancing your book club. The suggested questions are intended to help your reading group find new and interesting angles and topics for your discussion. We hope that these ideas will enrich your conversation and increase your enjoyment of the book.*

# INTRODUCTION

From the *USA Today* bestselling author of *Behind Every Lie* and *The Night Olivia Fell* comes an unforgettable and heart-wrenching novel about the lengths one woman will go to save her son.

Emma loves her life. She's the mother of a precocious kindergartner, married to her soulmate—a loyal and loving police detective—and has a rewarding career as a doctor at the local hospital.

But everything comes crashing down when her son, Josh, is diagnosed with a rare form of cancer.

Determined to save him, Emma makes the risky decision to sell opioids to fund the lifesaving treatment he needs. But when somebody ends up dead, a lethal game of cat and mouse ensues, her own husband leading the chase. With her son's life hanging in the balance, Emma is dragged into the dark world of drugs, lies, and murder. Will the truth catch up to her before she can save Josh?

A timely and moving exploration of a town gripped by the opioid epidemic, and featuring Christina McDonald's signature "complex, emotionally intense" (*Publishers Weekly*) prose, *Do No Harm* examines whether the ends ever justify the means . . . even for a desperate mother.

# TOPICS & QUESTIONS
## FOR DISCUSSION

1. Emma often reflects on her dad's advice, including "You don't get to choose what cards you're dealt"; "Sometimes you're dealt a losing hand, and that really sucks. But if you always fold, you'll have a pretty tough time in life"; "Keep your hand close to your chest"; and "Never get caught drawing dead." In which instances in the book do you think Emma uses this advice to justify her actions?

2. Throughout the book McDonald paints the opioid epidemic as a complex problem. Her characters recognize that opioids can provide lifesaving pain relief, but that they can also cause lifelong addiction that endangers people. When Emma discovers that her colleague and friend Julia has been stealing opioids, she thinks, "[Addicts] needed help, not criticism and ridicule." How does Emma's opinion of using opioids for pain management evolve?

3. Nate once said of Josh and Emma, "You need him as much as he needs you." Do you think this is an accurate assess-

ment of their relationship as mother and son? Why or why not?

4. When Emma encounters someone from Moira's church who expresses her sympathy for Josh and their family, Emma has a particularly negative reaction: "Thoughts and prayers. . . . Like that does any good." Why do you think she has that reaction to the church's response to Josh's illness?

5. When Emma visits Julia and sees her in pain, Julia tells her, "I'm not an addict. Maybe I'm addicted, but I'm not an addict." What do you think the difference is for Julia? Compare her addiction to that of other characters in the story, such as Ben or Violeta.

6. Nate often feels pressure to provide for his family, at times relying on traditional roles of masculinity and, in moments of failure, thinking, "What kind of man am I?" Why do you think Nate has this idea of fatherhood? How do you think Nate's vision of fatherhood drives his actions?

7. Emma states that her job as a doctor is "to help people, not watch them suffer." However, at times Emma's actions cause her to do both. Discuss points when Emma's actions cause unintended pain or suffering.

8. When thinking about her brother, Ben, and the anger and resentment that he developed during his life, Emma asks herself, "What makes people go to war with themselves?" What are the reasons that the characters in this book "go to war with themselves"? What commonalities do you think Ben and Emma have as siblings?

9. In *Do No Harm*, the family receives some small donations through a GoFundMe account set up to help pay for Josh's treatments. Do you think GoFundMe accounts and community donations should play a role in paying for medical care?

10. Do you agree with Emma that "the ends justify the means"? Why or why not?

11. One of the overarching themes in *Do No Harm* is sacrifice. Emma sacrifices her oath as a doctor to save her son's life. Nate sacrifices his life to protect Emma. Discuss other sacrifices that characters make. Which do you think are justified?

12. Did Emma's final choice surprise you? Why or why not?

# ENHANCE YOUR BOOK CLUB

1. In 2017, the Department of Health and Human Services (HHS) declared the opioid crisis a public health emergency in the United States. Research the interventions the government is currently taking and discuss the different means of intervention. Do you think these interventions are working?

2. In *Do No Harm*, Josh's leukemia diagnosis forces his family to take extreme measures in order to afford his treatments. Is there someone in your community who is facing similar circumstances? With your book group, organize a donation to their GoFundMe to help provide some support.

3. Author Christina McDonald captures many of the complexities of the opioid epidemic. Did the book change the way you view opioid addiction? Why or why not?